ROBERT CRAIS

Free Fall

Indigo Slam

D0727029

Free Fall
First published in Great Britain by Orion Books Ltd in 1990

Indigo Slam
First published in Great Britain by Orion Books Ltd in 1998

This omnibus edition published in 2009
by Orion Books Ltd
Orion House, 5 Upper St. Martin's Lane,
London
WC2H 9EA

An Hachette UK company

A CIP catalogue record for this book is available
at the British Library.

ISBN 9781407221106

Printed and bound in the UK by
Clays Ltd, St. Ives plc

The Orion Publishing Group's policy is to use papers that are
natural, renewable and recyclable products and made from wood
grown in sustainable forests. The logging and manufacturing
processes are expected to conform to the environmental
regulations of the country of origin.

www.orionbooks.co.uk

Free Fall

CHAPTER 1

Jennifer Sheridan stood in the door to my office as if she were Fay Wray and I was King Kong and a bunch of black guys in sagebrush tutus were going to tie her down so that I could have my way. It's a look I've seen before, on men as well as women. 'I'm a detective, Ms Sheridan. I'm not going to hurt you. You may even find that you like me.' I gave her my best Dudley Do-Right smile. The one with the twinkle.

Jennifer Sheridan said, 'Is what we say privileged, Mr Cole?'

'As in attorney-client?' I was holding the door, but Jennifer Sheridan couldn't seem to make up her mind whether to come in or leave.

'Yes.'

I shook my head. 'No. My records and my testimony can be subpoenaed, and under California law, I must provide them.'

'Oh.' She didn't like that.

'But there is latitude. I sometimes forget things.'

'Oh.' She liked that better, but she still wasn't convinced. I guess there's only so much you can do with the Dudley.

Jennifer Sheridan said, 'This isn't easy for me, Mr Cole. I'm not sure I should be here and I don't have much time. I'm on my lunch hour.'

'We could talk over sandwiches, downstairs.' There was a turkey and Swiss on a French baguette waiting for me in the deli on the ground floor. I had been thinking about it for most of the morning.

'Thank you, no. I'm engaged.'

'That wasn't a sexual proposition, Ms Sheridan. It was a simple offer to share lunch and perhaps more efficiently use both our times.'

'Oh.' Jennifer Sheridan turned as red as a beating heart.

'Also, Ms Sheridan, I'm getting tired of holding the door.'

Jennifer Sheridan made up her mind and stepped past me into the office. She walked quickly and went to one of the two director's chairs across from my desk. There's a couch, but she didn't even consider it.

Jennifer Sheridan had sounded young on the phone, but in person she looked younger, with a fresh-scrubbed face and clear healthy skin and dark auburn hair. Pretty. The kind of happy, innocent pretty that starts deep inside, and doesn't stop on the way out. That kind of pretty. She was wearing a light blue cotton skirt with a white blouse and a matching light blue bolero jacket and low-heeled navy pumps. The clothes were neat and fit well, and the cuts were stylish but not expensive. She would have to shop and she would have to look for bargains, but she had found them. I liked that. She carried a black imitation leather purse the size of a Buick, and when she sat, she sat with her knees and her feet together, and her hands clutching the purse on her lap. Proper. I liked that, too. I made her for twenty-three but she looked eighteen and she'd still be carded in bars when she was thirty. I wondered if I looked old to her. Nah. Thirty-nine isn't old.

I closed the door, went to my desk, sat, and smiled at her. 'What do you do, Ms Sheridan?'

'I'm a secretary for the law firm of Watkins, Okum, & Beale. We're in Beverly Hills.'

'Is that how you found me?' I work for Marty Beale,

time to time. A little skip-tracing, a little missing persons. That kind of thing.

'I peeked in Mr Beale's reference file. He thinks highly of you.'

'You don't say.'

'They don't know that I'm here and I would appreciate it if you didn't say anything.'

I nodded. 'On the phone you said something about your boyfriend.'

'My fiancé. I think that he's mixed up in some kind of criminal thing. I've asked him, and he denies it, but I know that something's going on. I think he's scared, and that worries me. My fiancé is not scared of very much.'

I nodded again and tucked that away. Fearless Fiancé. 'Okay. What kind of crime are we talking about?'

'I don't know.'

'Is he stealing cars?'

'I don't think so.'

'Is he embezzling?'

'No. It wouldn't be that.'

'How about fraud?'

She shook her head.

'We're running out of choices, Ms Sheridan.'

She glanced into the big purse as if there were something inside it that she was hoping she wouldn't have to show me, as if the purse were somehow a point of no return, and if she opened it and let out whatever was inside, she would never be able to close it again or return the elements of her life to a comfortable or familiar order. Pandora's Purse. Maybe if I had a purse like that, I'd be careful of it, too.

I said, 'I know it's hard, Ms Sheridan. If it was easy, you wouldn't need me. But if you don't tell me about him, or what you think he is up to, I can't help you. Do you see that?'

She nodded and held the purse tighter.

I took out a yellow legal pad, a black SenseMatic pencil, and made as if I were poised to copy the rush of information she was about to provide. I drew a couple of practice marks on the page. Subliminal prompting. 'I'm ready. Fire away.'

She swallowed.

'Anytime.'

She stared at the floor.

I put the pad on the desk and the pencil on the pad. I put my fingertips together and looked at Jennifer Sheridan through the steeple, and then I looked at the Pinocchio clock that I've got on my wall. It has eyes that swing from side to side as it tocks, and it's always smiling. Happiness is contagious. It was twelve twenty-two, and if I could get down to the deli fast enough, the turkey would still be moist and the baguette would still be edible. I said, 'Maybe you should go to the police, Ms Sheridan. I don't think I can help you.'

She clutched the purse even tighter and gave miserable. 'I can't do that.'

I spread my hands and stood up. 'If your fiancé is in danger, it is better to get in trouble with the police than it is to be hurt or killed.' Twelve twenty-three. 'Try the police, Ms Sheridan. The police can help you.'

'I can't do that, Mr Cole.' The misery turned into fear. 'My fiancé *is* the police.'

'Oh.' Now it was my turn. I sat down.

Jennifer Sheridan opened the purse and took out a 3x5 color snapshot of herself and a tall good-looking kid in a navy blue LAPD summer-weight uniform leaning against a squad car. They were smiling. 'His name is Mark Thurman. He doesn't work uniform anymore. Last year he was chosen for a plainclothes position at the Seventy-seventh Division in South Central Los Angeles.'

'What kind of plainclothes?'

'They call it a REACT team. They monitor career

4

criminals and try to stop them before they hurt people. It's an elite unit, and he was the youngest man chosen. He was very proud of that.' She seemed proud of it, too. 'Everything was fine for the first few months, but then he changed. It happened almost overnight.'

'What kind of change?' I was thinking Kevin McCarthy. *Invasion of the Body Snatchers.*

'He became anxious and scared and secretive. We never keep secrets from each other and now there are things that he won't talk about with me.'

I looked closer at the picture. Thurman had long forearms and a ropey neck and a country boy's smile. He must've been fourteen inches taller than Jennifer Sheridan. I said, 'I know a lot of police officers, Ms Sheridan. Some of them are even my friends. It can be a hard job with unusual hours and you see too much of what's wrong with people. You don't want to go home and chat about it.'

She shook her head, telling me that I didn't get it. 'It isn't just him not talking about the job. He was in uniform for three years and I know to expect that. It's the way he acts. We used to talk about getting married, and having children, but we don't anymore. I ask him what's wrong, he says nothing. I say tell me about your day, he says that there's nothing to say. He was never like that before. He's become irritable and snappish.'

'Irritable.'

'That's right.'

'He's irritable, and that's why you think he's involved in crime?'

She gave me exasperated. 'Well, it isn't just that.'

'Have you seen him perform a criminal act, or heard him speak of it, or seen the results of it?'

'No.'

'Has he exhibited signs of an income other than his police salary?'

'No.'

I tapped the desk. 'Sounds like you think he's up to something because he's irritable.'

She gave me more of the impatience. 'You don't understand. Mark and I have known each other since the seventh grade. We fell in love in the ninth grade. That's how long we've been going together. I love him and he loves me and I know him better than anyone else in all the world.'

'All right,' I said. 'Do you have any clues?'

She frowned at me.

'Clues,' I said. 'An overheard snatch of conversation. A subrosa glimpse of a secret bank account. Something that I can use in ascertaining the nature of the crime.' I hadn't used *ascertaining* in three or four weeks.

She said, 'Are you making fun of me?'

I was getting one of those headaches that you get when your blood sugar starts to drop. 'No, I'm trying to make you consider what you want and why you want it. You claim that Mark Thurman is involved in criminal activity, but you have no direction in which to point me. That means that you're asking me to surveil an active-duty police officer. Police officers are paranoid by nature and they move around a lot. This will be expensive.'

She looked uncertain. 'How expensive?'

'Two thousand dollars. In advance.'

You could see her swallow. 'Do you take Visa?'

'I'm afraid not.'

She swallowed a second time. 'That seems an awful lot.'

'Yes,' I said. 'It is.'

She put the photograph of Mark Thurman back in her purse and took out a red doeskin wallet. She dug in the wallet and got a faraway look like she was working with numbers. Then she pulled out two twenties and put them

6

on my desk. 'I can pay you forty dollars now, and forty dollars per month for forty-nine months.'

I said, 'Jesus Christ, Ms Sheridan.'

She clenched her jaw and brought out another ten. 'All right. Fifty dollars.'

I raised my hands, got up, and went to the glass doors that lead out to the little balcony. The doors that came with the office were aluminum sliders, but a couple of years ago I had them changed to a nice set of double-glazed French doors with brass handles. I opened the doors, set them so that the breeze wouldn't blow them closed, and that's when I saw two guys sitting across the street in a brown unmarked sedan four stories below. A tall guy with shaggy, thick-cut hair sat behind the steering wheel and a shorter guy with a ragged face slouched in the passenger's side. The tall guy had long forearms and a ropey neck and looked a lot like Mark Thurman. Sonofagun. I turned away from the doors and looked at Jennifer Sheridan. Nope. She didn't know that they were out there. 'Mark work today?'

She looked surprised that I'd ask. 'That's right. He works Monday through Friday, from eleven until six.'

'He let his hair grow since he went to REACT?'

Jennifer Sheridan smiled, trying to figure me. 'Why, yes. He had to, for the undercover work.'

Thurman, all right.

I walked back to the desk and looked at her. You could see how much she loved him. You could see that she trusted him, and that she'd never think that maybe he was following her. I said, 'Do you and Mark live together?'

She made a tiny headshake and a bit of the red again touched her cheeks. 'We've talked about it, but we decided to wait.'

'Uh-huh. So you believe that he's hiding something, and you want me to find out what.'

7

'Yes.'

'What if I find out that Mark Thurman isn't who you think he is? What if I look, and I find something that changes the way that you feel about him, and the way that he feels about you?'

Jennifer Sheridan made a little move with her mouth, and then she cleared her throat. 'Mark is a good man, Mr Cole. If he's involved in something, I know it's not because he wants to be. I trust him in that, and I love him. If we find out that he is in trouble, we will help him.' She had thought about these things. Probably lay awake with them.

I went back to the doors and pretended to adjust them. Thurman and the other guy were still in the sedan. Thurman had been looking up, but ducked back when he realized that I had come back onto the balcony. Fast moves are bad. Another couple of years on the job and he'd know better. You just sort of casually look away. Shift the eyes without moving the head. Eye contact can kill you.

I went back into the office and sat, and Jennifer Sheridan said, 'Will you help me, Mr Cole?'

I said, 'Why don't we do this? I'll nose around and see if there is anything worth pursuing. If there is, I will work for you and pursue it. If there isn't, I will return your money, and you won't owe me anything.'

Jennifer Sheridan said, 'That will be fine,' and then she smiled. Her tanned skin dimpled and her white teeth gleamed and there came a quality of warmth to the room as if a small sun had risen from beneath my desk. I found myself returning the smile. I wrote a receipt in her name for the amount of forty dollars, and noted that it was paid against a due balance of one thousand, nine hundred sixty dollars, payable in monthly installments. I gave back the extra ten with her receipt, then put the forty dollars into my wallet. My wallet didn't feel any fatter than it had without the forty. Maybe if I went down to the bank and had the forty changed to ones, it would feel like more.

Jennifer Sheridan took a folded sheet of paper from the huge purse and handed it to me. 'This is where Mark lives, and his home phone number, and his license plate, and his badge number. His partner's name is Floyd Riggens. I've met Floyd several times, but I don't like him. He's a mean-spirited man.'

'Okay.' Riggens would be the other guy in the car.

She took back the paper and scribbled something on the back. 'This is where I live and this is my work number. It's a direct line to Mr Beale's office, and I answer his phone, so I'll be the one who picks up when you call.'

'Fine.'

She stood, and I stood with her. She put out her hand. I took it. I think we were in a contest to see who could smile the most. She said, 'Thank you, Mr Cole. This is very important to me.'

'Elvis.'

'Elvis.' She smiled even wider, and then she gathered her things and left. It was twelve forty-six, and I stopped smiling. I sat at my desk and looked at the paper that she had given me with the information about Mark Thurman and herself, and then I put it into the desk's top right-hand drawer along with my copy of the receipt.

I leaned back and I put my feet up, and I wondered why Mark Thurman and his mean-spirited partner Floyd Riggens were following Jennifer Sheridan while they were on duty. I didn't like the following, but I didn't have very long to wonder about it.

At twelve fifty-two, Mark Thurman and Floyd Riggens came in.

CHAPTER 2

They didn't kick the door off its hinges and they didn't roll into the office with their guns out like Crockett and Tubbs used to do on *Miami Vice*, but they didn't bother to knock, either.

The guy I figured for Floyd Riggens came in first. He was ten years older than Thurman and maybe six inches shorter, with a hard, squared-off build and weathered skin. He flashed his badge without looking at me and crossed to Joe Pike's office. I said, 'It's empty.' He didn't pay attention.

Mark Thurman came in after him and went out onto the balcony, like maybe a couple of Colombian drug lords had ducked out only seconds ago and were hanging off the side of the building with grappling hooks and Thurman wanted to find them. He looked bigger in person than he had in the pictures, and he was wearing faded khaki fatigue pants and a red jersey that said LANCASTER HIGH VARSITY. Number 34. He looked younger, too, with a kind of rural innocence that you rarely find in cops, sort of like *Dragnet* as played by Ronnie Howard. He didn't look like a guy who'd be into crime, but then, what does a criminal look like? Boris Badenov?

Riggens came out of Pike's office and scowled at me. His eyes were red and swollen and I could smell the scotch on his breath even though he was standing on the other side of the chairs. Hmm. Maybe he didn't have the weathered look, after all. Maybe he had the drunk look. Riggens said, 'We need to talk about the girl.'

I gave him innocent. 'Girl?'

Riggens squinted like I'd spit on his shirt and grinned out the corner of his mouth. Mean-spirited. 'Oh, I like it when jerks like you get stupid. It's why I stay on the job.'

'What are you drinking to get eyes like that – Aqua Velva?'

Riggens was wearing a baggy beachcomber's shirt with the tail out, but you could still make out the butt of his piece riding high on his right hip. He reached up under the shirt and came out with a Sig 9-mil and said, 'Get your ass against the goddamned wall.'

I said, 'Come on.'

Mark Thurman came in off the balcony and pushed the gun down. 'Jesus Christ, Floyd, take it easy. He doesn't know what this is about.'

'He keeps dicking with me, he won't make it long enough to find out.'

I said, 'Let me guess. You guys work for Ed McMahon and you've come to tell me that I've won the Publisher's Clearing House sweepstakes for a million bucks.'

Riggens tried to lift his gun but Thurman kept the pressure on. Riggens's face went red to match his eyes and the veins swelled in his forehead, but Thurman was a lot stronger, and sober, so it wasn't much of a problem. I wondered if Riggens acted like this on the street, and if he did, how long he had been getting away with it. Stuff like this will get you killed. Thurman said, 'Stop it, Floyd. That's not why we're here.'

Riggens fought it a little longer, then gave it up, and when he did Thurman let go. Riggens put the Sig away and made a big deal with the hand moves and the body language to let everyone know he was disgusted. 'You want to do it, then do it, and let's get out of here. This asshole says she wasn't even here.' He went to the couch and sat down. Petulant.

Thurman sort of shook his head, like he couldn't figure

Riggens out, like he had tried for a long time and was maybe getting tired of trying. He turned back to me. 'My name is Mark Thurman. This is my partner, Floyd Riggens. We know she was up here because Floyd followed her up.'

I glanced at Floyd again. He was staring at the Pinocchio clock. 'Maybe Floyd got confused. There's an insurance office across the hall. Maybe she went there.'

Floyd said, 'Okay, she wasn't here. We're not here, either, you want to play it that way. You fell asleep and you're dreaming all this.' He got up and went to the clock for a closer look. 'Hurry up, Mark. I don't wanna spend the day.' Like a little kid.

Thurman looked nervous, but maybe he was just uncomfortable. His partner was looking bad and that made him look bad. He said, 'We called in about you and the word is that you're a straight shooter, so I thought we should talk.'

'Okay.'

'Jennifer and I are having some trouble.'

'You mean, this isn't official police business?'

Riggens went back to the couch and sat down. 'It could be, you want. We could have information that you been up to something. We could even find a snitch to back it up. That would look real good for your license.'

Thurman's face went dark and he said, 'Shut up, Floyd.'

Riggens spread his hands. What?

Thurman came to the front of my desk and sat in the right-side director's chair. He leaned forward when he sat and stared at me the way you stare at someone when you're trying to figure out how to say something you don't want to say. 'I'm here for personal reasons, and they have to do with me and Jennifer. You want to pretend she wasn't here, that's fine. I understand that. But we still have to talk. See?'

'Okay.'

Riggens went, 'Jesus Christ, get on with it.'

Thurman's face clouded again and he once more looked at Riggens and said, 'If you don't shut the fuck up, I'm going to clock you, Floyd.' Enough's enough.

Riggens frowned and crossed his arms and drew himself into kind of a knot. Drunk enough to be pissed, but sober enough to know that he'd stepped over the line. These guys were something.

Thurman turned back to me and sat there, his mouth working. He was having trouble with it, and he didn't strike me as a guy who'd have trouble with a lot. He made a little blowing move with his lips, then laced his fingers and leaned forward. 'We followed her because she's been pressing me pretty hard about some stuff, and I knew she'd try something like this. She's pretty strong-willed, and she gets a head on about things, if you know what I mean.'

Riggens made a snorting sound, then recrossed his arms and put his feet up on the little coffee table I have in front of the couch. I didn't like it, but I didn't say anything.

Thurman said, 'Jennifer and I have been going together since we were kids. I've been acting kind of distant with her for the past couple of months and I haven't told her why, and Jennifer has it figured that I'm mixed up in something. I know that's what she talked to you about, because that's what she talks to me about. Only, that isn't it at all.'

'No?'

'No.' Mark Thurman looked down at his feet and worked his jaw harder and then he looked up at me. 'I've got another girlfriend.'

I stared at him.

'I knew that if she hired someone, they'd find out and tell her, and I don't want that. Do you see?'

I said, 'Another woman.'

He nodded.

'You've been seeing another woman and Jennifer knows something is up, but she doesn't know what. And you're trying to head me off so I won't blow the whistle.'

He nodded again.

Riggens uncurled his arms and pushed up from the couch. 'You don't need to know anything else. The word is that you're a straight shooter and we're looking for a break. It was me I'd slap the bitch down and move on, but he doesn't want to play it that way. Why don't you give the kid a hand?'

I said, 'Jesus Christ, Riggens, why'd you come along? Moral support?'

Riggens said, 'No one's trying to muscle you, smart guy. Everyone's playing straight up.' Riggens jerked his head toward Thurman. 'Tell him we're playing straight up.'

Mark Thurman looked back at me, only now there was a lost quality to his eyes. 'I didn't want you telling Jennifer. When it comes, it's got to come from me.' He was leaning forward so far I thought he'd fall out of the chair. 'Do you see?'

'Sure. I see.'

'It's personal. That's how it should stay.'

'Sure.'

Riggens said, 'No one's asking you to turn down the fee. Just play it smart. Do us the favor and someday you'll get a payback.'

'But I can keep the fee.'

'No problem.'

I looked at Thurman. 'Some right guy you've got as a partner, Thurman, saying it's okay for me to stiff your girlfriend.'

Riggens said, 'Fuck you,' and banged out. Thurman sat in the director's chair, not saying anything, and then he pushed himself up. He was twenty-four years old and he looked like a baby. When I was twenty-four I looked a million years old. Vietnam. He said, 'You do what you want, Cole. No one's telling you what to do. But I'm asking you not to tell her what I said. I get ready, I should be the one tells her. Shouldn't I?'

'Sure.'

'I just got to work this out, that's all I'm saying.' Like he was in the principal's office, like he had been caught throwing eggs at the class geek's house, and now he was ashamed of it. He went to the door. Riggens was already down the hall.

I said, 'Thurman.'

He stopped and looked back at me with his right hand on the handle.

'Why don't you just tell her?'

He didn't answer. He stood there, sort of staring, like he didn't know what to say. Maybe he didn't.

I said, 'She didn't say anything to me about crime. She said that she thought you were seeing another woman. She said that she always knew you were that way.'

Mark Thurman went as red as Jennifer Sheridan when I told her that I hadn't been making a pass. He stared at me with the sort of look you'd have if you were in a hurry one day and backed out your drive without looking and ran over a child. Like someone had pushed an ice spike through your heart. He stared at me like that, and then he went out. He didn't close the door.

I went to the little balcony and stood back from the rail and watched the street. Mark Thurman and Floyd Riggens came out of my building, climbed back into the brown sedan, and drove away. Neither of them spoke, as far as I could tell, and neither of them looked particularly happy. It was six minutes after one, and it looked as if my case was solved.

I closed the glass doors, sat on my couch, and thought about what I might say when I was inducted into the Detective's Hall of Fame. Perhaps they would bill me as

Elvis Cole, World's Fastest Detective. Wouldn't Jennifer Sheridan be pleased. She could say *I knew him when.* At six minutes after one, Jennifer Sheridan would be sitting in Marty Beale's outer office, not expecting a phone call in which the detective that she had hired only moments before would crush her heart with one fell blow, service with a smile, *thank you, ma'am, and the bill is in the mail.* Of course, since I had made such a big deal to Jennifer Sheridan about her lack of proof, she might enquire as to mine, and I had none. I had only Mark Thurman's word, and maybe he had lied. People do.

I put aside my thoughts of the Hall of Fame and called a guy I know named Rusty Swetaggen. For twenty-four years he drove a black-and-white in and around the city of Los Angeles, then his wife's father died and he inherited a pretty nice restaurant in Venice, about four blocks from the beach. He likes it better than being a cop. He said, 'Rusty's.'

I made hissing and cracking noises into the phone. 'I'm calling from the new car phone. Pretty good, huh?'

Rusty Swetaggen said, 'Bullshit, you got a car phone.' Then he yelled at someone in the background. 'It's the big-time op, making like he's got a car phone.' Someone said something and then he came back on the line. 'Emma says hey.'

'Hey back. I need to find out about an officer and I don't want him to know.'

'This guy active duty?'

'Yeah. His name is Mark Thurman. He works a REACT team out of the Seventy-seventh.'

Rusty didn't say anything. I guess he was writing. Then he said, 'Is this guy dirty?' He didn't like asking. You could hear it in his voice. You ride the black-and-white for twenty-four years and you don't like asking.

'I want to find out. Can you do this for me?'

'Sure, Elvis. I'd do anything for you. You know that.'

'I know. I'll be by in a couple of hours. That okay?'

'Fine.'

Rusty Swetaggen hung up, and then I hung up.

I took the shoulder holster out of my bottom left drawer and put it on. It's a nice brushed-leather Bianchi rig that cost a fortune, but it's comfortable, and it's made for the Dan Wesson .38 revolver that I carry. Stylish detectives often carry automatics, but I have never been a slave to fashion.

I took the Dan Wesson out of its drawer and seated it into the shoulder holster and then I covered the works with a light gray cotton sport coat. It looks great over my black-and-maroon Hawaiian beach shirt, and is ideal for hiding firearms in L.A.'s summer weather. I took the Watkins, Okum, & Beale stationery out of my desk, put it in the inside pocket of the sport coat, then called the deli and asked them if they still had my turkey and Swiss on baguette. They did.

I walked the four flights down to the deli, ate my sandwich at a little table that they have by the door, then left to find out whether or not LAPD Officer Mark Thurman was telling the truth, or telling a lie.

Either way, Jennifer Sheridan wouldn't like it.

CHAPTER 3

Driving along Santa Monica Boulevard through West Hollywood and Beverly Hills is a fine thing to be doing in late March, just at the end of the rainy season. It was warmer than it should have been, with highs in the mid-eighties and mare's-tail cirrus streaking the sky with feathery bands, and there were plenty of men in jogging shorts and women in biking pants and Day-Glo head-bands. Most of the men weren't jogging and most of the women weren't biking, but everyone looked the part. That's L.A.

At a traffic light in Westwood I pulled up next to a woman in pristine white biking pants and a white halter workout top sitting astride a white Japanese racing bike. I made her for Jennifer Sheridan's age, but maybe she was older. The line of her back was clean and straight, and she leaned to the right, her right toe extended down to kiss the street, her left toe poised on its pedal. Her skin was smooth and tanned, and her legs and body were lovely. She wore a ponytail and bronze-tinted sunglasses. I gave her the big smile. A little Dennis Quaid. A little Kevin Costner. She stared at me through the bronze lenses and said, 'No.' Then she pedaled away. Hmm. Maybe thirty-nine is older than I thought.

At the western edge of UCLA, I climbed the ramp onto the 405 freeway and headed north into the San Fernando Valley. In another week the smog and haze would build and the sky would be bleached and obscured, but for now the weather was just right for boyfriends tailing girl-friends and girlfriends hiring private eyes to check up on boyfriends and private eyes spending their afternoons on long drives into the valley where they would risk life and limb snooping around police officers' apartments. If Randy Newman were here, he'd probably be singing *I Love L.A.*

I edged off the 405 at Nordhoff and turned west, cruising past the southern edge of Cal State, Northridge, with its broad open grounds and water-conscious land-scaping and remnants of once-great orange groves. In the prewar years before freeways and super-highways the valley was mostly orange trees, but after the war the orange groves began to vanish and the valley became a bedroom community of low-cost family housing tracts. When I came to L.A. in the early seventies, there were still small bits of orchard dotted around Encino and Tarzana and Northridge, the trees laid out in geometric patterns, their trunks black with age but their fruit still sweet and brilliant with color. Little by little they have melted away into single-family homes and minimalls with high vacancy rates and high-density apartment complexes, also with high vacancy rates. I miss them. Minimalls are not as attractive as orange trees, but maybe that's just me.

Mark Thurman lived in a converted garage apartment in the northwestern part of the San Fernando Valley, about a mile west of Cal State, Northridge, in an older area with stucco bungalows and clapboard duplexes and mature landscaping. Though the structures are old, the residents are not, and most of the apartments are rented to college students or junior faculty from the university or kids out on their own for the first time. Lots of bikes around. Lots of small foreign cars. Lots of music.

I parked across the street from a flat-topped duplex and looked down the drive. The sheet of Watkins, Okum stationery said that Thurman drove a 1983 blue Ford Mustang as his personal car, but the Mustang wasn't around, and neither was the dark brown cop-mobile. Still out fighting crime, no doubt. Or tailing Jennifer Sheridan. A chain-link fence ran parallel to the drive along a row of eight-foot hedges. About halfway back, a little wrought-iron gate ran from the fence to the duplex, cutting the drive in half. Thurman's converted garage was in the rear yard behind the gate, snuggled against the hedges. A set of sliding glass doors had been installed where the garage door used to hang and someone had built a little sidewalk out of stepping-stones that ran around the side of the place by the hedges. A curtain of vertical blinds was drawn across the glass doors and pulled closed. It was a nice, neat, well-kept place, but it didn't look like the kind of place a cop taking down heavy graft would keep. Of course, maybe Mark Thurman was smart, and the outward appearance of his home was just a dodge to throw off unsuspecting PIs. Maybe the inside of the place looked like Uncle Scrooge's money bin and the walls were lined with cash and bricks of gold. Only one way to find out.

I got out of the Corvette, strolled up the drive, and let myself through the little wrought-iron gate. A young German shepherd was lying by the gate beneath the hedges next door. He watched me come and when I let myself through the gate he lifted his head. I said, 'Woof.' He got up and walked with me. Police dog. If Thurman came home I'd have to go over the fence. Hope he didn't bite.

There were three young women lying on towels in the little yard that separated the duplex from the guest house. One was on her belly, the other two were on their backs, and the one nearest to me was up on an elbow, adjusting a radio. U-2. Nobody was wearing very much in the way of clothes, and you could smell the suntan oil. The one with the radio saw me first and made a little gasping noise. I said, 'Hi, ladies. Is Mark around?' Elvis Cole, the Smooth Detective.

The one with the radio relaxed and the other two looked over. The one without the radio was wearing little round sunglasses and the one on her belly smiled. The two on their backs were brunette, the one on her belly a blonde.

The one with the radio said, 'He's at work.'

I glanced at my watch and made a big deal out of looking disappointed. 'He said he'd meet me here. I guess he got hung up.'

The one on her belly said, 'Are you a cop, too?'

I said, 'Do I look like a cop?'

The three of them nodded.

I spread my hands. 'I'd do great undercover, hunh?'

The one on her belly said, 'I don't know. You might.'

The other two laughed.

The one with the little round glasses covered her mouth and said, 'Ohmygod, do you know who he looks like? He looks like Mel Gibson in *Lethal Weapon*. Don't you think so?'

I was liking the one with the glasses just fine. Maybe thirty-nine wasn't so old after all.

The one with the radio said, 'If Mark told you he'd be here, he's probably on his way. He's pretty good about that kind of stuff.'

I said, 'I've just got to drop something off. You think he'd mind?'

Radio said, 'You could leave it with us.'

'Couldn't do that. It's business-related. And it's sort of a surprise.'

The one on her belly looked interested. 'Evidence.'

The one with the little round sunglasses said, 'Allie likes cops. She wants to see your gun.'

Allie slugged Sunglasses in the leg, and all three of them laughed.

The one with the radio said, 'Go ahead. Mark's cool. He keeps a spare key in a little Sucrets box to the left of the landing behind a plant pot.'

'Thanks.'

The German shepherd was waiting for me when I went around the side of the guest house, and followed me to the door. The Sucrets box and the key were exactly where Radio said they'd be. Some neighbors, hunh? I took out the key and let myself in. The German shepherd sat on his haunches and stared after me and whined. Helluva police dog, too.

Mark Thurman's garage had been converted into a pretty nice apartment. The side door opened into a living room, and from the door you could see the kitchen and another door that led to a bedroom and a bath. A brown cloth couch rested against the west wall and a shelving unit stood against the north. The east wall was the glass doors. A CD player and a Sony TV and a VCR and about a zillion CDs were in the wall unit, but the CD player and the VCR were low-end Pioneer and neither was a bank breaker, even on a police officer's take-home. There was an overstuffed chair at either end of the couch, and a coffee table of bright white pine that matched the wall unit. He would've bought the set from one of those discount places. Imported, they would have told him. Danish. There wasn't a sea of gold coins that you could dive into, or mounds of money bags scattered around, but I hadn't yet seen the bedroom. One shouldn't jump to conclusions.

I glanced through the kitchen, then went into the bedroom. It was small, with a single window and a door that led into the bath, and it wasn't any more lavishly appointed than the living room. I went into the bath first, then came back into the bedroom. There was a king-sized bed without a headboard, a nightstand, and a dresser with a large curved mirror that didn't match any of the other furniture. Garage sale. The bed was made and neat, and the spread was pulled tight across its surface. I went through the dresser drawers and then I looked under the bed. Under the bed there was a red Lily of France brassiere. Thirty-six C. I pulled it out and looked at it, but there was nothing to suggest the owner. Jennifer Sheridan might be a thirty-six C, but I hadn't asked and I hadn't thought about it. I put the brassiere back where I had found it, and then I looked in the nightstand. There was a New Balance shoe box in the large cabinet at the bottom of the nightstand with Mark Thurman's diploma from the police academy, a couple of letters from someone named Todd, and Thurman's credit card and banking receipts. Thurman held a checking account and savings account with Cal Fed, one MasterCard, one Visa card, plus gas cards from both Chevron and Mobil. He kept the billing statements from the Visa and MasterCard in a legal-sized envelope marked *VISA*. Neither card showed recent purchases for anything out of the ordinary, but the most recent bill was three weeks old. His savings account held $3,416.28. I copied the account numbers for the Visa and the MasterCard and then I put the box back as I had found it and went to the closet.

A summer-weight LAPD uniform and a set of navy winters hung with the sport shirts and the jeans and the slacks. They hadn't been worn in a while. A single blue suit looked like it didn't get worn much, either. There were shoes and a spinning rod and a set of golf clubs that looked so old they had probably been handed down from father to son. Above the clothes, a high shelf ran around the perimeter of the closet, weighted down with old issues of *Sports Illustrated*, a motorcycle helmet that looked like it had never been used, and a cardboard box containing an outsized scrapbook with yellowed clippings of Mark Thurman playing football and baseball and basketball and track for the Lancaster Wildcats. Four letter man. Mark had played fullback and strong side linebacker, going both ways for sixty minutes a game. There were newspaper photos of Mark in action, and Mark celebrating with teammates, but there were also snapshots of Mark alone and Mark with Jennifer and Jennifer alone, here Mark eating ice cream at the Tastee Freeze, here Jennifer posing shyly in the empty bleachers, here the two of them at the Sophomore Prom and the Junior-Senior and at graduation. I don't know how old they were in the earliest photographs, but they looked like babies. You got the feeling that Jennifer had taken the photos of Mark and Mark had taken the photos of Jennifer, and that there had never been anyone else in their lives, that they had been complete and whole since that moment when they'd fallen in love in the ninth grade, and, in some wonderful way, always would be. But maybe not. The clippings and the photographs began in ninth grade and ended with graduation. Maybe all those years of oneness had become oppressive to Mark and he had decided that there had to be more and, like the photos in the scrapbook, the oneness had to end. Maybe he had told me the truth. Maybe, after all those years, it was finally over.

I put the scrapbook back as I had found it and finished going through his things, but there were no keys to a newly purchased Porsche, no hastily scrawled map to bags of money buried in the high desert, and no unexplained series of numbers for the Swiss accounts. There was only the thirty-six C. That's the way it goes, sometimes.

I made sure the rooms were like I had found them, then I let myself out, locked the door, and went around to the drive. The German shepherd was gone. So was Allie. The other two were still on their backs. I said, 'Allie get bored?'

The one with the radio said, 'She said she was hot. She went in to cool off.'

The one with the little round glasses said, 'What took you so long?'

'Pit stop.' Elvis Cole, Man of a Thousand Lies. 'You guys know Mark's friend, Jennifer?'

'Sure.'

'She come around lately?'

'Not for a couple of weeks, but she used to.'

The one with the glasses said, 'She's so flat. I don't know what he sees in her.'

The one with the radio said, 'Puh-lease, Brittany.' Brittany. Whatever happened to the women's movement?

I said, 'Mark said he's got another friend. Have you met her?'

The one with the radio said, 'We haven't seen her.'

Brittany sat up and wrapped her arms around her knees. 'You mean he's available?'

I shrugged.

Michael Bolton started singing about how much being in love hurt and the one with the radio turned it up. Brittany lay back and stretched, making a thing out of lifting her ribs and showing her body. She looked thoughtful. Making plans, no doubt. Devising strategies.

The one with the radio said, 'Let me get Allie. She wanted to say good-bye.' Then she got up and went into the house. Brittany was mumbling to herself and Allie was probably mumbling, too. I left before they got back.

Women in heat are frightening to behold.

CHAPTER 4

I let myself out through the little gate, walked back to my car, and drove two blocks to a 7-Eleven where I used their pay phone to call a friend of mine who works in the credit department of Bank of America. I gave her Mark Thurman's name, social security number, and account numbers from both his Visa and MasterCard. I told her that I wanted to know if the charge totals for the month exceeded two thousand dollars and, if they did, how many separate purchases exceeded five hundred dollars and where and when they had been made. I also told her that I wanted to know if Thurman had applied for or received any additional credit cards during the past year. She asked me who the hell did I think I was, calling up out of the blue and asking for all of that? I told her that I was the guy who was going to take her to see Sting at the Greek Theater, then take her to dinner at Chinois on Main afterwards. She asked if tomorrow was okay, or did I want the information later tonight? She called me Chickie when she said it.

I drove back to the 405, then went south, back across the floor of the valley, then through the Sepulveda Pass and into the basin, heading toward Venice and Rusty Swetaggen's place. I left the freeway at Wilshire and turned west to San Vicente Boulevard in Brentwood. It would've been faster to stay on the 405, but San Vicente was nicer, with interesting shops and elegant cafes and palatial homes that somehow seemed attainable, as if the people within them got there by working hard, and were

26

still the type of folks who would give you a smile if you passed them on the sidewalk. Sort of like the Cleavers or the Ricardos.

Bike paths bordered the east- and westbound lanes, and an expansive center island with a row of mature coral trees divided the traffic. Bicyclists and joggers and power walkers flock to San Vicente for its pleasant surroundings and two-mile straightaway from Brentwood to the ocean. Even at midday, the bike paths were crowded and runners pounded along the center island. A man who might've been Pakistani ran with a dust mask, and a red-haired woman with a Rottweiler stopped to let the dog piddle on a coral tree. The woman kept her legs pumping as she waited for the dog. Both of them looked impatient.

Brentwood became Santa Monica and the nice homes became nice apartment buildings, and pretty soon you could smell the ocean and pretty soon after that you could see it. Santa Monica has rent control, and many of the apartment buildings had little signs fastened to their walls that said PEOPLE'S REPUBLIC OF SANTA MONICA. Protest by the apartment owners.

San Vicente ended at Ocean, which runs along a sixty-foot bluff separating Santa Monica proper from the sand and the water and Pacific Coast Highway. Most of the joggers turned back at Ocean, but most of the riders turned left to continue on the bike paths that run along the top of the bluff. I turned with the riders. The top of the bluff sports green lawns and roses and a comfortable parklike setting. There are benches, and some of the time you can sit and watch the ocean and the volleyball games down below on the beach. The rest of the time the benches are used by the thousands of homeless who flock to Santa Monica because of its mild climate. Santa Monica encourages this. The People's Republic.

A block and a half up from the Venice boardwalk I aced out a flower delivery van for a parking spot, fed the meter, and walked two blocks inland to Rusty Swetaggen's place between a real estate office and an architectural firm where they specialized in building houses on unbuildable building sites. You could eat at Rusty's during the day, and people did, but mostly they went there to drink. The real estate salespeople were all politically correct women who believed in Liz Claiborne and the architects were all young guys in their thirties who dressed in black and wore little round spectacles. Everyone was thin and everyone looked good. That's the way it is in Venice. Rusty Swetaggen is a short, wide guy with a body like a bulldog and a head like a pumpkin. If you didn't know that he owned the place, you'd think he was there to rob it. Venice is like that, too.

Six years ago, Rusty and Emma's fifteen-year-old daughter, Katy, took up with a guy from the Bay Area who introduced her to the joys of professional loop production and crack-inspired public sex performance. Katy ran away and Rusty asked me to help. I found her in the basement of a three-bedroom house in the San Francisco hills, sucking on a crack bong to kill the pain of the beating that her Bay Area hero had just given her because she wasn't quite enthusiastic enough in the multiple-partner sex she'd just been forced to have in front of a Hitachi 3000 Super-Pro video camera. I got Katy and all copies of the fourteen sex loops she'd made in the previous three days. None of her performances had as yet been distributed. I destroyed the tapes and brought Katy to a halfway house I know in Hollywood. After eight months of hard family therapy, Katy moved back home, returned to high school, and began to put her life on track. She met a guy named Kevin in a support group during her second year of college, and fourteen months later they were married. That was seven months ago, and now she was finishing a business degree at Cal State, Long Beach. Rusty Swetaggen cried for a week after I brought her back, said he'd never be able to repay me, and refused to let me or anyone who was with me pay for a drink or for anything else that he might provide. I stopped going to Rusty's because all the free drinks were embarrassing.

Rusty was sitting at the bar, reading a copy of *Newsweek*, when I walked in. It was twenty-six minutes past two, but the place was still crowded with the lunch-hour rush. The real estate salespeople and the architects were vying for bar space with a lot of businessmen sporting bow ties and very short hair. The real estate people were getting the best of it. More practice, I guess. I pushed in beside Rusty and said, 'I can't believe a guy with your money hangs around the job. I had your bucks, I'd be on the beach in Maui.'

Rusty squinted at the kid who worked the bar and said, 'It's a cash business, Hound Dog. You don't watch'm, they'll rob you blind.'

The kid showed Rusty his middle finger without looking up. 'I don't have to steal it. I'm going to own it one day.' The kid's name was Kevin. Rusty's son-in-law.

Rusty shook his head and looked back at me. 'The day I get any respect around here I'll drop dead and be buried.'

I said, 'Eat the food around here and it'll happen sooner rather than later.'

Rusty Swetaggen laughed so hard that an architect looked over and frowned.

Kevin said, 'You want a Falstaff, Elvis?'

'Sure.'

Rusty told him to bring it to the table and led me to an empty window booth where someone had put a little *Reserved* sign. People were waiting by the maitre d', but Rusty had saved the booth.

After Kevin had brought the beer, I said, 'You get anything on my guy?'

Rusty hunkered over the table. 'This guy I talked to, he says the people from the Seventy-seventh like to hang at a

29

bar called Cody's over by LAX. It's a shitkicker place. They got dancers in little chicken-wire cages. They got secretaries go in to get picked up. Like that.'

'Is Thurman a regular?'

'He didn't give it to me as a fact, but a REACT unit is a tight unit, sort of like SWAT or Metro. They do everything together, and that's where they've been hanging.'

'You got the address?'

He told me and I wrote it down.

'Your guy know if Thurman is mixed up in anything dirty?'

Rusty looked pained, like he was letting me down. 'I couldn't push it, Hound Dog. Maybe I could've gotten more, but you want Mr Tact. The rest is going to take a couple days.'

'Thanks, Rusty. That's enough for now.'

I finished the Falstaff and took out my wallet. Rusty covered my hand with his. 'Forget it.'

I said, 'Come on, Rusty.'

Rusty's hand squeezed. 'No.' The squeeze got harder and Rusty's jagged teeth showed and suddenly the pumpkin head looked like a jack-o'-lantern from hell and you could see what had kept Rusty Swetaggen alive and safe for twenty-four years in a black-and-white. It was there for only a second and then it was gone, and he gently pushed my wallet toward me. 'You don't owe me anything, Elvis. I'm glad to help you, and I will always help you in any way I can. You know that.' There was something in his voice and his eyes and the way he held his hand that said that my not paying was profoundly important, as profound as anything had been or ever would be in his life.

I put the wallet away and stood. 'Okay, Rusty. Sure.'

He looked apologetic. 'I've got a couple more calls to make, and I'm waiting to hear from a guy. You want tact.'

'Sure.'

'You hungry? We got a pretty good halibut today.' Like nothing would make him happier than to feed me, to give to me.

'I'll see you around, Rusty. Thanks.'

One hour and forty minutes later I parked in a McDonald's lot about three-quarters of a mile from LAX and walked across the street to Cody's Saloon. Mid-afternoon was late for lunch and early for quitting time, but a dozen men were lining the bar and sipping cold beer out of plain glasses. There weren't any female real estate agents and none of the guys at the bar looked like architects, but you never know. Maybe they were politically incorrect and wanted to keep it a secret. There was a big sign on the roof of a neon cowgirl riding a bucking horse. The cowgirl looked sort of like a cheerleader from Dallas. Maybe she was politically incorrect, too.

A young guy with a lot of muscles was behind the bar, talking with a couple of women in skimpy cheerleader outfits who were hanging around at the waitress station. A red-haired woman in an even skimpier outfit danced without enthusiasm in a chicken-wire cage behind the bar. Neither the bartender nor the waitresses were looking at the dancer, and neither were most of the guys lining the bar. Guess it's tough to get motivated with the chicken wire. They were playing Dwight Yoakam.

I went to a little table across from the dancer's cage and one of the waitresses came over with her little pad. I ordered another Falstaff. When you've got a forty-dollar retainer, the sky's the limit.

When she came back with it, I said, 'What time do things pick up?' I gave her the nice smile. The Kevin Costner.

She smiled back and I saw her eyes flick to my hands. Nope. No wedding ring. I made the smile wider. She said, 'Mostly after dinner. We get a lot of cops in here and they don't get off until later.'

31

I nodded. 'You know an officer named Mark Thurman?'

She tried to remember. 'What's he look like?'

'Big. Like a jock. He probably comes around with a guy named Floyd Riggens. They work together.'

Now she remembered and her face grew hard. 'I know Floyd.' Floyd must be a real pip all the way around.

I grinned like it was an old joke. 'That Floyd is something, isn't he?'

'Uh-huh.' She wasn't seeing much humor in it.

'What time do they usually get here?'

'I don't know. Maybe eight. Something like that.' Like she was getting tired of talking about it. Maybe even pissed. Floyd must be something, all right. 'Look, I've got to get back to work.'

'Sure.'

She went back to the bar and I sipped the beer and pretty soon I ordered another. There didn't seem to be a lot to do until eight o'clock, so sipping Falstaff seemed like a good way to pass the time.

Dwight Yoakam stopped and Hank Williams, Jr, came on and pretty soon the day-shift waitresses left and the night shift cranked up the Garth Brooks and the Kentucky Headhunters. The night-shift dancers were younger and moved better in the cage, but maybe that was because of the music. Or maybe it just seemed that way because of the Falstaff. Maybe if you drank enough Falstaff your personal time scale would grind to a stop and everyone around you would move faster and faster until they looked like a Chip'n Dale cartoon running at fast forward and you looked like a still picture frozen in time. Maybe they would continue to age but you would stay young and pretty soon they'd be dead and you'd have the last laugh. That Falstaff is something, isn't it? Maybe I was just drunk. Occupational hazard.

By seven o'clock the crowd had grown and I didn't want to be there if Riggens or Thurman walked in early, so I paid for the beer, went back to the McDonald's, and bought a couple of cheeseburgers to eat in the car.

At fourteen minutes after eight, Mark Thurman's blue Ford Mustang turned into Cody's parking lot. There were three other people in the car. A brown-haired woman was sitting in the front passenger seat beside Thurman. Riggens and an overweight blonde were shoehorned into the back. The overweight blonde was loud and laughing and pulling at Riggens's pants as they got out of the car. The brown-haired woman was tall and slender and looked like a thirty-six C. They walked across the parking lot, Riggens and the blonde together, Thurman and the brunette together, and then the four of them went into the bar.

I sat in my car for a long time after they disappeared, smelling the McDonald's and tasting the beer and watching the neon cowgirl blink. My head hurt and I was tired from all the sitting, but I wasn't anxious to get home. Getting home meant going to bed and sleep wouldn't come easy tonight. Tomorrow I would have to speak with Jennifer Sheridan and tell her what I had found.

Sleep never comes easy when you're going to break someone's heart.

CHAPTER 5

I woke the next morning with a dull ache behind my right eye and the sound of finches on my deck. I have a little A-frame off Woodrow Wilson Drive in Laurel Canyon, in the hills above Hollywood. I don't have a yard because the A-frame is perched on a hillside, but I've got a deck, and a nice view of the canyon. A woman I know gave me a build-it-yourself bird-feeder kit for Christmas, so I built it, and hung it from the eve of my roof high enough to keep the birds safe from my cat. But the birds scratch the seed out of the feeder, then fly down to the deck to eat the seed. They know there's a cat, but still they go down to pick at the seed. When you think about it, people are often like this, too.

I rolled out of bed, pulled on a pair of shorts, then went downstairs and out onto the deck. The finches flew away in a gray, fluttery cloud.

I did twelve sun salutes from the hatha-yoga to loosen my muscles, then moved to the tai chi, and then to the tae kwon do, first the Tiger and Crane *katas*, and then the Dragon and Eagle. As I worked, the finches returned to eat and watch as if I were now elemental to their world and no longer a threat. I worked for the better part of an hour, driving through the *katas* faster and faster, breathing deep to well my energy, then unloading that energy with long explosive moves until my muscles burned and the sweat spotted the deck as if there had been a passing rain shower. I finished with another twelve sun salutes, and then I went in. Penance for the Falstaff. Or maybe just client avoidance.

My cat was staring at the finches. He's large and he's black and he carries his head sort of cocked to the side from when he was head-shot by a .22. He said, 'Naow?'

I shook my head. 'Not now. Got a call to make.'

He followed me into the kitchen and watched while I called my friend at B of A. You know you're serious when you call after an hour's worth of *katas* before you shower. Good thing we don't have smell-o-phones.

I said, 'You get anything out of the ordinary on Mark Thurman?' The detective makes a desperate last-ditch attempt at linking Mark Thurman to Criminal Activity.

'Doesn't look like it. Thurman's outstanding credit charges on both Visa and MasterCard appear typical. Also, he has not applied for higher credit limits nor additional credit cards through any facility in the state of California.' The desperate attempt fails.

'That's it, huh?'

'You sound disappointed.'

'What's disappointment to a hard guy like me?'

'Tell me about it. Are these good seats for Sting, or are we going to camp in the back of the house like last time?'

'Did I mention that you're not aging well?'

She hung up. So did I. These dames.

I took a deep breath, let it out, and then I called Jennifer Sheridan at Marty Beale's office. She answered on the second ring. 'Watkins, Okum, & Beale. Mr Beale's office.'

'This is Elvis Cole. I have uncovered some things, and we should speak.' The cat came over and head-bumped me.

'Well. All right.' She didn't sound happy about it, like maybe she could hear something in my voice. 'Can you tell me now?'

'It's better if we meet for lunch. Kate Mantilini's is very nice.'

More of the pause. 'Is it expensive?'

'I'll pay, Ms Sheridan.'

'Well, I only have the hour.' Nervous.

'I could pick up a couple of cheeseburgers and we could sit on the curb.'

'Maybe the restaurant would be all right. It's only a few blocks from here, isn't it?'

'Three blocks. I'll make a reservation. I will pick you up in front of your building or we can meet at the restaurant.'

'Oh, I don't mind walking.'

'Fine.'

I put the receiver down and the cat looked up at me. He said it again. 'Naow?'

I picked him up and held him close. He was warm against me and his fur was soft and I could feel his heart beat. It was good to hold him. He often doesn't like it, but sometimes he does, and I have found, over the years, that when I most need to hold him, he most often allows it. I like him for that. I think it's mutual.

I scrambled two eggs, put them in his bowl, then went upstairs to shower and dress. At seven minutes after twelve, I walked into Kate Mantilini's and found Jennifer Sheridan already seated. The waiters were smiling at her and an older woman at the next table was talking to her and all the lights of the restaurant seemed focused on her. Some people just have lives like that, I guess. She was wearing a bright blue pant suit with a large ruffled tie and black pumps with little bows on them, and she looked even younger than the first time I'd seen her. Maybe she wasn't twenty-three. Maybe she was seventeen and the people around us would think I was her father. If she looked seventeen and I looked thirty-eight, that would work out. Bummer.

She said, 'I hope this won't take long.'

'It won't.'

I motioned to the waiter and told him that we were in a

hurry and would like to order. He said fine and produced a little pad. I ordered the niçoise salad with sesame dressing and an Evian water. Jennifer Sheridan had a hamburger and french fries and a diet Coke. The waiter smiled at me when she ordered. Probably thought I was a lecher. When the waiter had gone, Jennifer Sheridan said, 'What have you found out, Mr Cole?' The mister.

'What I have to tell you will not be pleasant, and I want you to prepare yourself for it. If you'd rather leave the restaurant so that we might go someplace private, we can do that.'

She shook her head.

I said, 'Typically, when an officer is profiting from crime, it shows up in his lifestyle. He'll buy a boat or a time-share or maybe a high-end sound system. Something like that.'

She nodded.

'Mark hasn't. In fact, I checked his bank balances and his credit card expenses and there is no indication that he has received any undue or inordinate sums of money.'

She looked confused. 'What does that mean?'

'It means that he has not been acting strangely because he's involved in crime. There's a different reason. He's seeing another woman.'

Jennifer Sheridan made a little smile and shook her head as if I'd said three plus one is five and she was going to correct me. 'No. That's not possible.'

'I'm afraid that it is.'

'Where's your proof?' Angry now. The older woman at the next table looked over. She frowned when she did. She had a lot of hair and the frown made her look like one of those lizards with the big frill.

I said, 'Five minutes after you left my office yesterday, Mark came to see me. He had been following you. He explained to me that he was seeing someone else, and that he had not been able to bring himself to tell you. He asked me not to tell you this, but my obligation and my loyalty are to you. I'm sorry.' The detective delivers the death blow.

Jennifer Sheridan didn't look particularly devastated, but maybe that was just me.

The waiter brought our food and asked Jennifer Sheridan if she'd like catsup for her french fries. She said yes and we waited as he went to the counter, found a bottle, and brought it back. Neither of us said anything and Jennifer Sheridan didn't look at me until he had gone away. He seemed to know that something was wrong and frowned at me, too. The woman with the big hair was keeping a careful eye on our table.

When the waiter was gone, Jennifer Sheridan ate two french fries, then said, 'For Mark to come to you and make up a story like this, he must be in bigger trouble than I thought.'

I stared at her. 'You think he's making it up?'

'Of course.'

I put down my fork and I looked at the niçoise. It was a good-looking salad with freshly grilled ahi tuna, and I think I would've enjoyed eating it. Jennifer Sheridan had asked me for proof and I told her about my visit from Mark Thurman, but I hadn't told her the rest of it and I hadn't wanted to. I said, 'He's not making this up.'

'Yes, he is. If you knew Mark, you'd know that, too.' Confident.

I nodded, and then I looked at the salad again. Then I said, 'What size bra do you wear?'

She turned a deep shade of crimson. 'Now you're being ugly.'

'I put you at a thirty-four B. I went into Mark's apartment to look through his bank papers and I found a thirty-six C-cup brassiere.'

She looked shocked. 'You broke into his apartment? You went through his things?'

'That's what private detectives do, Ms Sheridan.'

She put her hands in her lap. 'It isn't real.'

'It was a red Lily of France brassiere. I held it. It was real.'

She shook her head. 'That's not what I mean. They knew you would look so they planted it there to make you think he was seeing another woman. What do they call it? A false lead?'

'Later that evening, I staked out a country-and-western bar called Cody's. It's a place where the police officers who work with Mark tend to gather. At a little bit after eight last night, Mark and his partner Floyd Riggens arrived. Mark was with a tall woman with dark brown hair.' I felt bad telling her and the bad feeling was oily and close, but there didn't seem to be any other way.

'And?'

'I wish I had better news, but there it is. I have looked into the matter and this is what I have found. I think my work here is done.'

'You mean you're quitting?'

'The case is solved. There's nothing left to do.'

Jennifer Sheridan's eyes welled and her mouth opened and she let out a long loud wail and began to cry. The woman with the big hair gasped and looked our way and so did most of the other people in the restaurant.

I said, 'Maybe we should leave.'

'I'm all right.' She made loud whooping sounds like she couldn't catch her breath and the tears rolled down her cheeks, making dark tracks from the mascara. The waiter stormed over to the maitre d' and made an angry gesture. The woman with the big hair said something to an elderly man at an adjoining table and the elderly man glared at me. I felt two inches tall.

'Try to see it this way, Jennifer. Mark being involved with another woman is better than Mark being involved in crime. Crime gets you in jail. Another woman is a problem you can work out together.'

Jennifer Sheridan wailed louder. 'I'm not crying because of that.'

'You're not?'

'I'm crying because Mark's in trouble and he needs our help and you're *quitting*. What kind of crummy detective are you?'

I spread my hands. The maitre d' said something to the waiter and the waiter came over.

'Is everything all right, sir?'

'Everything is fine, thank you.'

He looked at Jennifer Sheridan.

She shook her head. 'He's a quitter.'

The waiter frowned and went away. The woman with the big hair made a *tsk*ing sound like she thought they should've done something.

Jennifer said, 'I want to be sure, that's all. If he's seeing this other woman, then who is she? Do they work together? Does he love her? Did you follow them home?'

'No.'

'Then you don't know, do you? You don't know if they slept together. You don't know if he kissed her good night. You don't even know if they left the bar together.'

I rubbed my brow. 'No.'

The woman with the big hair whispered again to the elderly man, then stood and went to three women sitting in a window booth. One of the women stood to meet her.

Jennifer Sheridan was crying freely and her voice was choking. 'He needs us, Mr Cole. We can't leave him like this, we *can't*. You've *got* to help me.'

The woman with the big hair shouted, 'Help her, for God's sake.'

The three women at the window booth shouted, 'Yeah!'

I looked at them and then I looked back at Jennifer Sheridan. She didn't look seventeen anymore. She looked fifteen. And homeless. I dropped my napkin into the niçoise. I'd had maybe three bites. 'You win.'

Jennifer Sheridan brightened. 'You'll stay with it?'

I nodded.

'You see how it's possible, don't you? You see that I'm right about this?'

I spread my hands. The Defeated Detective.

She said, 'Oh, thank you, Mr Cole. Thank you. I knew I could depend on you.' She was bubbling now, just like Judy Garland in *The Wizard of Oz*. She used her napkin to dry her eyes, but all she did was smear the mascara. It made her look like a raccoon.

The woman with the big hair smiled and the elderly man looked relieved. The waiter and the maitre d' nodded at each other. The three women in the window booth resumed their meal. The restaurant returned to its normal course of lunchtime events, and Jennifer Sheridan finished her hamburger. Everybody was happy.

'Jesus Christ,' I said.

The waiter appeared at my elbow. 'Is something wrong with the niçoise, sir?'

I looked at him carefully. 'Get away from me before I shoot you.'

He said, 'Very good, sir,' and he got.

CHAPTER 6

At twelve fifty-five, I gave Jennifer Sheridan a lift the three blocks back to her office and then I headed back toward mine, but I wasn't particularly happy about it. I felt the way you feel after you've given money to a panhandler because the panhandler has just dealt you a sob story that both of you knew was a lie but you went for it anyway. I frowned a lot and stared down a guy driving an ice cream truck just so I could feel tough. If a dog had run out in front of me I probably would've swerved to hit it. Well, maybe not. There's only so much sulking you can do.

The problem was that Jennifer Sheridan wasn't a panhandler and she wasn't running a number on me. She was a young woman in pain and she believed what she believed, only believing something doesn't make it so. Maybe I should spend the rest of the afternoon figuring out a way to convince her. Maybe I could rent one of those high-end, see-in-the-dark video cameras and tape Mark Thurman in the act with the brown-haired woman. Then we could go back to Kate Mantilini's and I could show everyone and what would the woman with the big hair think then? Hmm. Maybe there are no limits to sulking, after all.

I stopped at a Lucky market, bought two large bottles of Evian water, put one in my trunk, then continued on toward my office. Half a block later two guys in a light blue four-door sedan pulled up behind me and I thought I was being followed. A Hispanic guy in a dark blue

Dodgers cap was driving and a younger guy with a light blond butch cut was riding shotgun. His was the kind of blond that was so blond it was almost white. I looked at them, but they weren't looking at me, and a block and a half later they turned into a Midas Muffler shop. So much for being followed.

When I got up to my office I opened the French doors off the little balcony, then turned on the radio, and lay down on my couch. KLSX on the airwaves. Howard Stern all morning, classic rock all afternoon. We were well into classic rock and I liked it just fine. Lynyrd Skynyrd. What could be better than that?

It was a cool, clear afternoon and I could be at the beach but instead I was here. Portrait of a detective in a detective's office. When a detective is in a detective's office, shouldn't he be detecting? One of life's imponderables. The problem was that I didn't suspect Mark Thurman of a crime, and crime still didn't look good to me as the answer to Jennifer Sheridan's problems. If you're talking cops and crime, you're talking motive, and I didn't see it. I had been in Thurman's home and I had talked to his fiancée and his neighbors, and the crime part just didn't fit. When you're talking cops and crime, you're talking conspicuous consumption. Cops like to buy cars and they like to buy boats and they like to buy vacation homes and they explain it all by saying that the wife came into a little money. Only Thurman didn't have a wife and, as near as I could tell, he didn't have any of the other things, either. Of course, there could always be something else. Debt and dope are popular motives, but Thurman didn't seem to fit the profile on those, either. I had witnessed events and gathered evidence, and an examination of same had led to certain conclusions which seemed fair to me but not to the client. Maybe the client was crazy. Maybe I was crazy. Maybe the client was just confused and maybe I should have done more to alleviate her confusion, but I had not. Why? Maybe she should be the detective and I should be the client. We couldn't be any more confused than we were now.

Sometime later the phone rang. I got up, went to my desk, and answered it. 'Elvis Cole Detective Agency. We never lie down on the job.'

'Caught you sleeping, huh?' It was Rusty Swetaggen.

'Ha. We never sleep.'

Rusty said, 'I talked to a guy who knows about REACT.'

'Yeah?' I sat in the chair and leaned back and put my feet up. It was quiet in the office. I looked at the water cooler and the couch and the two chairs opposite my desk and the file cabinet and the Pinocchio clock and the closed door to Joe Pike's office. The water machine hummed and little figures of Jiminy Cricket and Mickey Mouse stared back at me and the coffee machine smelled of old coffee, but something was missing.

Rusty said, 'Maybe I shouldn't even mention this.'

'You've rethought our friendship and you want me to pay for lunch?'

'Nothing that important. This guy I talked with, he said something that's maybe a little funny about the REACT guys down at Seventy-seven.'

'Funny.' I have seen these things in my office ten thousand times, and today something was different.

'Yeah. It's like he wouldn't't've even mentioned it if I hadn't pushed him, like it's one of those things that doesn't matter unless you're looking, and it probably doesn't matter even then.'

'Okay.' I was only half listening. I picked up the phone and carried it around to the file cabinet and looked back at my desk. Nope. Nothing was off with the desk.

'He says their arrest pattern is maybe a little hinky for the past few months, like maybe these guys aren't making

44

the arrests that they should be, and are making a lot of arrests that they shouldn't.'

'Like what?' I looked at the file cabinet. I looked at the Pinocchio clock.

'REACT was always big on dope and stolen property, and they've always posted high arrest rates, but the past couple of months they haven't been making the big numbers. They've mostly been booking gang-bangers and stickup geeks. It's a different level of crime.'

'We're not just talking Thurman? We're talking the team?'

'Yeah. It's a team thing. What I hear, Thurman's got a great record. That's why he got the early promotion.' I looked at the French doors. I looked at the little refrigerator. Nope.

Rusty said, 'Hell, Elvis, maybe it's just the off-season. I hear anything else, I'll let you know.'

'Sure, Rusty. Thanks.' I looked back at the Pinocchio clock.

Rusty Swetaggen hung up and then I hung up and that's when I saw it. The Pinocchio clock was still. Its eyes weren't moving. It wasn't making the tocking sound. The hands were stopped at eleven-nineteen.

I followed the cord to where it plugs into the wall behind the file cabinet. The plug was in the socket, but not all the way, as if someone had brushed the cord and pulled it partway out of the wall and hadn't noticed. I stood very still and looked around the office and, in the looking, the office now felt strange, as if an alien presence were a part of it. I went back to my desk, opened each drawer and looked at it without touching it. Everything appeared normal and as I had left it. Ditto the things on the desk top. I got up again and opened the file cabinet and looked at the files without touching them and tried to recall if they were positioned as I had last seen them, but I couldn't be sure. I keep all active files in the office cabinet as well as all cases in the current quarter. At the end of every quarter I box the closed files and put them in storage. There were twenty-seven files in the cabinet drawer. Not much if you're the Pinkertons but plenty if you're me. Each file contains a client sheet and day book entries where I've made notes along the way, as well as any photographs or paperwork I accumulate, and a conclusion sheet, which is usually just a copy of the letter I write to the client when the job is over. I hadn't yet made a file for Jennifer Sheridan. I fingered through the twenty-seven files that were there, but nothing seemed to be missing. I closed the cabinet and looked at the little figurines of Jiminy Cricket and Mickey Mouse and Pinocchio on my desk and on top of the file cabinet. Jiminy doffing his top hat had been moved, but Mickey and Minnie riding in a Hupmobile had not. Sonofagun. Someone had searched my office.

I put Jiminy in his proper place, plugged in the Pinocchio clock and set it to the correct time, then went back to my desk and thought about Mark Thurman. The odds were large that whoever had come into my office wasn't Mark Thurman or anyone who knew Thurman, and that the timing had just been coincidental, but the timing still bothered me. I had thought the case was over, but apparently it wasn't. I wasn't exactly sure that the case was still on, but maybe that's what I had to prove. Hmm. Maybe I should ask Jennifer Sheridan to be a partner in the firm. Maybe she gave detective lessons.

I called this reporter I know who works for the *Examiner* named Eddie Ditko. He's about a million years old and he loves me like a son. He said, 'Jesus Christ, I'm up to my ass in work. What the fuck do *you* want?' You see?

'I need to find out about the REACT unit deployed out of the Seventy-seventh Division down in South Central L.A.'

Eddie said, 'You think I know this shit off the top of my head?' Isn't Eddie grand?

'Nope. I was thinking maybe you could conjure it in your crystal ball.'

'You got crystal balls, always imposing like this.' Eddie went into a coughing fit and made a wet hacking noise that sounded like he was passing a sinus.

'You want I should call 911?'

'That's it. Be cute.' I could hear keys tapping on his VDT. 'This'll take some time. Why don'tchu swing around in a little while. I might have something by then.'

'Sure.'

I put on my jacket, looked around my office, then went to the door and locked up. I had once seen a James Bond movie where James Bond pasted a hair across the seam in the doorjamb so he could tell if anyone opened the door while he was gone. I thought about doing it, but figured that someone in the insurance office across the hall would come out while I was rigging the hair and then I'd have to explain and they'd probably think it was stupid. I'd probably have to agree with them.

I forgot about the hair and went to see Eddie Ditko.

CHAPTER 7

The *Los Angeles Examiner* is published out of a large, weathered red-brick building midway between downtown L.A. and Chinatown, in a part of the city that looks more like it belongs in Boston or Cincinnati than in Southern California. There are sidewalks and taxis and tall buildings of cement and glass and nary a palm tree in sight. Years ago, enterprising developers built a nest of low-rise condominiums, foolishly believing that Angelenos wanted to live near their work and would snap the places up to avoid the commute. What they didn't count on is that people were willing to work downtown but no one wanted to live there. If you're going to live in Southern California, why live in a place that looks like Chicago?

I put my car in the lot across the street, crossed at the light, then took the elevator up to the third floor and the pretty black receptionist who sits there. 'Elvis Cole to see Eddie Ditko. He's expecting me.'

She looked through her pass list and asked me to sign in. 'He's in the city room. Do you know where that is?'

'Yep.'

She gave me a peel-and-stick guest badge and went back to talking into the phone. I looked at the badge and felt like I was at a PTA meeting. *Hello! My name is Elvis!* I affixed the badge to my shirt and tried not to look embarrassed. Why risk the hall police?

I went through a pair of leather upholstered swinging doors, then along a short hall that opened into the city

48

room. Twenty desks were jammed together in the center of the room, and maybe a dozen people were hanging around the desks, most of them typing as fast as they could and the rest of them talking on the phone. Eddie Ditko had the desk on the far left corner, about as close to the editors' offices as you could get without being one of the editors. A woman in her late twenties was working at a terminal next to him. She was wearing huge round glasses and a loud purple dress with very wide shoulders and a little purple pillbox hat. It was the kind of clothes you wore when you were establishing your identity as a retro-hip urban intellectual. Or maybe she was just odd. She glanced up once as I approached, then went on typing. Eddie was chewing on an unlit Grenadiers cigar and scowling at his VDT when I got there. He had to be forty years older than her. He didn't bother glancing up. 'Hey, Eddie, when are they going to make you an editor around here and get you off the floor?'

Eddie jerked the cigar out of his mouth and spit a load of brown juice at his wastebasket. He never lit them. He chewed them. 'Soon's I stop saying what I think and start kissing the right ass, like everybody else around here.' He said it loud enough for most of the room to hear. The purple woman glanced over, then went on with her typing. Tolerant. Eddie grimaced and rubbed at his chest. 'Jeez, I got chest pains. I'm a goddamned walking thrombo.'

'Lay off the fats and exercise a little.'

'What're you, my fuckin' mother?' Eddie leaned to the side and broke wind. Classy.

I pulled up a chair and sat on it backwards, hooking my arms over its back. 'What'd you find on the REACT guys?'

Eddie clamped the wet cigar in his teeth, leaned toward the VDT, and slapped buttons. The little VDT screen filled with printing. 'I put together some stuff from our morgue files, but that's about it. REACT is an elite

surveillance unit, and that means the cops block their
files. They can't do their jobs if everybody knows who
they're surveilling.'

'How many guys we talking about?'

'Five. You want the names?'

'Yeah.'

He hit a couple of buttons and a little printer beside his
VDT chattered and spit out a page. He handed it to me.
Five names were listed in a neat column in the center of
the page.

> LT. ERIC DEES
> SGT. PETER GARCIA
> OFF. FLOYD RIGGENS
> OFF. WARREN PINKWORTH
> OFF. MARK THURMAN

I looked over the names. They meant nothing. 'They
any good?'

Eddie grinned like a shark with his eye on a fat boy in
baggy shorts. 'They wouldn't be a REACT team if they
weren't any good. They target felons and they've got a
ninety-nine-point-seven per cent conviction rate. Dees
has been down there almost six years, along with Garcia
and Riggens. Pinkworth joined a couple of years back and
they picked up Thurman a year ago. He's the baby.'

'How'd Thurman make the squad?'

Eddie hit more buttons and the printing on the screen
changed. 'Same as everybody else. Top ten of his academy
class, a string of outstandings in his quarterly evaluations,
Officer of the Month four times. You remember that nut
pulled a gun on the RTD bus and threatened to start
killing people unless Madonna gave him a blow job?'

'Sort of.'

The purple woman looked over. Interested.

'Hell, I wrote about that one. Guy stops the bus in the

middle of Hollywood Boulevard, and Thurman and a guy named Palmetta were the first cops on the scene. Thurman was, what, maybe twenty-two, twenty-three years old?'

The purple woman shrugged.

'Yeah, he was just a kid. That was part of the story. Anyway, the nut shoots this fat guy in the leg to make his point, then grabs this nine-year-old girl and starts screaming he's going to do her next. He wants Madonna, right? Palmetta puts the call in for a hostage negotiator and the SWAT team but Thurman figures there ain't time. He takes off his gun and goes into the bus to talk to the guy. The nut tries to shoot him twice but he's shaking so bad both shots miss, so he puts the gun to the girl's head. You know what happened then?'

The purple lady was leaning forward, frowning because she wanted to know.

Eddie said, 'Thurman tells the guy he's had Madonna and Madonna's a lousy lay, but he knows Rosanna Arquette and Rosanna Arquette is the best blow job in town. Thurman tells the guy if he puts down the gun, as soon as he's out on bail, he'll set it up with Rosanna Arquette 'cause she owes him a couple of favors.'

The purple woman said, 'And he went for that?'

Eddie spread his hands 'Here's a nut believes he's gonna get Madonna, why not? The guy says only if she blows him *twice*. Thurman says, okay, she'll do it twice, but not on the same day, she's got a thing about that. The nut says that's okay with him 'cause he's only good for once a week anyway, and puts down the gun.'

The purple lady laughed, and she didn't look so odd anymore.

Eddie was smiling, too. 'That was, what, a couple years ago? Thurman gets the Medal of Valor and six months later he wins the early promotion to plain-clothes and the REACT team. They're top cops, pal. Every one of those guys has a story like that in his file else he wouldn't be on the team.'

'Eddie, what if I didn't want the good stuff? What if I was a reporter and I was looking for something that maybe had a smell to it?'

'Like what?'

'Like maybe I'm looking to see if they've crossed over.'

Eddie shook his head and patted the VDT. 'If it's in here, it's already public record. Someone would've had to lodge the complaint, and it would've had to come out through LAPD PR or one of the news agencies or the courts. It wouldn't be a secret and no one would be trying to hide it.'

'Okay. Could you check for allegations?'

'Substantiated or otherwise?'

I looked at him.

'Reporter humor. It's probably over your head.' Eddie hit more keys and watched the screen, and then did it again. When he had filled and wiped the screen three times, he nodded and leaned back. 'I had it search through the files keying on the officers' names for every news release during the past year, then I threw out the junk about them saving babies and arresting the Incredible Hulk and just kept the bad stuff. This is pretty neat.'

I leaned forward and looked at the screen. 'What's it found?'

'Excessive-force complaints. "Suspect injured while resisting arrest." "Suspect filed brutality charges." Like that. 'Course, these guys are busting felons and felons tend to get nasty, but check it out, you've got twenty-six complaints in the past ten months, and eleven of them are against this guy Riggens.'

'Any charges brought?'

'*Nada*. IAD issued letters of reprimand twice, and dealt a two-week suspension, but that's it.'

I read the list. Twenty-six names ran down the left side

of the page, and next to each name there was a booking number and the arresting charge and the claims levied by the defendants and the accused officer or officers. Riggens had all or part of eleven of the charges, and the remainder were divided pretty evenly between Pinkworth and Dees and Garcia and Thurman. Thurman had part of three.

Eddie said, 'You've got to understand, cops on these special tac squads get charges filed all the time, so most of these really are garbage, but if I'm looking for tuna I'm looking for losers, and that's Riggens.'

'Thanks, Eddie.'

Eddie stuck the cigar in his mouth and rolled it around and looked at me. 'What you got going here, kid? It any good?'

'I don't know. I'm still just running down the leads.'

He nodded and sucked on the cigar, and then he gazed at the editors' offices. He wasn't getting any younger. 'If there's a story here, I want it.'

'You bet, Eddie.'

Eddie Ditko spread his hands, then hacked up something phlegmy and spit it into the basket. No one looked and no one paid any mind. I guess seniority has its privileges.

I went back the way I came, took the elevator down to the lobby, then used the pay phone there to call Jennifer Sheridan in Marty Beale's office. I asked her for Floyd Riggens's address. She said, 'Which one?'

'What do you mean, which one?'

'He's divorced. He used to live in La Cañada, but now he's got a little apartment somewhere.'

I told her that if she had them both, I'd take them both. She did. She also told me that Riggens's ex-wife was named Margaret, and that they had three children.

When I had the information that I needed, I said, 'Jennifer?'

'Yes?'

'Did Mark ever complain to you about Floyd?'

There was a little pause. 'Mark said he didn't like having Floyd as a partner. He said Floyd scared him.'

'Did he say why?'

'He said Floyd drank a lot. Do you think Floyd is involved in this?'

'I don't know, Jennifer. I'm going to try to find out.'

We hung up and I went out of the building and across the street to my car.

CHAPTER 8

Floyd Riggens was living in a small, six-unit stucco apartment building on a side street in Burbank, just about ten blocks from the Walt Disney Studio. There were three units on the bottom and three on top, and an L-shaped stair at the far end of the building. It was a cramped, working-class neighborhood, but working class was good. Working class means that people go to work. When people go to work, it makes things easier for private eyes and other snoopers who skulk around where they shouldn't.

I parked three houses down, then walked back. Riggens had the front apartment, on top. Number four. None of the units seemed to belong to a manager, which was good, but the front door was open on the bottom center unit, which was bad. Light mariachi music came from the center unit and the wonderful smells of simmering *menudo* and fresh-cut cilantro and, when I drew closer, the sound of a woman singing with the music. I walked past her door as if I belonged, then took the stairs to the second level. Upstairs, the drapes were drawn on all three units. Everybody at work. I went to number four, opened the screen, and stood in Riggens's door with my back to the street. It takes longer to pick a lock than to use a key, but if a neighbor saw me, maybe they'd think I was fumbling with the key.

Floyd Riggens's apartment was a single large studio with a kitchenette and a closet and the bath along the side wall. A sleeping bag and a blanket and an ashtray were lined against the opposite wall and a tiny Hitachi portable television sat on a cardboard box in the corner. A carton of Camel Wides was on the floor by the sleeping bag. You could smell the space, and it wasn't the sweet, earthy smells of *menudo*. It smelled of mildew and smoke and BO. If Floyd Riggens was pulling down graft, he sure as hell wasn't spending it here.

I walked through the bathroom and the closet and the kitchenette and each was dirty and empty of the items of life, as if Riggens didn't truly live here, or expect to, any more than a tourist expects to live in a motel. There was a razor and a toothbrush and deodorant and soap in the bathroom, but nothing else. The sink and the tub and the toilet were filmed with the sort of built-up grime that comes of long-term inattention, as if Riggens used these things and left, expecting that someone else would clean them, only the someone never showed and never cleaned.

There were four shirts and three pants hanging in the closet, along with a single navy dress uniform. Underwear and socks and two pairs of shoes were laid out neatly on the floor of the closet, and an empty gym bag was thrown in the far back corner. The underwear and the socks were the only neat thing in the apartment.

An open bottle of J&B scotch sat on the counter in the kitchenette, and three empties were in a trash bag on the floor. The smell of scotch was strong. A couple of Domino's pizza boxes were parked in the refrigerator along with four Styrofoam Chicken McNuggets boxes and half a quart of lowfat milk. An open box of plastic forks and a package of paper plates sat on the counter beside the sink. The sink was empty, but that's probably because there were no pots or pans or dishes. I guess Riggens had made the choice to go disposable. Why clutter your life with the needless hassle of washing and cleaning when you can use it and throw it away?

It had taken me all of four minutes to look through

Riggens's apartment. I went back into the main studio and stood in the center of the floor and felt oily and somehow unclean. I don't know what I expected, but it wasn't this, and it left me feeling vaguely depressed, as if this wasn't a place where someone lived, but more a place where someone died. I went to the sleeping bag and squatted. A photograph had been pushpinned to the wall. It was an older picture and showed Riggens with a plain woman about his age and three kids. A boy and two girls. The boy looked maybe fourteen and sullen. The oldest girl was maybe twelve, and the youngest girl was a lot younger. Maybe four. She was tiny compared to the others, with a cute round face and a mop of curly hair and she was holding up a single bluegill on a nylon cord. She looked confused. Riggens was smiling and so was his wife. Margaret. They were standing in front of the bait shop at Castaic Lake, maybe twenty miles north of L.A. in the Santa Susana Mountains. The picture looked worn around the edges, as if it had been handled often. Maybe it had. Maybe Riggens lived here but maybe he didn't. Maybe he brought his body here, and drank, and slept, but while the body was here he looked at the picture a lot and let his mind go somewhere else. Castaic, maybe. Where people were smiling.

I closed the apartment as I had found it, went down the stairs, and picked up the Ventura Freeway east through the Glendale Pass and into La Cañada in the foothills of the Verdugo Mountains.

It was mid-afternoon when I got there, and knots of junior high school kids were walking along the sidewalks with books and gym bags, but no one looked very interested in going home or doing homework.

Margaret Riggens lived in a modest ranch-style home with a poplar tree in the front yard in the flats at the base of the foothills. It was one of those stucco-and-clapboard numbers that had been built in the mid-fifties when a developer had come in with one set of house plans and an army of bulldozers and turned an orange grove into a housing tract to sell 'affordable housing' to veterans come to L.A. to work in the aerospace business. The floor plan of every house on the block would be the same as every other house. The only differences would be the colors and the landscaping and the people within the houses. I guess there is affordability in sameness.

I parked at the curb across the street as a girl maybe thirteen with limp blonde hair walked across the Riggenses' front lawn and let herself into their home without knocking. That would be the older daughter. A white Oldsmobile Delta 88 was parked in the drive. It needed a wash. The house looked like it needed a wash, too. The stucco was dusty and the clapboard part was peeling and needed to be scraped and painted. I crossed the street, then went up the drive to the front door and rang the bell. It would have been shorter to cut across the lawn, but there you go.

A tired woman in a sleeveless sun shirt and baggy shorts opened the door. She was smoking a Marlboro. I said, 'Hello, Ms Riggens. Pete Simmons, Internal Affairs, LAPD.' I took out my license and held it up. It would work, or it wouldn't. She would read the ID, or she wouldn't.

Margaret Riggens said, 'What'd that sonofabitch do now?' Guess she didn't bother to read it.

I put the license away. 'I'd like to ask you a couple of questions. It won't take long.'

'Ain't that what they all say.' She took a final pull on the Marlboro, then flipped it into the front yard and stepped out of the door to let me in. I guess visits by guys like Pete Simmons were an inevitable and expected part of her life.

We went through the living room into an adjoining dining area off the kitchen. The girl who had come in before me was sitting cross-legged on the living room floor, watching *Geraldo* and reading a copy of *Sassy* magazine. There was a hard pack of Marlboros beside her and a green Bic lighter and a big clay ashtray that looked like she'd made it in pottery class. She was smoking. Loud music came from the back of the house, but there was a muffled quality to it as if a door was closed. The music suddenly got louder, and a boy's voice screamed, 'I told you to stay out of my room, you little shit! I don't want you here!' Then the boy came out of the back hall, pulling the younger girl by the upper arm. He was maybe sixteen now, with most of his father's growth, and she was maybe six. The little girl's face was screwed up and she was crying. The boy shouted, 'Mom, make her stay out of my room! I don't want her back there!'

Margaret Riggens said, 'Jesus Christ, Alan.'

I said, 'You're holding her too tight. Let go.'

Alan said, 'Who in the hell are you?'

The little girl was staring at me. 'You're hurting her,' I said. 'Let go.'

Margaret Riggens said, 'Hey, I don't need any help with my kids.'

I was looking at Alan and Alan was looking at me, and then he suddenly let go and bent over the little girl and screamed, 'I *hate* you!' He stomped back down the hall and the music went soft as the door closed. The little girl didn't seem too upset by what had happened. Guess it happened so often she was used to it. Probably even a game by now. She rubbed at her arm and ran back down the hall. The music didn't change pitch, so I guess she went into her own room.

Margaret Riggens said, 'These kids,' then stooped down, took a cigarette from her older daughter's pack, and turned away to sit at the dining room table.

I said, 'Maybe it'd be better if we had a little privacy.'

Margaret Riggens used a book of paper matches to light

the Marlboro, and put the spent match in a little beanbag ashtray she had on the table. 'Is Floyd going to get fired?' Guess the privacy didn't matter.

'No, ma'am. This is just follow-up on a couple of things.'

'That alimony is all I have. He pays it on time. Every month.'

I took out the little pad I keep in my jacket and made a big deal out of taking that down. 'That's good to hear. The Department frowns on a man if he ducks his responsibility.'

She nodded and sucked on the cigarette. Out in the living room, the oldest girl was sucking on a cigarette, too.

I tried to look sly. 'We hear enough good things like that, and it makes it easy to overlook a bad thing. Do you see?'

She squinted at me through the smoke. 'I don't understand.'

I made a little shrugging move. Conversational. 'Everybody thinks we're looking to chop heads, but that's not true. We hear a guy does right by his family, we don't want to throw him out in the streets. We find out he's gotten himself into trouble, we'll try to counsel him and keep him on the payroll. Maybe suspend him for a while, maybe demote him, but keep him employed. So he can take care of his family.'

She drew so hard on the Marlboro that the coal glowed like a flare. 'What kind of trouble?'

I smiled. 'That's what I want you to tell me, Ms Riggens.'

Margaret Riggens turned toward her older daughter. 'Sandi. Shut off the TV and go to your room for a little while, okay?'

Sandi gathered up her things, then went down the same

hall the other kids had used. Margaret turned back to me. 'I don't know what you're talking about.'

'You and Floyd talk?'

'Maybe once a week. There's always something with one of the kids.'

'He's supporting two households, Ms Riggens. Kids need things. So do adults.'

'Jesus Christ, have you seen where he lives?'

I spread my hands. 'Has money seemed a little easier to come by?'

'Ha.'

'Has Floyd maybe hinted around that he has something going?'

'Absolutely not.'

I leaned forward and I lowered my voice. 'If an officer crosses the line and someone aids and abets in that crossing, they can be charged. Did you know that, Ms Riggens?'

She drew on the cigarette and now her hands were trembling. 'Are you telling me that Floyd has stepped over the line?'

I stared at her.

She stood up, dribbling cigarette ash. 'I've had enough with that sonofabitch. I really have. I don't know anything about this. I don't know what the hell you're talking about.'

'Sit down, Ms Riggens.'

She sat. Breathing hard.

'I'm making no accusations. I'm just curious. Floyd has a problem with the drinking. Floyd has a problem with the excessive-force complaints. Floyd has money problems. Pretty soon problems become a way of life. You see how these things add up?'

She crushed out the cigarette in the little beanbag ashtray and lit another. The first continued to smolder.

'I'm not accusing Floyd, and I'm not accusing you. I'm

just wondering if maybe you've heard anything, or noticed a change in Floyd's behavior, that's all.'

She nodded. Calmer, now, but with eyes that were still frightened and weak. The look in her eyes made me feel small and greasy, and I wanted to tell her it had all been a mistake and leave, but you don't learn things by leaving. Even when the staying smells bad.

She said, 'He's been out of his mind ever since that guy died. The past couple of years have been tough, but since then has been the worst. That's when he went back to the bottle.'

I nodded like I knew what she was saying.

'He was in AA before that, and he was getting better, too. He'd come over sometimes, we'd have dinner, like that.'

'But then the guy died?'

She rolled her eyes. 'Well, everyone's still thinking about Rodney King and this black guy dies when they're trying to arrest him and then the family files a lawsuit and it was awful. Floyd started drinking worse than ever. He was angry all the time, and he'd blow up over the tiniest thing. They told me it was a stress reaction.'

'About how long ago was that?'

She gestured with the cigarette. 'What was it? Three or four months?'

I nodded. 'Did Floyd feel responsible?'

She laughed. 'Floyd doesn't feel responsible for hitting the bowl in the morning. I thought he was worried about the suit, but then the suit went away and I thought he'd relax. You know those suits cost a fortune. But he still stayed drunk all the time. Eric would call and check on him to make sure he was holding it together. Things like that. Eric was a godsend.' Eric Dees.

I nodded.

'Floyd hasn't been acting right since then. If he's gotten

himself mixed up in something, I'll bet that's why. I'll bet it's all part of the stress reaction.'

'Maybe so.'

'That should qualify for disability, shouldn't it?'

There were about ten million questions I wanted to ask, but I couldn't ask them without tipping her that I wasn't from LAPD. I patted her hand and tried to look reassuring. 'That'll be fine, Ms Riggens. You've been a big help, and that will be in the record.'

'Why don't you people make him go back to AA? When he was in AA he was doing a lot better.'

'Let's just keep this our little secret, all right, Ms. Riggens? That way it looks better for you all the way around.'

She crushed out the cigarette into the over-full ashtray and pushed ashes out onto the table. 'Look, I don't know what Floyd's mixed up with, and I don't want to know. I'm not aiding and abetting anything. I got enough to worry about.'

'Sure. Thank you for your time.'

I got up and went to the door. Margaret Riggens stayed at the table and lit another Marlboro and drew the smoke deep off the match and stared out through the windows into her shabby backyard. You could hear the kids screaming over the loud bass throbbing of the music and I imagined that it went on without end, and that her living hell wasn't a whole lot different from Floyd's.

Out in the living room there was an upright Yamaha piano that looked like it hadn't been played in a long time. A schoolbag was sitting on one end of it, and half a dozen wilting yellow roses were floating in a glass jar on the other end. Between the two was a framed picture of Floyd and Margaret Riggens standing together at his police academy graduation. They were fifteen years younger, and they were smiling. It was a photograph very much like the one that Jennifer Sheridan had, only

Jennifer and Mark still looked like the people in their picture, and Floyd and Margaret didn't.

I guess romance isn't for everyone.

CHAPTER 9

When I pulled away from the house that Floyd Riggens once shared with his wife and children, the sun was low in the west and the ridgeline along the Verdugo Mountains was touched with orange and pink. I worked my way across the valley, letting the rush hour traffic push me along, and enjoyed the darkening sky. I wondered if Margaret Riggens found much in the mountains or the sky to enjoy, but perhaps those things were too far away for her to see. When you're hurting, you tend to fix your eyes closer to home.

I cut across the northern edge of Burbank and Pacoima, and then dropped down Coldwater to a little place I know called Mazzarino's that makes the very best pizza in Los Angeles. I got a vegetarian with a side of anchovies to go and, when I pulled into my carport fifteen minutes later, the pizza was still warm.

I opened a Falstaff and put out the pizza for me and the anchovies for the cat, only the cat wasn't around. I called him, and waited, but he still didn't come. Off doing cat things, no doubt.

I ate the pizza and I drank the beer and I tried watching the TV, but I kept thinking about Margaret Riggens and that maybe I had come at all of this from the wrong direction. You think crime, and then you think money, but maybe that wasn't it. Maybe Mark Thurman had gotten himself involved in another type of crime. And maybe it wasn't Mark alone. Maybe it was Mark and Floyd. Maybe it was the entire REACT team. For all I knew, it was the full and complete population of the state of California, and I was the only guy left out of the loop. Me and Jennifer Sheridan. I was still thinking about that when I fell asleep.

At ten oh-six the next morning I called this cop I know who works in North Hollywood. A voice answered the phone with, 'Detectives.'

'Is that you, Griggs?' It was this other cop I know, Charlie Griggs.

'Who's this?'

'Guess.'

Griggs hung up. Some sense of humor, huh?

I called back and Griggs answered again. I said, 'Okay, I'll give you a hint. I'm known as the King of Rockin' Detectives, but I wasn't born in Tupelo, Mississippi.'

'I knew it was you. I just wanted to see if you'd call back. Heh-heh-heh.' That's the way Griggs laughs. Heh-heh-heh.

'Lemme speak to Lou.'

'What's the magic word?'

'C'mon, Charlie.'

'What do you say, wiseass? You wanna speak to Lou, tell me what you say? Heh-heh-heh.' This guy's an adult.

'I'm going to get you, Griggs.'

'Heh-heh-heh.' Griggs was killing himself.

'I'm going to give your address to Joe.'

The laughing stopped and Griggs put me on hold. Maybe forty seconds later Lou Poitras picked up. 'I don't pay these guys to goose around with you.'

'Griggs hasn't done a full day's work in fifteen years.'

'We don't pay him to work. We keep'm around because he's such a scream. Sort of like you.' Another comedian.

I said, 'Four months ago, a guy died during a REACT arrest down in South Central. You know anyone I can talk to about it?'

'Hold on.' Poitras put me on hold again and left me

there for maybe eight minutes. When he came back he said, 'Suspect's name was Charles Lewis Washington.'

'Okay.' I wrote it down.

'There's a guy working Hollywood named Andy Malone used to be a partner of mine. He's a uniform supervisor on the day shift. He just came out of the Seventy-seventh. You wanna go down there now?'

'Yeah.'

'I'll call him and set it up.'

'Thanks, Lou.'

'You got that twelve bucks you owe me?'

I made a staticky noise and pretended we had been cut off. Works every time.

Forty minutes later I parked in a diagonal parking place outside the glass front door of the Hollywood Police Division, and went past three black women who were standing on the sidewalk into a trapezoidal public room with a high ceiling and a white tile floor. There was a pay phone on the wall up by the front glass and padded chairs around the perimeter of the wall for your waiting comfort. The walls were aqua, the glass was bulletproof. A Formica counter cut off the back third of the room, and three uniformed officers sat on stools behind the counter. Two women and a man. One of the women and the man were talking on telephones, and the other woman was writing in a small black notebook. A Hispanic man and woman sat in the chairs under the pay phone. The Hispanic man sat with his elbows on his thighs and rocked steadily. He looked worried. The Hispanic woman rubbed his back as he rocked and spoke softly. She looked worried, too.

I went past them to the officer writing in the little black notebook and said, 'Elvis Cole to see Sergeant Malone.'

'He expecting you?'

'Yes.'

'Have a seat.'

67

She left the counter and went back through a door into the bowels of the station house. There was another door on the customer side of the counter. It was heavy and dense and if no one buzzed you through it'd probably take a rocket launcher to get past it. I sat opposite the door and waited. In a couple of minutes the female officer reappeared behind the counter and said, 'He's finishing up a couple of things. He'll be with you in a minute.'

'Sure.'

I waited some more.

A well-dressed black woman came in and asked the people behind the counter if Officer Hobbs was in. The same officer who had gone to see Malone said something into a phone, and a couple of minutes later a tall muscular black officer came through the heavy door. He smiled when he saw the woman and she smiled when she saw him. He offered his hand and she took it and they went out through the glass door to hold hands in the privacy of the sidewalk. Love at the station house. Two Pakistani men came in past the lovers. One of them was maybe in his fifties and the other was maybe in his forties. The older one looked nervous and the younger one wore a loud pink shirt and leather sandals. The younger one went to the counter and said, 'We would like to speak with the chief of police.' He said it so loud the Hispanic man stopped rocking. The two desk officers glanced at each other and smiled. The desk officer on the phone kept talking like it was nothing. Guess you work the desk at Hollywood, nothing surprises you. The male desk officer leaned back on his stool and looked through the doorway behind the counter and yelled, 'We got a citizen out here wants to see the chief.' A uniformed lieutenant with silver hair came out and stared at the Pakistanis, then frowned at the desk officer. 'Knock off the shit and take care of these people.'

The younger Pakistani said, 'Are you the chief?'

The lieutenant said, 'The chief's busy with the city council. How can I help you?'

Just as he said it the heavy door opened and a hard-shouldered uniformed sergeant looked out at me. 'You Cole?'

'Yeah.' He had sandy hair and thick, blocky hands and a deep tan because most of his time would be spent on the street. He wore a little red and green and gold Vietnam service ribbon beneath the badge on his left breast and a marksmanship pin beside the ribbon.

'Andy Malone,' he said. 'We can talk back here.' He put out his hand and I stood and took it, and then I followed him through the door.

We went down a long hall past three candy machines and a soft-drink machine and a couple of rest rooms for people who weren't cops to use. At the far end of the hall there was a booking desk where a couple of cops were processing a tall skinny black kid. The kid's hands were cuffed. One of the cops was white and the other was black, and they both were thick across the chest and back and arms, like they spent a lot of time in the gym. Guess you work in a war zone, you want to be as threatening as possible. The white cop was trying to unlock the cuffs and the black cop was shaking his finger about two inches from the kid's nose, saying, 'Are you listening to me?' The kid was giving with attitude and you knew he wasn't listening and wasn't going to. Your bad guys are often like that.

There were a couple of varnished wood benches in the hall opposite a door that said SERGEANT'S OFFICE. We went into the office and Malone closed the door. 'You want coffee?'

'Sure. Thanks.'

Malone filled a couple of paper cups, handed one to me, then went behind a cluttered desk and sat. He didn't offer cream or sugar. Maybe they didn't have any.

I sat across from him in a hard chair, and we looked at each other and sipped our coffee. He said, 'My buddy Lou Poitras says you want to know about Charles Lewis Washington.'

'Uh-huh.'

'You're a private investigator.'

'That's it.' The coffee was hot and bitter and had probably been made early this morning.

'Make any money at it?'

'No one's getting rich.'

He took more of the coffee and made a little smile. 'The wife's been after me to leave the force since the riots. All this time, she's still after me.' He made a shrugging move with his head, then set the cup on his desk. 'So tell me why you're digging around Charles Lewis.'

'His name came up in something I'm working on and I want to run it down.'

Malone nodded and had more of his coffee. He didn't seem to mind the taste, but then, he was used to it. 'How do you know Poitras?'

'Met on the job. Got to know each other.'

He nodded again and leaned back. When he did, the old swivel squealed. 'Lou says you pulled time in Vietnam.'

'Yep.'

He put down his coffee and crossed his arms. 'I was there in sixty-eight.'

'Seventy-one.'

The chair squealed again. The nod. 'People think the Nam they think the sixties. Lot of people forget we still had guys there till March twenty-nine, 1973.'

'Lot of people don't care.'

He made a little smile. 'Yeah. We kicked ass in Saudi. That sort of makes up for things.'

'Don't forget Panama and Grenada.'

The smile got wider. 'Kick enough ass, and pretty soon

you forget the losers. Who wants to remember losers when you got so many winners running around?'

I said, 'Hell, Malone, we're not that damned old, are we?'

Malone laughed, uncrossed his arms, and said, 'What do you want to know about Washington?'

I told him.

Malone went to a battered gray cabinet, took out a manila folder, and brought it back to the desk. He skimmed through it for a couple of minutes, then he closed it. He didn't offer to let me see. 'Washington worked in a pawnshop over on Broadway, down in South Central. We had information that the shop was being used as a fence drop for some of the guns looted during the riots, so REACT put eyes on the place, then went in with a sting.'

'And it went bad.'

'That's a way to say it. Washington thinks he's making a buy on ten thousand rounds of stolen ammo, the officers think it's under control, but when they flash the badges he goes a little nuts and decides to resist. Washington dives behind a counter, and comes up with a piece, but our guys are thinking Rodney King, so they don't shoot him. There's a scuffle and Washington hits his head and that's it.'

'I hear it was controversial.'

'They're all controversial. This one less than most.'

'What do you have on Washington?'

Malone checked the report again. 'Twenty-eight. A longtime Double-Seven Hoover Crip with multiple priors.'

'He there alone in the store?'

'Sure. The family went nuts. We had the pickets, the wrongful-death suit, all of that, but they backed off.'

'Did the city settle?'

'Nope. They dropped it.'

'Can I read the report?'

Malone stared at me for a while and you could tell he didn't like it, then he shrugged and shoved it across the desk at me. 'Here in my presence. I can't let you copy it and I can't let you take it.'

'Sure.'

I read the report. It told me what Malone had told me, only with more words. Lieutenant Eric Dees, the REACT team leader, had written the report. Garcia and Pinkworth and Riggens had gone in to front the sale, and Thurman and Dees were the outside men. When it was clear that the transaction would be consummated, Garcia identified himself as a police officer, told Washington that he was being placed under arrest, and Dees and Thurman entered the premises. As the cuffs were being applied, Washington broke free from Pinkworth and Riggens and lunged for a weapon. The officers attempted to subdue the suspect without the use of deadly force, and Pinkworth and Riggens received substantial injuries. Washington was struck repeatedly by all officers involved, but refused to succumb, and died when team leader Eric Dees tackled him, causing his head to strike the corner of a metal display case. Dees assumed full responsibility. There were copies of the IAD investigation report and a letter of final disposition of the case. The letter of disposition released the officers involved from any wrongdoing. Copies of the death report, the coroner's findings, and Charles Lewis Washington's arrest record were appended to the finding.

'What about Riggens?'

'What can I say? Riggens has his problems, but you read the report. It was a team effort.'

I said, 'Does it seem odd to you that five officers couldn't apprehend this guy without letting him kill himself?'

'Hell, Cole, you know what it's like out there. Shit

happens. This kid was a felon gangbanger and he picked the wrong time to pull a gun. Our guys tried to do the right thing, but it went wrong. That's all there is to it. Nobody wants another Rodney King.'

I nodded. 'Mind if I copy down Washington's address?'

'No problem.'

'Any idea why they dropped the suit?'

Malone shrugged. 'People down there are tired. I spent four years in South Central. God knows I can tell you *we* are.' He made the shrug again. 'Nobody ever drops a wrongful death against LAPD. Too many shysters are willing to take the case on a contingency, and the city council's always ready to settle out, but who can tell.'

'Yeah. Who can tell. Thanks, Malone. I appreciate it.'

I handed back the file and went to the door. He said, 'Cole.'

'Yeah?'

'I know the kind of press South Central gets, but the people down there, most of the people down there are good people. That's why I stayed the four years.'

'Most folks everywhere are good people.'

He nodded. 'I don't know what you're doing, or where you're going, but watch yourself around the gangs. LAPD owns the streets, but the gangs keep trying to take'm away. You understand?'

'More than I want.'

I showed myself out, picked up my car, and took the long drive down to South Central Los Angeles.

Home of the body bag.

CHAPTER 10

I dropped down through West Hollywood and the southwest corner of Beverly Hills through La Cienega Park to the 1-10 freeway, then picked up the 10 east to the Harbor, then went south on the Harbor past USC and Exposition Park, and into South Central.

Even on the freeway, the world begins to change. The cinderblock sound walls and ramp signs show more graffiti, and, if you know how to read it, you can tell that it isn't just young Hispanic taggers out to get famous all over town, it's gangbangers marking turf and making challenges and telling you who they've killed and who they're going to kill. Just the thing you want to see when you're looking for an exit ramp.

I left the freeway at Florence, looped under to Hoover, then turned south to Eighty-second Street. Broadway and Florence show liquor stores and neighborhood groceries and gas stations and other businesses, but Hoover and the cross streets are residential. Up by the businesses you get out-of-work men hanging around and a lot of graffiti and it looks sort of crummy, but the residential streets will surprise you. Most of the houses are stucco or clapboard bungalows, freshly painted and well maintained, with front yards as neat and pretty as anything you'd find anywhere.

Elderly people sat on porches or worked in yards trimming roses and, here and there, small children played on tricycles. Satellite dishes sprouted from poles like black aluminum mums and clean American cars sat in the drives. There were a lot of the dishes, and they looked identical, as if a satellite-dish salesman had gone door-to-door and found many takers.

There was no graffiti on the houses and there was no litter in the streets or the yards, but every house had heavy metal bars over windows and door fronts and sometimes the bars encircled a porch. That's how you knew there was a war on. If there wasn't a war, you wouldn't need the protection.

According to the police report, Charles Lewis Washington had lived with his mother in a rose-colored bungalow on Eighty-second Street, just west of Hoover. His mother, Ida Leigh Washington, still lived there. It was a nice-looking place, with a satellite dish on a tower in their backyard and a well-kept Buick LeSabre in the drive. An open-air front porch was boxed in by a redwood trellis and bright yellow vine roses. The vine roses were healthy and vibrant.

I parked at the curb in front of their home, went up the narrow walk, and onto the porch. The roses threw off a heavy scent and smelled wonderful. The front door opened before I got there, and a slender young black man looked out at me. I could hear music, but it was coming from another house, not this one. He said, 'May I help you?'

I gave him the card. 'My name is Elvis Cole. I'm a private investigator, and I was hoping to speak with Mrs Ida Leigh Washington.' He was wearing a plain white crewneck tee shirt and blue Navy work pants and white sneakers and an imitation gold watchband. The band was bright against his dark skin. He read the card and then he looked back at me.

'About what?'

'Charles Lewis Washington.'

'Lewis is dead.'

'I know. That's what I want to talk about.'

He stared at me a couple of seconds longer, like he had to make up his mind, but like he was making it up about things that had nothing to do with me. After a little of that, he stepped back out of the door and held the screen. 'All right. Please come in.'

I went past him into a small, neat living room. An old man maybe three hundred years old and a young woman who couldn't have been more than sixteen were watching TV. The girl was sitting on a burgundy velveteen couch and the old man in a hardwood rocker. He was holding a can of Scrapple. They both looked at me with a sort of curious surprise. The white man comes to call. A little boy maybe three years old pulled at the girl's legs, but she ignored him. Crocheted doilies were spread on the arms of the couch and the headrest, but you could make out the worn spots through the gaps in the doilies. The girl didn't look a whole hell of a lot older than the baby, but there you go. Toys appropriate to a three-year-old were scattered about the floor. I smiled at them. 'Hi.'

The old man nodded and the girl picked up a remote control and clicked off the TV.

The younger man said, 'Go tell Mama we got company.'

The girl slipped off the couch and went down a little hall into the back of the house. I said, 'Your wife?'

'Lewis's girlfriend, Shalene. This is their son, Marcus, and this is my grandfather, Mr Williams. Say hello, Marcus.'

Marcus covered his eyes with his fingers and sat down on the floor, then rolled over onto his belly. He giggled as he did it. The old man started rocking.

Lewis's girlfriend came back with a heavy, light-skinned woman in her fifties. Ida Leigh Washington. There was a friendly half smile on her face, and a fine film of perspiration as if she'd been working.

The younger man held the card toward her. 'Man wants to ask you about Lewis.'

The older woman froze as if someone had put a gun to her head, and the half smile died. 'Are you with the police?'

'No, ma'am. I'm a private investigator, and I had some questions about what happened to Charles Lewis Washington. I was hoping you could help me.'

She looked at the card, and then she looked at me, and then she looked at her son. He crossed his arms and stared at her with the sort of look that said you're on your own. She shook her head. 'I'm very sorry, but you've come at a bad time.'

'Please, Mrs Washington. This won't take long, and it would be terribly inconvenient to come back later.' I thought about saying *aw, shucks*, but I figured that would be overboard.

She fingered the card and looked at the younger man. 'James Edward, did you offer the man a cool drink?'

James Edward said, 'You want a Scrapple?'

'No, thank you. I won't take any more of your time than necessary.'

Mrs Washington offered me a seat in the overstuffed chair. It was worn and comfortable and probably had belonged to Mr Washington. She sat on the couch with the girl and the baby. James Edward didn't sit.

I said, 'Was Lewis in a gang, Mrs Washington?'

Her foot began to move. Nervous. 'No, he was not. The police said he was, but that wasn't so.'

'I saw his arrest record. He was arrested for stealing electronics equipment with three other young men when he was sixteen years old. All four kids, including Lewis, admitted to being members of the Double-Seven Hoover Crips.'

'When he was a baby.' The foot stopped moving and she made an impatient gesture. 'Lewis got out of all that. That Winslow Johnston was the troublemaker. They put him in the penitentiary and he got killed there and Lewis

77

gave it up. He joined the Navy and got away from all this. When he came back he found Shalene.' Mrs Washington reached out and patted Shalene on the thigh. 'He was trying to make something of himself.'

Shalene was staring at me the way you stare at someone when you're thinking that a good time would be punching little holes in their head with an ice pick.

'The report also said Lewis owned the pawnshop.'

'That's right.'

'Where'd he get the money to buy an ongoing business like that, Mrs Washington?'

There were lovely crocheted doilies on the couch's arms. She straightened the one nearest her, then began to twist it. 'He had money from the Navy. And I co-signed some papers.'

Marcus climbed down off the couch and toddled out of the living room and into the kitchen. Mrs Washington leaned forward to see where he was going but Shalene didn't. Mrs Washington straightened and looked at her. 'You'd better see where he's going.'

Shalene went into the kitchen after him.

I said, 'Mrs Washington, I don't want to offend you, and I promise you that nothing you say to me will be repeated to police or to anyone else. Was Lewis fencing stolen goods?'

Her eyes filled. 'Yes,' she said. 'I believe that he was. But that gave them no call. Lewis didn't carry no gun. Lewis wouldn't have done what they said.'

'Yes, ma'am.'

'I know my boy. I know him the way only a mother can know a son. They had no call to hurt my boy.' Jennifer Sheridan knowing Mark Thurman.

'Yes, ma'am.' She was twisting the crocheted doily into a high, tight peak.

I said, 'If you believe that, then why did you drop the wrongful-death suit against the officers who killed him?'

Mrs Washington closed her eyes against the tears, and the old man spoke for the first time. He said, 'Because Lewis was always looking for trouble and he finally found it. There's nothing else to it, no reason to keep it alive.' His voice was deep and gravelly, and more like a bark than a voice. His eyes blinked rapidly as he said it. 'It was right to let it go, just let it go and walk away. Let the dead lie. There's nothing more to say to it.' He put the Scrapple can carefully on the floor, then, just as carefully, he pushed himself up and walked from the room. He took very short steps, and used first the couch and then the wall to steady himself. Shalene had come back with Marcus in her arms to stand in the door to the kitchen, staring at me and hating me. Mrs Washington was staring into the folds of her lap, eyes clenched, her body quivering as if it were a leaf in the wind. I sat there in the warm living room and looked at them and listened and I did not believe them. Mrs Washington said, 'You should go. I'm sorry, now, but you should go.'

'You really, truly believe he was murdered.'

'You have to go.'

I said, 'Did the officers threaten you?'

'Please, go.'

'The officers who shot Lewis. Did they come here and threaten you and make you drop the suit?'

'Please leave.'

James Edward said, 'What're you going to tell him, Mama?'

'Don't you say anything, James Edward. There's nothing more to say.' Ida Leigh Washington pushed to her feet and waved me toward the door. 'I want you out of my house. You're not the police and you have no paper that says you can be here and I want you out.'

Marcus began to wail. For a moment, everything was still, and then I stood. 'Thank you for your time, Mrs Washington. I'm sorry about your son.'

James Edward went to the door and followed me out. Mrs Washington hurried after us, but stopped in the door. 'Don't you go out there with him, James Edward. They'll see you, out there.'

James Edward said, 'It's all right, Mama.'

He pushed her gently back into the house and closed the door. It was cooler on the porch, and the rose smell was fresh and strong. We stood like that for a moment, then James Edward went to the edge of the porch and peered out between the roses and looked at his neighborhood. He said, 'I wasn't here when it happened.'

'The Navy?'

He nodded. 'Missed the riots, too. I was away for four years, first in the Med, then the Indian.'

'How long have you been out?'

'Five weeks, four days, and I gotta come back to this.' He looked at me. 'You think it's the cops, huh?'

I nodded.

He gave disgusted, and moved into the shade behind the trellis. 'The cops killed my brother, but a nigger named Akeem D'Muere made'm drop the suit.'

I gave him stupid. 'Who's Akeem D'Muere?'

'Runs a gang called the Eight-Deuce Gangster Boys.'

'A black gang made your family drop the suit?' I was taking stupid into unexplored realms.

'You're the detective. I been away for four years.' He turned from the street and sat on the glider and I sat next to him.

'So why's a black gang force a black family to drop a wrongful-death suit against a bunch of white cops?'

He shook his head. 'Can't say. But I'm gonna find out.'

'There has to be some kind of connection.'

'Man, you must be Sherlock fuckin' Holmes.'

'Hey, you get me up to speed, I'm something to watch.'

He nodded, but he didn't look like he believed it.

I said, 'This is your 'hood, James Edward, not mine. If

there's a connection between these guys, there's going to be a way to find out, but I don't know what it is.'

'So what?'

'So they don't have a detective's-mate rating in the Navy, and maybe I can help you find out. I find out, and maybe we can get your mother out from under this thing.'

James Edward Washington gave me a long, slow look, like maybe he was wondering about something, and then he got up and started off the porch without waiting for me. 'C'mon. I know a man we can see.'

CHAPTER 11

We walked out to the Corvette and James Edward Washington gave approval. I got in, but James Edward took a slow walk around. 'Sixty-five?'

'Sixty-six.'

'I thought private eyes were supposed to drive clunky little cars like Columbo.'

'That's TV.'

'What about if you follow somebody? Don't a car like this stand out?' James Edward was liking my car just fine.

'If I was living in Lost Overshoe, Nebraska, it stands out. In L.A., it's just another convertible. A lot of places I work, if I drove a clunker it'd stand out more than this.'

James Edward smiled. 'Yeah, but this ain't those places. This is South Central.'

'We'll see.'

James Edward climbed in, told me to head east toward Western, and I pulled a K-turn and did it.

We drove north on Western to Slauson, then turned east to parallel the railroad tracks, then turned north again. James Edward told me that we were going to see a guy he knew named Ray Depente. He said that Ray had spent twenty-two years in the Marine Corps, teaching hand-to-hand down at Camp Pendleton before tendering his retirement and opening a gym here in Los Angeles to work with kids and sponsor gang intervention programs. He also said that if anyone knew the South Central gang scene, Ray did. I said that sounded good to me.

Four blocks above Broadway I spotted the same two

guys in the same blue sedan that I'd suspected of following me two days ago. They stayed with us through two turns, and never came closer than three cars nor dropped back farther than six. When we came to a 7-Eleven, I pulled into the lot and told James Edward that I had to make a call. I used the pay phone there to dial a gun shop in Culver City, and a man's voice answered on the second ring. 'Pike.'

'It's me. I'm standing in a 7-Eleven parking lot on San Pedro about three blocks south of Martin Luther King Boulevard. I'm with a black guy in his early twenties named James Edward Washington. A white guy and a Hispanic guy in a dark blue 1989 sedan are following us. I think they've been following me for the past two days.'

'Shoot them.' Life is simple for some of us.

'I was thinking more that you could follow them as they follow me and we could find out who they are.'

Pike didn't say anything.

'Also, I think they're cops.'

Pike grunted. 'Where you headed?'

'A place called Ray's Gym. In South Central.'

Pike grunted again. 'I know Ray's. Are you in immediate danger?'

I looked around. 'Well, I could probably get hit by a meteor.'

Pike said, 'Go to Ray's. You won't see me, but I'll be there when you come out.' Then he hung up. Some partner, huh?

I climbed back into the car, and fourteen minutes later we pulled into a gravel parking lot on the side of Ray Depente's gymnasium. James Edward Washington led me inside.

Ray's is a big underground cavern kind of place with peeling paint and high ceilings and the smell of sweat pressed into the walls. Maybe forty people were spread around the big room, men and women, some stretching, some grinding through *katas* like formal dance routines, some sparring with full-contact pads. An athletic woman with strawberry hair was on the mats with a tall black man with mocha skin and gray-flecked hair. They were working hard, the woman snapping kick after kick at his legs and torso and head, him yelling c'mon, get in here, c'mon, I'm wide open. Every time she kicked, sweat flew off her and sprayed the mat. Each of them was covered with so many pads they might've been in space suits. James Edward said, 'That's Ray.'

I started fooling around with the martial arts when I was in the Army and I got pretty good at it. Ray Depente was good, too, and he looked like an outstanding teacher. He snapped light punches and kicks at the woman, making her think defense as well as offense. He tapped them on the heavy pad over her breasts and taunted her, saying stop me, saying Jesus Christ protect yourself, saying you mine anytime I want you. She kicked faster, snapping up roundhouse kicks and power kicks, then coming in backwards with spin kicks. He blocked most of the kicks and slipped a few and taunted her harder, saying he ain't never had a white woman but he was about to get one now. As fast as he said it she hooked his left knee and he stumbled to catch himself and when he did she got off a high fast spin kick that caught him on the back of the head and bowled him over and then she was on him, spiking kicks hard at his groin pad and his spine and his head and he doubled into a ball, covering up, yelling that he gives, he gives, he gives, and laughing the big deep laugh. She helped him up and they bowed to each other, both of them grinning, and then she gave a whoop and jumped up to give him a major league hug. Then she hopped away to the locker rooms, pumping her fist and yelling 'Yeah!' Ray Depente stepped off the mat, unfastening the pads, and then he saw us standing on the hardwood at the edge of the mat. He grinned at James

Edward and came over, still pulling off the pads. He was two inches taller than me and maybe fifteen pounds heavier. 'Welcome back, Admiral. I've missed you, young man.'

He grabbed James Edward in a tight hug, and the two men pounded each other on their backs. When James Edward stepped back, he said, 'You ain't never had a white woman but you're about to get one now?'

Ray grinned. 'Thirteen months ago two assholes followed her into a parking lot in Rancho Park. One of them raped her in the backseat of her MB. The second one was just getting ready to mount up when a couple of women came along and scared'm off. What you think would happen if those guys came back today?'

'Testicular transplant?'

'Uh-huh.'

I said, 'She's come along fast.'

'Motivation, baby. Motivation is all.'

James Edward said, 'Ray, this is Elvis Cole. He's a private investigator.'

'Do tell.' We shook. Ray Depente had a hand like warm steel. 'What do you investigate?'

'I'm working with something that's bumped up against a gang called the Eight-Deuce Gangster Boys. James Edward says that you know about those guys.'

Ray peeled away the rest of his body pads and used his sweatshirt to wipe his face and neck. Everybody else in the place was wearing heavy canvas karate *gies*, but not Ray. Ray wore desert-issue combat pants and an orange Marine Corps tee shirt. Old habits. 'Bumping up against the Crips isn't something you want to do if you can help it. Crips got sharp edges.'

I gave him shrug. 'Occupational hazard.'

'Uh-huh. Be tough and see.'

'The Gangster Boys a Crip set?' People hear Crips or Bloods and they think it's just two big gangs, but it isn't.

85

Both the Crips and the Bloods are made up of smaller gang sets. Eight-Deuce Gangster Boys, Eight-Trey Swan Crips, Rolling Sixties Crips, Double-Seven Hoover Crips, East Coast Crips, like that.

Ray nodded. 'Yeah. From down around Eighty-second and Hoover. That's where they get the name. You want to be a Gangster Boy, you got to do a felony. You want to be OG, you got to pull the trigger. It's as simple as that.'

James Edward said, 'O.G. means Original Gangster. That's like saying you're a made man in the Mafia.'

'Okay.'

Ray said, 'What are you messing around with that's got you down here in South Central with a goddamned Crip set?'

'Charles Lewis Washington.'

Ray's smile faded and he looked at James Edward. 'How's your mama doing, son?'

'She's okay. We got a little problem with the Eight-Deuce, though.'

Ray looked back at me. 'You working for the family?'

'Nope. But maybe what I'm doing gets us to the same place.'

Ray looked at James Edward and James Edward nodded. Ray said, 'I hadn't seen Lewis for a couple years, but when I heard about him dying, I didn't like it, and I didn't like how it happened. I worked with that boy out of youth services. It was a long time ago and he didn't stay with it, but there it is. Once you're one of my young men, you're one of my young men. Just like this one.' Ray Depente put a warm steel hand on James Edward's shoulder and gave him a squeeze. 'I tried to point this one toward the Marines but he liked the idea of ships.' Ray and James Edward grinned at each other, and the grins were as warm as the hand.

I said, 'The cops say that Lewis was a Double-Seven gangbanger. His mother says no.'

Ray frowned. 'Lewis used to mess around with the Double-Sevens, but that was years ago. That's how he came to me.'

'He ever have anything to do with the Eight-Deuce Gangster Boys?'

'Not that I know.'

'The family filed a wrongful death after Lewis was killed, but James Edward here tells me that a guy named Akeem D'Muere made them back off.'

Ray looked at James Edward again. 'You sure?'

James Edward nodded.

I said, 'Why would Akeem D'Muere go to bat for a bunch of white LAPD officers?'

Ray shook his head. 'I know Akeem. Akeem D'Muere wouldn't go to bat for anybody unless there's something in it for him.'

'When Lewis Washington died, every news service in town was looking into it, smelling Rodney King all over again. Maybe Akeem D'Muere wanted all the looking to stop. Maybe there was something going on at the Premier Pawn Shop that he didn't want anyone to find out.'

'You think?'

I shrugged. 'I think there's a connection. I just don't know who to ask to find out.'

James Edward said, 'That's why I brought him here, Ray. Figured you'd be the guy to know.'

Ray Depente smiled at James Edward. 'You want me to ask around, young mister, I can do that. Know a man who'll probably be able to help. But you stay away from those Eight-Deuce. The Navy doesn't teach you what you need to know to mess with that trash.'

James Edward said, 'Hell Ray.'

The strawberry-haired woman came out of the dressing room, showered and changed, and gave Ray a ten-megawatt smile as she bounced out of the gym and into the sunshine. I said, 'Pretty.'

Ray said, 'Uh-huh.'

An older woman pushed her head out of a little glass cubicle that served as an office at the rear of the gym. She called, 'Ray, it's somebody from Twentieth Century-Fox. They say it's some kind of emergency and they need you to come over and show Bruce Willis how to do something for a movie they're making.'

James Edward grinned. 'Bruce Willis. Damn.'

Ray didn't look as thrilled with Bruce Willis as did James Edward. 'Now?'

'They said right away.'

James Edward said, 'These studio dudes hire Ray to set up fight scenes and teach his moves to their actors. Arnold been here, man. Sly Stallone useta come here.'

Ray shook his head. 'I can do it tonight, but I can't do it now. I've got a class coming in, now.'

The woman said, 'They said right away.'

Ray shook his head. 'Movie people.' He called back to her. 'Tell'm I gotta pass.'

James Edward Washington gave impressed. 'Is this fuckin' righteous or what? Tellin' Bruce Willis to pass.'

The older woman went back into the glass cubicle.

Ray said, 'Jesus Christ, James Edward. It ain't no big thing.' Ray Depente looked my way and gave embarrassed. 'These kids think this movie stuff is a big deal. They don't know. A client's a client.'

'Sure.'

'I've got a class.'

'Sure.'

A dozen little girls came in, shepherded by a tall erect black woman in a neat dress suit. Most of the little girls were black, but a couple were Hispanic. They all wore clean white karate *gies* and tennis shoes. They took off their shoes before they stepped onto the mat. Ray uncrossed his arms and smiled. 'Here they are, now.'

James Edward Washington laughed and said, 'Damn.'

Ray Depente squeezed James Edward's shoulder again, then told me that it had been a pleasure to meet me, and that if he learned something he would give James Edward a call. Then he turned away and walked out onto the mat to face his class.

The little girls formed a neat line as if they had done it a thousand times before and bowed toward Ray Depente and shouted *kun hey* with perfect Korean inflection. Ray said something so quietly that I could not hear, and then he bowed to them.

Ray Depente gets five hundred dollars an hour from movie stars, but some things are more important.

CHAPTER 12

James Edward Washington wanted to chill with Ray for a while, so he stayed, and I walked out to my car, making a big deal out of taking off my jacket so that I could look up and down the street and across the intersections. Joe Pike drives an immaculate red Jeep Cherokee, and I was hoping to spot him or the blue sedan, but I saw neither. Of course, maybe they weren't there. Maybe the blue sedan hadn't really been following me and I was making a big deal with the jacket for nothing. Elvis Cole, Existential Detective. On the other hand, maybe the guys in the blue sedan were better than me and I wasn't good enough to spot them.

Not.

I climbed the ramp to the I-10 freeway and went west, changing lanes to avoid slower traffic and speeding up when the traffic allowed and trying to play it normal. Just another Angeleno in the system. It paid off. A quarter mile past the La Brea exit I spotted the blue sedan hiding on the far side of a Ryder moving van, two lanes over. The guy with the Dodgers cap was still driving and the guy with the butch cut was still riding shotgun.

I took the La Cienega exit and went north, timing the lights to get a better view, but always just missing. They were good. Always three or four cars back, always with plenty of separation, and they didn't seem worried that they'd lose me. That meant they knew they could always pick me up again, or that they were working with a second car. Cops always use a second car.

La Cienega is four lanes, but Caltrans was at it again, and as La Cienega approached Pico, the two northbound lanes became one. There's a 20/20 Video in a large shopping center on the northeast corner, and the closer I got to the 20/20, the slower I drove. By the time I cleared the work in the intersection, a guy behind me in a Toyota 4x4 had had enough and roared past, giving me the finger. I stayed in the right lane as I crossed Pico, and the remaining two cars behind me turned. Then there was just me and the blue sedan. The driver swung right, making the turn with the two other cars as if they had never intended anything else, and that's when I picked up the slack car. Floyd Riggens was driving his dark brown sedan two cars back, sitting in traffic behind a couple of guys on mopeds. My, my.

I stayed north on La Cienega and three blocks later the blue sedan sat at a side street ahead of me, waiting. As soon as they made the turn onto Pico they must've punched it like an F-16 going into afterburner, then swung north on a parallel side street to come in ahead of me. Floyd would've radioed that he still had me in sight, and that we were proceeding northbound, and that's how they'd know where to wait. Floyd hung back, and after I passed, the blue sedan pulled in behind me again. Right where I wanted them.

I turned east on Beverly, then dropped down Fairfax past CBS Television City to the Farmer's Market. The Market is a loose collection of buildings surrounded on all sides by parking lots used mostly by tour buses and people from Utah, come to gawk at CBS.

I turned into the north lot and made my way past the buses and about a million empty parking spots toward the east lot. Most of the traffic stays in the north lot, but if you want to get from the north lot to the east, you have to funnel through a cramped drive that runs between a couple of buildings where people sell papayas and framed pictures of Pat Sajak. It's narrow and it's cramped and it's lousy when you're here on a Saturday and the place is jammed with tourists, but it's ideal for a private eye looking to spring an ambush.

When I was clear of the little drive, I pulled a quick reverse and backed my car behind a flower truck. A teenaged girl in a white Volkswagen Rabbit came through the gap after me, and, a few seconds later, the blue sedan followed. It came through at a creep, the guy in the passenger seat pointing to the south and the driver sitting high to see what he was pointing at. Whatever he saw he didn't like it, because he made an angry gesture and looked away and that's when they saw me. I jumped the Corvette into their path and got out of the car with my hands clear so they could see I had no gun. The kid with the butch bounced out and started yelling into a handi-talkie and the Hispanic guy was running toward me with his badge in one hand and a Browning 9mm in the other. Floyd Riggens was roaring toward us from the far end of the lot. Thurman wasn't with him. Thurman wasn't anywhere around.

The Hispanic guy yelled, 'Get your hands up. Out and away from your body.' When the guns come out there's always a lot of yelling.

The guy with the butch ran over and patted me down with his free hand. I made him for Pinkworth. The other guy for Garcia. While Pinkworth did the shakedown, some of the people from the tour buses began to gather on the walk and look at us. Most of the men were in Bermuda shorts and most of the women were in summer-weight pant suits and just about everyone held a camera. Tourists. They stood in a little group as they watched, and a fat kid with glasses and a DES MOINES sweatshirt said, 'Hey, neat.' Maybe they thought we were the CBS version of the Universal stunt show.

Garcia said, 'Jesus Christ, we've got a goddamned crowd.'

I smiled at him. 'My fans.'

Pinkworth looked nervous and lowered his gun like someone might see it and tell. Garcia lowered his, too.

Riggens's car screeched to a stop and he kicked open the door. His face was flushed and he looked angry. He also looked drunk. 'Stay the fuck away from my wife.'

Garcia yelled, 'Floyd,' but Floyd wasn't listening. He took two long steps forward, then lunged toward me with his body sort of cocked to the side like he was going to throw a haymaker and knock me into the next time zone.

He swung, and I stepped outside of it and snapped a high roundhouse kick into the side of his head that knocked him over sideways.

The fat kid said, 'Look at that!' and the fat kid's father aimed a Sony video camera at us.

When Riggens fell, Garcia's gun came up and Pinkworth started forward, and that's when Joe Pike reared up from behind their car, snapped the slide on a 12-gauge Ithaca riot gun, and said, 'Don't.'

Garcia and Pinkworth froze. They spread their fingers off their pistol grips, showing they were out of it.

The crowd went, 'Ooo.' Some show, all right.

Joe Pike stands six-one and weighs maybe one-ninety, and he's got large red arrows tattooed on the outside of each deltoid, souvenirs from his days as a Force Recon Marine in Vietnam. He was wearing faded blue jeans and Nike running shoes and a plain gray sweatshirt with the sleeves cut off and government-issue sunglasses. Angle the sun on him just right, and sometimes the tattoos seem to glow. I think Pike calls it his apparition look.

I said, 'Gee, and I thought you'd got lost in traffic.'

Pike's mouth twitched. He doesn't smile, but sometimes he'll twitch. You get a twitch out of Pike, he's gotta be dying on the inside. In tears, he's gotta be.

I took Garcia's and Pinkworth's guns, and Pike circled the blue sedan, finding a better angle to cover Riggens. When he moved, he seemed to glide, as if he were flowing over the surface of the earth, moving as a panther might move. To move was to stalk. I'd never seen him move any other way.

Garcia said, 'Put down that goddamned gun. We're LAPD officers, goddamn it.'

Pike's shotgun didn't waver. An older woman with a lime green sun hat and a purse the size of a mailbag looked at the other tourists and said, 'Does the bus leave after this?'

I pulled Riggens's gun and then I went back to Pinkworth and Garcia and checked their IDs. Pinkworth said, 'You're marked fuck for this, asshole. You're going down *hard*.'

'Uh-huh.'

Riggens moaned and sort of turned onto his side. His head was bleeding where it had bounced on the tarmac, but it didn't look bad. I took the clips out of the three police guns, tossed them into the blue sedan's backseat, then went back to Riggens. 'Let me see.'

Riggens pushed my hand off and tried to crab away, but he didn't do much more than flop onto his back. 'Fuck you.'

Pinkworth said, 'You're in a world of shit. You just assaulted a Los Angeles police officer.'

I said, 'Call it in and let's go to the station. Maybe they'll give Riggens a Breathalyzer while you guys are booking me.' You could smell it on him a block away.

Garcia said, 'Quiet, Pink.'

A green four-door sedan identical to the other two cop sedans came toward us across the lot. Riggens was still trying to get up when the green car pulled in behind him and a tall guy with short gray hair got out. He was wearing chino slacks and a striped short-sleeve shirt tucked neatly into his pants and short-topped Redwing trail shoes. He was tanned dark, like he spent a lot of time in the sun, and his face was lined. I made him for his mid-forties, but he could've been older. He looked at Riggens, then the two cops by the blue sedan, and then at Joe Pike. He wasn't upset and he wasn't excited, like he knew what he'd find when he got here and, when he got here, he knew that he could handle it. When he saw Joe Pike he said, 'I didn't know you were in on this.'

Pike nodded once.

I gave them surprised. 'You guys know each other?'

Pike said, 'Eric Dees.'

Eric Dees looked at me, then looked back at Pike. 'Pike and I rode a black-and-white together for a couple of months maybe a million years ago.' Pike had been a uniformed LAPD officer when I'd met him. 'Put away the shotgun, Joe. It's over, now. No one's going to drop the hammer.'

Pike lowered the shotgun.

Pinkworth craned around and stared at Pike. 'This sonofabitch is Joe Pike? *The* Joe Pike?' Pike had worn the uniform for almost three years, but it hadn't ended well.

Riggens said, 'Who?' He was still having trouble on the ground.

Dees said, 'Sure. You've just been jumped by the best.'

Pinkworth glowered at Pike like he'd been wanting to glower at him for a long time. 'Well, fuck him.'

Joe's head sort of whirred five degrees to line up on Pinkworth and Pinkworth's glower wavered. There is a machine-like quality to Joe, as if he had tuned his body the way he might tune his Jeep, and, as the Jeep was perfectly tuned, so was his body. It was easy to imagine him doing a thousand pushups or running a hundred miles, as if his body were an instrument of his mind, as if his mind were a well of limitless resource and unimaginable strength. If the mind said start, the body would start.

When the mind said stop, the body would stop, and whatever it would do, it would do with precision and exactness.

Dees said, 'Long time, Joe. How's it going?'

Pike's head whirred back and he made a kind of head shrug.

'Talkative, as always.' Dees looked at the people from Des Moines. 'Pink, move those people along. We don't need a crowd.' Pinkworth gave me tough, then pulled out his badge and sauntered over to the crowd. The fat kid's father didn't want to move along and made a deal out of it. Dees turned back to me. 'You're this close to getting stepped on for obstruction and for impersonating an officer, Cole. We drop the hammer, your license is history.'

I said, 'What's your connection with Akeem D'Muere and the Eight-Deuce Gangster Boys?'

Dees blinked once, then made a little smile, like maybe he wasn't smiling at me, but at something he was thinking. 'That's an official police investigation. That's what I'm telling you to stay away from. I'm also telling you to stay the hell out of Mark Thurman's personal life. You fuck with my people, you're fucking with me, and you don't want to do that. I'm a bad guy to fuck with.'

Riggens made a sort of a coughing sound, then sat up, squinted at me, and said, 'I'm gonna clean your ass, you fuck.' He got most of his feet under himself but then the feet slipped out and he sort of stumbled backwards until he rammed his head into the green sedan's left front wheel with a *thunk*. He grabbed at his head and said, 'Jesus.'

Dees stared hard at me for another moment, then went to Riggens. 'That's enough, Floyd.'

Floyd said, 'He hit me, Eric. The fuck's takin' the ride.' There was blood on Riggens's face.

Dees bunched his fingers into Riggens's shirt and gave a

single hard jerk that almost pulled Riggens off the ground and popped his head back against the sedan. 'No one's going in, Floyd.'

Riggens got up, took out a handkerchief, and dabbed at his head. The handkerchief came back red. 'Shit.'

I said, 'Better get some ice.'

'Fuck you.'

Dees made a little hand move at Garcia. 'Pete, take Floyd over there and get some ice.'

Floyd said, 'I don't need any goddamn ice. I'm fine.'

Dees said, 'You don't look fine. You look like a lush who got outclassed.' When he said it his voice was hard and commanding and Floyd Riggens jerked sideways as if he had been hit with a cattle prod. Garcia went over to him and took him by the arm. Floyd shook his hand off but followed him into the Market.

Joe Pike said, 'Elite.'

Eric Dees's face went hard. 'They're good, Joe. They didn't cut and walk away.'

Pike's head whirred back to lock onto Eric Dees.

I said, 'That's the second time I've seen Riggens and the second time I've seen him drunk. Your people always get shitfaced on duty?'

Dees came close to me. He was a little bit taller than me, and wider, and maybe six or eight years older. He reminded me of a couple of senior NCOs that I had known in the Army, men who were used to leading men and taking care of men and exercising authority over men. He said, 'I take care of my people, asshole. You'd better worry about taking care of you.'

Joe Pike said, 'Easy, Eric.'

Eric Dees said, 'Easy what, Joe?' He looked back at me. 'This is your wake-up call, and you're only going to get one. The little girl's problems with Mark are going to be solved. She's not going to need you anymore. That means you're off the board.'

'Is that why four LAPD officers have nothing better to do than follow me around?'

'We followed you to talk to you. It was either talk to you or kill you.'

'I'm shaking, Dees.' The detective plays it tough. 'What did Akeem D'Muere have to do with Lewis Washington's death?'

When I said *Lewis Washington*, Dees's eyes went hard and I wondered if I'd pushed too hard. 'I'm trying to play square with you, Cole. Maybe because of Joe, or maybe because I'm a square guy, but if you're not smart enough to listen, there are other ways I can solve the problem.'

'Where's Mark Thurman? You give him the day off?'

Dees looked at the ground like he was trying to think of the magic word, and then Pinkworth came back with Riggens and Garcia. As soon as Pinkworth turned away, the crowd came back. The fat kid's father was smiling. Riggens got into his sedan and Pinkworth and Garcia went back to the blue. Dees looked up at me with eyes that were profoundly tired. 'You're not helping the girl, Cole. You think you are, but you're not.'

'Maybe she has nothing to do with it anymore. Maybe it's larger than her. Maybe it's about Lewis Washington and Akeem D'Muere and why five LAPD officers are so scared of this that they're living in my shorts.'

Dees nodded. Like he knew it was coming, but he wasn't especially glad to see it arrive. 'It's your call, bubba.'

Then he went back to his car and drove away.

Riggens cranked his sedan and took off after him with a lot of tire squealing. Garcia fired up the blue, and as they pulled out after Riggens, Pinkworth gave me the finger. When he gave me the finger the fat kid in the DES MOINES

98

sweatshirt laughed and shook his dad's arm so that his dad would see.

A Kodak moment.

CHAPTER 13

Thirty-five minutes later I pulled up the little road to my house and saw Pike's red Jeep Cherokee under the elm by the front steps. I had left the Farmer's Market before Pike, and I had made good time, but when I got home, there he was, as if he had been there for hours, as if he had been both here and there at the same time. He does this a lot, but I have never been able to figure out how. Teleportation, maybe.

Pike was holding the cat and the two of them were staring at something across the canyon. Looking for more cops, no doubt. I said, 'How'd you beat me?'

Pike put down the cat. 'I didn't know it was a race.' You see how he is?

I turned off the alarm and let us into the kitchen through the carport. I was uncomfortable moving into and through the house, as if I expected more cops to be hiding in a closet or behind the couch. I looked around and wondered if they had been in the house. People have been in my house before. I didn't like it then, and I liked it even less, now.

Pike said, 'We're clear.'

One minute he's across the room, the next he's right behind you. 'How do you know?'

'Went down to the end of the road. Checked the downslope and the upslope. Walked through the house before you got here.' He made a little shrug. 'We're clear.'

A six-thousand-dollar alarm, and it's nothing to Pike. He said, 'You want to tell me about this?'

I took two Falstaffs out of the refrigerator, gave one to Pike and kept one for myself, and then I told him about Jennifer and Thurman and Eric Dees's REACT team. 'Four months ago Dees's team was involved in an arrest in which a man named Charles Lewis Washington died. Washington's family filed a suit against Dees and the city, but they dropped it when a street gang called the Eight-Deuce Gangster Boys pressed them.'

Pike took some of the Falstaff and nodded. 'So what's the connection between a street gang and Eric Dees?'

'That's the question, isn't it?'

I went upstairs, got the notes I had made on the case, and brought them down. 'You hungry?'

'Always.'

'I've got some of the venison left.'

Pike made a face. 'You got something green?' Two years ago he had gone vegetarian.

'Sure. Tuna, also, if you want.' He'll sometimes eat fish. 'Read the notes first, then we'll talk after.'

Pike took the notes, and I went into the freezer for the venison. In the fall, I had hunted the hill country of central California for blacktail deer and had harvested a nice buck. I had kept the tenderloins and chops, and had the rest turned into smoked sausage by a German butcher I know in West L.A. The tenderloins and the chops were gone, but I still had three plump sausage rings. I took two of the rings from the freezer, put them in the microwave to thaw, then went out onto the deck to build the fire. The cat was sitting out there, under the bird feeder. I said, 'Forget the birds. We're making Bambi.'

The cat blinked at me, then came over and sat by the grill. Venison is one of his favorite things.

I keep a Weber charcoal grill out on the deck, along with a circular redwood picnic table. The same woman who had given me the bird feeder had also helped me build the picnic table. Actually, she had done most of the building and I had done most of the helping, but that had probably worked out better for the table. I scraped the grill, then built a bed of mesquite coals in the pit and fired them. Mesquite charcoal takes a while, so you have to get your fire going before you do anything else.

When the coals were on their way, I went back into the kitchen.

Pike looked up from the report. 'We're squaring off against five LAPD officers, and all we're getting paid is forty bucks?'

'Nope. We're also getting forty dollars per month for the next forty-nine months.'

Pike shook his head.

'Think of it as job security, Joe. Four years of steady income.'

Pike sighed.

I opened another Falstaff, drank half of it on the way upstairs to the shower, and the other half on the way back down. When I got back down, Pike had built a large salad with tuna and garbanzo beans and tomatoes and onions. We brought the salad and the venison out onto the deck.

The sky had deepened, and as the sun settled into a purple pool in the west, the smells of budding eucalyptus and night-blooming jasmine mingled with the mesquite smoke. It was a clean, healthy smell, and made me think, as it always does, of open country and little boys and girls climbing trees and chasing fireflies. Maybe I was one of the little boys. Maybe I still am. There are no fireflies in Los Angeles.

I put the venison on the grill, then sat with Pike at the table and told him about Charles Lewis Washington and the Washington family and what I had learned from Ray Depente about Akeem D'Muere and the Eight-Deuce Gangster Boys.

Pike sipped his beer and listened. When I finished he

said, 'You think the family was telling the truth about Charles Lewis going straight?'

'They believed it.'

'Then where'd a guy like that get the cash to buy a solvent business?'

'There is that, yes.'

'Maybe he had a partner.'

I nodded. 'D'Muere funds the pawnshop to front a fence operation, and Lewis's working for D'Muere. I can see that, but why does D'Muere front off the Washington family from pressing their lawsuit? The pawnshop is shut down. The fence operation is history.'

'If there's a suit, there's an investigation. There was something else there that he wants to hide.'

'Something that Eric Dees knows?'

Pike shrugged.

'If Dees knows about it, it's not hidden.'

Pike angled his head around and stared at me. 'Unless it's something Eric wants hidden, too.'

'Ah.' I turned the sausages. Fat was beginning to bubble out of the skin and they smelled wonderful. 'Akeem D'Muere and Eric Dees are sharing a secret.'

Pike nodded.

'The question arises, how far will they go to protect it?'

Pike stared at me for a moment, then got up and went into the house. I heard the front door open, then I heard his Jeep's door, and then he came back out onto the deck. When he came back, he was wearing his pistol. It's a Colt Python .357 with a four-inch barrel. Eternal vigilance is the price of freedom. I said, 'Guess that means they'll go pretty far.'

Pike said, 'If five cops are on you, then it's important to them. If they're with you, then they're not doing the work they're supposed to be doing, and that's not easy to cover. Dees's people can't just go to the beach. He has to account for their time to his boss, and he has to produce results with whatever cases they're working.'

'And all five guys have to be on board with it.'

Pike nodded. 'Everybody has to be on board.'

I turned the sausages again. The skins were taking on a crunchy texture and the cat had hopped up on the rail that runs around the edge of the deck so he could be as close to the sausage as possible. Any closer and we could serve barbecued cat.

Pike said, 'Eric was nervous. That's not like him. Maybe even scared, and that's not like him, either.'

'Okay.'

'Scared people do atypical things. He was thinking maybe that he could scare you off. Now that he knows that I'm in, it will change what he thinks. He knows that I won't scare.'

'Great. That will make him all the more dangerous.'

'Yes,' Pike said. 'It will.'

'Maybe Dees is telling the truth. Maybe we're just stepping on a case and he's pissed.'

Pike shook his head. 'He wants you out, it's easy. He tells his boss and his boss calls you in and you sit down together. You know that.' The sky darkened and the hillside below us grew speckled with lights. Pike adjusted his sunglasses, but did not remove them. He never removes them. Even at night. 'If he's not playing it straight, then he can't play it straight. That's the first rule every cop learns.'

I turned the sausage rings a last time, then took them off the grill and put them onto a maple cutting board. I sliced them at an angle, then put half the meat on my plate and a serious portion on a saucer for the cat. I blew on his to cool it. Pike went into the house and came out with two more Falstaffs and what was left of a loaf of rosemary bread. I took some of the salad and tasted it.

Pike had made a dressing of soy sauce, rice vinegar, and minced garlic. I nodded. 'Good.'

He nodded back.

We ate without speaking for several minutes, and Pike didn't look happy. Of course, since Pike never smiles, it's sometimes tough to tell when he is happy, but there are ways. I said, 'What?'

Pike picked up a piece of tuna with his fingers, took a small bite, then held out the rest to the cat. The cat stepped forward and ate with enthusiasm. Pike said, 'I haven't seen Eric in many years.'

'Was he good?'

'Yes.'

'Was he honest?'

Pike turned his head and the dark lenses angled toward me. 'If I saw it any other way, I wouldn't have ridden with him.'

I nodded. 'But people change.'

Pike wiped his fingers on his napkin, then turned back to his meal. 'Yes. People change.'

We ate the rest of the meal in silence, and then we brought the dirty dishes into the kitchen and flipped a nickel to see who would wash. I lost. Midway through the load the phone rang and Joe Pike answered. He said, 'Jennifer Sheridan.'

I took the phone and said, 'Elvis Cole, Personal Detective to Jennifer Sheridan.'

Jennifer Sheridan said, 'Floyd Riggens just left me. He was here with another officer. They said that I was going to get Mark killed. They said that if I didn't make you stop, something bad would happen.' Her voice was tight and compressed and the words came quickly, as if she were keeping a close rein, but just.

'Are you all right?'

'I called Mark, but he's not home.'

'What about you? Are you all right?'

I could hear her breathe. She didn't say anything for a time, and then she said, 'I'd like someone with me, I think. Would you mind?'

'I'm leaving now.'

I hung up. Pike was staring at me, his glasses reflecting the kitchen lights. 'Riggens paid her a visit. I'd better go over there.'

Pike said, 'This isn't going to work out the way she wants it to.'

I spread my hands. 'I don't know. Maybe we can make it work out that way.'

'If Dees and Thurman and these guys are mixed up with Akeem D'Muere, it'll be ugly. She may find out something about him that she wished she didn't know.'

I spread my hands again. 'Maybe that's the price for being in love.'

Pike said, 'I'll finish the dishes.'

I told him thanks, then I put on the Dan Wesson and drove to see Jennifer Sheridan.

CHAPTER 14

Twenty-six minutes later I parked on the street across from Jennifer Sheridan's apartment building and buzzed her number on the security phone. The speaker came to life and Jennifer Sheridan said, 'Who is it?'

'Elvis Cole.'

The door lock buzzed open and I went in and took the elevator to the third floor.

Jennifer Sheridan lived in one of those stucco ant farms just off the freeway in Woodland Hills that caters to attractive young singles, attractive young couples, and the not-so-young-but-almost-as-attractive newly divorced. There would be a lot of grabass around the pool and something called a 'fitness room' where men and women would watch each other work out, but I guess it was a fair trade for a secure building at an affordable price in a low-crime area. Unless the cops were doing the crime.

Apartment 312 was down a long hall with a lot of shag carpeting and textured wallpaper and cottage-cheese ceilings. Jennifer Sheridan was peeking out of a two-inch crack in her door, waiting for me. When she saw me, she closed the door to unhook the chain, then opened it again. 'I'm sorry for calling you like that, but I didn't know what else to do. I feel so silly.'

I gave her the benevolent detective smile. 'It's no trouble and you did the right thing by calling me.' Maybe it was the six-pack-of-Falstaff smile.

She stepped out of the door and led me through an entry past her kitchen and into the living room. She was wearing an oversized white sweatshirt that hung low over black tights and white Keds tennis shoes. Comfortable. Just the kind of thing to be lounging around in in the apartment when Floyd Riggens came to call. She said, 'I tried calling Mark again, but there's still no answer. I left a message on his machine.'

'Okay.'

'There was another man with Floyd, but I don't know his name. He was a police officer, also.'

'What did he look like?'

'Bigger than Floyd, with very short hair. Blond.'

'Pinkworth.'

She nodded. 'Yes, that's right. Floyd called him Pink but I didn't realize that was a name.' She was trying to be brave and she was doing a good job.

'Did Floyd threaten you?'

She nodded.

I said, 'Did they hurt you?'

'Not really.' She made an uneasy smile, as if she didn't want to say anything that would cause trouble. 'He sort of grabbed me a little, that's all. I think he'd been drinking.' When she said it, she sort of brushed at her right arm. She wore the sweatshirt with the sleeves pushed above her elbows and on her forearm where she brushed there were angry red marks, the way there might be if someone grabbed hard and twisted.

I touched her forearm and turned it to look at the marks and a sharp pain throbbed behind my eyes. I said, 'Floyd.'

She took her arm back, and made a sort of dismissive laugh. 'I don't think he meant to. It just surprised me, that's all.'

'Of course.' The throbbing pain was worse.

It was a nice apartment, with inexpensive oak furniture and the kind of large overstuffed couch and matching chairs that you would buy on sale at Ikea or Home Club. A Sony television sat on a long white Formica table opposite the couch, along with a lot of plants and a portable CD player. A little forest of photographs stood between the plants and Mark Thurman was in most of the photographs. Many of the shots were duplicates of ones I had seen in Mark Thurman's album but many were not. An enormous stuffed Garfield stood sentry by the dining room table and a half-dozen smaller stuffed animals rested on the couch. Everything was neat and clean and in its proper place. I said, 'Why don't you sit, and I'll get something for us to drink, and then we can figure out what to do.'

She shook her head. 'I'm not helpless. Besides, the activity is good. Would you like a diet Coke or a glass of wine? I've got a Pinot Grigio.'

'The Pinot.'

She said, 'You sit, and I'll be right back.'

'Yes, ma'am.'

She smiled and went into the kitchen.

There was a pass-through between the kitchen and the living room so you could see from one into the other. I sat in the overstuffed chair at the far end of the living room and watched her get the wine. Jennifer Sheridan stood on her toes to reach two flute glasses out of her cupboard, then put them on the counter beside her sink. She opened the fridge, took out the bottle of Pinot, and worked out the cork. The Pinot had been opened earlier and was missing maybe a glass. She worked with her back to me. I watched the shape of her calves when she went up onto her toes and the line of her thighs and the way the oversized sweatshirt hung low over her bottom and draped from her shoulders. She didn't look so young from the back and I had to turn away to make myself stop looking at her. Jesus Christ, Cole. Portrait of the detective as a lecher. I looked at the pictures on the white table instead. Mark Thurman. Watching me. I crossed my eyes and made a face at him. Screw you, Mark. I looked at the

Garfield, instead. Maybe you shouldn't drink a six-pack of Falstaff before you visit a client.

Jennifer Sheridan came out with the two glasses of wine, handed one of them to me, and went to the couch. She must've seen me looking at the Garfield. 'Mark won that for me. Isn't it cute?'

'How nice.' I smiled. 'Tell me about Riggens and Pinkworth. Tell me everything they said. Don't leave anything out.'

She shook her head. 'The other guy didn't say very much. He just stood by the door, and every once in a while said something like "You oughta listen to him" or "We're only trying to help."'

'Okay. Then tell me about Floyd.'

She sipped her wine and thought about it, as if she wanted to be very careful and get it right. As she told me she picked up a stuffed lion from the couch and held it. 'He told me that Mark didn't know they were here, but that he was Mark's partner and he said that someone had to straighten me out because I was going to get Mark killed. I asked him to tell me what was going on but he wouldn't. He said that I didn't love Mark and I said that I did. He said I had a funny way of showing it. I told him to get out, but he wouldn't. He said that I never should have hired you because all you're doing is making trouble.'

'Floyd and I had a run-in today.' I told her about the Farmer's Market.

She blinked at me. 'You hit him?'

'No. I kicked him.'

She said, 'Kicked?'

'Yeah. Like Bruce Lee. You know.'

'You can get your foot up that high?'

I spread my hands. 'I am a man of profound talents.'

She touched her left cheek between the ear and the eye. 'He had a bruise right here.' Sort of awed.

I spread my hands again and she smiled, maybe

thinking how he had grabbed her. When she smiled I wanted to drop one wing and run in a circle. Guess we aren't so mature, after all.

I said, 'You don't get four active-duty REACT cops on your tail unless they're very scared of what you're doing. They didn't want me to know that they were on me, and now they know that I do, and they didn't want you to know that something is going on, and now Riggens has come here and threatened you. They've been trying to control the program but that isn't working, and things are beginning to fall apart. The gloves are coming off.'

She nodded, and looked thoughtful, like maybe whatever she was thinking wasn't easy to think about. She said, 'Was Mark there? At the Market?'

'No.' I was watching her. The thing that was hard to think about was even harder to say.

'He said Mark was in trouble. He said that they've been trying to help Mark, but that I was messing everything up and Mark was going to be hurt. He started yelling. He said maybe somebody ought to show me what it was like. I got scared then, and that's when he grabbed me.' She suddenly stopped speaking, went into the kitchen, and came back with the bottle of Pinot. She added more to her glass, then put the bottle on the table. 'Do you think Mark knew that Floyd was coming here?'

'I don't know. Probably not.' The detective answers a cry for support with a resounding maybe.

'I asked him why he was doing this. I asked him to tell me what had happened or what was going on. I told him I would help. He thought that was funny. He said that I didn't want to know. He said that Mark had done bad things and now they were fucked. I said Mark wasn't like that and he said I didn't know anything about Mark.' She stopped as if someone had pulled her plug, and stared into the forest of photographs.

I said, 'And you're scared he's right?'

She nodded.

'You're scared that you don't know anything about Mark, and that if you find out, you might not love him anymore.'

She pursed her lips and shook her head, then looked directly at me. 'No. I will always love him. No matter what. If he did something, it's because he believed he had to. If I can help him, then I will help him. I will love him even if he no longer loves me.' She blinked hard several times, and then took more wine. I watched her drink, and I wondered what it would be like to have someone love me with that commitment and that intensity, and, in that moment, I wished that it were me.

I said, 'Jennifer, did Mark ever mention someone named Lewis Washington?'

'No.'

'It might've been three or four months ago.'

'Maybe he said the name in passing and I wasn't paying attention, but I don't think so.'

I said, 'Four months ago, Mark's REACT team went into a place called the Premier Pawn Shop to arrest Lewis Washington for fencing stolen goods. There was a struggle, and Lewis Washington died of massive head injuries.'

She stared at me.

'The REACT team statement is that Washington pulled a gun and the head injuries resulted accidentally when team members tried to subdue Washington without the use of firearms. Washington's family said that Lewis didn't own a gun and was trying to go straight. The Washingtons sued the city and the LAPD, claiming wrongful death. The LAPD investigated, but found that there had been no wrongdoing.'

Jennifer Sheridan didn't move. She was staring at the far pictures. Mark and Jenny at the prom. Mark and Jenny after the big game. See them smile. See them laugh. 'Was it Mark?'

'The REACT team statement was that it was a combination of all five officers present, though Eric Dees, the team leader, took responsibility.'

She took a deep breath. 'Mark never told me any of that.'

'How about the name Akeem D'Muere?'

'No.'

'Akeem D'Muere is a gangbanger in South Central Los Angeles. He bosses a street gang called the Eight-Deuce Gangster Boys. Lewis Washington's family dropped their lawsuit because Akeem D'Muere told them that he'd kill them if they didn't.'

'He didn't tell me any of this. You think Mark has something to do with these people?'

'I don't know if these two things are connected or not. Maybe they're not. Maybe Mark didn't tell you about Akeem D'Muere because he doesn't know.'

'He didn't tell me about any of this.' She was shaking her head.

'This isn't going to be easy, Jennifer. What we find out about Mark might be a bad thing, just like Riggens said. It might be something that you'll wish you didn't know, and what you find out might change forever what you feel about Mark and about you with Mark. Do you see that?'

'Are you telling me that we should stop?'

'I'm not telling you one way or the other. I want you to know what you're dealing with, that's all.'

She turned away from me and looked at the pictures on the white Formica table, the pictures that had charted her life from the ninth grade until this moment. Her eyes turned pink and she rubbed at them. 'Damn it, I didn't want to cry anymore. I'm tired of crying.' She rubbed her eyes harder.

I leaned forward and touched her arm. The arm that Riggens had hurt. I said, 'Crying is dangerous. It's wise of you to avoid it this way.'

She said, 'What?' Confused.

'First, there's the dehydration, and then the lungs go into sob lock.'

She stopped the rubbing. 'Sob lock?'

I nodded. 'A form of vapor lock induced by sobbing. The lungs lose all capacity to move air, and asphyxiation is only moments away. I've lost more clients to this than gunshot wounds.'

'Maybe,' she said, 'that doesn't so much speak to the clients as to the detective.'

I slapped a hand over my chest. 'Ouch.'

Jennifer Sheridan laughed, forgetting about the tears. 'You're funny.'

'Nope. I'm Elvis.' You get me on a roll, I'm murder.

She laughed again and said, 'Say something else funny.'

'Something else funny.'

She laughed again and made a big deal out of giving me exasperated. 'No. I meant for you to *say* something funny.'

'Oh.'

'Well?' Waiting.

'You want me to say something funny.'

'Yes.'

'Something funny.'

Jennifer Sheridan threw the stuffed lion at me but then the laughter died and she said, 'Oh, my God. I am so scared.'

'I know.'

'I've got a college education. I have a good job. You're supposed to go out a lot, but I don't do that. You're supposed to be complete and whole all by yourself, but if I can't have him I feel like I'll die.'

'You're in love. People who say the other stuff are saying it either before they've been in love or after the love is over and it hasn't worked out for them, but no one says it when they're in the midst of love. When you're in love, there's too much at stake.'

She said, 'I've never been with anyone who makes me feel the way that he makes me feel. I've never tried to be. Maybe I should've. Maybe it's all been a horrible mistake.'

'It's not a mistake if it's what you wanted.' I was breathing hard and I couldn't get control of it.

She stared down into her flute glass, and she traced her fingertip around its edge, and then she stared at me. She didn't look sixteen, now. She was lean and pretty, and somehow available. She said, 'I like it that you make me laugh.'

I said, 'Jennifer.'

She put down the flute glass. 'You're very nice.'

I put down my glass and stood. She went very red and suddenly looked away. She said, 'Ohmygod. I'm sorry.'

'It's all right.'

She stood, too. 'Maybe you should go.'

I nodded, and realized that I didn't want to go. The sharp pain came back behind my eyes. 'All right.'

'This wine.' She laughed nervously, and still didn't look at me.

'Sure. Me, too.'

I backed away from her and went into the entry hall by the kitchen. I liked the way the tights fit her calves and her thighs and the way the sweatshirt hung low over her hips. She was standing with her arms crossed as if it were cold. 'I'm sorry.'

I said, 'Don't be.' Then I said, 'You're quite lovely.'

She flushed again and looked down at her empty glass and I left.

I stood in the street outside her apartment for a long time, and then I drove home.

Pike was gone and the house was cool and dark. I left it that way. I took a beer from the refrigerator, turned on the radio, and went out onto my deck. Jim Ladd was conning the air waves at KLSX. Playing a little George Thorogood. Playing a little Creedence Clearwater Revival. When you're going to listen to radio, you might as well listen to the best.

I stood in the cool night air and drank the beer and, off to my left, an owl hooted from high in a stand of pine trees. The scent of jasmine now was stronger than it had been earlier in the evening, and I liked it. I wondered if Jennifer Sheridan would like smelling it, too. Would she like the owl?

I listened and I drank for quite a long while, and then I went in to bed.

Sleep, when it finally came, provided no rest.

CHAPTER 15

At ten-forty the next morning I called my friend at B of A. She said, 'I can't believe this. Two calls in the same week. I may propose.'

'You get that stupid, I'll have to use the Sting tickets on someone else.'

'Forget it. I'd rather see Sting.' These dames.

'I want to know who financed the purchase of a place called the Premier Pawn Shop on Hoover Street in South Central L.A.' I gave her the address. 'Can you help me on that?'

'You at the office?'

'Nope. I'm taking advantage of my self-employed status to while away the morning in bed. Naked. And alone.' Mr Seduction.

My friend laughed. 'Well, if I know you, that's plenty of company.' Everybody's a comedian. 'Call you back in twenty.'

'Thanks.'

She made the call in fifteen. 'The Premier Pawn Shop was owned in partnership between Charles Lewis Washington and something called the Lester Corporation. Lester secured the loan and handled the financing through California Federal.'

'Ah ha.'

'Is that "ah ha" as in this is important, or "ah ha" as in you're clearing your throat?'

'The former. Maybe. Who signed the papers?'

'Washington and an attorney named Harold Bellis.

Bellis signed for Lester and is an officer in that corporation.'

'Bellis have an address?'

'Yeah. In Beverly Hills.' She gave it to me, then I hung up, showered, dressed, and charged off to deepest, darkest Beverly Hills. Portrait of the detective in search of mystery, adventure, and a couple of measly clues.

The Law Offices of Harold Bellis were on the third floor of a newly refurbished three-story office building a half block off Rodeo Drive and about a million light-years from South Central Los Angeles. I found a parking space between a Rolls-Royce Corniche and an eighty-thousand-dollar Mercedes two-seater in front of a store that sold men's belts starting at three hundred dollars. Business was brisk.

I went into a little glass lobby with a white marble floor and a lot of gold fixtures and took the elevator to the third floor. Harold Bellis had the front half of the building and it looked like he did very well. There was a lot of etched glass and glossy furniture and carpet about as deep as the North Atlantic. I waded up to a receptionist seated behind a semicircular granite desk and gave her my card. She was wearing one of those pencil-thin headphones so she could answer the phone and speak without having to lift anything. 'Elvis Cole to see Mr Bellis. I don't have an appointment.'

She touched a button and spoke to someone, then listened and smiled at me. There was no humor in the smile, nor any friendliness. She said, 'We're sorry, but Mr Bellis's calendar is full. If you'd like an appointment, we can schedule a time next week.'

I said, 'Tell him it's about the Premier Pawn Company. Tell him I have a question about the Lester Corporation.'

She said it into the microphone, and a couple of minutes later a rapier-thin woman with prominent cheeks and severely white skin came out and led me through a long common office where secretaries and aides and other people sat in little cubicles, and then into her office, and then into his. Her office held a bank of designer file cabinets and fresh-cut tulips and the entrance to his office. You want to see him, you've got to get past her, and she wouldn't be easy to beat. She'd probably even like the fight.

Harold Bellis had the corner office and it was big. She said, 'This is Mr Cole.'

Harold Bellis stood up and came around his desk, smiling and offering his hand. He was short and soft with pudgy hands and a fleshy face and thinning gray hair that looked as soft as mouse fur. Sort of like the Beverly Hills version of Howdy Doody. 'Thanks, Martha. Harold Bellis, Mr Cole. Martha tells me you're interested in the Premier Pawn Shop. Would you like to buy it?' He sort of laughed when he said it, like it was an obvious joke and we both knew it. Ha ha.

'Not today, Mr Bellis, thanks.'

Martha looked down her nose at me and left.

Harold Bellis's handshake was limp and his voice was sort of squeaky, but maybe that was just confidence. An original David Hockney watercolor and two Jésus Leuus oils hung on the walls. You don't get the Hockney and the Leuus by being sissy in the clinches. 'I'm working on something that brought me across the Premier and I learned that you're an officer in the company that owns it.'

'That's correct.' Bellis offered me a seat and took the chair across from me. The decor was Sante Fe, and the seating was padded benches. Bellis's chair looked comfortable, but the benches weren't. He said, 'I have a meeting with a client now, but she's sorting through records in the conference room, so we can squeeze in a few minutes.'

'Great.'

'Does this involve Mr Washington's death?'

'In part.'

Bellis gave me sad and shook his head. 'That young man's death was a tragedy. He had everything in the world going for himself.'

'The police say he was fencing stolen goods. His family suspects that, too.'

'Well, that was never established in a court of law, was it?'

'Are you saying he wasn't?'

'If he was, it was unknown to the co-owners of the shop.' Bellis's smile grew tighter and he didn't look so much like Howdy Doody now.

I smiled at him. 'Who are the co-owners, Mr Bellis?'

Harold Bellis looked at my card as if, in the looking, something had been confirmed. 'Perhaps if you told me your interest in all of this.'

'Mr Washington's family implied that he was the sole owner of the Premier, but upon checking, I found that something called the Lester Corporation arranged the financing and carried the paper.'

'That's right.'

'Since Mr Washington had no credit history, and was working at a minimum-wage job at the time, I was wondering why someone would co-sign a loan with him for such a substantial sum of money.'

Harold Bellis said, 'The Lester Corporation provides venture capital for minority businessmen. Lewis Washington made a proposal, and we agreed to enter into partnership. That's all there is to it.'

'To the tune of eighty-five thousand dollars.'

'Yes.'

'You co-signed a loan for a man with no formal education, a criminal record, and no business experience, because you like to help underprivileged entrepreneurs?'

'Someone has to, don't you think?' He leaned forward

out of the Sante Fe chair and the Howdy Doody eyes were as hard as a smart bomb's heart. Nope, he wouldn't be sissy in the clinches.

I said, 'Does Akeem D'Muere own the Lester Corporation?'

Bellis didn't move for a long moment and the eyes stayed with me. The smart bomb acquiring its target. 'I'm afraid I'm not at liberty to discuss the Lester Corporation or any other client, Mr Cole. You understand that, don't you?'

'I understand it, but I was hoping that you'd make an exception.'

The hard eyes relaxed and some of the Howdy Doody came back. Howdy Doody billing at a thousand dollars an hour. 'Do you suspect that this Mr D'Muere has something to do with Lewis Washington's death?'

'I don't know.'

'If you suspect someone of criminal activity, you should report it to the police.'

'Perhaps I will.' Elvis Cole makes his big threat.

Harold Bellis glanced at his watch and stood up. The watch was a Patek Philippe that wholesaled out at maybe fourteen thousand dollars. Maybe if you could blow fourteen grand on a watch and keep Hockney originals around for office decorations, you didn't think twice about giving eighty-five thousand to a total stranger with no credentials and a spotty past. Of course, you didn't get rich enough for the watch and the Hockneys by not thinking twice. Harold Bellis said, 'I'm sorry I couldn't be more help to you, Mr Cole, but I really have to see my client now.' He looked at my card again. 'May I keep this?'

'Sure. You can have a couple more, if you want. Pass'm out to your friends. I can use the work.'

Harold Bellis laughed politely and showed me to the door. The thin woman reappeared and led me back through the office and out to the lobby. I was hoping she'd walk me down to my car, but she didn't.

Outside, my car was still bracketed by the Rolls and the Mercedes, and gentlemen of indeterminate national origin were still going into Pierre's to buy three-hundred-dollar belts and twelve-hundred-dollar shoes. Slender women with shopping bags and tourists with cameras crowded the sidewalks, and foreign cars crept along the outside lanes, praying for a parking space. I had been inside maybe fifteen minutes and not much had changed, either with Beverly Hills or with what I knew, but I am nothing if not resourceful.

I fed quarters into the parking meter and waited. It was eleven twenty-five.

At sixteen minutes after noon, Harold Bellis came out of his building and walked north, probably off to a business lunch at a nearby restaurant. Eleven minutes later, his assistant, Martha, appeared out of the parking garage driving a late-model Honda Acura. She turned south.

I ran back across the street, rode the elevator up to Bellis's floor, and hurried up to the receptionist, giving her the Christ-my-day-is-going-to-hell smile. 'Hi. Martha said she'd leave my calendar with you.'

She gave confused. 'Excuse me?'

'When I was here this morning, I left my date book in Harry's office. I called and Martha said she'd leave it with you for me.'

The receptionist shook her head. 'I'm sorry, but she didn't.'

I gave miserable. 'Oh, man. I'm screwed. It's got all my appointments, and my account numbers. I guess it just slipped her mind. You think it'd be okay if I ran back there and checked?' I gave her expectant, and just enough of the little boy so that she'd know my fate in life rested squarely on her shoulders.

'Sure. You know the way?'

'I can find it.'

I went back past the assistants and the cubicles to Martha's office. It was open. I went in and closed the door, then looked over the files until I found the client index. It took maybe three minutes to find the client index and twenty seconds to find the Lester files.

The articles of incorporation of the Lester Corporation, a California corporation, were among the first documents bound in the Lester Corp files. The president of the Lester Corporation was listed as one Akeem D'Muere. D'Muere's address was care of The Law Offices of Harold Bellis, Attorney-at-Law. Sonofagun.

I flipped through the files and found records of the acquisitions of nine investment properties throughout the South Central Los Angeles area, as well as two properties in Los Feliz and an apartment building in Simi Valley. The purchases included two bars, a laundromat, and the pawnshop. The rest were residential. I guess the weasel-dust business pays.

The Premier Pawn Shop location was purchased nine months and two days prior to Charles Lewis Washington's death. There was a contract with a property management firm for six of the businesses, as well as receipts from contractors for maintenance and renovation work performed on seven of the businesses. Each property had a separate file. The Premier showed plumbing and electrical work, as well as a new heating and air conditioning unit, and there was also a receipt from something called Atlas Security Systems for the installation of an Autonomous Monitoring System, as well as a Perimeter Security Alarm. Similar systems had also been purchased for the two bars. I wasn't sure what an Autonomous Monitoring System was, but it sounded good. The cost of these things and their installation was $6,518.22, and there had been no mention of them in the police reports. Hmm.

I wrote down the phone number of Atlas Security Systems, then closed the file, and borrowed Martha's phone to call them. I told a guy named Mr Walters that I was a friend of Harold Bellis's, that I owned a convenience store in Laguna Niguel, and that I was thinking of installing a security system. I told him that Harold had recommended Atlas and something called an Autonomous Monitoring System, and I asked if he could explain it. Mr Walters could. He told me that the Autonomous Monitoring System was perfect for a convenience store or any other cash business, because it was an ideal way to keep an eye on employees who might steal from you. The AMS was a hidden video camera timed to go on and off during business hours, or whenever a motion sensor positioned to my specifications told it to. He gave me cost and service information, and then I thanked him and told him that I'd get in touch.

I hung up the phone, returned the files to their cabinets, left the door open as I had found it, then walked out past the receptionist and drove to my office.

As I drove, I thought about the video equipment.

No one shot at me on the way, but maybe they were saving that for later.

CHAPTER 16

When I got to my office at five minutes past one, there was a message on my machine from James Edward Washington, asking me to call. I did.

James Edward said, 'You know a taco stand called Raul's on Sixty-five and Broadway?'

'No.'

'Sixty-five and Broadway. I'm gonna be there in an hour with a guy who knows about what's going on. Ray came through.'

'I'll meet you there.'

I hung up, then called Joe Pike. He answered on the first ring. 'Pike.'

'I'm going to meet James Edward Washington at a place called Raul's on Sixty-five and Broadway in about one hour. He says he's got a guy who maybe knows something.'

'I'll be there.'

'There's more.' I told him about the Lester Corporation and Harold Bellis and the contract with Atlas Security. I told him about the video equipment.

Pike grunted. 'So Akeem D'Muere saw what happened to Charles Lewis.'

'It's possible.'

'And maybe it shows something different than the police report claims.'

'Yeah. But if that's the case, why doesn't Akeem use it to fry these guys? Why is he protecting them?'

Pike fell silent.

'Joe?'

'Watch your ass out there, Elvis. It's getting too hot for these guys to sit by. They're going to have to move.'

'Maybe that's how we finally crack this. Maybe we make it so hot that they've got to move, and when they move we'll see what they're doing.'

'Maybe. But maybe their idea of a move is to take us out.'

Nothing like a little inspiration.

Thirty-two minutes later I exited the freeway and turned north on Broadway past auto repair shops and take-out rib joints and liquor stores that had been looted in the riots and not yet rebuilt.

Raul's Taco was a cinderblock stand on the west side of Broadway between a service drive and an auto parts place that specialized in remanufactured transmissions. You ordered at a little screen window on one side of the stand, then you went around to the other side to wait for your food. There was a tiny fenced area by the pick-up window with a couple of picnic benches for your more elegant sit-down diners and a couple of little stand-up tables on the sidewalk for people in a rush. A large sign over the order window said WE HAVE SOUL-MAN TACOS. An hour before noon and the place was packed.

I drove up to Sixty-fourth, pulled a U-turn at the light, then swung back and parked at the curb in front of the transmission place. James Edward Washington and a young black guy maybe Washington's age were sitting across from each other at one of the picnic tables, eating tacos. The second guy was wearing a neon orange hat with the bill pointed backwards, heavy Ray Ban sunglasses, and a black Los Angeles Raiders windbreaker even though it was ninety degrees. Washington saw me and nodded toward the table. The other guy saw him nod and turned to watch me come over. He didn't look happy. Most of the other people in Raul's were watching me, too.

Guess they didn't get many white customers. Washington said, 'This is the guy Ray was talking about. Cool T, this is the detective.'

Cool T said, 'You say his name Elvis I thought he a brother.'

I said, 'I am. Amazing what a marcel and skin lightener will do, isn't it?'

Cool T shook his head and gave disgusted. 'And he think he funny, too.'

Cool T started to get up but Washington put a hand on his forearm and held him down. 'He's white, but he's trying to help about Lewis. That means he can be all the funny he wants.'

Cool T shrugged without looking at me. Aloof.

Washington took a taco wrapped in yellow paper out of the box and offered it to me. He said, 'This is a Soul-Man taco. These Mexicans grill up the meat and the peppers and put barbecue sauce on it. You like barbecue?'

'Sure.' I unwrapped the taco. The paper was soaked through with oil and barbecue sauce, but it smelled like a handful of heaven. The taco was two handmade corn tortillas deep-fried to hold their shape, and filled with meat and chili peppers and the barbecue sauce. The sauce was chunky with big rings of jalapeño and serrano peppers.

Cool T finished off the rest of his taco, then pointed out the peppers. 'It's pretty hot, you ain't used to it. They probably make one without the peppers, you ask.' He was showing a lot of teeth when he said it.

I took a bite, and then I took a second. It was delicious, but it wasn't very hot. I said, 'You think they'd give me more peppers?'

Cool T stopped showing the teeth and went sullen. Shown up by the white man.

Washington said, 'Cool T's been living on these streets

while I've been swabbing decks. He's seen what's going on.'

Cool T nodded.

'Okay. So what's Cool T know?' I finished my taco and eyed the box lustily. There were three more tacos in it. Washington made a little hand move that said help yourself. I did.

Cool T said, 'Those cops ain't cops no mo'. They just passin'.'

'What's that mean?'

'Mean they in business and they use the Eight-Deuce as what we call sales representatives.' He grinned when he said it.

I looked at Washington. 'Is this for real?'

Washington shrugged. 'That's what his girlfriend says.'

Cool T said, 'I friendly with this bitch used to live with a Gangster Boy.'

I said, 'Are you telling me that these officers are in the crack trade?'

Cool T nodded. 'They in the everything trade. Whatever the Eight-Deuce in, they in.' He selected another taco. 'Ain't been an Eight-Deuce home boy locked down in four or five months. Pigs take off the Rolling Sixties and the Eight-Trey Swans and all these other nigguhs, but not the Eight-Deuce. They look out for each other. They share the wealth.'

'The cops and the Eight-Deuce Gangster Boys.'

'Uh-hunh. They in business together.' He finished the taco and licked his fingers. 'Eight-Deuce point out the competition and the cops take it down. You wanna see it happen, I can put you onto something.'

'What?'

Cool T said. 'Nigguh been sellin' dope out a ice cream truck over by Witley Park. He at the park every Thursday and the park in Eight-Deuce turf and they tired of it. The cops going over there today to run him off.'

Washington said, 'I figured we could go over there and see what's what. I figure if it's our guys, maybe we can do something with it.'

I was liking Washington just fine. 'Okay.'

Cool T said, 'Not me. Anybody see me over there and something happen, I be meetin' up with Mr Drive-By.'

Cool T stood up. Washington held out his fist and Cool T brushed his own fist against it, back and top and sides, and then he walked away.

I looked at Washington. Well, well. 'You did okay.'

Washington nodded. Cool.

CHAPTER 17

When we walked out to the car, I saw Joe Pike parked at a fire hydrant a block and a half north. We made eye contact, and he shook his head. No one was following.

James Edward said, 'What're you looking at?'

'My partner.'

'You work with someone?' He was looking up Broadway.

'If you look for him like that, people will know someone's there.'

James Edward stopped looking and got into the car. I slid in after him. 'Use the mirror. Angle it so that you can see. He's in a red Jeep.'

James Edward did it. 'Why's he back there?'

'The men who killed your brother have been following me. He's there to follow the followers.'

James Edward readjusted the mirror and we pulled away. 'He any good?'

'Yes.'

'Are you?'

'I get lucky.'

James Edward settled back and crossed his arms. 'Luck is for chumps. Ray knows a couple of people and he asked them about you. He says you're a straight up dude. He says you get respect.'

'You can fool some of the people some of the time.'

James Edward shook his head and stared at the passing buildings. 'Bullshit. Any fool can buy a car, but you can't buy respect.'

I glanced over, but he was looking out at the streets.

James Edward Washington told me where to go and I went there and pretty soon we were on streets just like James Edward Washington's street, with neat single-family homes and American cars and preschool children jumping rope and riding Big Wheels. Older women sat on tiny porches and frowned because teenagers who should've been in school were sitting on the hood of a Bonneville listening to Ice Cube. The women didn't like the kids being on the Bonneville and they didn't like Ice Cube but they couldn't do anything about it. We drove, and after a while I knew we weren't just driving, we were taking a tour of James Edward Washington's life. He would say turn, and I would turn, and he would point with his chin and say something like *The girl I took to the prom used to live right there* or *Dude I knew named William Johnston grew up there and writes television now and makes four hundred thousand dollars every year and bought his mama a house in the San Gabriel Valley* or *My cousins live there. I was little, they'd come to my street and we'd trick-or-treat, and then I'd come back here with them and we'd do it all over again. The lady that lived right over there used to make caramel-dipped candy apples better'n anything you ever bought at the circus.*

We drove and he talked and I listened, and after a while I said, 'It has to be hard.'

He looked at me.

I said, 'There are a lot of good things here, but there are also bad things, and it's got to be hard growing up and trying not to let the bad things drag you down.'

He looked away from me. We rode for a little bit longer, and then he said, 'I guess I just want you to know that there's more to the people down here than a bunch of shiftless niggers sopping up welfare and killin' each other.'

'I knew that.'

'You think it, maybe, but you don't know it. You're down here right now cause a nigger got beaten to death. We're driving to a park where a nigger gonna be selling drugs and niggers gonna be buying. That's what you know. You see it on the news and you read it in the papers and that's all you know. I know there's people who work hard and pay taxes and read books and build model airplanes and dream about flying them and plant daisies and love each other as much as any people can love each other anywhere, and I want you to know that, too.'

'Okay.' He wasn't looking at me, and I wasn't looking at him. I guess we were embarrassed, the way men who don't know each other can get embarrassed. 'Thanks for telling me.'

James Edward Washington nodded.

'It's important.'

He nodded again. 'Turn here.'

At the end of the block was a playground with a basketball court and six goals, and, beyond the court, a softball diamond with a long shallow outfield. A few teenaged guys were on the court, but not many, and a guy in his early thirties was running wind sprints in the outfield, racing from second base to the far edge of the outfield, then walking back, then doing it all again. A row of mature elms stood sentry along the far perimeter of the outfield, then there was another street and more houses. A sky blue Sunny Day ice cream truck was parked at the curb in the shade of one of the elms and a tall guy in a Malcolm X hat was leaning against it with his arms crossed, watching the sprinter. He didn't look interested in selling ice cream.

James Edward Washington said, 'That's our guy.'

We turned away from the park, made the block, and came back to a side street that gave an unobstructed view of the basketball players and the outfield and the ice cream truck on the far street. I parked on the side street so we'd have an easy, eyes-forward view, and then I shut the engine. If the neighbors saw us sitting there, maybe they'd think we were scouting for the NBA.

Maybe eight or nine minutes later four guys in a white Bel Air turned onto the far street, slowed to a stop, and the guy with the X hat went over to them. One of the guys in the backseat of the Bel Air gave something to the X, and the X gave something to the guy in the Bel Air. Then the Bel Air drove away and the X went back to his leaning. A little bit later a kid on a bike rolled up the sidewalk, jumped the curb down to the street, and skidded to a stop. The kid and the X traded something, and the kid rode away. Washington said, 'Cool T better be giving it to us straight about those cops.'

I pointed at the X. 'He's here, isn't he?'

'He's here, but will the cops come, and if they come are they coming because they're cops or because they're working with the Eight-Deuce?'

'We'll find out.'

'Yes. I guess we will.' James Edward shifted in the seat, uncomfortable, but not because of the seat. 'They don't come and run this muthuhfuckuh off, maybe I'll do it myself.'

'Maybe I'll help you.'

Washington glanced at me and nodded.

A couple of minutes later Joe Pike came up along the sidewalk and squatted beside my window. I said, 'Joe Pike, this is James Edward Washington. James, this is my partner, Joe Pike.'

Pike canted his head to lock onto James Edward Washington and reached in through the window. You can't see his eyes behind the dark glasses, but it's always easy to tell where he's looking. His whole being sort of points in that direction, as if he were totally focused on you. James Edward took his hand, but stared at the tattoos. Most people do.

I told Pike about the X at the ice cream truck and what Cool T had said about Thurman's REACT team and their involvement with the Eight-Deuce Gangster Boys.

Pike nodded. 'Dees and his people are supposed to thump this guy?'

James Edward said, 'That's the word.'

Pike looked at the X. 'It's a long way across the playground to the ice cream truck. If Dees moves the action away from us, we've got too much ground to cover to catch up. We might lose them.'

I said, 'Why don't you set up on that side, and we'll stay here. If Dees moves that way, you've got them, and if he moves in this direction, we've got him.'

Pike stared behind us up the street, then twisted around and looked at the park. 'You feel it?'

'What?'

Pike shook his head. 'Doesn't feel right.'

He stepped away from the car and stood without moving for a time and then he walked away. I thought about what Joe had said. *They're going to have to make a move.*

James Edward watched Pike leave. 'He's sorta strange, huh?'

'You think?'

A few minutes later we saw Pike's Jeep pass the ice cream truck and turn away from the park. James Edward looked at me. 'You don't think he's strange?'

We moved deeper into the afternoon, and business was good for the man in the ice cream truck. Customers came by in cars and trucks and on motorcycles and bicycles and on foot. Some of the cars would slow as they passed and the X would stare and they would make the block a couple of times before they finally stopped and did their deal, but most folks drove up and stopped without hesitating. The X never hesitated, either. Any one of these people could've been undercover cops but no one seemed to take that into consideration. Maybe it didn't matter. Maybe business was so good and profits were so large that the threat of a bust was small relative to the potential gain. Or maybe the X just didn't care. Some people are like that.

Once, two young women pushing strollers came along the far sidewalk. The X made a big deal out of tipping his cap with a flourish and giving them the big smile. The women made a buy, too. The one who did the talking was pregnant. Washington rubbed his face with both hands and said, 'Oh, my Jesus.'

School let out. More players joined the basketball games. The guy running wind sprints stopped running, and the time crept past like a dying thing, heavy and slow and unable to rest.

James Edward twisted in the seat and said, 'How you stand this goddamn waiting?'

'You get used to it.'

'You used to be a cop?'

I shook my head. 'Nope. I was a security guard for a while, and then I apprenticed with a man named George Fieder. Before that I was in the Army.'

'How about that guy Pike?'

'Joe was a police officer. Before that, he was a Marine.'

James Edward nodded. Maybe thinking about it. 'You go to college?'

'I had a couple years, on and off. After the Army, it was tough to sit in a classroom. Maybe I'll go back one day.'

'If you went back, what would you study?'

I made a little shrug. 'Teacher, maybe.'

He smiled. 'Yeah. I could see you in a classroom.'

I spread my hands. 'What? You don't think there's a place for a thug in the fourth grade?'

He smiled, but then the smile faded. Across the park, a

girl who couldn't have been more than sixteen pulled her car beside the ice cream truck and bought a glassine packet. She had a pretty face and precisely cornrowed hair in a traditional African design. Washington watched the transaction, then put his forearms on his knees and said, 'Sitting here, seeing these brothers and sisters doing this, it hurts.'

'Yes, I guess it does.'

He shook his head. 'You aren't black. I see it, I see brothers and sisters turning their backs on the future. What's it to you?'

I thought about it. 'I don't see brothers and sisters. I don't see black issues. Maybe I should, but I don't. Maybe because I'm white, I can't. So I see what I can see. I see a pretty young girl on her way to being a crack whore. She'll get pregnant, and she'll have a crack baby, and there will be two lifetimes of pain. She'll want more and more rock, and she'll do whatever it takes to get it, and, over time, she'll contract AIDS. Her mother will hurt, and her baby will hurt, and she will hurt.' I stopped talking and I put my hands on the steering wheel and I held it for a time. 'Three lifetimes.'

Washington said, 'Unless someone saves her.'

I let go of the wheel. 'Yes, unless someone saves her. I see it the only way I can see it. I see it as people.'

Washington shifted in the bucket. 'I was gonna ask you why you do this, but I guess I know.'

I went back to watching the X.

James Edward Washington said, 'If I wanted to learn this private eye stuff, they got a school I could learn how to do it?'

James Edward Washington was looking at me with watchful, serious eyes. I said, 'You want to learn how to do this, maybe we can work something out.'

He nodded.

I nodded back at him, and then Floyd Riggens's sedan

turned onto the far street and picked up speed toward the ice cream truck.

I said, 'Camera in the glove box.'

Mark Thurman was in the front passenger seat and Pinkworth was in the backseat. The sedan suddenly punched into passing gear and the X jumped the chain-link fence and ran across the outfield toward the basketball court. He was pulling little plastic packs of something out of his pockets and dumping them as he ran.

James Edward opened the glove box and took out the little Canon Auto Focus I keep there. I said, 'You see how to work it?'

'Sure.'

'Use it.'

I started the Corvette and put it in gear in case the X led Riggens across the park toward us, but it didn't get that far. Riggens horsed the sedan over the curb and cut across the sidewalk at the far corner where there was no fence and aimed dead on at the running X and gunned it. The X tried to cut back, but when he did, Riggens swung the wheel hard over and pegged the brakes and then Riggens and Thurman and Pinkworth were out of the car. They had their guns out, and the X froze and put up his hands. Thurman stopped, but Riggens and Pinkworth didn't. They knocked the X down and kicked him in the ribs and the legs and the head. Riggens went down on one knee and used his pistol, slamming the X in the head while Pinkworth kicked him in the kidneys. Mark Thurman looked around as if he were frightened, but he didn't do anything to stop it. There were maybe a hundred people in the park, and everybody was looking, but they didn't do anything to stop it, either. Next to me, James Edward Washington snapped away with the little Canon.

Riggens and Pinkworth pulled the X to his feet, went through his pockets, then shoved him away. The X fell, and tried to get up, but neither his legs nor his arms were much use. His head was bleeding. Pinkworth said something sharp to Mark Thurman and Thurman walked back across the park, scooping up the little plastic envelopes. Riggens climbed the chain link and went into the ice cream truck and that's the last we saw of it because a burgundy metal-flake Volkswagen Beetle and a double-dip black Chevrolet Monte Carlo playing NWA so loud that it rocked the neighborhood pulled up fast next to us and three guys wearing ski masks got out, two from the backseat of the Monte Carlo and one from the passenger side of the Volkswagen. The guy from the Volkswagen was wearing a white undershirt maybe six sizes too small and baggy pants maybe forty sizes too big and was carrying what looked to be a Taurus 9mm semiautomatic pistol. The Taurus fit him just right. The first guy out of the Monte Carlo was tall and wearing a black duster with heavy Ray Ban Wayfarers under the ski mask and was carrying a sawed-off double-barrel 20-gauge. The second guy was short and had a lot of muscles stuffed into a green tee shirt that said LOUIS. He was holding an AK-47. All of the guns were pointed our way.

James Edward Washington made a hissing sound somewhere deep in his chest and the tall guy stooped over to point the double twenty through my window. He looked at me, then James Edward, and then he gestured with the double twenty. 'Get out the muthuhfuckin' car, nigger.'

James Edward got out of the car, and then the tall guy pointed the double twenty at me. 'You know what you gonna do?'

'Sure,' I said. 'Whatever you say.'

The tall guy smiled behind the ski mask. 'Tha's right. Keep doin' it, and maybe you see the sun set.'

CHAPTER 18

The guy with the Taurus brought James Edward Washington to the metal-flake Beetle and put him in the right front passenger seat. The Beetle's driver stayed where he was, and the guy with the Taurus got into the back behind Washington.

The guy in the long coat said, 'They gonna take off and you gonna follow them and we gonna follow you. You get outta line, they gonna shoot your nigger and I gonna shoot you. We hear each other on this?'

'Sure.'

'M'man Bone Dee gonna ride with you. He say it, you do it. We still hear each other?'

'Uh-huh.' While the tall guy told me, the shorter guy in the Louis Farrakhan tee shirt walked around and got into my car. When he walked he held the AK down along his leg, and when he got in, he sort of held the muzzle pointed at the floorboard. The AK was too long to point at me inside the car. The guy in the long coat went back to the Monte Carlo and climbed into the back. There were other guys in there, but the windows were heavily tinted and you couldn't see them clearly. If Pike was here, he might be able to see them, but Pike was probably on the other side of the park, still watching the cops. But maybe not.

Bone Dee said, 'You got a gun?'

'Left shoulder.'

Bone Dee reached across and came up with the Dan Wesson. He didn't look under my jacket when he did it

139

and he didn't look at the Dan Wesson after he had it. He stared at me, and he kept staring even after he had the Dan Wesson.

I said, 'I always thought the AK was overrated, myself. Why don't you buy American and carry an M-16?'

More of the staring.

I said, 'You related to Sandra Dee?'

He said, 'Keep it up, we see whether this muthuh-fuckuh overrated or not.'

No sense of humor.

The Beetle started rolling and the guy in the shotgun seat of the Monte Carlo motioned me out. I tucked in behind the Bug and the Monte Carlo eased in behind me. I stayed close to the Beetle, and the Monte Carlo stayed close to me, too close for another car to slip between us. There was so much heavy-bass gangster rap coming out of the Monte Carlo, they shouldn't have bothered. No one would come within a half mile for fear of hearing loss.

We went west for a couple of blocks, then turned south, staying on the residential streets and avoiding the main thoroughfares. As we drove, Bone Dee looked through the glove box and under the seats and came up with the Canon. 'Thought you liked to buy American?'

'It was a gift.'

Bone Dee popped open the back, exposed the film, then smashed the lens on the AK's receiver and threw the camera and the exposed film out the window. So much for visual evidence.

The Bug drove slowly, barely making school zone speeds, and staying at the crown of the street, forcing oncoming cars to the side. Rolling in attack mode. Kids on their way home from school clutched their books tight to their chests and other kids slipped down driveways to get behind cars or between houses in case the shooting would start and women on porches with small children hurried them indoors. You could see the fear and the resignation, and I thought what a helluva way it must be to live like this. *Does South Central look like America to you?* A short, bony man in his seventies was standing shirtless in his front yard with a garden hose in one hand and a can of Pabst Blue Ribbon in the other. He glared at the guys in the Bug and then the guys in the Monte Carlo. He puffed out his skinny chest and raised the hose and the Pabst out from his sides, showing hard, letting them have him if they had the balls to take him and saying it didn't scare him one goddamn bit. Dissing them. Showing disrespect. An AK came out of the Volkswagen and pointed at him but the old man didn't back down. Hard, all right. We turned again and the AK disappeared. With all the people running and hiding, I began to think that running and hiding was a pretty good idea. I could wait until we were passing a cross street, then backfist Bone Dee, yank the wheel, and probably get away, but that wouldn't work too well for James Edward Washington. Not many places to hide inside a Volkswagen Beetle.

Two blocks shy of Martin Luther King Boulevard we turned into an alley past a '72 Dodge with no rear wheels and stopped at a long, low unpainted cinderblock building that probably used to be an auto repair shop. The alley ran behind a row of houses along to a train track that probably hadn't been used since World War II. Most of the railroad property was overgrown with dead grass, and undeveloped except for the cinderblock building. The houses all had chain-link fences, and many had nice vegetable gardens with tomato plants and okra and snap beans, and most of the fences were overgrown with running vines so the people who lived there wouldn't have to see what happened in the alley. Pit bulls stood at the back fences of two of the houses and watched us with small, hard eyes. Guess the pit bulls didn't mind seeing what happened. Maybe they even liked it.

The guy in the long coat got out of the Monte Carlo and

went to one of four metal garage doors built into the building and pushed it open. No locks. There were neither cars nor signs nor other evidence of human enterprise outside the building, but maybe inside was different. Maybe this was the Eight-Deuce clubhouse, and inside there would be pool tables and a soda fountain and clean-cut kids who looked like the Jackson family playing old Chubby Checker platters and dancing like the white man. Sure. Welcome to The Killing Zone.

When the door was open the Bug drove into the building.

Bone Dee said, 'Follow him.'

I followed. The Monte Carlo came in after me and then the guy in the long coat stepped through and pulled the door down. Nothing inside, either. The building was as empty and as uncluttered as a crypt.

When the door was down Bone Dee reached over, turned off the ignition, and took the keys. The guy in the long coat came over with the double-barreled twenty. There were no lights and no windows in the place, and the only illumination came from six industrial skylights built into the roof. No one had washed the skylights since they had been installed, so the light that came down was filtered and dirty and it was hard to see. One of the skylights was broken.

The guy in the coat made a little come-here finger gesture with his free hand and said, 'Get outta there, boy.'

I got out. Bone Dee got out with me.

The guy in the coat said, 'I like that old Corvette. You get dead, can I have it?'

'Sure.'

He ran his hand along the fender as if it were something soft, and would appreciate tenderness.

The doors on the Beetle opened and the two guys in there got out with James Edward Washington and pushed him toward me. The Monte Carlo opened up at the same time and three guys came out of there, two from the front and one from the back. The guy from the Monte Carlo's backseat was holding a Benelli combat shotgun and the two from the front were carrying AKs like Bone Dee. The guy who'd been in the backseat of the Beetle had put away the Taurus and come up with an old M-1 carbine. You count the double twenty and figure for handguns, and these guys were packing serious hurt. I spent fourteen months in Vietnam on five-man reconnaissance patrols, and we didn't carry this much stuff. Of course, we lost the war.

I said, 'Okay, are you guys going to give up now or do I have to kick some ass?'

Nobody laughed. James Edward Washington shifted his weight from foot to foot and looked as tight as a hand-me-down shirt. A fine sheen of sweat slicked his forehead and the skin beneath his eyes, and he watched the Monte Carlo like he expected something worse to get out. Something worse did.

A fourth guy slid out of the back of the Monte Carlo with the lethal grace of an African panther. He was maybe a half inch shorter than me, but with very wide shoulders and very narrow hips and light yellow skin, and he looked like he was moving in slow motion even though he wasn't. There was a tattoo on the left side of his neck that said *Blood Killer* and a scar on the left side of his face that started behind his eye, went back to his ear, then trailed down the course of his cheek to his jaw. Knife scar. He was wearing a white silk dress shirt buttoned to the neck and black silk triple-pleated pants and he looked, except for the scar, as if he had stepped out of a Melrose fashion ad in *Los Angeles Magazine*. Bone Dee handed him the Dan Wesson. The other three guys were watching me but were watching the fourth guy, too, like maybe he'd say jump and they'd race to see who could jump the highest. I said, 'You Akeem D'Muere?'

D'Muere nodded like it was nothing and looked at the Dan Wesson, opening the chamber, checking the loads, then closing the chamber. 'This ain't much gun. I got a nine holds sixteen shots.'

'It gets the job done.'

'I guess it does.' He hefted the Dan Wesson and lined up the sights on my left eye. 'What's your name?'

'Elvis Cole.'

'What you doin' here?'

'My buddy and I were looking for a guy named Clement Williams for stealing a 1978 Nissan Stanza.' Maybe a lie would help.

Akeem D'Muere cocked the Dan Wesson. 'Bullshit.' Nope. Guess a lie wasn't going to help.

I said, 'Why'd you force the Washington family to drop their wrongful-death suit against the LAPD?'

He decocked the Dan Wesson and lowered it. 'How much you know?'

I shook my head.

D'Muere said, 'We see.' He wiggled the Dan Wesson at Bone Dee and the other guy with an AK. 'Get on this fool.'

Bone Dee hit the backs of my knees with his AK and the other guy rode me down and knelt on my neck. Bone Dee knelt on my legs. The guy on my neck twisted my head around until I was looking up, then put the muzzle of his AK under my ear. It hurt.

Akeem D'Muere stood over me. 'It be easy to kill you, but easy ain't always smart. The people I know, they say you got friends at LAPD and you turnin' up dead maybe make'm mad, maybe make things even worse.'

Something moved across the skylights. Pike, maybe.

'Still, I can't let you keep runnin' around, you see? Things gettin' outta hand and they got to stop. *You* got to stop. You see that?'

'Sure.' It was hard to breathe with the guy on my back.

Akeem D'Muere shook his head. 'You say that, but it just talk, so I gotta show you how things are.' Akeem D'Muere went over to James Edward Washington, touched the Dan Wesson to James Edward's left temple, and pulled the trigger. The explosion hit me like a physical thing and the right side of James Edward Washington's face blew out and he collapsed to the concrete floor as if he were a mechanical man and someone had punched his off button. He fell straight down, and when his face hit the cement, a geyser of blood sprayed across the floor and splattered onto my cheeks.

I went as stiff and tight as a bowstring and pushed against the men on my back but I could not move them. James Edward Washington trembled and twitched and jerked on the floor as a red pool formed under his head. His body convulsed and something that looked like red tapioca came out of his mouth. The guy in the long coat who had opened and closed the big door went over to James Edward and squatted down for a closer look. He said, 'Look at this shit.'

The convulsing peaked, and then the body grew still.

Akeem D'Muere came back, squatted beside me, and opened the Dan Wesson's chamber. He shook out the remaining cartridges, then wiped down the Dan Wesson and dropped it next to me. He said, 'The fuckin' bitch next. She started this.'

I blinked hard five or six times, and then I focused on him. It was hard to focus and hard to hear him, and I tried to think of a way to shake off the men on my back and get to him before the AKs got to me.

Akeem D'Muere smiled like he knew what I was thinking, and like it didn't really worry him, like even if I tried, and even if I got out from under the men and past the AKs, he still wouldn't be worried. He looked over at the others. 'You got the keys?'

Bone Dee said, 'Yeah,' and held up my keys.

Akeem sort of jerked his head and Bone Dee went to the guy with the carbine and they went out of my field of view to my car.

Maybe thirty seconds later Bone Dee came back and Akeem D'Muere went over to James Edward Washington's body. He touched the body with his toe, then shook his head and looked at me. 'Don't matter none. This just another dead nigger.'

I tried to say something, but nothing came out.

Akeem D'Muere turned away. 'Let's get the fuck out of here.'

Bone Dee and the guy with the carbine got back into the Volkswagen and Akeem D'Muere and the guy with the Benelli riot gun went to the Monte Carlo. The guy on my shoulders stayed there and another guy with an AK went to the Monte Carlo and stood by the open passenger door, ready to cover me. The tall guy with the double twenty opened the big doors. When he did, something outside made a loud BANG and the tall guy was kicked back inside and Joe Pike came through fast, diving low and rolling toward the Volkswagen, then coming up and snapping off one shot at the guy on my shoulders and two shots through the Volkswagen's driver's-side window. The bangs were loud and would've been Pike's .357. The first bullet rolled the guy off my shoulders and the two in the Volkswagen pushed the driver over into the passenger side on top of Bone Dee. Pike yelled, 'Down.'

I stayed down.

The guy standing guard by the Monte Carlo dove into the open passenger door, and the big Benelli came out over the top of him and cut loose, putting most of its pellets into the Volkswagen. Pike popped two fast shots at the Monte Carlo, and then the Monte Carlo roared to life and fishtailed its right rear into the Volkswagen and then into the side of the garage door and then it was gone.

I ran forward and pulled Bone Dee out of the VW. The

driver was dead. Bone Dee screamed when I grabbed him and yelled that he'd been shot and I told him I didn't give a damn. I pushed him down on the cement and made sure he wasn't armed and then I went to James Edward Washington but James Edward Washington was dead. 'Jesus Christ.'

Pike said, 'You okay?'

I shook my head. I took a deep breath and let it out and then I began to shake.

Pike said, 'We're going to have company.' He put his Python down carefully, so as not to mar the finish. 'You hear them?'

'Yes.'

I think Pike heard them before me, but maybe not. The sirens came in from both sides of the alley and then people were yelling and two cops I'd never seen before leapfrogged through the door. They were in street clothes and were carrying shotguns, and one took up a position in the doorway and the other rolled in and came up behind the Volkswagen's left front fender, much as Pike had. They screamed POLICE when they made their advance and told us to put down our weapons. Habit. Our weapons were already down. I said, 'Guy by the Volkswagen is wounded. The other three are dead.'

A third cop appeared in the opposite side of the door with another shotgun. 'Keep your hands away from your body and get down on the ground. Do it *now*.' He had long hair tied back with a blue bandana.

Pike and I did what they said, but they came in hard anyway, like we knew they would, one of them going to Pike and one of them coming to me and the third going to Bone Dee. The one who went to Bone Dee was short. More cars pulled up outside, and you could hear the *whoop-whoop* of the paramedics on their way in.

The cop who came to me put his knee into my back and twisted my hands around behind me and fit me with cuffs. You get knees in your back twice at the same crime scene, and you know it's not shaping up as a good day. I said, 'My wallet's on the floorboard of the Corvette. My name is Elvis Cole. I'm a private investigator. I'm one of the good guys.'

The cop with the bandana said, 'Shut the fuck up.'

They cuffed Pike and they cuffed Bone Dee and then the short cop said, 'I got the keys,' and went to my Corvette. The cop with the bandana went with him. They moved with clarity and purpose.

The other cop picked up my wallet and looked through it. He said, 'Hey, the sonofabitch wasn't lying. He's got an investigator's license.'

The cop with the bandana said, 'Not for long.'

A couple of bluesuits came in and said, 'Everything cool?'

The cop with the bandana said, 'We'll see.'

The short cop fumbled with the keys, then opened the trunk and made one of the world's widest grins. You'd think he'd won Lotto. 'Bingo. Just where they said.' He reached into the trunk and pulled out a baggie of crack cocaine worth about eight thousand dollars and tossed it to the cop with the bandana. What Bone Dee and the guy with the carbine had been doing behind me.

I looked at Joe Pike and Pike's mouth twitched.

I said, 'It isn't mine.' I pointed at Bone Dee. 'It's his.'

The cop with the bandana said, 'Sure. That's what they all say.' Then he took out a little white card, told us we were under arrest, and read us our rights.

After that he brought us to jail.

CHAPTER 19

The cop with the bandana was named Micelli. He put Pike into a gray sedan and me into a black-and-white, and then they drove us to the Seventy-seventh. Micelli rode in the sedan.

The Seventy-seventh Division is a one-story red brick building just off Broadway with diagonal curbside parking out front and a ten-foot chain-link fence around the sides and back. The officers who work the Double-seven park their personal cars inside the fence and hope for the best. Concertina wire runs along the top of the fence to keep out the bad guys, but you leave personal items in your car at your own risk. Your car sort of sits there at your own risk, too. The bad guys have been known to steal the patrol cars.

We turned through a wide chain-link gate and rolled around the back side of the building past the maintenance garage and about two dozen parked black-and-whites and up to an entry they have for uniformed officers and prospective felons. Micelli got out first and spoke with a couple of uniformed cops, then disappeared into the building. The uniforms brought us inside past the evidence lockers and went through our pockets and took our wallets and our watches and our personal belongings. They did me first, calling off the items to an overweight property sergeant who noted every item on a large manila envelope, and then they did Pike. When they did Pike, they pulled off the hip holster for his .357, the ankle holster for his .380, an eight-inch Buck hunting knife, four speed-loaders for the .357, and two extra .380 magazines. The overweight sergeant said, 'Jesus Christ, you expecting a goddamned war?'

The uniform who did Pike grinned. 'Look who it is.'

The sergeant opened Pike's wallet, then blinked at Pike. 'Jesus Christ. You're him.'

The uniformed cop took off Pike's sunglasses and handed them to the sergeant. Pike squinted at the suddenly bright light, and I saw for the first time in months how Pike's eyes were a deep liquid blue. My friend Ellen Lang says that there is a lot of hurt in the blue, but I have never been able to see it. Maybe he just hides it better with me. Maybe she sees his eyes more often than I.

Micelli came back as they were finishing and I said, 'Play this one smart, Micelli. There's a detective sergeant in North Hollywood named Poitras who'll vouch for us, and an assistant DA named Morris who'll back Poitras up. Give'm a call and let's get this straight.'

Micelli signed the property forms. 'You got connections, that what you telling me?'

'I'm telling you these guys know us, and they'll know we've been set up.'

Micelli grinned at the property sergeant. 'You ever hear that before, Sarge? You ever hear a guy we're bringing in say he was set up?'

The sergeant shook his head. 'No way. I've never heard that before.'

I said, 'For Christ's sake, Micelli, check me out. It's a goddamned phone call.'

Micelli finished signing the forms and glanced over at me. 'Listen up, pogue. I don't care if you've been hamboning the goddamned mayor. You're mine until I say otherwise.' He gave the clipboard to the property sergeant, and then he told the uniforms to bring us to interrogation. He walked away.

Pike said, 'Cops.'

The uniforms brought us through a heavy metal door and into a long sterile hall that held all the charm of a urinal in a men's room. There were little rooms on either side of the hall, and they put Pike into the first room and me into the second. The rooms sported the latest in interrogation-room technology with pus-yellow walls and water-stained acoustical ceilings and heavy-duty sound-proofing so passing liberals couldn't hear the rubber hoses being worked. There was a small hardwood table in the center of the floor with a single straight-backed metal chair on either side of it. Someone had used a broken pencil to cut a message into the wall. *In interrogation, no one can hear you scream.* Cop, probably. Detainees weren't allowed pencils.

They kept me waiting for maybe an hour, then Micelli and a cop in a gray suit came in. The new cop was in his late forties and looked to be a detective lieutenant, probably working out of homicide. Micelli took the chair across the table from me and the guy in the suit leaned against the wall. Micelli said, 'This conversation is being recorded. My name is Detective Micelli, and this is Lieutenant Stilwell.' You see? 'I'm going to ask you questions, and your answers will be used in court. You don't have to answer these questions, and if you want a lawyer, but can't afford one, we can arrange for a public defender. You want someone?'

'No.'

Micelli nodded. 'Okay.'

'Did you call Poitras?'

Micelli leaned forward. 'No one's calling anyone until we get through this.'

Stilwell said, 'How do you know Lou Poitras?'

Micelli waved his hand. 'That doesn't mean shit. What's it matter?'

'I want to know.'

I told him about me and Poitras.

When I finished, Stilwell said, 'Okay, but what were you doing down here?'

'I got a tip that a REACT cop named Eric Dees is involved with a gangbanger named Akeem D'Muere and I'm trying to find out how.'

Micelli grinned. Stilwell said, 'You got proof?'

'A guy named Cool T gave me the tip. He was a friend of James Edward Washington. Washington is one of the dead guys.'

Micelli said, 'That's fuckin' convenient.'

'Not for Washington.'

Micelli said, 'Yeah, well, we got a little tip, too. We got tipped that an asshole fitting your description and driving your car was down here trying to move a little Mexican brown to the natives. We got told that the deal was going down in an abandoned building off the tracks, and we went over there, and guess what?'

'Who gave you the tip, Micelli? Dees? One of the REACT guys?'

Micelli licked the corner of his mouth and didn't say anything.

I said, 'Check it out. Twenty minutes ago I saw Akeem D'Muere put a gun to James Edward Washington's head and pull the trigger. I'm working for a woman named Jennifer Sheridan. Akeem D'Muere has a mad on for her, and he said that she's next.'

Stilwell crossed his arms. 'Two of the dead men found in the garage were named Wilson Lee Hayes and Derek La Verne Dupree. Both of these guys had a history of trafficking in narcotics. Maybe you were down here to meet them and the deal went bad. Maybe you and your buddy Pike tried to rip those guys off.'

I spread my hands.

Micelli said, 'You own a 1966 Corvette?' He gave me the license number.

'Yeah.'

'How come there was a half kilo of crack in the trunk?'

'Akeem D'Muere's people put it there.'

'They dumped eight thousand dollars' worth of dope, just to set you up?'

'I guess it was important to them.'

'Eight-Deuce Gangster Boys buy and sell dope, they don't give it away. No profit in it.'

'Maybe it wasn't theirs. Maybe Dees gave it to them. Maybe it came from the LAPD evidence room.'

Micelli leaned forward across the table and gave me hard. 'You're holding out for nothing. Your buddy's already come clean.'

'Pike?'

Micelli nodded. 'Yeah. He gave it to us. He said you guys found a connection for the dope. He said you thought you could turn the trick with the Eight-Deuce for a little extra cash. He said that after you set the deal you got the idea that you could just rip these guys off, then you'd have the cash and the dope. Maybe sell it three or four times. Really screw the niggers.'

I gave them the laugh. 'You guys are something Micelli.'

Stilwell said, 'If you don't like our take on it, how about yours?'

I gave it to them. I told them about Mark Thurman and Eric Dees and Charles Lewis Washington. I described how I had been followed, and how Pike and I had boxed Riggens and Pinkworth at the Farmer's Market. I told them about Dees warning me off. I told them about the meeting with Cool T, and Cool T putting us onto the park, and the Eight-Deuce Gangster Boys lying in wait for us. Micelli squirmed around while I said it, like maybe he was bored with the nonsense, but Stilwell listened without moving. When I ran out of gas, Stilwell fingered his tie and said, 'So you're saying that Dees set you up to get you out of the way.'

'Yeah.'

'Why doesn't he just bump you?'

'Maybe he knows that if I get bumped, guys like Joe Pike and Lou Poitras will stay with it, and he doesn't want that. He wants to buy time so he can regain control of things.'

'But if he gets you jugged, he's got to know you're going to talk. He's got to know we're going to call him in and ask him about it.'

I said, 'He knows I'm going to be sitting here with a guy like Micelli. He knows I can't prove anything and all it looks like is that I'm trying to dodge the charge. If I'm alive, he's still got control. If I'm dead, guys like Pike and Poitras are a couple of loose cannons.'

Micelli made a big deal out of throwing up his hands. 'He's wasting our time with this crap. I got tickets to the Dodgers tonight. I want to get there before the stretch.'

I said, 'Listen to me, Stilwell. D'Muere said he's going for the girl. Even if you guys don't buy my end of it, send a car around to her apartment. What's that cost you?'

Stilwell stared at me another couple of seconds. Then he pushed away from the wall. 'Finish up, Paul.' Then he left.

Micelli and I stayed in the interrogation room for another hour. I would go through my story and then Micelli would ask me who was my connection and how much was I going to get for the dope, as if I had said one story but he had heard another. Then he would have me go through my story again. The room was bugged and there were probably a couple of guys listening in. They would be taking notes and a tape recorder would be recording everything I said. They'd be looking for discrepancies and Micelli would be waiting for my body language to change. He'd keep trying out scenarios until I seemed comfortable with one, even if it was one I denied. Then he'd know he struck pay dirt. Of course, since I was telling the truth, he wasn't going to get the body language when and where he wanted it. He probably wasn't too concerned about that, though. Time was on his side. Maybe I shouldn't have passed on the lawyer.

After about the sixth time through, the door opened and Stilwell came back, only this time Eric Dees was with him. Micelli said, 'You been listening to this stuff?'

Dees grinned. 'Yeah. He's pretty good at this.'

Stilwell said, 'You arrest the guy in the park?'

Dees nodded. 'Sure. He's down in cell four.'

'Cole said you ripped off his dope.'

Dees smiled wider. 'Gathered it for evidence, duly logged and checked in.'

I said, 'Come off it, Stilwell. He knew I was going to be in here. He knew I was going to be talking.'

Stilwell stayed with Dees. 'You got anything going with these gangbangers?'

Dees spread his hands. 'Trying to bust'm. Cole's been nosing around and I tried to warn him off and maybe that's when he got the idea for the dope deal. I don't know. I don't want to talk about an ongoing investigation in front of a suspected felon.'

Stilwell said, 'Sure.'

Dees said, 'I've got to go wrap it up with my guys. You need anything else?'

'That's it, Eric. Thanks.'

Dees left without looking at me.

I said, 'Jesus Christ, Stilwell, what do you expect him to say?'

'Just about what he said.'

'Then what are you going to do about it?'

Stilwell grabbed my upper arm and lifted. 'Book you on three murder counts and a dope. I think you're guilty as sin.'

CHAPTER 20

They took me out into the detectives' squad room and began the booking process. Dees wasn't around, and after Micelli spoke to a couple of uniforms, he and Stilwell left.

The processing cops had already begun with Pike and, as I watched, they used paraffin on his hands and took his picture and fingerprinted him and asked him questions so that they could fill out their forms. He nodded once and I nodded back. It was strange to see him without the glasses. He seemed more vulnerable without them. Less inviolate. Maybe that's why he wears them.

They led Pike away through a hall toward the jail and then they started with me. A uniform cop named Mertz led me from station to station, first using the paraffin, then getting my prints, and then taking my picture. I crossed my eyes when they took the picture and the cop who worked the camera said, 'No good, Mertz. He crossed his goddamned eyes.'

Mertz picked up a baton and tapped it against his thigh. 'Okay, smart ass. Cross'm again and I'll smack you so hard they'll stay crossed.'

They took the picture again but this time I didn't cross them.

When Mertz was filling out my personal history form, I said, 'When do I get a bail hearing?'

'Arraignment's tomorrow. One of the detectives ran over to the court to get a bail deviation so we could bind you over.'

'Jesus Christ. Why?'

'You see the crowding down there? You're lucky they'll arraign you by next Monday.'

When the processing was finished, Mertz turned me over to an older uniform with a head like a chayote squash and told him to take me to felony. The older uniform led me back along a hall to a row of four-by-eight-foot cages. Each cage had a seatless toilet and a sink and a couple of narrow bunks, and it smelled of disinfectant and urine and sweat, sort of like a poorly kept public men's room. 'No place like home.'

The older uniform nodded. Maybe to him it was home.

There were two black guys in the first cage, both of them sitting in the shadows of the lower bunk. They had been talking softly when we approached, but they stopped when we passed and watched us with yellow eyes. Once you were in the cells, there was no way to see who was in the next cell, and no way to reach through the bars and twist your arm around to touch someone in the next cell, even if someone in the next cell was reaching out to touch you. I said, 'Which one's mine?'

The uniform stopped at the second cell, opened the gate, and took off my handcuffs. 'The presidential suite, of course.'

I stepped in. A Hispanic guy in his early thirties was lying on the lower bunk with his face to the wall. He rolled over and squinted at me, and then he rolled back. The uniform closed the gate and locked it and said, 'You wanna make a call?'

'Yeah.'

He walked back down the hall and out the heavy door and was gone. One of the black guys in the cell next to me said something and the other laughed. Someone in one of the cells on the other side of me coughed. I could hear voices, but they sounded muted and far away. I said, 'Joe.'

Pike's voice came back. 'Fourth cell.'

Someone yelled, 'I'm trying to sleep, goddamn it. Shut the fuck up.' It was a big voice, loud and deep, and sounded as if it had come from a big man. It also sounded about as far away as Joe Pike.

I said, 'D'Muere said he's going for Jennifer Sheridan.'

Joe said, 'Dees wouldn't go for that.'

'Dees may not know. D'Muere wasn't talking like a guy who was worried about what Eric Dees thought.'

The big voice yelled, 'Goddamn it, I said shut up. I don't want to hear about your goddamn –' There was a sharp meat-on-meat sound and the voice stopped. Joe continued, 'Maybe he isn't. Maybe things aren't the way we were told.'

'You mean, maybe they aren't partners.'

Pike said, 'Maybe Dees is an employee. Maybe D'Muere is the power, and Eric Dees is just trying to control him. Maybe putting us in here is part of that.'

'Only maybe while we're in, Jennifer Sheridan gets offed.'

Pike said nothing.

The heavy door opened and the cop with a squash for a head came back pushing a phone that was bolted to a kind of a tripod thing on heavy rollers. The cop pushed it down to my cell and parked it close enough for me to reach the buttons. 'You can make as many calls as you want, but it won't take long distance, okay?'

'Sure.'

He went out and left the door ajar because of the phone cable.

I called Marty Beale's direct line and a male voice answered. It wasn't Marty, and it wasn't Jennifer Sheridan. 'Watkins, Okum, & Beale. Mr Beale's office.'

'Jennifer Sheridan, please.'

'She didn't come in today. May I take a message?'

'I'm a friend, and it's important that I speak with her. Do you know where I can reach her?'

'I'm sorry, sir. I'm an office temp, and I didn't get here until this afternoon.'

'Do you know why she didn't come in?'

'I'm sorry, sir.'

I hung up and called Jennifer Sheridan's apartment. On the third ring, the phone machine answered. After it beeped, I said, 'It's Elvis. If you're there, pick up.'

No one picked up.

I called Lou Poitras. A woman's voice answered, 'Detectives.'

'Lou Poitras, please.'

'He's out. You want to leave a message?'

'How about Charlie Griggs?'

'Hold on.' I heard her ask somebody in the background about Griggs. She came back on the line. 'He's with Poitras. You want to leave a message or not?'

I hung up and leaned against the bars. 'She didn't go to work and she's not at home.'

Pike said, 'Could mean anything.'

'Sure.' Mr Optimism.

'We could help her.'

'In here?'

Pike said, 'No. Not in here.'

'Joe.' I knew what he was saying.

'Wait.'

The cop with the squash head came back for the phone, and forty minutes after that the heavy door opened again and in came the squash with a Hispanic cop sporting a flattop crew cut. The squash said, 'You guys are going to be bused over to County. On your feet.'

You could hear the men in the cells coming off their bunks.

The squash went down the row, unlocking the doors and telling the prisoners to step out into the hall. When the squash got down to Pike's cell, he said, 'What in hell happened to you?'

The big voice said, 'Fell.'

Pike was three people behind me.

They lined us up and led us down another corridor past the booking area. The young Hispanic cop brought up the rear.

We went down another short hall and then out into a kind of outdoor alcove. Two uniformed cops were walking into the maintenance building to our right and a third uniformed cop was coming in from the parking lot to our left. A large blue bus that said SHERIFF on the side was parked maybe sixty feet away. The deputy sheriff who drove the thing was talking to a guy in the maintenance building. The cop coming in from the parking lot walked past us and went inside through the same door that we had just come out of. The deputy sheriff yelled, 'Hey, Volpe,' and went into the maintenance building. Pike said, 'Now,' then stepped out of the line and launched a roundhouse kick into the side of the Hispanic cop's head. The Hispanic cop went down. The squash heard it and turned and I hit him two fast straight rights low on the jaw, and he went down, too. The Hispanic guy who had shared my cell said, 'The fuck you guys doing?' He looked surprised.

The black guys with the yellow eyes held on to each other and smiled. The big guy who'd been with Pike said, 'Fuckin' A,' and ran to the right past the maintenance building and toward the front gate. Two other guys ran after him. Pike and I went to the left through the parking lot, keeping low and moving toward the street. We made the fence just as men began shouting. The fence ran back along the side of the building past a trash dumpster and maybe half a dozen fifty-five-gallon oil drums and a motorcycle that looked like somebody's personal property. We followed the fence back toward the oil drums, and pretty soon we were on the side of the building. The shouts got louder and there were the sounds of men running, but all of the noise seemed behind us.

We went up onto an oil drum, chinned ourselves to the roof, then jumped back across the concertina wire to the street. A couple of kids on mountain bikes watched us with big eyes.

We walked toward the houses just as an alarm buzzer went off at the police station. An older man rocking on a porch stood and looked at us. 'What's going on?'

I told him they were running tests.

We stayed on the street until he couldn't see us, and then we cut between two houses and started to run.

Somewhere behind us, there came the sound of sirens.

CHAPTER 21

We went over fences and through vegetable gardens and between houses. We checked each street for police, then crossed steadily and with purpose as if two white guys on foot were an everyday thing in South Central Los Angeles. Twice we had to pull back between houses for passing patrol units, and once we surprised an elderly woman coming out of her home with a basket of wet laundry. I gave her my best Dan Aykroyd. 'Gas company. We've had reports of a leak.' The Aykroyd works every time.

We moved from her yard to the next, and worked our way north.

More black-and-whites roared past, and sirens that started far away drew close. The cops knew that anybody who made it through the gates would be on foot, so they'd concentrate their people within a close radius. More and more cops would flood into the surrounding streets, and pretty soon there would be helicopters. Pike said, 'We need wheels.'

'They impounded my car. You think they got the Jeep?'

'I was on the next street over. They didn't know about it.'

'That makes it, what, ten or twelve blocks from here? Might as well be in Fresno.'

Pike said, 'If we have limits, they are self-imposed.' Always count on Pike for something like that.

Two black-and-whites sped east on Florence under the freeway. After they passed, we trotted west into an Arco station that had one of those little Minimart places. A couple of cars sat at the pumps, and a Hostess delivery van sat at the Minimart. A young black guy in his early twenties got out of the van with a box of baked goods and went into the Minimart. Pike said, 'Wheels.'

'Maybe he'll give us a ride.'

Pike frowned.

The delivery guy came out of the Minimart, threw his box into the van, and climbed in after it. I went up to his window and said, 'Excuse me. We need a lift about ten blocks west of here. Think you could help?'

The delivery guy said, 'Hey, sure. No problem.'

Only in L.A.

Maybe ten minutes later he dropped us off at Joe Pike's Cherokee. Joe keeps a spare key duct-taped to the inside of the front fender. He found it, unlocked the cab, and we climbed inside. Joe dug under the dash and came out with a plastic bag containing five hundred dollars in cash, a driver's license that said his name was Fred C. Larson, a Visa card in the same name, and a Walther TPH .22-caliber pocket gun. *Be prepared.*

I said, 'Fred?'

Pike headed toward the freeway. 'They'll cover our houses and our businesses.'

'We don't go home. We try for Jennifer Sheridan. We've got to get her off the street before D'Muere finds her.'

'Where does she live?'

I told him. Pike drove quickly, and neither of us spoke during the ride.

We parked in front of her building maybe forty minutes later and pressed her call button, but no one answered. We pressed more buttons until someone finally buzzed open the glass door and we went up to the third floor.

We were knocking on her door when a woman with two small children came out of the apartment across the hall. The woman was maybe in her forties and heavy across the hips. She made a *tsking* sound when she saw us and said, 'I'd appreciate it if you ask her not to make so much noise tonight. All the hammering woke up Teddi.'

I looked at her. 'What hammering?'

She pulled the door shut and locked it. The two children ran down the hall. I guess one of them was Teddi. 'Well, the knocking. It was so loud it woke Teddi and Teddi woke me and I had to look. It was after two.' She squinted at Pike. 'Was it you?'

Pike shook his head.

I said, 'Someone was hammering at her door after two in the morning?'

The woman nodded, but now she wasn't interested in talking. Her children had disappeared around a corner and she wanted to go after them. 'Yes, and someone got quite loud, too. It was very inconsiderate.'

'More than one voice?' I was thinking D'Muere.

'I don't believe so.' She glanced at Pike again. 'Well, I thought it was him but I guess not. Her boyfriend. That big guy. I think he's a police officer.'

'Mark Thurman?'

'I don't know his name. We just see him in the hall.'

'He was here at two this morning?'

She nodded. 'Making a terrible racket. Then they left together.' Now she frowned at me and looked at my hair.

I said, 'What?'

She gave embarrassed, and then she hurried away down the hall. 'I've got to find those damn kids.'

I looked at Pike. He said, 'You've got something in your hair.'

I touched my hair and felt something crusty. My fingers came away speckled red. James Edward Washington's blood. 'If she's with Thurman, she's running. If she's running, that means she's safe.'

'Until she gets found.'

'Yeah.'

Thirty minutes later we checked into a motel Pike knew two blocks from the beach in Santa Monica. It was called the Rising Star Motel. Fred C. Larson signed the register.

The room was simple, but functional, with two double beds and a bath and cheap wall paneling that had been scarred by years of transient use. There was a little round table and two chairs by the window, and a TV bolted to a dresser. The bolts looked thick and heavy enough to pin down a Saturn Five.

Pike left after a couple of minutes, and I went into the bathroom and inspected myself.

I went out to the ice machine, brought back a bucket of ice, then peeled off my shirt, put it in the sink, covered it with the ice, and ran in cold water. I wanted to call Mrs Washington and tell her about James Edward, but I didn't. James Edward Washington's blood was on my shirt and in my hair. How could I tell her about that? When the shirt was soaking, I took off the rest of my clothes, went into the shower, and let the water beat into me. The water was hot. I used the little motel soap and a washcloth, and I scrubbed hard at my face and my neck and my hands and my hair, and then at the rest of me. I washed my hair twice. The police had let me wash off; but that had been with Handi Wipes and paper towels and Borax soap. There's only so much you can do with a Handi Wipe. I scrubbed until my skin was pink and my scalp stung with the hot water, and then I got out to see about the shirt. I rubbed the fabric as hard as I had rubbed my skin, but it was too late. The bloodstains were set, and would always be there. How could I tell Ida Leigh Washington about that?

Twenty minutes later there was a double rap at the door and Joe Pike let himself in. He was carrying an olive green Marine Corps duffel and a large grocery bag and he was wearing new sunglasses. The sunglasses would've been the first thing he bought. He put the grocery bag on the little round table and the duffel bag on the bed. He looked at me and nodded. 'Better.'

'You went by the gun shop?'

He took waist holsters and handguns from the duffel. 'Called one of the guys and had him pick up some things. We met at the market.'

'Have the cops been by your shop?'

Pike nodded. 'They've got an undercover van parked down the block. It'll be the same at your place, too.'

Great.

Pike unwrapped the holsters and inspected them, and then tossed one to me. Clip holsters. We could snap them to our waistbands and wear our shirts out over them for that Miami thug look. Pike handed me a Smith & Wesson .38. He counted four hundred dollars out of a plain white envelope, handed half to me. 'There's food in the bags.'

He'd bought soap and deodorant and toothbrushes and paste and razors and the things you need to keep yourself up. He'd also bought a six-pack of cold Thai beer. I put the toiletries in the bathroom, and then we ate. While we ate I called my office to check for messages, but there were none. I called my home next and there were two messages from Jennifer Sheridan. In the first message she identified herself and asked if I was there and, when I didn't answer, she hung up. In the second, she again asked if I was there, but this time when I didn't answer she said that she would call back later tonight. She said that it was very important that she speak with me. She was speaking softly and she didn't sound happy.

Pike watched me listen. 'Jennifer?'

'She's going to call later tonight.'

Pike stared at me.

'I've got to be there, Joe.'

Pike's mouth twitched, and he stood up, ready to go. 'If it were easy, it wouldn't be fun.'

CHAPTER 22

We cruised the Mulholland Snake from Cahuenga Pass to Laurel Canyon, and then back again. It was after ten, and the traffic was light and getting lighter, mostly affluent stragglers who'd put in extra hours at the office or in the bar and were only now cresting the mountain in their effort toward home.

When we saw that there were no police stationed at either end of Woodrow Wilson Drive, Pike shut the lights and pulled over. 'You want me to take you in closer?' The turnoff to my house was maybe a mile in along Woodrow Wilson.

'Nope. Too easy to get boxed if we meet a black-and-white coming the other way.'

Pike nodded. 'I know. Just thought I'd offer.'

'There's a turnout about a mile and a half east that the kids use as a parking place, on the valley side overlooking Universal Studios. Wait there. If the police come I'll work my way downslope, then come back around onto Mulholland and meet you there.'

'If you don't get caught.'

Some support, huh?

I slipped out of the Jeep, then trotted off Mulholland and onto Woodrow Wilson Drive, taking it easy and slipping into bushes or shadows or behind parked cars whenever headlights showed around a curve. Woodrow Wilson Drive is narrow and winding and affects sort of a rural quality, even in the midst of high-density housing and fourteen million people. There are trees and coyotes and sometimes even deer, and, though there are many homes in the area, the houses are built for privacy and are often hidden from view. Frank Zappa lives there. So does Ringo Starr. Smaller streets branch off of Woodrow Wilson, and, like mine, lead to areas often more private, and even more rustic. If the police were waiting for me, or came while I was there, it would be easy to work my way downslope, then loop around and work back to Mulholland. Of course, it's always easy if you don't get caught.

I passed three joggers and, twice, couples walking dogs, once a man and woman with an Akita, and once two men with a black Lab. I nodded at them and they nodded back. Elvis Cole, the Friendly Felon, out for an evening's stroll.

I left Woodrow Wilson and turned up my road and moved into the trees. The mountain shoulders up there, and the road follows the shoulder into a little canyon. I crept through the scrub oak until the road curved around to my house, and then I saw the plain unmarked sedan sitting in the shadows beneath a willow tree, maybe sixty yards past my front door. I kept the trunk of an oak between myself and the car and I waited. Maybe eight minutes later someone on the passenger's side moved, then the driver moved, and then they were still again. Shadows within shadows. If there were cops outside the house, there might be cops inside the house. The smart thing to do would be to leave and forget about being in my living room when Jennifer Sheridan called. Of course, if I wasn't there when she called, maybe she'd never call again. For all I knew, Akeem D'Muere was closing in on her at this very moment and her last call would be a call for help and I wouldn't be there to answer it because I'd be off doing the smart thing. Whatever that was.

Across the canyon, headlights moved on mountain roads and someone somewhere laughed and it carried on the night breeze. A woman. I thought about it some more and then I moved down the slope toward my house. Sometimes there is no smart move.

I worked through the trees and the brush until I was beneath my house, and then I climbed up to the deck. There were no police posted along the back and, as best I could tell, none within the house. Of course, I wouldn't know that for sure until I went in, would I?

I checked to see if the two cops were still in their sedan, and then I went back downslope and found the spare key I keep beneath the deck. I moved back across the slope to the far side of the house, climbed up onto the deck, and let myself in through the glass doors.

The house was still and dark and undisturbed. No cops were lying in wait, and the SWAT team didn't rappel down from my loft. If the police had been here, they had come and gone without breaking the door and without abusing my possessions.

The message light on my machine was blinking. I played it back, worried that it was Jennifer and that I had missed her call, but it was Lou Poitras. He called me an asshole, and then he hung up. You've got to love Lou.

I went into the kitchen, opened a Falstaff, and drank some. The moon was waxing three-quarters, and blue light spilled through the glass steeples at the back of my A-frame to flood the living room. I didn't need the light. Behind me the cat door clacked and the cat walked into the kitchen. He went to his food bowl.

I said, 'It's been a pretty crummy day. The least you could do is say hello.'

He stared at his bowl.

I took out his dry food and fed him. I watched as he ate, and then I took down a larger bowl and put it on the floor and emptied the box into it. I didn't know when I would get back, so I figured that this would have to do. I turned on the kitchen tap just enough to drip. He could hop up and drink.

I went to each door to make sure it was locked, then found a nylon overnight bag and packed it with toiletry items and three changes of clothes. The police had my wallet and all the things in it, but I had spare American Express cards and Visa cards in my dresser, along with gas cards and three hundred dollars in cash. I packed that, too.

When I was done I called Charlie Bauman, a lawyer I know who has an office in Santa Monica. I called him at home. Charlie answered on the fourth ring and said, 'Hey, Elvis, how's it going, buddy?' There was music somewhere behind him and he sounded glad to hear from me.

I said, 'I'm sitting on the floor in my living room, in the dark, and I'm wanted on three murder counts and a dope charge.'

Charlie said, 'Shit, are you out of your nut?' He didn't sound so happy to hear from me anymore.

I told him about it. When I got to the arrest and the questioning, he stopped me.

'You should've called me. Never give up your right to an attorney. That was bush.'

'I'm calling you now, Charlie.'

'Yeah, yeah. *After* you fuck up.'

I gave him the rest of it. When I finished, he didn't say anything for a while.

'Charlie?'

'You assaulted a police officer, and you escaped?'

'Pike and I. Yeah.'

'Shit.'

I didn't say anything.

Charlie said, 'Okay. You've got to come in. Come to my place, and we'll go in together. I'm sure we can pull bail, even after this.'

'No.'

'What do you mean, no?'

'I can't come in yet, Charlie. There's something I've got to do.'

Charlie went ballistic. 'Are you *fucked*?'

I hung up.

The house was quiet with a stillness that went beyond the auditory or the visual. Outside, a police helicopter tracked across the horizon, overflying Hollywood. Closer, cars wound their way along mountain roads. The phone rang, but I did not answer it. The machine caught it, and Charlie said, 'Okay, so you're not going to go in. Shit, pick up, willya?'

I picked up.

He made a sigh. 'All right. I'll talk to the DA. I'll start trying to work things out.'

'Sure.'

'Shit, don't get killed.' He hung up. What a way to say good-bye.

I went back to the aloneness of my house and wondered if in fact Jennifer Sheridan was going to call. Maybe I was just wasting my time, and risking my freedom.

The cat came out of the kitchen and watched me for a while, the way cats will, but then he tired of it and left. I thought that, were I a cat, it might be nice to go with him. Creep through a little grass, stalk a few field mice, maybe hang with a couple of nice lady cats. I guess cats grow weary of human pursuits. So do humans.

Thirty-six minutes later gravel crunched outside my front door and a light played through the entry windows. The cops from the sedan, come to take a look-see.

Footsteps moved to the carport and a second light tracked along the opposite side of the house. I scrambled behind the couch, and tried to wedge myself under it. The footsteps came out onto the deck, and now both lights raked over the couch and the living room and the stairs that lead up to my loft. There was maybe eight feet and a couple of dust bunnies between me and the two cops. I held my breath. The lights worked over the couch again and then the footsteps went away. My, my. Nothing like an adrenaline jolt to help you wile away the hours.

Seventy-two minutes after the cops had come to call, the phone rang again, and this time it was Jennifer Sheridan. When I picked up, she said, 'Thank God you're there.'

'Where are you?' Her voice was low, as if maybe she were calling without Mark knowing. Or maybe because she was just tired.

'I'm with Mark.'

'Where with Mark?'

'I made a mistake getting you involved in this. You have to stop, now. You have to leave us alone.'

'It's too late to leave you alone, Jennifer.' I told her about the Eight-Deuce Gangster Boys. I told her about Eric Dees working through the Eight-Deuce to set me up and I told her about James Edward Washington getting his brains blown out. I said, 'They're killing people. That means Mark is involved. They set us up with the Eight-Deuce and Akeem D'Muere killed James Edward Washington and that's the same as if they had ordered him killed. They're accessories before the fact, and if you're a part of it now, then you're an accessory after the fact. Do you understand that?'

She was breathing hard, but she didn't sound frantic. She sounded resolved. 'We can't come back, yet. We have to stay away.'

'Because of Mark?'

'It's not like what you think. Eric is going to work everything out. We only have to be up here a little while.' Up here.

I said, 'Eric isn't going to work it out, Jennifer. D'Muere is out of control. You need to come in. Tell me where you are.'

'I can't do that. I'm calling to ask you to stop. I want you to leave us alone.'

'I can't do that. It's larger than you now, Jennifer. There's James Edward.'

Jennifer Sheridan hung up.

I stood in the dark with the phone in my hand, and then I replaced the receiver and reset the answering machine. I made sure all of the windows were locked and the alarm was armed and the faucet still dripped for the cat, and then I picked up the overnight bag, let myself out, and moved back down the slope to the trees.

It took just under an hour to work my way back to Mulholland and to the turnout where Joe Pike was waiting. It was a broad, flat area looking out on the valley. Pike's Jeep was there. So were a Toyota Celica and a Chevy van. Music came from the van.

I slipped into the passenger side of the Jeep and Pike looked at me. The smell of coffee was strong. 'She call?'

'Yes. She wouldn't tell me where she is.'

'You think she's in danger?'

'I think they're all in danger. I'm just not sure who they're in danger from.'

Pike's mouth twitched. 'It's often like that, isn't it?'

'Yes. Often.' I stared at the lights of the San Fernando Valley and listened to the music from the van. It sounded Spanish. I said, 'If we can't find her, then we have to stop Akeem. That means we go back to the source.'

Pike nodded. 'The guy who set us up.'

'Cool T. Cool T might know.'

Pike shook his head. 'What a name.'

Pike started the Jeep and we drove back down into the city and to the motel, and the next day we went for Cool T.

CHAPTER 23

Joe Pike and I left the motel for Ray Depente's place at five minutes after eight the next morning. We drove to Ray's much as you would drive anywhere. SWAT wasn't waiting on the roof, and the police hadn't cordoned off the area, and a squadron of black-and-whites with screaming sirens didn't give chase. We were just two guys in a Jeep. Wanted for murder, maybe, but there you are.

We stopped at a Denny's for breakfast, and while we were eating, two uniformed cops came in and sat in the smoking section. Pike and I paid, and walked out past them, but they never looked our way. Detective material.

At seven minutes before nine, we pulled into the little parking lot next to Ray Depente's, and went inside.

Ray Depente was sitting at his desk in the little glass cubicle, talking on the phone and leaning back with his feet up. The older woman who managed the office was behind him, peering into a file cabinet. When we stepped out of the door, Ray saw us and put down his feet and stood up. He mumbled something into the phone, then hung up and came around the desk and out onto the floor. The cops would've been here. They would've talked to him.

I said, 'Hi, Ray. This is a buddy of mine. Joe Pike.'

Ray stopped just outside of striking range and looked over Joe Pike and then squinted back at me. You could see him braining out what he'd have to do and how he'd have to do it to neutralize us. Pike slid two steps to the side, giving himself room if Ray made the move. There weren't many people in the gym. A young Asian guy sporting a black belt worked three women and a man through an intermediate *kata*, and a young Hispanic guy practiced roundkicks on a heavy bag in the far corner. Some of his leg moves were so fast you couldn't follow them.

Ray said, 'You've got no business here. Leave now, before I call the police.'

'I didn't kill James Edward, Ray. Akeem D'Muere set me up for the bust and D'Muere pulled the trigger.'

'Ain't the way the police tell it.' Ray took a half step back and turned so that his shoulders were angled to the plane of attack. 'Why don't we give'm a call, let everybody sit down and talk about it.' He made a little head move toward his office.

Pike said, 'That won't happen.'

Ray shifted again, adjusted his angle more toward Joe. 'Maybe not, but you never know.' Behind him, the class grunted and worked through their *kata*, and the heavy bag snapped with deep coughing *whumps*. 'I won't tell you again to leave, then we'll see what happens.' The woman in the little office closed the file and looked out at us and then came around the desk to stand in the door as if she could somehow read the tension.

I said, 'You don't know me, but you know James Edward. You think he was digging for a deal?'

Ray Depente canted his head like he'd been trying not to think of that, and his eyes flicked from me to Pike, then back. There was a physical quality to time, as if it were suddenly still, and moving through it was like moving through something dense and unyielding. 'Maybe you used him for a fool. Maybe you thought you could come down here and rip off the brothers, but it didn't work out that way. The police said you escaped. An innocent man don't escape.'

'Bullshit. James Edward and I came here to find out what happened at the Premier Pawn Shop. James Edward is dead because the cops involved didn't want us to find out, and neither does Akeem. Your man Cool T set us up.'

'I know you're lying. Cool T's righteous.'

'He set us up. He told us when and where to be, and the Eight-Deuce were there waiting for us.'

Ray was fighting it. You could see him starting to think that maybe I was being square. He wet his lips. 'Why in the hell did you come back here?'

'Because Akeem wants to kill a woman named Jennifer Sheridan, and I can't let that happen.'

'I don't know anything about it.'

'You don't, but maybe Cool T does, or knows somebody who does.'

Behind us, the Hispanic kid launched a flurry of kicks at the heavy bag, then collapsed to the mat, sweat falling like rain from the dark cloud of his hair. Ray Depente abruptly straightened from his fighting stance. 'I've got a class due in forty-five minutes.'

'This won't take long.'

'All right. Let's talk about it. If what you say makes sense, I'll see what I can do.'

Ray led us back across the wide parquet floor to the little cubicle and said, 'Miriam, I need maybe a few minutes alone with these gentlemen. Would you excuse us, please?' Miriam moved out of the door when she saw us coming and stood beside her desk. She peered at me and at Pike with obvious distaste. 'Who's going to answer the phones?'

'I will, Miriam. I remember how they work.'

'That fella from NBC is supposed to call.' She didn't like this at all.

'I can handle it, Miriam. Thank you.'

She *humphed* and bustled out, and then he closed the door, and went behind his desk. He took the phone off the hook.

A couple of hard chairs sat against a wall that was

mostly pictures and mementos of Ray Depente's Marine Corps years. I took one of the chairs, but Pike stayed on his feet, looking at the pictures. Ray in fatigues showing gunnery-sergeant stripes. An older Ray showing master sergeant. An 8×10 of Ray Depente screaming at a platoon of recruits. Another of him smiling and shaking hands with President Reagan. Ray in dress blues with enough ribbons on his chest to make him walk sideways. Pike shook his head at the pictures, and said, 'Jarhead.'

Ray Depente's eyes flashed. 'You got a problem with that?'

Pike's mouth twitched. 'I went through Pendleton.'

Depente's eyes softened and he settled back, maybe looking at Pike with a little more respect. *There are two basic types of individuals: Marines, and everybody else.* He gave a thin, tight smile. 'Yeah. You got the look, all right.' He crossed his arms and looked at me. 'Okay, we're here and I'm listening.'

I told him about Eric Dees and the REACT team, and that these guys were now apparently involved with the Eight-Deuce Gangster Boys. I told him about the meeting at Raul's Taco, and what Cool T had told us. 'Cool T said that the REACT cops were in business with the Eight-Deuce. He told us that the Eight-Deuce would hip the REACT cops to the competition, and the cops would bust the dealers. He knew we were looking for a connection, and that's what he gave us. He told us that the REACT cops were going to step on a dope dealer in the park. The cops showed up, but so did the Eight-Deuce. They knew that we were there, and they were looking for us.'

Ray shook his head. 'I believe what you say, but I know Cool T to be a right brother. If he told you this, it's because he believed it.'

I spread my hands.

Ray gave me certain. 'Bet your life on it.'

Pike said, 'James Edward did.'

Ray's jaw flexed and he shifted in the chair. 'Yeah. I guess he did.' He fixed the sharp eyes on me again. 'Least, that's what you say.'

I said, 'Cool T said that the Eight-Deuce are working for the REACT cops, but it's not tracking out like that. These cops are acting like they're scared of Akeem, and they're trying to handle him, but they don't have the horsepower. That puts a woman I know in jeopardy. She's hiding with one of the officers involved, and if she's hiding, it's because the cops don't think they can control Akeem. I need to find out how this thing fits together. If I find out how it fits, maybe I can find her, or maybe I can stop Akeem.'

'And you think Cool T's the way.'

'Yes.'

Ray rubbed at the hard ridges above his eyes and looked out at the students on his mat. A couple of men in their forties had come in and were watching the class spar. Two of the women were sparring, and the remaining woman and man were doing the same. They danced forward and back, punching and kicking and blocking, but none of the punches and kicks landed. They weren't supposed to land. Ray shook his head. 'My goddamned Christ, first Charles Lewis, and now James Edward. How long you figure Akeem D'Muere and these officers been lying down together?'

'Since Charles Lewis.' I told him about the video equipment. I told him how, after Charles Lewis, the REACT team stopped arresting members of the Eight-Deuce Gangster Boys, and that they hadn't arrested any since.

'You figure those officers wrongfully killed that boy, and Akeem got it on tape, and he's holding it over them.'

'I'm not sure, but that's what I think.'

Ray Depente picked up his phone and punched a

number. He stared at me while it rang, and kept his eyes on me when he spoke. 'This is Ray. Cool T over there?'

I crossed my arms and tilted back the chair and watched Ray Depente watch me.

He made seven calls, and when Ray Depente found what he was looking for, he put down the phone, stood up, and said, 'I know where he is. Let's go find out what the fuck is going on.'

CHAPTER 24

The three of us took Pike's Jeep, and drove south on Hoover to a row of low industrial buildings on the west side of the street. A two-way alley ran from the street between the buildings to a little truck yard in the rear. Ten-wheel trucks like they use for local deliveries moved in and out of the alley, but a couple of eighteen-wheelers were parked at the curb. Guess the big trucks wouldn't fit through the little alley.

The eighteen-wheelers had their sides open, and men with hand trucks moved between the trucks and one of the warehouses, going into the eighteen-wheelers empty and coming out full like ants raiding a pantry. Ray said, 'Park across the street. Cool T got him a temp job unloading those things. If he's here, we'll see him.'

Pike drove past, made a U-turn, and parked so that we had a clear view of the action.

Maybe ten minutes later Cool T came out of the warehouse with an empty hand truck. I nodded. 'That's him.'

Cool T still wore the neon orange cap turned backwards, but the sunglasses were gone, and he had a little yellow Sony Walkman clipped to his belt and a set of headphones in place over the cap. His lips were moving, singing along with something on the Sony. He pushed the hand truck up a long metal ramp and disappeared into the near truck, but a couple of minutes later he reappeared with maybe eight cases of power steering fluid and went back down the ramp and into the warehouse. I said, 'Let's go.'

We trotted across Hoover, then around the side of the warehouse and up a little flight of stairs onto the loading platform. Freestanding metal industrial shelves towered maybe fifteen feet high, jammed with crates of shock absorbers and air filters and transmission fluid. Guys with loaded hand trucks were coming in through a big door on the side and working their way down the long aisles between the shelves. Once they got inside, everybody seemed to be going in different directions, but I guess they knew what they were doing. The crates already stacked on the shelves looked neat and orderly.

A bald guy maybe in his late fifties was sitting at a little desk, digging through receiving forms with a rat-tail file, and shouting at the men with the hand trucks. He looked over when he saw us and said, 'I got all the muscle I need. Come back tomorrow.'

Ray said, 'Myron Diggs is expecting us.'

Pike said, 'Myron.'

Ray looked at Joe. 'You think Cool T is his Christian name?'

The guy at the desk said, 'Oh. Well, if Myron is expecting guests, who am I to object?' Everybody's a comedian. Everybody's got an act they want to sell. 'I hire a guy to do a full day's work. He don't want to work, he can find himself another goddamn job. That's all I got to say about it.' A peach, this guy.

Ray said, 'It won't take long.'

The bald guy didn't look satisfied. 'Yeah, right. It never takes long.' He made a gesture toward the back quarter of the warehouse. 'Try over around E-16. He's doin' auto parts.'

We moved past the bald guy and into the aisles and back toward E-16. The warehouse covered maybe twelve thousand square feet, and most of it was mazed with shelves and aisles that had little letters and numbers on them just like the sections in a parking garage. When we found the Es, Pike said, 'Better if we split up.'

'Okay.'

Ray and Joe Pike turned off at the first intersection, and I continued back to the third. I had gone maybe six aisles when I found Cool T wrestling the eight cases of power steering fluid off of his hand truck. I said, 'Hey, Cool T. Let's take a walk.'

Cool T made a noise when he saw me, and then he looked nervous and pulled off the headset. 'What you doin' here?' He began backing away. 'I don't wanna be seen with you, man. Lot of these guys are gangbangers.'

Joe and Ray came into the aisle behind him, cutting him off. When he saw Ray he frowned. 'Ray, what you doin' here?' He looked back at me. 'What the fuck goin' on?'

Ray said, 'We've got to talk, Cool.'

Cool T was waving us away. 'You tryin' to get my ass killed? This muthuhfuckuh after the Eight-Deuce. They see I with him, they'll be treatin' me to Mr Drive-By.' He was looking down the other aisles, seeing who was there. 'You know better'n this, Ray. James Edward know better than this.' He tried to push past me.

I grabbed his arm. 'James Edward died yesterday.'

It stopped him the way a heavy caliber rifle bullet will stop you. It brought him up short and his breath caught and his eyelids fluttered and he sort of blinked at me. 'Fuck you sayin'?'

'We went over to the park, like you said. We saw the ice cream guy selling dope, and then the cops came, but the Eight-Deuce came, too. They knew we were there, Cool. They were gunning for us.'

'Bullshit.'

'They took us to a little place by the railroad tracks. Akeem D'Muere put a Dan Wesson thirty-eight-caliber revolver to James Edward's temple and blew his brains out.'

Cool T's mouth opened and closed and his eyes made little jerky moves. 'That's a fuckin' lie.'

I said, 'You fed us a bullshit story to get us there so they could set us up for a phony dope bust. It was a setup.'

'You a muthuhfuckin' liar.' Cool T lunged at me and threw a straight right hand. I stepped to the outside and hooked a left up and inside under his ribs. He stumbled sideways and when he tried to come back at me Ray Depente tied him up and twisted his arms behind his back. 'That's enough, boy.'

Cool T's eyes were red and he struggled against Ray, but a Sherman tank could probably struggle against Ray and it wouldn't do any good. Cool T said, 'He fuckin' lyin'. I didn't set'm up. I love James Edward like a goddamned brother.' The red eyes began to leak.

Ray Depente looked at me. 'He didn't know. He wasn't part of it.'

'No. I guess he wasn't.'

Ray Depente turned Cool T loose, and Cool T wiped at the wet around his eyes and smeared it over his cheeks. He shook his head. 'James Edward dead because of me.'

'You didn't know.'

'This shit ain't happenin'.'

I said, 'It's happening.'

'They feedin' me stuff to set you up, that means they know I with you. They know I was askin' about them, and that means they'll be comin' for me. They'll kill me just like they killed James Edward.'

There didn't seem to be a whole lot to say to that.

He shook his head. 'I can't believe the goddamned bitch lied to me. I got all that stuff from a woman I diddle. She run around with some of those niggers in the Eight-Deuce. She get rock from some of those niggers.'

I said, 'We need to talk to her, Cool T.'

Cool T looked at Joe. 'Who this guy?'

'This is Joe Pike. He's with me.'

Cool T nodded. 'Then he gonna die, too.'

Pike's mouth twitched.

I said, 'Akeem wants to kill a woman named Jennifer Sheridan. I've got to find out what Akeem knows and doesn't know, and if he has a line on the woman. Do you see?'

'Okay.'

'Maybe the girl who set us up, maybe she knows.'

Cool T put his hands together and pressed them against his mouth like he was praying. He looked tall and gaunt, and the sort of loose-jointed energy that he'd had only a few minutes ago seemed gone, as if he had pulled himself inward and, in the pulling, had made himself hard and fierce. He let his hands drop to his sides. 'She a sister named Alma Reeves.'

'You know where to find her?'

'I know.' He turned back to the hand truck and wrestled it from under the stack of boxes and rolled it to the side of the aisle and left it neatly against the wall. 'I take you over there.'

'What about your job?'

'Fuck the job. This for James Edward.'

CHAPTER 25

Alma Reeves lived in a small stucco bungalow with a nice flagstone walk and a single car in the drive and a little picket fence that needed painting. We cruised the block once so that we could check out the house and the street. I said, 'Does she live alone?'

Cool T was sitting behind me, next to Ray Depente. 'She live with her mama and sister. The sister got a pretty good job with State Farm, so she won't be around, but the mama be there. She old.'

'Okay.'

Across the street and two houses down, three teenaged guys in cutoff baggies and gold chains and backwards baseball caps sat on a low brick wall, laughing about something. Pike said, 'What about the three guys on the wall?'

'The one in the middle Eight-Deuce. The other two are wanna-bes.'

Pike didn't like it. 'No good. They see us go in, it'll be bad for the family.'

Cool T said, 'Fuck'm.'

Pike looked at him.

Cool T said, 'These niggers used to me. I here all the time.'

Ray said, 'Don't use that word again.'

Cool T gave hands. 'What?'

Ray put hard eyes on him. 'I'm looking where you're looking, and I don't see any. I'm looking in this car, and I don't see any in here, either.'

The hard eyes got heavy and Cool T looked away.

Ray said, 'I just want to get that straight.'

Cool T nodded.

I cleared my throat. 'Oh, boys.'

They both looked at me. Pike looked at me, too.

'Sorry. That didn't come out right.'

Pike shook his head and turned away. You can't take me anywhere. I said, 'If Joe and I go in through the front, it won't take a rocket scientist for those guys to figure out who we are. We can let Cool T out here like we're dropping him off, then we'll park on the next street over and come in through the backyard.' I looked at Cool T. 'Will she let you in?'

'I get in.'

Pike stopped at the drive and Cool T got out, and then Pike kept going. One of the guys on the low wall pointed at Cool T and Cool T pointed back, and then we turned the corner. Pike turned right, then right again, and we counted houses until we were in front of a tiny saltbox that would butt against the back of Alma Reeves's place. Joe said, 'Here,' and pulled to the curb.

Ray said, 'Let me get out first and go up to the house. Folks inside see a couple of white men sneaking up the drive, they'll call the police for sure.'

Ray got out and walked up the drive to the front door and knocked. After a little bit, Ray shook his head and motioned us forward. Nobody home.

We went up the drive and through a neatly kept backyard and over a low chain-link fence and onto Alma Reeves's property. Cool T was standing in the back door, waiting for us and holding by her left forearm a young woman who couldn't have been more than seventeen. She looked scared.

We trotted past two rows of nicely set tomato plants and across their yard and up three cement steps and into a small yellowed kitchen with a picture of Jesus on the wall. A heavy woman with gray hair was leaning against the doorjamb between the kitchen and the dining room, saying, 'Y'all stop that and get out of here. Y'all get out of here, now.'

Cool T pulled the door closed after us. He locked it. The heavy woman's voice got higher, and she said, 'Cool T! Cool, what you doin', boy? I'm talking to you, Myron.'

Ray Depente said, 'It's all right, Mama. Nothing bad is gonna happen here.'

Cool T jerked Alma Reeves's arm. ''Less it has to.'

I said, 'Cool.'

'Goddamn it. She the reason James Edward dead.' He shook her arm again. 'Fuckin' bitch, set me up like I'm some kinda chump, lie to me like that so a brother gets killed.' Cool T raised his hand and Alma fell back against the refrigerator with a whimper and Pike stepped in and caught Cool T's arm.

'No.'

The heavy woman said, 'Alma, what is he talking about? Alma, you talk to me!' Nobody was looking at the heavy woman.

Cool T glared at Pike, but then he let go of the girl and stepped back. When he let go, she stumbled back and fell. Cool T was so angry that he was trembling. He was so angry that his eyes were rimmed red again, and filled with tears, but the tears weren't because she had lied to him. 'Goddamn it, this outrageous shit has been goin' on too long down here, brother on brother. This shit got to stop.'

Alma Reeves was shouting. 'He *made* me, Cool. He said you was asking and he told me what to say. I didn't know he was gonna *kill* anyone. I swear to *Jesus* I didn't know.'

Alma Reeves was sitting on the floor, looking up at us, and I wondered how frightening it must be for these two women to have four men push into their home and act in this manner. I squatted down by her. 'How did Akeem know that Cool was working with us?'

She jerked away from me. 'I can't be talkin' about all this. Don't you understand anything? I be talkin' about this and it gets back, I'm dead for sure.'

The heavy woman was pulling at her hair. 'What do you mean, dead? Alma, what have you gotten yourself messed with?'

Alma looked at her mother. Then she closed her eyes.

I said, 'Ray, why don't you take Mrs Reeves into the living room.'

Ray took the heavy woman away. She begged us not to do anything to her baby. She said it over and over as Ray pulled her away, and hearing it made me feel small and foul and ashamed of myself. I said, 'Look at me, Alma.'

She didn't move.

I said, 'Akeem doesn't know that we're here. No one but the people in this room knows that we're here, and no one else is going to know. Do you understand that?'

She opened her eyes.

'No one saw us come in, and no one will see us go out. We are going to move against Akeem. If you help us, no one will know. If you don't help us, I'll make sure Akeem believes that you turned on him. Do you see?' Small and foul and mean.

She said, 'Oh, you muthuhfuckuh.'

I nodded.

Alma Reeves said, 'I got what you call a little dependency problem.'

Cool T said, 'She went along with Akeem for the rock. She a crack 'ho.'

She flared at him. 'I ain't no 'ho. Don't you call me that.'

I said, 'Cool.'

He said, 'She say she want to quit, so I got her in a program, but she didn't stay. That's why she diddle around with trash like the Eight-Deuce. 'Ho'ing for the rock.'

Alma Reeves was the kind of unhealthy thin that doesn't come from dieting. Who needs protein and vitamin B when you can suck on a crack bong? Ray came back in the room. I said, 'What did Akeem tell you to say to Cool T?'

'That the cops was gonna lean on a brother be sellin' rock at the park. He say I was supposed to tell Cool, then call him and tell him right away.'

'Alma, this is important. Did Akeem say anything about a girl named Jennifer Sheridan?'

She shook her head. 'I don't know.'

'It's very important, Alma. He's already killed James Edward, and I think he wants to kill her.'

'I don't know. I'm not over there that much. I don't know.'

Pike said, 'Where does Akeem live?'

'He in a place just off Main over here.' She made a little hand wave toward the east. 'Used to be a rock house.' She told us where it was and what it looked like.

Ray said, 'Shit. That means it's built like a fort. There'll be reinforced walls and steel on the doors and windows.'

Cool T laughed. 'What you fools thinkin' about doin', stormin' the 'hood like at Normandy?' He laughed louder.

I said, 'Reconnoiter. We go, we watch, we learn whatever we can learn, and we maybe try to pick up Akeem when he's alone. If someone comes, we follow them. Whatever we can do.'

Cool T said, 'What about Alma?'

We looked at her. 'I didn't know Akeem was gonna kill that boy. I swear I didn't. Why I wanna tell Akeem now I told you?'

Cool T said, 'Crack. Crack 'ho do anything for the rock.'

Alma screamed, 'I can't help it. Don't you call me that.'

Cool T went to the little dinette and pulled out a chair. 'Maybe I'll just set a spell.' He gave me sleepy eyes, eyes that were tired maybe from seeing too many brothers killed by other brothers. James Edward Washington eyes. 'Make sure she don't call up old Akeem.'

Ray said, 'Thanks, Cool.'

I looked back at Alma, and then I found a notepad and a Bic pen on one of the counters. I wrote down a name and a phone number. 'You want to get into a program and try to get off this stuff?'

She stared at me.

I dropped the pad into her lap. 'There's a woman I know named Carol Hillegas. She runs a halfway house in Hollywood. If you want to get into a program, give her a call.' I looked at Cool T. 'If she wants to go, call Carol and take her over there. It won't cost anything.'

Alma Reeves stared down at the pad.

Cool T got up from his chair, came over, and took the notepad out of her lap. 'Crack 'ho ain't gonna do nothin' to help herself. Maybe I'll give a call for her.'

We went out as we came, through the backyard and over the little chain-link and out the rear neighbor's drive to Pike's Jeep. Ray Depente gave directions and we made the short drive to Akeem D'Muere's.

D'Muere's house was maybe five houses from an intersection, and we could see it well. It was a small cinderblock with an ill-kept front lawn and a couple of overgrown roses that looked like they needed water and heavy steel grates over the windows. Rock house. When we edged to a stop at the intersection, Floyd Riggens came out of the house, punched a black guy who was maybe nineteen years old, and knocked him down.

Then Warren Pinkworth was running out of the house and pulling Riggens away, and Eric Dees was coming out of the house, too.

I said, 'Well, well.'

Pike's mouth twitched.

More of the Gangster Boys came out of the house and Pinkworth shook Riggens like he was an idiot. Riggens did a lot of finger jabbing toward the kid, but he didn't try to get back into it. He walked out to the street and got into a sedan. Akeem D'Muere came out after Dees, and the two of them argued, but they probably weren't arguing about Riggens.

Pike said, 'If these guys are willing to risk being seen here, whatever they've got going must be falling apart.'

Ray Depente twisted in his seat. 'What are we going to do?'

'Watch.'

Ray didn't like that. 'There the motherfuckers are, right there. Shouldn't we call the police? They can see for themselves.'

'See what, Ray?' I looked at him. 'Dees is conducting an investigation. He's questioning Akeem D'Muere and other members of the Eight-Deuce Gangster Boys for information they might have as to my whereabouts, or the drug deal James Edward and I were trying to put together.'

Pike said, 'Uh-huh. And these guys might know. Two of them were found dead at the scene. Probably been a parade of cops through here.'

Ray's jaw worked and his eyes were wide.

I said, 'Can you get back from here okay, Ray?'

He looked at me.

'We have to find Jennifer Sheridan, and Dees knows where she is. Dees would've told Thurman to hide her, and he's worried, so he'll make contact. We're going to follow him when he leaves. Do you see?'

Ray Depente didn't move.

Akeem D'Muere said something sharp to Eric Dees, then went back into his house. Dees stood for a moment like he wanted to do something, but then he walked out to the street. Pinkworth and Riggens were out there, sitting in Riggens's sedan. There was another car behind them, but that was probably Dees's.

I said, 'Ray.'

Ray stared past me at the crack house, and then he nodded, maybe more to himself than to me. He said, 'Tell me that this sonofabitch is going to pay for James Edward.'

'He'll pay. I promise.'

Ray Depente turned heat-seeker eyes my way. 'Bet your ass he will.'

Ray Depente got out of the Jeep and walked back the way we had come.

Pike shook his head. 'Hate to have that sonofabitch mad at me.'

'Uh-hunh.'

Eric Dees finished speaking to Pinkworth and Riggens, then climbed into his own car. Pinkworth drove away first, and when Dees drove away, Pike and I followed.

CHAPTER 26

It didn't take long.

Eric Dees went west toward LAX, then climbed onto the San Diego Freeway and headed north, up through Los Angeles and the Sepulveda Pass and into the San Fernando Valley.

He left the freeway at Roscoe, turned west again toward Van Nuys Airport, then pulled into the parking lot of a Tommy's hamburger stand where Mark Thurman was sitting at a window table, waiting for him. Jennifer Sheridan wasn't around.

We snapped a turn into a Nissan dealership next to the Tommy's just as Mark Thurman left his window table and came out to meet Eric Dees. Pike eased the Jeep toward them along one of the aisles of new Nissans, and parked behind a row of vans. We got out of the Jeep and moved up between two of the vans and watched.

Dees got out of the car, and Thurman hugged him, and Dees hugged him back, slapping Mark Thurman's shoulder the way you do when you're moved to see someone that you haven't seen in a while and they are someone you care about. Cars moved in and out of the lot, and Hispanic guys who looked like they did yard work and women who looked like they worked in offices came out of or went into the Tommy's, and looked at Dees and Thurman as they did, but Thurman and Dees seemed not to notice, nor to care. Dees put out his hand and Thurman gripped it tight, as if he were using it to anchor himself.

Thurman seemed tired and drawn, but then, so did Eric

Dees. They looked nervous, and they looked glad to see each other, and they didn't look like homicidal co-conspirators rendezvousing to foil justice and commit evil. I wasn't sure what they should look like, but they didn't look like that. Pike said, 'What?'

I shook my head. 'I don't know. It's not the sort of meeting I expected.'

Pike nodded and maybe his mouth twitched.

A balding salesman in a bright blue Miles Vandeveer sport coat smiled his way over and said, 'That's an outstanding little van you're looking at there, gentlemen. You wanna trade in this old clunker, I'll give you a fair deal.' He slapped the side of Pike's Jeep. Hard.

Pike's head swiveled toward the salesman. 'Clunker.'

I stepped in front of him. 'We're just looking, thanks. If we have any questions, I'll come get you.'

The salesman gestured at the van. 'Great new five-year, fifty-thousand-mile warranty with these vehicles.' He looked back at the Jeep, and this time slapped the hood. 'Be a big step up from a maintenance hog like this old bitch.'

I said, 'Oh, man.'

Pike leaned toward the salesman and said, 'Look at me.'

The salesman looked.

Pike said, 'Touch the Jeep once more, and I will hurt you.'

The salesman's smile faltered, then failed. He swallowed hard. 'Yes, well. I'll be in the showroom if you gentlemen have any questions.'

I said, 'That will be fine.'

He made a last stab at the smile, couldn't quite manage it, and walked backwards until he bumped into a green Stanza. When he hit the Stanza, the impact turned him around, and the fast walk became a sort of skipping hop, as if he had to go to the bathroom. Then he ducked into the showroom and peered out at us through the glass. A saleswoman with red hair came up beside him, and he started with the big gestures, filling her in.

I said, 'Great, Joe. Nothing like a little restraint. What if he calls the cops?'

Pike gave sullen. 'Clunker.'

Thurman and Dees went into Tommy's and bought a couple of Cokes and returned to Thurman's window table. Eric Dees did most of the talking. Thurman nodded a lot, and occasionally said something, but mostly he just sipped at his drink. Thurman looked scared. He looked like Eric Dees was telling him things that were maybe hard to understand, but necessary to hear. At one point, Thurman got agitated and spread his hands, gesturing broadly, but Dees reached across the table and gripped his shoulder to explain something, and after a while Mark Thurman calmed.

The meeting didn't last long. Ten minutes later they came back into the parking lot and went to Eric Dees's sedan. Dees put his hand on Thurman's shoulder again, and said something else, and this time Mark Thurman smiled. Bucking up. Hanging tough. With Eric Dees telling him everything would be fine if he just hung in a little while longer. You could see it on his face. The pep talk by the old man. Then they shook hands and Eric Dees got into his sedan and drove away. Pike said, 'Now what?'

'We stay with Thurman.'

Mark Thurman crossed the parking lot to his blue Mustang even before Eric Dees had pulled away. He tossed his cup into a big cement trash container, climbed into the Mustang, and pulled out onto Roscoe heading east. Pike and I trotted back to the Jeep and roared through the car dealership and out into traffic after him. The salesman in the blue sport coat watched us go, then made a big deal out of saying something to the saleswoman who'd come up beside him. I think he gave us the finger.

We followed Thurman up onto the 405 and climbed north through the valley past Mission Hills and the Simi Freeway interchange and the San Fernando Reservoir. I kept waiting for him to exit, and maybe head west toward his apartment, but he didn't. We continued north into the Newhall Pass and the Santa Susana Mountains until the 405 became the Golden State, and when we came to the Antelope Valley Freeway just before Santa Clarita, Mark Thurman exited and followed it east, up through the San Gabriels. I said, 'Thurman's from Lancaster.'

Pike glanced at me.

'Mark Thurman is going home.'

The landscape became parched and barren and more vertical than not. Pockets of condominiums clung to the mountains, and fields of low-cost housing spread across creek beds, and huge billboards proclaimed YOU COULD BE HOME NOW IF YOU LIVED HERE. Ten years ago, only rattlesnakes and sagebrush lived here.

Thurman followed the freeway through the mountains past quarries and rock formations and drop sites for dead bodies, and then we were out of the mountains and descending into the broad flat plain of Antelope Valley. The valley up there is high desert, and the communities there grew up around top-secret military projects and government funding. Chuck Yeager broke the sound barrier up there. Edwards Air Force Base is there, with its shuttle landings and Stealth fighters, and, beyond that, the Mojave Desert spreads out to the north and east, a hot dry desolate plain that is ideal for crashing top-secret government hardware. In the foothills of the San Gabriels there is water and fruit orchards, and, in the winter, there is even snow. But the valley is different. In the valley, there is only scrub brush and heat and cactus, and secret things that no one is supposed to know.

Maybe six miles after we descended out of the San Gabriels, Mark Thurman left the highway and turned into a flat middle-class housing tract with stucco houses and azalea bushes and two-car garages so filled with the clutter of life that at least one of the family's cars had to stay in the drive. We turned in after him, and Pike shook his head. 'No traffic and no movement. We follow him in there, he'll make us.'

'Then let him go.'

We let Mark Thurman draw ahead and turn and disappear from sight.

We pulled to the side of the street and waited, and maybe five minutes later we started again. We made the same turn that Mark Thurman made, and then we drove slowly, crisscrossing the subdivision streets, and looking for his blue Mustang.

Two streets over, we found it, parked in the open garage of a pleasant two-story house with a neatly kept lawn and a fig tree in the front yard.

We parked in the drive behind the Mustang, walked up to the front door, and rang the bell. Footsteps came toward the door, the door opened, and Mark Thurman looked out at us. I said, 'Hi, Mark.'

Mark Thurman tried to shove the door shut. He was big, and strong, but he started the move too late and we had the angle.

The door crashed open, and Joe Pike went in first and I went in after him. Thurman threw a fast straight right, but it was high over Joe Pike's left shoulder. Pike hit Mark Thurman three times in maybe four-tenths of a second. Once in the neck and twice in the solar plexus.

Mark Thurman made a choking sound, then sat down and grabbed at his throat.

Somewhere deeper in the house a voice called, 'Who is it, Mark?'

I called back. 'Mark lost his voice, Jennifer. Better come out here and give him a hand.'

CHAPTER 27

Jennifer Sheridan came out of a door off the back of the entry and saw Mark Thurman on the floor. When she saw Thurman she ran to him, yelling, 'What did you do to him?'

Pike said, 'Hit him.'

We pulled Thurman to his feet and helped him into the living room. He tried to push away from us, but there wasn't a lot of *umphf* in it. I said, 'Take it easy. We've got the gun.'

Jennifer gave confused. 'What gun?'

Pike showed her Mark's revolver, then stuck it in his belt. 'Is anyone else here?'

Jennifer followed us into the living room, hovering around Mark Thurman as we put him into a green Naugahyde Ez-E-Boy. 'No. The house belongs to Mark's aunt, and she's away. That's why we're using it.'

Pike grunted approval, then pulled the drapes so that no one could see in from the street.

Jennifer Sheridan touched Mark Thurman's face with her fingertips. His face was already starting to puff. 'I'd better get some ice.'

He tried to push her away. 'Goddamn it, why'd you tell them?'

She stepped back. 'I didn't.'

I said, 'I'm a detective, Mark. I did a little detective work and found you.' I told him about watching Akeem D'Muere's, and about picking up Dees and following him to Tommy's.

Thurman tried to act like it was no big deal. 'So what? That doesn't prove anything.' He looked at Jennifer. 'Jesus Christ, Jen, this guy is a wanted fugitive.'

She said, 'No, Mark. He wants to help us. He got into trouble trying to help.'

Mark yelled, 'Don't tell this guy anything.' Panicked. 'He's just making guesses. He doesn't know anything.' He tried to push up from the chair, but Joe Pike shoved him down.

I said, 'I know that the Premier Pawn Shop is owned by Akeem D'Muere. I know that eleven weeks before Charles Lewis Washington died, D'Muere hired a security contractor called Atlas Security to install a hidden surveillance camera at the Premier.' When I said it, his face dropped maybe a quarter of an inch. He tried not to show it, but there it was. 'The camera was there when you guys pulled the sting. It would've recorded what happened.' I felt like Perry Mason, laying out my summation for the court. Did that make Jennifer Della Street? Was Pike Paul Drake? 'Akeem D'Muere has a tape of what happened that night, and because he has the tape he has you.'

Jennifer moved behind him and put her hand on his back. 'It's killing him.'

'For Christ's sake, Jennifer, be quiet.' He was looking scared.

Jennifer said, 'That's why it went so bad for us. They made him swear to keep quiet and he did, but he just isn't like that.'

Mark said, 'Eric's taking care of it. Don't admit anything. What if he's wired?'

Jennifer Sheridan pulled at him, trying to make him see, trying to make him come to his senses. 'He's not wired and Eric's getting you into trouble.' She turned from him and looked at me. 'He thinks he's protecting them. He wasn't part of all that. He's not like the others.'

'Nothing happened, goddamn it.' Thurman pointed at me. 'I'm telling you that nothing happened.'

'Damn it, Mark,' she shouted. 'Stop protecting them. *Stop lying for them.*'

I said, 'Leave him.'

They looked at me as if I'd fired a shot into the floor.

I said, 'He doesn't love you, Jennifer. He's willing to take you down with him, just because he isn't strong enough to stand up to the guys he works with.'

Mark Thurman boiled up out of the chair like an angry bull and hit me with his shoulder, driving me back across the living room. Jennifer Sheridan shrieked and yelled, 'Mark,' but then Pike was next to her, wrapping her in his arms.

I stayed high on Thurman's shoulders and let him carry me across the room and into the wall. He was angry and scared and probably not thinking too well, but he was also large and strong. We hit the wall and he backed away to throw a punch, and when he did I spun left and kicked him on the right side of his face and then I slipped to the side, and kicked him behind the left knee. He went down. I could've kicked him on the outside of his knee and broken the ligaments, but I didn't want to do that. I said, 'Don't be stupid, Mark. You're not helping you and you're not helping Jennifer.'

He shoved his way up and this time he sort of crabbed in sideways, like he wanted to box. He feinted with his left and threw a straight right and when he did, I pushed it past and snapped a side kick to his head that made him stumble back and drop his hands. I kicked him twice more, and punched him hard once in the solar plexus, and he went down. I'd hit him hard enough to keep him there.

I squatted beside him and said, 'You're going to listen to this.'

He shook his head. Like a five-year-old. His nose was

swelling and there was a smear of blood along his lower lip.

I said, 'Eric Dees and Akeem D'Muere conspired to set me up for this dope bust. In the course of that action, Akeem D'Muere murdered James Edward Washington. That makes Dees a co-conspirator to murder.'

Thurman was breathing hard. Sucking deep breaths and letting them out.

'You tried to keep all of this from Jennifer, but Jennifer hired me, and you finally brought her in. You told Jennifer about Charles Lewis Washington and Akeem D'Muere, and that means you've implicated her. You're a cop. You know what that means.'

Mark Thurman looked at her.

'She's become an accessory after the fact to murder. She can be charged, and she can be tried. Do you see that? Do you see what you've done to her?'

Jennifer Sheridan frowned. 'Mark?'

I said, 'Who are you going to protect, boy? Eric Dees, or Jennifer?'

Mark Thurman raised his hands as if he were about to say something, but the something didn't come and he lowered them. He looked from me to Jennifer Sheridan, and then back to me. He said, 'It was Floyd.'

You'd know it was Floyd. It'd have to be.

'I'm not even sure what happened. Floyd was hitting him, and then Pinkworth was hitting him, and he just died.' Jennifer Sheridan knelt down beside him and put her hand on his arm.

I said, 'You told yourselves it was an accident. Everybody's thinking Rodney King, and you decide to cover up.'

He nodded. 'Only a couple of days later, here comes the tape. Just like Rodney. Only this time the bad guys had the tape, and not the good guys. Akeem had the tape.'

There was quiet in the small house.

Jennifer Sheridan said, 'He went along because he didn't know what else to do. You can see that, can't you?'

I didn't answer.

'He didn't do it for himself. Don't you see that?'

I looked at Pike and Pike looked at me.

Mark Thurman said, 'What are you going to do?'

I shook my head. 'I don't know.'

He said, 'It was just an accident.' I looked at him and he wasn't a cop anymore. He was a big handsome kid who looked confused and scared, and more than a little bit lost. He said, 'I dream about it every night, and I just don't know. It got out of hand, and we didn't know what to do. Even Floyd was surprised. Floyd didn't expect to kill him. It just happened.' He tried to think of another way to say it. His mouth opened and closed a couple of more times. His brow knotted. Then he just shook his head.

'So you decided to protect each other.'

'You think I'm proud of this? You think I don't see that poor guy? Jesus God, I don't know what to do.' He was shaking his head. Jennifer Sheridan looked like she wanted to hold him and take care of him and make it all better even though she knew it was wrong. Maybe that's what love is.

I said, 'How many copies of the tape are there?'

'We got one. I don't know how many D'Muere has. Maybe a million.'

'Who has the copy you saw?'

'Eric.' Jennifer Sheridan put out her hand and Mark Thurman took it. Jennifer smiled, and Mark Thurman smiled back at her. They looked relieved, as if by finally sharing this the weight was becoming bearable. Mark said, 'I know where he hides it.'

I took a deep breath and then I let it out. I felt tired and my back hurt where the muscles lace over the shoulder blades. Tension, I guess. Stress.

Jennifer Sheridan said, 'Will you help him?'

I looked at Jennifer Sheridan looking at me and I nodded. 'Okay,' I said. 'I want to see the tape.'

CHAPTER 28

Jennifer Sheridan helped Mark Thurman to the couch and sat next to him. He could've made it on his own this time, but he let her help.

I said, 'Has everyone on the REACT team seen the tape?'

'Yeah.'

'Has anyone else?'

He shook his head. 'Not on our side. Who would we show it to?'

Pike went to the window and looked out the curtain. He said, 'Eric would have a plan. Akeem pops up with the tape, says do what I want or I burn you, Eric isn't going to just roll over.'

Thurman nodded. 'Eric said we should play along until we could find something to make Akeem back off.'

'Like what?'

'We started running intelligence on him and doing twenty-four-hour surveillance. We even went out and bought these video cameras. We figured if we got him doing a capital offense on tape, we could trade him. You burn us, we burn you, like that.'

Pike moved to the other side of the window and looked out the curtain from that side. 'Dorks.'

Thurman gave him hard. 'Hey, what would you do?'

Pike didn't bother to look at him. 'I wouldn't be where you are. I wouldn've killed Charles Lewis Washington, and then lied about it. I would've done the right thing.'

Jennifer Sheridan frowned. 'You don't need to be so harsh.'

I said, 'A man died, Jennifer. It doesn't get much harsher than that.'

She put her hand on Mark Thurman's thigh.

I said, 'Okay. So you were looking for something to press Akeem. Did you get anything?'

'Not yet.'

'So the five of you went along with him, committing crimes.'

'That's right.' Thurman made a tiny nod, the kind where your head barely moves, and he wouldn't look at me.

'And Eric figured you guys would keep on like that until you found something to use against Akeem?'

'Yeah.'

'Committing crimes.'

'Yeah.' He stared at the floor and looked even more ashamed. He was a guy with a lot to be ashamed of.

Jennifer said, 'Why do you have to keep asking him about these things? He feels bad enough.'

I said, 'I have to ask him because I don't know the answers. I have to know what he's done so that I'll know how to help him or even if I can help him. Do you see?'

She saw, but she didn't like it. 'I thought you said that you'd help.'

'I'm deciding. Maybe I'll help him, but maybe I won't. Maybe I can't.'

She liked that even less. I looked back at Thurman, and then I stood up. 'Where does Dees keep the tape?'

'He's got it hidden in his garage.'

'You know where?'

'Yeah. If he hasn't moved it.'

'Let's go see.'

We took Thurman's Mustang, and Thurman drove. Joe Pike stayed with Jennifer Sheridan.

Forty-two minutes later we left the freeway in Glendale and turned onto a pleasant residential street lined with mature trees and sidewalks and the sort of modest middle-class houses that more suggested Indiana or Iowa than Southern California. Mark Thurman said, 'Are you sure about this?'

'I'm sure. Which one?'

Thurman pointed out a white frame Cape Cod with a tiny front yard and a couple of nice magnolia trees and lots of surrounding shrubbery. The drive ran along the left side of the house to the garage. Like the rest of the houses on Dees's street, it was prewar, and the garage was detached. Someone had bolted a basketball goal above the garage door, and the net was yellowed and frayed. It had been there a long time. Thurman said, 'We can't just ask him, you know.'

'We're not going to ask him. We're going to steal it.'

Thurman nodded and frowned, like he knew I was going to say that. 'What if it's not there?'

'If it's not there, we'll find out where it is, and then we'll figure a way to get it from there.' A 1984 Nissan 4×4 sport truck sat in the drive beneath the basketball goal. One of those heavy roll bars with a row of lights across the top was mounted in the bed behind the cab, and the suspension was jacked up about eight inches too high so the little truck could sport oversized knobby tires. 'Who belongs to the truck?'

'Eric Junior. I guess he's home from school.'

'How about Mrs Dees? Would she be home?'

Thurman cruised past the house without my having to tell him. 'She works at Glendale General. She's a nurse, but I don't know if she works today, or when she gets home, or any of that.'

'Okay.'

'Would the kid recognize you?'

'Yeah, I think so. I've been here a few times, but not many.'

'How about the neighbors?'

He shook his head. 'No.'

We K-turned in someone's drive, went back, and parked one house away on the driveway side. I said, 'I'm going to see what the boy's up to. You're going to wait for my signal, then go into the garage and get the tape.'

Thurman looked nervous. 'Jesus Christ, it's broad daylight.'

'During the day, we look like we belong. At night, we look like crooks. You're a cop.'

'Well. Sure.'

'Give me the keys.'

He looked at me, then he took out the keys and gave them over. I put them in my pocket, then got out of the car and went up the Deeses' sidewalk to the front door. I pretended to ring the bell, though I didn't, and then I pretended to knock, though I didn't do that, either. If the neighbors were watching, it would look good for them.

I stood at the door and listened, and heard voices deep in the house, but they were the kind of voices that come from a television, and not from real people. The front door was under an overhang, and there was a long brick veranda that ran along the front of the house under the overhang, and a couple of large frame windows. The windows were open to let in the light. I went to the near window and looked in and tried to see the boy and the television, but I couldn't. The way the hall and the entry were laid out from the living room, it was a good bet that the boy and the TV were on the side of the house opposite from the garage. I went back to the edge of the porch and motioned to Thurman. He got out and went down the drive to the garage, and he didn't look happy about it. I stood by the front windows and watched. If the boy came through the house, I could always knock on the door for real and pretend like I was selling aluminum siding. If Mrs Dees drove up, I could pretend I was a real estate agent, and make a big deal out of listing her house, and maybe keep her away from the garage until Thurman made his getaway. If Eric Dees drove up, maybe I could run like hell before he shot me to death. There are always options.

It didn't take Mark Thurman long.

Less than three minutes later he came back along the driveway, and made a short quiet whistle to get my attention. When I looked, he held up an ordinary TDK half-inch VHS cassette. I walked away from the front door and got back into the Mustang maybe ten seconds after Mark Thurman.

He sat behind the wheel in the keyless Mustang with both hands on the cassette. He held it tightly. 'Now what?'

We went to the motel.

The sky had turned a deep violet by the time we got into Santa Monica, and the air was cooling nicely. The room had a VCR hooked to the TV, and that's where we'd screen the tape.

Thurman said, 'Is this where you've been holed up?'

'Yeah.' Like we were outlaws.

When we got into the room, Thurman looked around and saw the four left over Thai beers. They were warm. 'Say, could I have one of those?'

'Sure.'

'You?' He held out a bottle.

'No.'

I turned on the TV. Nightly News with Peter Jennings came on, and I loaded the cassette. Peter Jennings vanished in a flash of static, and a grainy high-angle shot of the interior of the Premier Pawn Shop filled the screen. Black and white. A muscular black guy maybe in his late twenties sat in a swivel chair behind the counter, watching a tiny TV. He wore a white Arrow shirt with the sleeves rolled up, and his hair was cut close with a couple of racing stripes carved above each ear. Charles Lewis Washington. There was no one else in the shop.

As I watched, Mark Thurman came up behind me and drank deep on the beer. He shifted his weight from foot to foot, not fast like he had to pee, but enough to show he wasn't comfortable. He said, 'There's a lot of this kind of stuff at first.'

'Okay.'

'We could maybe fast forward it.'

'Let's just watch.'

He went to the machine and turned it off. 'Look, this isn't easy.'

'I know.'

'You don't have to treat me like a piece of shit.'

I stared at him for maybe ten seconds. 'It doesn't matter if I like you or not, and it doesn't matter how I treat you or not. Whatever it is that I'm doing, I'm doing for Jennifer. Not for you.'

Mark Thurman stared at me for another couple of seconds, then he said, 'Can I have another of those beers?'

I turned on the VCR and watched the rest of the tape. Mark Thurman went into the bathroom and drank.

CHAPTER 29

The image was sort of overexposed and blurry, and not nearly as nice as your basic home video. From the angle the camera must've been maybe nine or ten feet up, and was mounted so that it framed the length of the shop. The tape ran without incident for another couple of minutes before Floyd Riggens and Warren Pinkworth entered from the bottom of the frame. There was no sound. Charles Lewis got out of his chair and went to the counter, and the three of them spoke for a few minutes. Then Pinkworth took two cardboard boxes out of his pocket and put them on the counter. Each box was about the size of a bar of soap, but they weren't Ivory. Washington opened the top box and shook out twenty rounds of what looked to be 5.56mm rifle cartridges. Same kind of stuff you pop in an M-16. He examined the bullets, and then he put them back into the box and pushed both boxes toward Pinkworth. The three of them talked some more, and Riggens left the frame. In a couple of minutes he came back, only now Pete Garcia was with him, carrying a pretty good-sized pasteboard box. It looked heavy. Garcia put the larger box on the counter and Charles Lewis looked inside. Whatever was there, you couldn't see it, but it was probably more of the little cardboard ammo boxes. Washington nodded as if he were agreeing to something, and when he did Riggens and Garcia and Pinkworth were all screaming and pulling out badges and guns. Charles Lewis Washington jumped back so far that he fell over the swivel chair. Riggens went over the counter after him. Riggens raised his pistol twice and brought it down twice, and then he jerked Washington to his feet and moved to hit him again. Washington covered up and pulled away. The narrow aisle behind the counter opened into the shop, and Washington, still holding his arms over his head, stumbled from behind the counter and into Pete Garcia. Maybe you could say it looked like he was attacking Garcia, but it didn't look like that to me. It looked like Washington was trying to get away from Riggens. Garcia hit Washington on the upper back and the arms four times, and then pushed him down. Pinkworth was pointing his gun in a two-handed combat stance, and shouting, and he stomped at Washington's head and back. Riggens came from behind the counter and waded in beside Pinkworth. Garcia was pointing his gun at Washington's head. Washington seemed to reach for him and Garcia kicked at his arm. At the bottom of the screen, Mark Thurman ran in wearing a tee shirt that said POLICE on the front and back. He stopped beside Garcia and aimed his gun, also in the two-handed combat stance. Charles Lewis Washington pushed up to his knees and held out his right arm like maybe he was begging Riggens and Pinkworth to stop. They didn't. Washington rolled into sort of a ball, but Riggens continued to hit him. Thurman started forward, then stopped and said something to Garcia, but Garcia made a hand move telling him to stay back. Thurman lowered his gun and stepped back. He looked confused. Eric Dees ran in then, also wearing a POLICE tee shirt, and stopped midway between Garcia and Pinkworth to assess the situation. Garcia shouted and pointed at Washington, and Dees pulled Pinkworth back. He tried to train his gun on Washington, but Riggens kept getting in the way. Washington was on his stomach now, trying to crawl under a shelf. The white Arrow shirt was streaked with blood. He was moving slowly, the way you might if you were stunned and unable to think clearly.

Thurman raised his gun, then lowered it. He looked like he wanted to move forward, maybe do something, but he didn't. Washington again raised his hand as if begging Riggens to stop. Riggens hit his hand. Dees grabbed Riggens's arm and pulled him back, but Washington started crawling away again. I guess if I was hurt bad, and confused, I'd try to crawl away, too. Riggens pointed at him and shouted, and went back to hitting him, and this time he was swinging for the head. Pinkworth moved in and swung for the legs, but he needn't have bothered. Charles Lewis Washington had already stopped moving. Dees pulled Riggens off again and Garcia moved in, gun first as if he thought maybe Washington was faking it and might suddenly jump up and mow them all down. He checked Washington's neck for a pulse, then shook his head. Garcia holstered his gun and said something to Dees, and now he checked Washington's wrist, but he didn't find a pulse there, either. Eric Dees came over and checked for himself. Mark Thurman holstered his gun, leaned against the counter, and threw up. Eric Dees went to him, said something, and then went back to the body. Mark Thurman moved out of the frame.

I let the tape play for another thirty seconds or so, and then I turned it off.

Mark Thurman said, 'Let it play and it shows us figuring out what to do. You can see Floyd planting a gun so we could say he was armed.'

I looked over at him. Thurman was in the bathroom door. I said, 'I've seen enough for now.'

'Yep.' He killed the rest of the beer. 'When I came into it everybody was screaming. I thought maybe the guy had a gun or something. It wasn't like I was scared, I just didn't know what to do.' He went to the little round motel table and took another beer. Twenty-five years old, looking for a friend, and there were no friends around. 'What could I have done?'

'You could have stopped them.'

He pulled at the warm beer and nodded. 'Yes. I'd say that's pretty clear. But I didn't, did I?'

'No. That's something you'll have to live with. You had an opportunity to behave well, but you behaved poorly. Had you behaved well, Charles Lewis Washington might still be alive.'

He sucked down the rest of the beer and you could tell that he was living with that, too.

I said, 'You're going to have to give up Dees and the other guys.'

'I can't do that.' There was one beer left. He went for it.

'You don't have a choice, Mark.'

'The hell I don't.' Angry now. Walled in by circumstances and goddamned tired of it. 'Jesus Christ, I feel bad enough. Now you want me to be a traitor? You want me to sell out my friends?'

'I want you to do what you should've done when it began. I want you to do the right thing.'

He raised his hands like he didn't want to hear it and he turned away.

I took two fast steps toward him, grabbed the back of his shirt, and shoved him across the little table. He said, 'Hey,' and dropped the beer.

I said, 'Charles Lewis Washington was living with a woman named Shalene. They had a baby named Marcus. Now that baby is going to grow up without a father. Do you understand that?'

'Let me up.' He grabbed my wrists, trying to pry my hands off and push up off the table, but I wouldn't let him.

'He had a brother named James Edward and a mother and a grandfather.' The muscles across my back and the tops of my shoulders felt tight and knotted. I dug my fingers into his face and neck and pressed. 'You have been part of something bad. It's unfair, and it's ugly, and you didn't know what you were supposed to do, but now you do, and you have to be man enough to stand up. If you don't, Ida Leigh Washington will have lost two sons for nothing and I will not allow that.'

He wasn't trying to pry me off anymore. He still gripped my wrists, but it was more as if he were holding on than pushing away.

I let go of him and stepped back, but he stayed on the table. He covered his face with his hands and then he sobbed. The sobs grew louder, and his body jerked, and he said things that I could not understand. I think he said that he was sorry.

I went into the bathroom, wet a towel, and brought it out to him. I helped him to sit up and gave him the towel, but it didn't do much good. He sat in one of the cheap motel chairs, bent over with his face in his hands, crying.

Finally, I held him close.

He would hurt for a long time, though not as long as Ida Leigh Washington. Still, he would hurt, and maybe this was his way of getting used to it.

CHAPTER 30

At twelve minutes after seven the next morning, I phoned Lou Poitras at home. Thurman didn't want to listen, so he went outside and stood in the parking lot. Crime is certainly glamorous, isn't it?

Poitras's middle daughter, Lauren, answered and asked who I was. I told her Maxwell Smart. She said, 'Nyuh-uh. You're Elvis Cole.' She's nine, and we'd known each other maybe seven years.

'If you knew who I was, why'd you ask?'

'Mommy told me always ask.' These kids.

'Lemme speak to your daddy.'

'Daddy was talking about you last night. He said you were an asshole.' She giggled when she said it. These kids are something, aren't they?

'Let me speak to him.'

The phone got put down and you could hear her running away, yelling for Lou and yelling that it was me. Lou Poitras came on maybe twenty seconds later, and said, 'Where you calling from?' His voice was tight in a way I hadn't heard it before.

'Why, Lou? You going to have me arrested?'

'Maybe I should. You screwed up bad, Hound Dog.'

'If not me, who? If not now, when?'

'Stop with the goddamn jokes. This isn't funny.' There was a kind of fabric sound that made me think he was moving with the phone, maybe getting away from his family.

I said, 'I need to see you, and I need to be certain that I'm not going to be taken into custody when I do.'

'You gonna turn yourself in?'

'No. I'm going to talk to you about cutting a deal that involves myself and Joe Pike and an LAPD officer, and I need someone to take it up the line to the DA.'

His voice went harder, and low, like maybe he didn't want his wife or kids to hear. 'Are you telling me that an LAPD officer is involved in this?'

'I've got visual proof that Charles Lewis Washington was unarmed when he was beaten to death five months ago. I've also got eyewitness proof that since that time, Eric Dees and his REACT team have been participating with the Eight-Deuce Gangster Boys in an ongoing series of misdemeanor and felony crimes.'

Lou Poitras didn't say anything for maybe forty seconds. Behind him, I heard his wife yelling for the kids to quit dogging it and get ready for school. Lou said, 'You're sure?'

'Sure enough to call you. Sure enough to think I can get the deal.' Nobody a good cop wants to bust more than a bad cop.

Poitras said, 'What kind of visual proof?'

'Videotape from a black-and-white surveillance camera.'

'There wasn't a tape in the Washington thing.'

'It was a hidden camera.'

'And this tape shows the incident?'

'Yes.'

'In its entirety?'

'Yes.'

'Can I see it?'

'You going to come alone?'

'You know better than that.' Giving me pissed. Giving me Had Enough. 'There's a video repair place called Hal's on Riverside just east of Laurel in Studio City. The guy owns it knows me. It's early, but he'll open up to let us use a unit. Can you meet me there in forty minutes?'

'Sure.' Most of the traffic would be coming this way.

Lou Poitras hung up without saying good-bye.

I put the cassette into a plastic Hughes Market bag, locked the room, and went out to the parking lot. Thurman was waiting in his car.

Thirty-five minutes later we pulled off the freeway in Studio City and found Hal's Video in a shopping center on the south side of the street. Lou Poitras's car was in the parking lot, along with a couple of other cars that looked abandoned and not much else. Eight A.M. is early for a shopping center. We parked next to Poitras's car, but Thurman made no move to get out. He looked uneasy. 'You mind if I stay out here?'

'Up to you.'

He nodded to himself and seemed to relax. 'Better if I stay.' It was going to be hard, all right.

I took the plastic bag with the videocassette and went into Hal's. It was a little place, with a showroom for cheap VCRs and video cameras made by companies you'd never heard of and signs that said AUTHORIZED REPAIR. Lou Poitras was standing in the showroom with a Styrofoam cup of coffee, talking to a short overweight guy with maybe four hairs on his head. Hal. Hal looked sleepy, but Lou didn't.

I said, 'Hi, Lou.'

Poitras said, 'This is the guy.' Some greeting, huh?

Hal led us into the back room where he had a VCR hooked to a little Hitachi television on a workbench. The Hitachi had been turned on. Its screen was a bright, motionless blue. Waiting for the tape. 'Everything's set up. You want me to get it going?'

Poitras shook his head. 'Nah. Go have breakfast or something. I'll lock up when we leave.'

'Forget breakfast. I'm gonna go home and go back to sleep.'

Hal left, and when we heard the front door close, Lou said, 'Okay. Let's see it.'

I put the tape in the VCR and pressed PLAY and Charles Lewis Washington appeared in the swivel chair behind the counter at the Premier Pawn Shop. I fast-forwarded the tape until Riggens and Pinkworth entered, and then I let it resume normal play. I said, 'You know those guys?'

Poitras said, 'No. They the officers?'

'There were five guys in Eric Dees's REACT team. Dees, Garcia, Thurman, Riggens, and Pinkworth. That's Riggens. That's Pinkworth.'

'Is there sound?'

'Unh-unh.'

A couple of minutes later Riggens left and came back with Garcia and the case of bullets. I said, 'That's Pete Garcia.'

Poitras's face was flat and implacable as a stretch of highway. He knew where we were going, and he didn't like it.

Charles Lewis Washington nodded to conclude the deal, and the three onscreen officers produced their guns and badges. Riggens went over the counter, and the beating began. I said, 'You see Washington go for a gun, Lou?'

Poitras kept his eyes on the screen. 'They're behind the counter part of the time. You can't see behind the counter.'

Washington came from behind the counter, and Garcia whacked him into Pinkworth. Riggens and Pinkworth beat him as he held up his hand and begged them to stop. If he had a gun behind the counter, he didn't have one now. Thurman entered the picture. 'That's Mark Thurman.'

Poitras nodded.

'Here comes Dees.'

'I know Dees.'

'I don't see the gun, Lou. I don't see any aggressive or threatening behavior.'

'I can see that, Hound Dog.' His voice was soft and hoarse, and the planes of his jaw and temples flexed and jumped and he had grown pale. I quit while I was ahead.

Pete Garcia checked Charles Lewis Washington for a pulse and shook his head, no, there was none.

I pressed the fast-forward again and we watched the men moving and talking at high speed, like in a cartoon. Riggens left the shop, then came back with a paper bag. He took a gun out of the bag. He put it in Charles Lewis Washington's hand. I said, 'There's the gun, Lou.'

Lou Poitras reached out and touched the off button, and the merciful blue reappeared. 'How'd you get this?'

'Mark Thurman and I stole it from Eric Dees's garage.'

'How'd Dees get it?'

'A gangbanger in South Central named Akeem D'Muere has the original. He's using it to blackmail Dees and the REACT team into supporting his drug trade.' I told him how Akeem D'Muere owned the Premier Pawn Shop, how he had had a surveillance camera installed, and how he had forced the Washington family to drop their suit against the city to protect Dees's team.

Poitras said, 'Okay. What's all this got to do with you and the charges against you?'

I gave him the rest of it, from the time Jennifer Sheridan hired me to James Edward Washington and Ray Depente and Cool T, and being set up by Eric Dees and the Eight-Deuce Gangster Boys so it would look like I was trying to pull down a drug deal. Poitras said, 'That's shit. Why set you up? Why not just kill you?'

'Akeem's a killer, but Dees isn't. He got into this mess trying to cover up for his people because of what happened to Charles Lewis Washington, and he's been looking for a way to get out. He's trying to control

Akeem. He doesn't want to make it worse. He just wants to survive it.'

Poitras's face split with a feral grimace. 'What a great guy.'

'Yep.'

'So what's the deal?'

'All charges against Joe and myself are dropped, and the city has to do right by the Washington family.'

Poitras shook his head, and the grimace came back. 'You and Pike we can handle, but when you start talking a wrongful-death suit, you're talking the mayor's office and the city council. You know what that's like. They're gonna ask how much. They're going to try to weasel.'

'Weaseling isn't in the deal. They have to negotiate in good faith. No weaseling, no disrespect.'

Lou said, 'Jesus Christ, they're lawyers. Weaseling is all they know how to do.'

'If the Washingtons sue, they'll win big. The city can fight them and drag it out, but they'll still win and the city will look bad because of the fight. So will the department. Do it my way, and no one has to know about the deal. The department can claim they uncovered the tape as a result of an internal investigation, and use going public as proof that the police can be trusted to wash their own dirty laundry. The city makes a big deal out of apologizing to the Washingtons, and everybody ends up looking like a hero. Jesus Christ, Lou, those people have lost two sons.'

Poitras gave a shrug. 'I don't think they'll go for it, but I'll try. What else?'

I said, 'Thurman skates and stays on the job.'

Poitras's face went as flat as a stone wall. 'Every one of these officers is taking the hard fall. Every one of them will do time.'

'Not Thurman. You can fine him, you can demote him, whatever you want, but he stays on the job.'

Poitras's eyes sort of flickered and his sport coat pulled across his shoulders as his muscles swelled. A fine ribbon-work of veins appeared on his forehead. I have known Lou Poitras for almost ten years, and I couldn't recall having seen him so angry. 'These guys shit on the badge, Hound Dog. I don't want guys like this in my department.'

'Thurman's young, Lou. He didn't have a hand in it. You saw.'

'He's sworn to protect. That means you protect even from other officers. He just stood there.'

'He froze. His team is like his family. Dees is like a father. He wants a second chance.'

'Fuck him.'

'You get four out of five, Lou. That's the way it works.'

Lou Poitras's jaw danced and rippled and he looked at the tape in the VCR, maybe thinking he should just take the tape, but maybe not, maybe thinking he should just arrest my ass. But maybe not. He let out a deep, hissing breath and his jacket smoothed as the heavy muscles in his shoulders and chest relaxed. Making peace with it. He said, 'Okay. Maybe we can make it fly. I'll have to run it up the line. It'd help if I had the tape.'

'Sorry, Lou. It's all I've got.'

He nodded and put his hands in his pockets. Wouldn't have to shake hands with me, his hands in his pockets. 'You going to be around?'

'No place in particular. We escaped fugitives lead nomadic lives.'

'Yeah. I guess you do.' He thought about it, then said, 'Call me at one o'clock. If I'm not in the office, Griggs will be there. I should know by then.'

'Okay, Lou. Thanks.' I took the tape from the VCR and we went out to the showroom toward the door. You could look out the glass there. You could see the cars, and who was in the cars. Poitras said, 'Is that Thurman?'

'Yeah.'

He stared at Thurman with empty eyes. He wet his lips and he stared.

I went to the door, but Lou Poitras didn't go with me. I guess there weren't many escaped felons he'd let walk away.

I stopped in the door and looked back at him. 'Tell me the truth, Lou. When you heard about the charges, did you doubt me?'

Lou Poitras shook his head. 'Nope. Neither did Griggs.'

'Thanks, Lou.'

When I turned away, he said, 'Try not to get stopped for a traffic violation. Our orders are shoot to kill.'

Ha ha. That Lou. Some kidder, huh?

CHAPTER 31

Thurman said, 'How'd it go?' He didn't look at me when he asked.

'We'll know by one o'clock.'

'I want to call Jennifer.'

'Okay. You hungry?'

'Not especially.'

'I am. We've got to kill time and not get caught until one. We'll grab something to eat. You can call Jennifer. We'll move around.'

'Fine.'

We drove over the hill into Hollywood. I drove, and Thurman sat in the passenger seat. Neither of us said very much or looked at the other, but there wasn't any tension in the car. There was more an awkwardness.

We followed Laurel Canyon down out of the hills, then turned east on Hollywood Boulevard. As we drove, Thurman's eyes raked the sidewalks and the side streets and the alleys, just like they had done when he was riding a black-and-white here, just like they had done when he saved the nine-year-old girl from the nut on the bus. He said, 'Hollywood was my first duty assignment when I left the academy.'

'Yeah.'

'My first partner was a guy named Diaz. He had twelve years on the job and he used to laugh a lot. He used to say, Jesus Christ, why you wanna do this for a living? A good-looking white guy like you, why don't you get a real job?'

I looked over at him.

Thurman laughed at the memory. 'I said I wasn't born on Krypton like Clark Kent and I wasn't good enough to be Batman like Bruce Wayne, so this was the next best thing. You get to wear a uniform and drive around in a fast car and put the bad guys behind bars. Diaz got a kick out of that. He started calling me Clark Kent.' Thurman fell silent and crossed his arms and stared ahead into Hollywood. Maybe remembering Diaz. Maybe remembering other things. 'You think they'll let me stay on the department?'

'We'll see.'

'Yeah.' We rode like that for a while, and then he said, 'I know you're not doing it for me, but I appreciate what you're doing in this.'

'They haven't gone for it yet, Thurman. A lot could go wrong.'

We went to Musso & Frank Grill for breakfast and used the pay phone there to call Lancaster. Mark Thurman spoke to Jennifer Sheridan and I spoke to Joe Pike. I said, 'It's happening fast. We should know by one o'clock.'

'You want us to come down?'

'No. If it goes right, we'll call you, and then we'll come up. Once we turn over the tape, they'll move on Akeem and the Eight-Deuce. I don't want Jennifer down until those guys are off the street.'

'Sounds good.'

We took our time with breakfast and didn't leave Musso's until the waiters and the busboys were giving us the glare treatment. When we left, we walked down Hollywood Boulevard to Vine, and then back again, looking at the people and the second-rate shops and trying to kill time. We passed the place where Thurman had gone onto the bus to save the nine-year-old girl. He didn't bring it up.

We picked up the car and drove east to Griffith Park where you can rent horses and ride along trails or in carefully controlled riding pens. The park was crowded, and most of the trail riders were families and kids, but most of the pen riders were serious young women with tight riding pants and heavy leather riding boots and their hair up in buns. We bought diet Cokes and watched them ride.

At eleven minutes before one that afternoon, we pulled into the parking lot at Griffith Observatory at the top of the Hollywood Hills and went into the observatory's great hall to use their pay phone. I figured it was a pretty safe place from which to make the call. You don't find a lot of cops browsing through the meteorite display or admiring the Chesley Bonestell paintings.

At exactly one o'clock by the observatory's time, I called Lou Poitras at his office. Charlie Griggs answered. Mark Thurman stood next to me, watching people come in and go out of the hall. Griggs said, 'North Hollywood detectives. Griggs.'

'This is Richard Kimball. I've been falsely accused. A guy with one arm did it.'

Griggs said, 'Let's see you smart off like that when they put you in the gas chamber.' Always a riot, Griggs.

'Is Lou there, or do I have to deal with the B team?'

Griggs put me on hold and maybe six seconds later Poitras picked up. 'I brought in Baishe, and we talked to a woman named Murphy at the DA.' Baishe was Poitras's lieutenant. He didn't much like me. 'Murphy brought in someone from the chief's office and someone else from the mayor's office, and we got together on this. Everybody's pretty anxious to see the tape.'

'What about Thurman?' When I said his name, Thurman looked at me.

'They'd like to have him, but they're willing to give him up to get the other guys. They don't like it much.'

'They don't have to like it, they just have to guarantee it. Does he stay on the job?'

227

'Yeah.'

'Do I have their word?'

'Yes.'

When Poitras said yes, I nodded at Thurman and he closed his eyes and sighed as if the results had just come back negative. I said, 'Are they going to deal square with the Washington family?'

'Shit, this comes out, the Washingtons are going to own City Hall.'

'Are they going to deal square?'

'Yes. That came from the DA's person and the mayor's person.'

'Okay. What's the next step?'

'They want Thurman to come in with the tape. They've made a lot of promises with nothing to go on except my word, and they don't like that. It all hinges on the tape. As soon as they see the tape, they'll move on Dees and those other assholes, and they'll move on Akeem D'Muere and anyone wearing Eight-Deuce colors. Everybody comes in.'

'Okay.'

'We can do it whenever you say. Sooner is better than later.'

I looked at Thurman. We would have to call Jennifer and Pike, and then we'd have to go get them and come down. It was eight minutes after one. 'How about your office at six?'

'Make it Baishe's office. Let him feel like he's in charge.'

'Done.'

I hung up the phone and told Mark Thurman the way it was going to be. I said, 'We have to call Lancaster.'

Thurman said, 'Let's not. I want to be the one to tell Jennifer. I want to see her face when I tell her that it's over.'

'I told her we'd call.'

'I don't care. I want to get flowers. Do you think we

228

could stop for flowers? She likes daisies.' He was like a cork that had been pulled down very far into deep water and suddenly released. He was racing higher and higher, and the higher he got the faster he moved. The sadness and the shame were momentarily forgotten and he was grinning like a kid who'd just won first prize in one of those contests they're always having in the backs of comic books.

I said, 'Sure. We can get daisies.' I guess I was grinning, too.

He said, 'Oh, boy.' Oh, boy.

We took the four-mile drive down out of Griffith Observatory and stopped at a flower shop in Hollywood for the daisies and then we hopped on the freeway and went north toward Lancaster and the house where Mark Thurman and Jennifer Sheridan had been hiding. It didn't take very long at all.

The neighborhood was alive with kids on skateboards and men and women working on their lawns and teenagers washing cars and the varied stuff of a Saturday afternoon. Joe Pike's Jeep was in front of the house where we had left it, and the drapes were still closed. We pulled into the drive and parked and Thurman got out first. He said, 'I want to go in first.' He held the flowers like a sixteen-year-old going to his first prom.

I followed him up the walk and stood beside him when he rang the bell once, then unlocked the door, and went in yelling for Jennifer Sheridan. He needn't have bothered.

Pete Garcia was sitting on the couch and Floyd Riggens was sitting in the green Ez-E-Boy. Riggens had his legs crossed and a cold Pabst in his right hand. He made a nasty grin when we walked in and said, 'Jennifer's not here, asshole. We've got her, and we want the goddamned tape.'

CHAPTER 32

No one said anything for maybe three seconds, and in that time you could feel the silence in the house, and the emptiness. There was me and Thurman and Riggens and Garcia, but no one else. I knew without looking. No one else. Garcia seemed nervous.

Thurman squinted, like maybe he hadn't heard right. 'Jennifer?' Loud.

Riggens said, 'You think I'm kidding?'

Thurman yelled toward the back of the house, then went to the foot of the stairs. 'Jennifer?' Getting frantic.

Riggens grinned. 'He thinks I'm kidding, Pete.'

I said, 'What did you do with her, Riggens?'

'Put her someplace safe until we get this straight. There's the copy of the tape, there's the copy of Jennifer. You see where we're going with this?'

'Where's Pike?'

Garcia said, 'Fuck him.' When Garcia moved, he seemed to jerk, and when he wasn't moving he rubbed his palms on his thighs like they were wet.

'What happened to Pike?' Maybe something in my voice.

Riggens made a little shrug, but he'd heard it, too. 'Who the fuck knows. They separated in town and we got her. He's not so much. He wasn't so goddamn much.'

Thurman came back from the stairs, his eyes nervous and his face flushed. 'She's gone.'

Riggens said, 'What did I say?'

'You bastard.' Thurman threw the flowers at Riggens

and started for him, but Riggens lifted his left hand and showed a 9-mil Browning. His face went cold as an ax blade. 'You wanna fuck with me? You want to see how far it'll push?'

Thurman stopped. He didn't look like a kid going to the prom anymore. He looked like an oversized street cop with a serious mad on. He looked dangerous.

I said, 'Mark.'

Riggens straight-armed the Browning and told Thurman to back up, but Mark Thurman didn't move.

I said, 'Mark.'

Garcia's eyes flicked from Thurman to me and then to Riggens. Beads of sweat had risen on Garcia's forehead and he wiped his palms again. I didn't like that.

I stepped close behind Thurman, then eased him back.

Riggens said, 'You sold us out, you fuck.'

Mark Thurman said, 'If she's hurt, I'll kill you, Floyd.' He looked at Garcia. 'I'll kill every one of you.'

Floyd nodded. 'You shoulda thought about that before you decided to sell us out, you prick.' He gestured again with the Browning. 'Where's the tape?'

I said, 'What tape?'

Pete Garcia said, 'Oh, fuck this.' He jerked up from the couch so quickly that Mark Thurman stepped back.

Garcia said, 'Just shoot the sonofabitch, Floyd. Jesus Christ.'

I said, 'Oh, that tape.'

Riggens shifted the muzzle from Thurman to me. 'Come on. You guys give us the tape, and we'll give you the girl. That's the way it's going to work.'

I shook my head. 'Too late, Riggens. We gave it to IAD.'

Garcia said, 'Then the broad's dead.' He shouted it, as if what little control he had over himself was going.

Mark Thurman said, 'That's not true. We still have it.'

I looked at him.

Thurman said, 'It's in the car. Floorboard behind the

driver's side.' He looked at me. 'I'm not going to risk Jennifer.'

Riggens said, 'Go see, Pete.'

Garcia went outside and came back maybe two minutes later with the tape. 'Got it.'

Riggens cocked his head toward a large-screen Zenith in the corner. 'Check it out.'

Garcia took the tape to the VCR and fumbled with the controls. His hands were shaking so badly that it took him a couple of tries to get the cassette into the machine. I didn't like all the shaking. Garcia wasn't the nervous type, but he was nervous today. I thought about why he might be nervous, and I didn't like that, either.

When the Zenith filled with Charles Lewis Washington and the Premier Pawn Shop, Riggens said, 'Fine. Eric's waiting. We'll take your car.'

The four of us went out to Mark Thurman's Mustang. Floyd Riggens asked if Thurman knew how to get to something called the Space Age Drive-In, and Thurman said that he did. Riggens told Thurman to drive and me to ride in the shotgun seat. Riggens and Garcia sat in back.

We worked our way out of the subdivision and onto the Sierra Highway, driving up through the center of town. It took maybe ten minutes to cross through Lancaster, and pretty soon we were away from the traffic and the traffic lights and into an area that the local cognoscenti probably called the outskirts of town. Not as many houses out here. Less irrigated lawn, more natural desert.

Maybe a quarter mile past a Tastee-Freez, Floyd Riggens said, 'There it is.'

The high sail of the Space Age Drive-In Movie Theater's screen grew up out of the desert maybe two hundred yards from the highway behind a marquee that said CL SED. It was surrounded by barren flatland and overgrown scrub brush and yucca trees. A narrow tarmac road branched off the highway and ran up past the marquee and a little outbuilding where people had once bought tickets to giant-ant movies, and disappeared along a high fence beside the movie screen that had probably been built so that people couldn't park on the side of the road and watch the movies for free.

Riggens said, 'Turn in just like you were going to the movies.'

We turned up the little road and followed it up past the marquee and the ticket booth and toward the entrance between the screen and the fences. The fences shouldered off of the movie screen and seemed to encircle the perimeter of the drive-in. A chain-link gate had been forced out of the way.

The Space Age Drive-In looked like it had been closed for maybe a dozen years. The tarmac road was potholed and buckled, and the outbuilding had been boarded over, and the fences had wilted and were missing boards. A long time ago someone had painted a cowboy in a space suit riding an X-15 on the back of the screen, tipping his Stetson toward the highway, but like the fences and the ticket booth and the marquee, he hadn't been maintained and he looked dusty and faded. Much of his face had peeled.

We went through the gate and passed into a large open field of crushed rock and gravel with a series of berms like swells on a calm sea. Metal poles set in cement sprouted maybe every thirty feet along the berms, speaker stands for the parked cars. The speakers had long since been cut away. A small cinderblock building sat in the center of the field with two cars parked in front of it. Concession stand. Eric Dees's green sedan and its blue stable mate were parked in front of the stand. The concession stand's door had been forced open.

Riggens said, 'Let's join the party.'

Pinkworth came out of the stand as we rolled up and said, 'They have it?' He was holding a shotgun.

Riggens grinned. 'Sure.'

Garcia got out with the tape and went into the concession stand without saying anything. More of the nervous, I guess.

Pinkworth and Riggens told us to get out of the car, and then the four of us went inside through an open pair of glass double doors. There were large windows on either side of the doors, but they, like the doors, were so heavy with dust that it was like looking through a glass of milk.

The concession stand was long and wide with a counter on one side and a little metal railing on the other. A sort of kitchen area was behind the counter, and a couple of single-sex bathrooms were behind the railing. I guess the railing was there to help customers line up. The kitchen equipment and metalwork had long since been stripped out, but tattered plastic signs for Pepsi and popcorn and Mars candy bars still spotted the walls. There was graffiti on some of the signs, probably from neighborhood kids breaking in and using the place as a clubhouse. Pete Garcia and Eric Dees were standing together by another pair of glass double doors at the back of the stand. Garcia looked angry and maybe even scared. Jennifer Sheridan was sitting on the floor outside the women's bathroom. When Jennifer and Mark saw each other, she stood and he ran to her, and they hugged. They stood together and held hands and she smiled. It was an uneasy smile, but even with all of this, she smiled. Love.

Eric Dees took the tape from Pete Garcia, then grinned at me. 'Sonofabitch if you didn't cause some trouble.'

I said, 'How'd you figure it, Dees?'

'You put in eighteen years on the job, you make a few friends.' As he spoke he put the tape on the floor, then stepped on it. He took a can of Ronson lighter fluid out of his pocket, squirted the fluid on the cassette, then lit it. Once it was going, he used more of the fluid. 'They heard the talk, and they let me know there's an investigation

234

going down. They said there's something about a tape, so I check and find out the tape is gone.' The fire was going pretty good, so he put away the fluid and came over and stood close to Mark Thurman. 'You fucked up bad, Mark. You should've just let it sit.'

Mark Thurman said, 'Jesus Christ, Eric, we were wrong.' The smell of the burning plastic was strong.

Riggens said, 'Hey, we went through that. We agreed. *You* agreed. You gave your word.'

Thurman shook his head. 'It was wrong. We did the bad thing together, and then we covered it up together. We should've stood up together, Floyd. Doesn't that bother you?'

'Going to fuckin' jail bothers me more!' Riggens was yelling. 'Losing the job and the pension and getting raked through the papers bothers me a helluva lot more!'

Garcia was pacing near the doors, glancing out like he expected something.

Dees said, 'You think I like this? You think I want it?' He looked at the fire. It was already dying away. 'You should've trusted me, Mark. I was going to work it out. I'm *still* going to work it out.'

Riggens said, 'Fuckin' A.'

I said, 'How, Dees? You going to bring Charles Lewis Washington back to life?'

Riggens screamed, 'Fuck you. With no tape, no one can prove anything. So maybe you showed it. Big fuckin' deal. Without the tape it's just hearsay, and we can ride that out.'

I nodded. 'Unless there's a copy.'

Garcia stopped the pacing and looked at me. Pinkworth shifted behind Eric Dees and Riggens sort of let his mouth open. Dees said, 'I'm willing to bet that you haven't made a copy. I figure you take the tape, you're thinking about cutting a deal, why do you need a dupe? You got a dupe, why make a big deal out of holding out? You'd just say, okay, here's the tape. You see?' Garcia was looking from Dees to me, Dees to me.

I spread my hands. 'But it's still a bet. You bet, sometimes you lose.'

Dees nodded. 'Yeah, but probably not this time.'

Guess you didn't earn command of a REACT team if you weren't smart. Of course, if you were smart, you didn't get yourself into a fix like this, either.

Mark Thurman said, 'Okay, the tape is gone and you're going to work things out. Let us out of here.'

Dees shook his head. 'Not yet.'

Jennifer said, 'You said if you got the tape back, you'd let us go. You said that.'

'I know.'

The crunching sound of tires over gravel came from outside, and Akeem D'Muere's jet black Monte Carlo eased between the fences and came toward the concession stand. Garcia said, 'He's here.' Pinkworth and Riggens went to the doors.

Eric Dees took out his 9mm Beretta service gun and Mark Thurman said, 'What the hell is D'Muere doing here, Eric?'

Floyd Riggens turned back from the doors. 'Akeem's pissed off about all the trouble. He wants to make sure it don't happen again.'

Jennifer said, 'What does that mean?'

I met Eric Dees's eyes. 'It means that Akeem wants to kill us, and Eric said okay.'

CHAPTER 33

Eric Dees said, 'Floyd. Pink. Get on them.'

Riggens drew his gun and Pinkworth worked the slide on his pump gun. Pete Garcia looked like he was about to pee in his pants. Jennifer Sheridan said, 'Oh, shit.'

Thurman shouted, 'Are you nuts? Have you lost your fuckin' mind?'

I took two steps forward, putting myself closer to Riggens and Pinkworth. 'You can't live it out, Dees. We come up dead, they're going to know. They'll backtrack the case and put it in bed with you.'

Dees nodded, but he nodded the way you nod when you're not really thinking about it. 'We'll see.'

Thurman said, '*Dees.*'

Eric Dees went outside and walked toward the Monte Carlo. The front passenger door opened and two black guys slid out with sawed-off Mossberg shotguns. They said something to Dees and the three of them came toward the concession stand.

Thurman yelled, 'Jesus Christ, Riggens. Pete.'

Pete Garcia said, 'Shut up. Just shut up.'

Pike moved across the cloudy glass at the back side of the concession stand. Everyone was looking toward the front, at Eric Dees with the hitters, so nobody saw him but me.

Eric Dees and the two Eight-Deuce hitters came in through the double doors, Dees squinting from the bright desert sun and the hitters stone-faced behind heavy-framed Wayfarer sunglasses. The hitters held their shotguns loosely, right hands on the pistol grips, left hands cradling the slides. Nothing like being comfortable with your work.

I said, 'Think it through, Dees. It's falling apart around you.'

Dees made a little gesture at Pinkworth and Riggens. 'Pink, you and Riggens take off.' He glanced at Garcia. 'Come on, Pete. We're outta here.'

Thurman shook his head, giving incredulous, still not believing that this could be happening. 'You're just giving us to these guys?'

Riggens said, 'Yeah.'

Riggens and Pinkworth holstered their guns and went to the door. Garcia wiped his hands on his thighs and hopped around some more, but he didn't move to leave. 'I can't believe we're doing this, Eric. We can't go along with this.'

Riggens stopped. Pinkworth was already outside, but he stopped, too, when he realized that Riggens wasn't with him.

Garcia looked at Dees, then Riggens. 'We can't do this. This is fuckin' nuts.'

Riggens went red in the face. 'What'd you say?'

Pinkworth came back and stood in the door.

Riggens screamed, 'You losing your fuckin' nut? We got a lot at stake here.'

Garcia screamed back at him. 'We know these people. This is fuckin' conspiracy. Fuckin' cold-blooded murder.'

The taller of the two hitters said, 'Shit.' He racked the slide on his shotgun.

Dees said, 'It's too late to back out, Pete. This is the only chance we have. You know that. Come on. All you have to do is let it happen.'

Pete Garcia said, 'No, Eric,' and reached under his shirt for his gun. When he did, the tall hitter lifted his shotgun and the shotgun went off with a sound that was as sharp and loud as a seismic shock. Pete Garcia was kicked back into the counter and then Joe Pike stepped into the glass doors at the back of the shack and fired his shotgun twice. The milky glass erupted inward and the tall hitter flipped backwards. Dees and Riggens came out with their pieces and fired at Pike, but Pike wasn't there anymore. The short hitter ran under their fire toward the broken doors, boomed his shotgun into the remaining glass, then looked out. 'Muthuhfuckuh gone.'

Something scuffed on the roof, and the short hitter let off another volley through the ceiling.

Warren Pinkworth ran for the blue sedan. Beyond him, the Monte Carlo kicked up a cloud of rocks and sand and fishtailed across the berms. Eric Dees dove out through the double doors and shot at something on the roof, but whatever he shot at he didn't hit. He said, 'Shit.'

I pushed Jennifer Sheridan down, and when I did, Mark Thurman went for Floyd Riggens. I yelled, 'No,' and Floyd Riggens shot him. Thurman spun to the left and sat down and Jennifer Sheridan screamed. She clawed past me, baring her teeth as if she'd like to tear out Riggens's throat.

I pushed her down again, then came up with the tall hitter's shotgun just as the short hitter turned and fired two times. Both of his shots went wide to the right. I shot him in the face, and then I fired out through the double doors at the Monte Carlo and hit it, but then it was behind the fence and away and Floyd Riggens was shooting at me. I dove behind the little wall that shielded the entrance to the bathrooms.

There were more gunshots outside, and then Eric Dees was in the double doors, yelling, 'Floyd, get your ass out here!' Outside, Pinkworth climbed into the blue sedan and ground it to life.

Riggens fired twice more at me, then went for the

doors. Riggens's eyes were wide and red and he looked like he was crying, but I wasn't sure why. He stopped over Mark Thurman. Mark Thurman looked up at him, and Riggens said, 'This is all your fault.' Then he raised his gun to fire. Jennifer Sheridan picked up Pete Garcia's pistol and shot Floyd Riggens in the chest. The bullet kicked him back, but he kept his feet. He opened his mouth and looked down at himself and then he looked at Jennifer Sheridan and fell.

Outside, Warren Pinkworth put the blue sedan in gear and sped away. Eric Dees shouted, 'You fuck,' fired two times at me, then dove behind the counter. Everything went still and quiet and stayed that way.

Pete Garcia rolled onto his side and moaned.

Jennifer Sheridan dropped Garcia's gun, then grabbed Mark Thurman by the shirt and dragged him toward the rest rooms. He had to outweigh her by a hundred pounds, but she kicked off her shoes for better traction and made a sort of groaning sound and did what she had to do. The floor was gritty with shattered glass, but she seemed not to notice.

Gravel crunched outside the concession stand, and Joe Pike took a position behind the broken double doors.

I said, 'That's it, Dees. It fell apart. It's over.'

Eric Dees moved behind the counter.

Pike looked in through the broken doors and I pointed at the counter. 'Dees.'

Eric Dees moved behind the counter again.

Pike said, 'Don't be stupid, Eric. Let's go home standing up.'

Dees said, 'What else have I got, Joe?'

Eric Dees charged around the near end of the counter, firing as he came, and when he did, Joe Pike and I fired back.

Dees went down hard, and I ran forward and kicked his pistol away, and then it was over. Dees was on his back, blinking at the ceiling and clutching at his chest. Most of the pellets had taken him there. A dozen feet away, Pete Garcia said, 'Oh, God,' but he didn't say it to anyone in the room.

Pike came up beside me and looked down. 'Hey, Eric.'

Eric Dees said, 'Joe.'

Pike said, 'There a radio in the unit?'

'Yeah.'

'I'll try to raise an ambulance.'

Pike went out to the green sedan.

Dees opened and closed his mouth and blinked up at the ceiling again. He said, 'How's Pete? Is Pete okay?'

I checked Pete Garcia and Floyd Riggens, and then I went to Mark Thurman. Jennifer Sheridan said, 'He's bleeding.'

The bullet had caught him low on the left side. She had ripped away part of her blouse and was using it to press on the wound. There was plenty of blood. Her hands were covered with it.

'Let me see.'

She pulled away the little compress and a steady rhythmic surge of blood pulsed from his abdomen. Artery.

He said, 'I gotta stand up.'

She said, 'You've got to stay down. You're bleeding, Mark. I think it's an artery.'

'I want to get up.' He pushed her off and flopped around and finally I helped him stand. When he was up he pushed me off and tried to walk. It was more of a sideways lurch, but he did okay.

Jennifer said, 'Damn it, Mark, *please*. We have to wait for the ambulance.'

Mark Thurman stumbled sideways. I caught him and helped him stay up. He said, 'You gotta help me.' He had lost a lot of blood.

Jennifer Sheridan said, 'Make him lie down.'

'He's okay.'

I helped Mark Thurman lurch across the concession stand to Eric Dees. Mark Thurman dug a slim billfold out of his back pocket, opened it, and held it out. It was his LAPD badge. He said, 'Do you see this?'

'What in hell are you doing?' Little bubbles of blood came out of Dees's nose when he said it and I wasn't sure if he was seeing the badge or not.

Mark Thurman breathed hard and sort of wobbled to the side but he kept his feet. His shirt and his pants were wet with his own blood. He said, 'I'm doing something that I should've done a long time ago, you sonofabitch. I am an LAPD officer, and I am placing you under arrest. You are under arrest for murder, and conspiracy to commit murder, and because you're a lousy goddamned officer.' Then Mark Thurman fainted.

Eric Dees was dead by the time the ambulance arrived.

CHAPTER 34

Jennifer Sheridan rode in the back of the ambulance when they brought Mark Thurman and Pete Garcia to the Lancaster City Hospital. Pike and I followed behind in Mark Thurman's Mustang.

The Lancaster cops assumed that something bad had gone down between a group of gangbangers and a group of LAPD officers, and neither Joe nor I told them different. The Lancaster police, as might be expected, assumed that the police officers on the scene had been there as the representatives of Truth and Justice. We didn't tell them different about that, either. Joe Pike got one of the Lancaster cops to give him a lift back to his Jeep.

The emergency room staff tried to keep Jennifer Sheridan out of the ER, but Mark Thurman woke up enough to say that he wanted her with him, and they relented. I went with him, too. Because of the nature of the bleeding, the ER staff prepared to take Mark Thurman into the operating room. One of the doctors grumbled about having no X rays, but I guess nobody wanted to wait. Pete Garcia was already on the table, and it didn't look good for him.

Jennifer and I stood beside Mark in a green tile hallway and waited for the orderlies to wheel him into the OR. Jennifer held his hand. Mark Thurman smiled at her, then his eyes moved to me. It was a sleepy smile. They had pumped him full of Demerol. 'What do you think will happen now?'

I made a little shrug. 'It'll come out. No way to keep it in.'

Mark looked lost and maybe a little fretful. 'The tape's gone. There's no more proof of what happened that night. They catch Pinkworth, all he's going to do is deny everything. Akeem D'Muere isn't going to offer anything.'

'There's Garcia.'

Mark Thurman sighed. 'If he makes it.'

'There's me and there's Pike.'

'Yeah. But that's just words. You weren't there that night.'

'No. But we'll offer what we can. If no one believes, then there it is.'

A nurse came and told Mark that it would be just a minute more.

I said, 'What do you want to do, Mark?'

He looked at Jennifer, and she nodded, and then he looked at me. 'I don't care about the tape. I want to go forward. I want to tell them what happened to Charles Lewis Washington. Can you set that up?'

I patted his shoulder and the orderlies came and took him away.

Jennifer Sheridan and I went into the little waiting room they have there and I bought her a cup of coffee. Then I went to the pay phone and called Lou Poitras. It was eighteen minutes after six, and he wasn't happy to hear from me. 'You're late. I got half a dozen people sitting here waiting for you and your boy Thurman. You getting cold feet?'

'The tape's gone, Lou. Dees burned it.'

Lou Poitras put me on hold. A couple of minutes later he picked up again. 'I had to change phones. I didn't want those people to see me have an aneurism.'

'Dees is dead. So is Riggens. Garcia and Thurman are under the knife now, and Pinkworth ran. I'd guess he'll go home. He'll think about it for an hour, then call in with a story.'

Lou Poitras said, 'Jesus Christ.'

'Thurman wants to come in, Lou. Tape or no tape. He wants to make a statement about what happened in the pawnshop, and what's been happening since, and he's willing to testify.'

Lou Poitras made a soft sound, but said nothing for several seconds. 'There's no deal without the tape, Hound Dog. None of these people will make a promise on verbal testimony. If he comes forward, he takes his chances.'

'He knows that. He wants to step forward anyway. If Garcia makes it, he'll probably be willing to corroborate.'

'That would help.'

'But even if Garcia doesn't, Thurman comes forward.'

'I understand.' There was maybe just a little bit more respect in Lou Poitras's voice than there had been. 'We're going to have to bring you in. Tell me where you are.'

I told him.

When I hung up, Joe Pike was sitting beside Jennifer Sheridan. He was holding her hand. I sat on the other side of her and took her free hand. She didn't look happy. She said, 'I can't believe I killed a man. I just shot him.'

'Yes.'

'A man I've known and talked to. Before they were divorced, the four of us had dinner once. We ate at the Sizzler.' She was staring at a point in the middle space, somewhere very far from here.

I said, 'You shot a man who was going to murder Mark Thurman. If you hadn't shot him, Mark would be dead. Do you see that?'

She nodded.

'It's what you have, and you must use it. You're going to hurt. You're going to miss sleep, and you're going to feel guilty, and it's going to get worse before it gets better, but you can survive it. You helped Mark survive, and now he will help you. He is alive because of you. When you hear him breathe, when you see him smile, it is because of you. Tell yourself that and know that it's true. Tell it to yourself as often as you need. If you forget, call me and I will tell you.'

She leaned her head against my shoulder and we sat like that. A few minutes later I told them about the call to Lou Poitras and the way it was going to be.

When I finished, Jennifer Sheridan said, 'I don't want to leave Mark.'

I rubbed her hand. Joe still had the other. 'You'll be fine. They're going to want to talk to you, and to Mark, but probably not until later. Joe and I will go now.'

She looked down at our hands, then up again. 'What will I say?'

'The truth.'

'Will they put him in jail?'

'I don't know. I don't think so, but I don't know. A lot of people out there are going to want his head.'

She nodded again, and this time smiled sort of sadly. 'He just wanted to be a police officer.'

'Yes. But now he'll have to move on, and so will you.'

'It's going to be such a big change. What will he do?'

'Something.'

'Well, we still have each other. We can make it.'

'Yes,' I said. 'If you want to make it, you can.'

She smiled again, and this time the smile didn't seem so sad. 'Thanks for sticking it out with me.'

'Jennifer, you're worth it.'

Twenty-two minutes later a couple of California Highway Patrol cops in khaki uniforms came into the waiting room. The shorter of the two said, 'Who's Cole?'

'Me.' I stood, and Pike stood with me. Jennifer got up with Pike and took my hand.

The same cop said, 'We're supposed to take you down to L.A. Is this guy Pike?'

Pike said, 'Yeah.'

'Okay. The both of you.'

The taller guy began to dig out his cuffs, but the shorter guy waved them away. 'We don't need that.'

Jennifer's grip on my hand tightened. I gave her the smile and squeezed her hand back and said, 'Everything's going to be fine.' Mr Confidence.

The high desert sky was turning a nice purple when the state cops loaded us into a black-and-white highway cruiser and blasted off down the Antelope Valley Freeway. Less than an hour later, the sky was dark when we pulled into the parking lot of the Seventy-seventh Division in South Central Los Angeles. I thought they'd take us to Parker Center, but there you go. Criminals always return to the scene of the crime. Even if we have to be taken.

They were expecting us. The Seventy-seventh's halls and squad rooms were jammed with cops and reporters and lawyers and handcuffed young black men who looked like they were Eight-Deuce gangbangers. A couple of them I recognized. I didn't see Akeem D'Muere, but Harold Bellis was talking to the homicide lieutenant, Stilwell. Stilwell looked bored, but Bellis looked confident. He also looked like he had just been called away from dinner. L'Orangerie, no doubt. *Des Oeufs de Poule au Beluga*, no doubt. The appetizer alone would've cost more than Stilwell's take-home for the day.

Stilwell saw me, went to a closed door that said WATCH COMMANDER, then opened the door and stuck in his head. Lou Poitras came out with two women and four men. The squad room was so crowded that if any more people came out of the office, they'd have to kick out the bad guys to make room for the good guys. One of the women was a prosecutor in the DA's office named Murphy, and one of the men was a uniformed captain who was probably the watch commander. I didn't recognize the others.

A guy in a wrinkled pinstripe with no tie said, 'Is this Cole?' He said it like he was in charge.

Lou Poitras pointed at me, then Pike. 'Cole. Pike.'

The pinstripe said, 'Let's go through it. I want to wrap this up.'

The pinstripe was a guy named Garvey from the chief's office and the other woman was a muck-a-muck named Greenberg from the city council. Of the two other guys, one was named Fallon, also from the DA's, and the other was from the mayor's office. The guy from the mayor was named Haywood. Fallon and Haywood took Joe Pike into an office down the hall, and Greenberg went with them. Garvey and everybody else took me into the watch commander's office. When we were settled, Murphy said, 'You're not under arrest at this time, Mr Cole, but we reserve the right to prosecute you for anything that you might admit to or say during this interview.'

Lou Poitras said, 'Jesus Christ, Murphy.'

Garvey made a take-it-easy gesture. 'At ease, Sergeant.'

Murphy said, 'Who's your attorney?'

'Charlie Bauman.'

She nodded. 'I know Charlie. I'd advise you to call him.'

I took her advice. An uncharacteristically smart move.

Everyone left for coffee while I called Charlie, told him where I was, and told him that I wouldn't say anything until he arrived. When I was done, I opened the door and saw Lou Poitras standing in the squad room with his boss from North Hollywood, a lieutenant named Baishe. Baishe has always looked shriveled and tight to me, sort of like a daddy longlegs, and he's never liked me much, but when I opened the door, he was jabbing the street cop Micelli in the chest and telling him that he'd acted like a goddamned bush-league asshole. Micelli said he didn't have to take this shit from some North Hollywood dick and jabbed back, and when he did Lou Poitras slapped his hand to the side and told him to step away. Poitras was maybe five inches taller than Micelli and eighty pounds heavier, and he looked like he was itching to use it. Micelli told Poitras to fuck himself, but he stepped away. Stilwell was over by a couple of uniforms, staying out of it. I said, 'Christ, Baishe, were you defending me?'

When Baishe saw me grinning, he scowled and said, 'Hell, no. I always knew you'd fuck up big time. I'm just surprised it took you this long.' A man with friends is the wealthiest man in the world.

Poitras told me to wait in the office, then asked if I wanted a cup of coffee. I told him that I did and waited in the open doorway for him to bring it. While I was waiting two Hispanic cops brought in Akeem D'Muere. His hands were cuffed, but he walked tall and defiantly, as if he were in some way larger than life, as if he were above all this and impervious to it and amused by it. Harold Bellis went to him, immediately complaining to the officers about the handcuffs. No one jumped to take them off. Stilwell went over to the uniforms, and they led D'Muere and Bellis toward the interrogation rooms. When they led D'Muere past, he saw me. I made my hand into a gun, pointed it at him, and dropped the hammer. He smiled. Amused.

Charlie Bauman came in maybe ten minutes later.

Murphy from the DA and Garvey from the chief saw him before I did, and then Charlie came to me. 'You say anything yet?'

'I learned my lesson last time.'

'Okay. These guys wanna have a powwow, so lemme see what I can work out.'

He went back to them, and pretty soon they were joined by Greenberg and Haywood. When Charlie came back, he said, 'They want a freebie, and I'm willing to give it to them, but it's up to you. You run through what you know and answer their questions, but it'll be off the record. If they decide to prosecute, they can't use your statements against you. Do you agree?'

'Yes.'

We went back into the watch commander's office, and I went through everything from the beginning, just as I had when I'd gone through it with Stilwell and Micelli, only this time there was more of it to tell. Everyone looked interested except the watch commander, who spent a lot of time saying things like, 'I've known Eric Dees for ten goddamned years. He's a fine officer,' or, 'Talk is cheap, but where's the goddamned evidence?' He said stuff like that until Murphy told him to shut up or leave the room.

I told them how Mark Thurman and I had stolen the tape from Eric Dees's garage, and described what I had seen on the tape and how I had tried to make the deal through Poitras. Poitras confirmed it. Then I told them what had happened at the Space Age Drive-In and what had happened to the tape. Murphy said, 'And the tape is destroyed?'

'Yeah. Dees burned it.'

The watch commander said, 'Ha.' As if that proved something.

Murphy ignored him and looked at Garvey. He shrugged. 'Might be possible to recover some of it. Won't know until we look.' Garvey picked up the phone and punched numbers. 'Where is it?'

I told him.

He repeated it into the phone.

We spent a total of three hours and fourteen minutes on it, and then Murphy said, 'Why don't you kick back for a while. We've got to talk with Pike, and then we've got to see where we stand.'

'Sure.' Mr Kick Back. That's me.

They let me stay in the commander's office. They left the door open and told me to help myself to coffee or the bathroom, but not to leave the building. Charlie Bauman went with them. The squad room had sort of settled down, with most of the reporters and lawyers gone, and most of the Gangster Boys in holding cells or interrogation rooms. It was closing on midnight, and from somewhere along one of the halls I could hear Jay Leno.

Maybe forty minutes later Charlie Bauman and the others came back. The people from the DA and the mayor and the city council stopped in the hall to talk, and Charlie and Pike came over to me. Charlie looked tired. 'There's a lot of little stuff, but they're not going to press on the Washington thing. They believe you didn't do it.'

'What about Lancaster?'

Charlie said, 'Man, Lancaster is nothing compared to this other stuff. They need to talk to Thurman, and they need him to testify, but as long as he backs up what you said, you guys can walk.'

'He will.'

'Then you're done. Go home and get some sleep.'

Lou Poitras broke away from the group and came over and offered his hand. 'Well, you've squeaked through another one, Hound Dog.'

I nodded. ''Tis better to be lucky than good.'

He looked at Joe Pike, and Pike looked back, but neither man offered a hand. 'How're you doing, Joe?'

Pike said, 'Fine. Thank you. And you?'

'Good.'

They stared at each other some more, and then Lou cleared his throat and turned away. Awkward.

Joe Pike and Lou Poitras have hated each other for almost twelve years, and in all of that time, this was the first that they had spoken civilly to each other. Crime makes for strange bedfellows.

Joe and I were walking out with Charlie Bauman when Harold Bellis and Akeem D'Muere came out of the interrogation hall. I thought maybe they were leading D'Muere to booking, but then I realized that no one was leading him and that they were heading for the exit. D'Muere saw me looking at him and made his hand into a pistol and dropped the hammer. He didn't smile. Then he and Bellis were gone. I looked at Murphy and Fallon and the big shots from the city. 'How come that sonofabitch is walking out?'

Murphy said, 'We can't file.' Her jaw was knotted and her mouth was a razor's slash.

Maybe I hadn't heard them right. 'He murdered James Edward Washington. You've got my statement.'

Fallon said, 'We can't use it.' He didn't seem any happier than Murphy.

I looked at Pike. 'Did I suddenly lose my grip on reality?'

Two uniforms came through with a young black kid in cuffs. The kid was smiling. Murphy watched him pass, her face set, and then she said, 'That young man says that he did it.' The kid was maybe fourteen.

'He didn't do it. I was there. I saw it. D'Muere pulled the trigger.'

'Three other young men admitted to being present and also said the kid did it. They pulled him out of a lineup.'

Pike said, 'Come on, Murphy. D'Muere found a kid to play chump. The boy does juvie time and comes home a hero.'

Murphy's hard jaw softened and she suddenly looked like a woman who wanted to go home, take off her shoes, and drink three or four glasses of some nice chardonnay. 'You know it and I know it, but that young man still says he did it and three eyewitnesses say he did it, too. We can't file against D'Muere, Elvis. That's just the way this one's going to work out.' She didn't wait for me or Pike or anyone else to speak. She and Fallon left, walking heavily as if the weight of the city were on them. Greenberg followed after them.

'But he murdered James Edward Washington.' I didn't know what else to say.

Garvey said, 'Go home, Cole. You've done a lot, and you've done it well, but there's nothing more to be done.'

CHAPTER 35

The watch commander authorized the release of my car and the personal possessions that had been taken from us at the time of our original arrests. He could have ordered a staff uniform to do it, but he did it himself, and we were out of there faster because of it. I guess that was his way of showing respect.

It was seventeen minutes before two that morning when we walked out of the Seventy-seventh, got into my car, and legally drove off the police grounds and onto the city's streets. We climbed onto the freeway, then worked our way north through the system toward Lancaster. There weren't many cars out, and the driving was easy.

Pike's Jeep was where he had left it, on a little circular drive outside the hospital. I parked behind it, and then we went inside to the waiting room and asked the nurses about Mark Thurman.

A nurse maybe in her early forties with a deep tan and a light network of sun lines checked his chart. 'Mr Thurman came through the surgery well.' She looked up at us, first Pike, then me. 'Are you the gentlemen who brought him in?'

'Yes.'

She nodded and went back to the chart. 'It looks like a bullet nicked a branch of the external iliac artery in his left side. No damage to any of the organs, though, so he's going to be fine.' She closed the chart as she said it.

Pike said, 'Is Jennifer Sheridan still here?'

A black nurse who'd been sitting with a young Chinese

orderly said, 'A couple Lancaster police officers came for her. That was at about eleven-thirty. She said to tell you that she would be fine. Mr Thurman was out of surgery by then, and she knew he was okay.'

Pike said, 'What about the other officer? Garcia?'

The two nurses stopped smiling, and the black nurse said, 'Were you close to Mr Garcia?'

'No.'

'He did not survive the surgery.'

We went out, Pike to his Jeep and me to my car, and we headed back through the rough barren mountains toward Los Angeles. The high desert air was cold and the surrounding mountains were black walls against the sky and the desert. At first we drove along together, but as the miles unwound we slowly grew apart, Pike with his drive and me with mine. Alone in my car, I felt somehow unfinished and at loose ends, as if there was still much unsaid, and even more unrealized. I wondered if Pike also felt that way.

I pulled into my carport just after four that morning and found a message on my machine from Ray Depente. He said that James Edward Washington was going to be buried at Inglewood Park Cemetery at eleven A.M. tomorrow, which made it today. He said that he thought I'd want to know.

I stripped off my clothes, showered, and climbed into bed, but the sleeping was light and unsatisfactory and I was up again before seven. I went out onto my deck and breathed deeply of the air and thought how sweet it smelled with a hint of wild sage and eucalyptus. I did twelve sun salutes from the hatha-yoga, then worked through a progression of *asanas* that left me sweating. At five minutes after nine I called Joe Pike and told him of James Edward Washington's funeral. He said that he would come. I called a florist I know in Hollywood and ordered flowers. I thought roses would be nice. It was late to order flowers, but the florist knows me, and promised to deliver the flowers to the church in time for the service.

I ate breakfast, then showered and dressed in a three-piece blue suit that I bought six years ago and have worn as many times. Once to a wedding and five times to funerals. Today would be number six.

It was a warm, hazy day, and the drive along the Harbor Freeway to South Central Los Angeles was relaxed and pleasant. I left the freeway at Florence, then went west to Inglewood, and then through the gates to the cemetery there just north of Hollywood Park. The cemetery is broad and green, with gently sloping grounds and well-kept headstones and winding gravel roads. A dark green canopy had been erected on the side of one of the slopes to protect the casket and the minister and the immediate family from the sun. A hearse and a family limo and maybe twenty cars were parked nearby. They had just arrived, and some of the older people were still being helped up the slope. I parked near Joe Pike's Jeep and moved up the slope to join the mourners. Joe was standing at the back of the crowd, and Cool T was four people away.

Twin rows of folding chairs had been placed under the canopy for the family. Ida Leigh Washington was seated in the center of the front row, with the elderly man to her right, and Shalene with the baby on her left. Ray Depente was behind Mrs Washington with a hand on her shoulder. He was wearing a dark brown herring-bone suit with a U.S.M.C. pin in his lapel. When Ray saw me, he said something into Mrs Washington's ear, then stood and waited for me. I went to Mrs Washington, offered my hand, and told her how sorry I was. She thanked me for the flowers and said, 'Someone from the police called my home this morning, as did one of those people from the city council. I understand that the truth about my boy Charles Lewis is going to come out because of you.'

I told her that I didn't know if it was because of me, but that it was going to come out, yes.

She nodded and considered me for quite a long time, and then she said, 'Thank you.'

I offered my condolences to the old man, and then to Shalene. Marcus said, 'I remember you,' loudly, and with a big smile. Shalene shushed him. She still didn't like me much.

Ray Depente led me away from the grave and Joe Pike drifted up behind us. Cool T watched from the crowd. Ray said, 'How come that bastard D'Muere is walking around free?'

I told him.

Ray listened, his face tight and contained. When I was done, he said, 'You remember what you said?'

'Yes.'

'You said we'd have justice. You said that bastard would pay for killing James Edward. Him getting a fourteen-year-old fool to take his place isn't what I call justice.'

I didn't know what to say. 'The DA's people know what's going on. They'll keep digging for a case against D'Muere, and when they find it, they'll file.'

Ray Depente said, 'Bullshit.'

'Ray.'

Ray said, 'That bastard called the Washingtons. He said that if they open their mouths about this, he'll kill that baby.' He pointed at Marcus. 'He called that poor woman on the day of her son's funeral and said that. What kind of animal does something like that?'

I didn't know what to say.

Ray Depente said, 'Fuck him and fuck the DA, too. I know what to do.' Then he walked away.

Joe said, 'I know what to do, too.'

I looked at him. 'Jesus Christ. Marines.'

Cool T came out of the crowd and met Ray Depente and they spoke for a moment, and then the minister began the service. Maybe five minutes into it, Akeem D'Muere's black Monte Carlo with the heavily smoked windows turned into the graveyard and slowly cruised past the line of parked cars, his tape player booming. The volume was cranked to distortion, and the heavy bass drowned out the minister. The minister stopped trying to speak over the noise and looked at the car, and everyone else looked at the car, too. Ray Depente stepped out from the row of chairs and walked toward the car. The Monte Carlo stopped for a moment, then slowly rolled away. When the car was on the other side of the cemetery, the minister went on with the service, but Ray Depente stayed at the edge of the dark green canopy and followed the car with his eyes until it was gone.

Guard duty. The kind of duty where your orders are to shoot to kill.

When the service was over and the people were breaking up and moving down the slope, Joe and I stood together and watched Ray Depente help Mrs Washington to the family's limo. Joe said, 'He's going to do something.'

'I know.'

'He's good, but there's only one of him.'

I nodded and took a breath and let it out. 'I know. That's why we're going to help.'

Pike's mouth twitched and we went down to our cars.

CHAPTER 36

At two oh-five that afternoon, Joe Pike and I found Ray and Cool T together in Ray's office. Cool T looked angry and sullen, but Ray looked calm and composed, the type of calm I'd seen on good sergeants when I was in Vietnam. Ray saw us enter and followed us with his eyes until we were at his door. 'What?'

'Are you going to kill him?'

'I don't know what you're talking about.' Innocent.

'Well, there are ways to do it. Get a good scoped hunting rifle, hang back a couple of hundred yards, and drop the hammer. Another way would be to drive around for a while until you see him, then walk up close with a handgun. There are more apt to be witnesses that way, but it's a matter of personal preference, I guess.'

Cool T shifted in his chair.

Ray leaned back and laced his fingers behind his head. 'Man, do you think I just fell off the watermelon truck?'

'What I think is that you've got a pretty good life doing well by a lot of folks, and you're about to mess it up.'

Ray looked at Cool T and Cool T grinned. Ray didn't. He gave me lizard eyes. 'That's what it is to you, that it?'

I spread my hands.

'So you come down here to point that out? Maybe set me straight?'

'Nope. We came to help.'

'Well, we don't need the white man coming down here to solve the black man's problems. We can manage that just fine, thank you.'

Pike's mouth twitched for the second time that day.

Ray gave the eyes to Pike. 'What?'

Pike shook his head.

I said, 'The DA would file if they thought they could win, and maybe there's a way we can give them that. Maybe not on James Edward, but on something.'

Ray Depente waited.

'If you want Akeem, you're going to have to go to him. That means his home, and it used to be a crack house. It's fortified like a bunker. But once we're in, I'm betting we can find something that the DA can use to put D'Muere away.'

Cool T said, 'Ain't no way we can get in there. Goddamn police use a goddamn batterin' ran to get in a crack house. Where we gonna get that?'

Ray glanced at Cool T. 'There are other ways.' He looked back at me. 'If it was worth it. If it would lead to that sonofabitch getting what he deserves.'

'We won't know until we get there, will we?'

Ray nodded. 'Why are you doing this, Cole?'

'Because I liked James Edward, Ray. Hell, I even like you.'

Ray Depente laughed and then he stood up and put out his hand. 'Okay. You want to help out on this, we'll let you help.'

Forty-two minutes later Joe Pike and I cruised past Akeem D'Muere's fortified home in Joe's Jeep. We parked six houses down on the same side of the street in an alley between a row of flowering azalea bushes and a well-kept frame house with an ornate birdbath in the front yard. Ray Depente and Cool T were one block behind us, sitting in Ray's LeBaron. Akeem D'Muere's black Monte Carlo and the maroon Volkswagen Beetle were parked at the front of his house, and a half-dozen Gangster Boys were hanging around on the Beetle. A couple of young women were with them. I wondered if they called themselves Gangster Girls.

Pike said, 'Brick house across the street. Clapboard two doors down, this side. Check it out.'

I looked at the brick house across the street and then at the clapboard house. A heavy woman with her hair in a tight gray bun was peeking from behind a curtain in the brick house and a younger woman, maybe in her early thirties, was peeking at us from the clapboard. The younger woman was holding a baby. 'They're scared. You live on a street with a gang for your neighbors and I guess peeking out of windows becomes a way of life. Never know when it's safe to venture out.'

Joe shifted in his seat. 'Helluva way to live.'

'Yes,' I said. 'It is.'

A tall kid leaning against the Bug's left front fender looked our way, but then went back to jiving with his buddies. All attitude, no brains.

Pike pulled a pair of Zeiss binoculars from the backseat and examined the front of D'Muere's house. 'Windows set close on both sides of the door. Bars on the windows.'

'What about the door?'

'Solid core with a couple of peepholes. No glass.'

'Does it open outward?'

'Yep.' Pike put down the glasses and looked pleased. Dope dealers often rebuild their doors to open outward instead of inward. Harder for the cops to bust in that way. It was something that we'd been counting on.

Fourteen minutes after we parked in the alley, Cool T turned onto the far end of the street in Ray Depente's LeBaron and drove slowly toward D'Muere's as if he were looking at addresses. He stopped in the middle of the street, and said something to the kids on the Volkswagen.

I said, 'Now.'

Joe and I rolled out of the Jeep and moved through the backyard of the near house and into the next yard toward

D'Muere's. We moved quickly and quietly, slipping past bushes and over fences and closing on D'Muere's while Cool T kept the gangbangers' attention. Akeem D'Muere's backyard was overgrown by grass and weeds and thick high hedges that had been allowed to run without care or trimming. A creaky porch jutted off the back of the house, and a narrow cement drive ran back past the house to a clapboard garage. The garage was weathered and crummy and hadn't been used in years. Why use a garage when you can park on the front lawn? Ray Depente appeared from the hedges on the far side of the yard and held up a finger to his mouth. He was wearing a black Marine Corps-issue shoulder sling with a Colt Mark IV .45-caliber service automatic. He pointed to himself, then gestured to the east side of the house, then pointed at us and then at our side of the house, and then he was gone.

Pike took the back of the house and I moved up the drive along the side. The windows along the back and sides of the house were barred, and many had been covered on the inside with tar paper, but there were gaps and tears in the paper and I moved from window to window, trying to see inside. Cool T drove away as I made the front corner of the house, and then I faded back to the rear. The rear was so crummy we could probably pitch a tent back there and no one would notice. Pike and Ray and I crouched in the bushes beside the porch.

Ray said, 'Two rooms and a bath on my side. Three full-sized windows, all barred, and a half-sizer on the bathroom. Someone was in the bathroom but the other two rooms were clear.' He looked at Pike. 'Will the door work?'

Pike nodded. 'No problemo.'

'How about the front?'

'No problemo.'

262

I said, 'Kitchen and two rooms on my side. I made six people, four male, two female. No children.'

Ray nodded. 'Any way out the windows?'

'Not unless they can squeeze through the bars.'

Ray smiled. 'This is going to work.'

Twelve minutes later Cool T once more turned onto the street and again stopped in front of the house. This time a couple of bangers slid off the Beetle and went toward him. When they did, Joe and I moved up the drive and across the front yard and Ray Depente trotted toward them from the opposite side of the house. One of the girls saw Ray Depente and said, 'What the hell?' and then the others saw me and Joe. The second girl ran and a short guy with too many muscles clawed at his pants for a piece. Joe Pike kicked him in the head with an outside spin kick, and then Ray Depente and I were at the Beetle with our guns out. The two guys out in the street started pulling for hardware, too, but Cool T came out with an Ithaca 12-gauge and they put up their hands. Ray said, 'Down.'

The Eight-Deuce Gangster Boys went down onto their stomachs.

Ray said, 'Make noise, and I'll bleed you.'

A tall skinny kid with a Raiders cap wiggled around and said, 'Why don't you kiss my goddamn ass?'

Ray punched him one time hard in the side of the head and he shut up.

Cool T opened the LeBaron's trunk and tossed me a bag filled with plastic wrist restraints. I passed a couple to Pike, and we tied them off. We worked quickly, and as we tied I glanced at the surrounding houses. You could see faces in the windows and behind doors. Watching. Wondering what in hell these fools were doing.

Ray gave two smoke grenades to Pike, kept two for himself, then pulled three ten-gallon metal gas cans from the trunk and four six-foot lengths of galvanized pipe from the backseat. When we finished with the tying, Pike took two lengths of the pipe and trotted to the back of the house. Cool T hefted the other two and started toward the front. When he was halfway there, the front door opened and a chunky guy with a thick neck and a thick belly stepped out and fired a Beretta 9 millimeter, *bapbapbapbap*. One of the rounds caught Cool T on the outside of his right arm. He screamed and went down, and then I had the Dan Wesson out and I was firing, and the heavy guy fell back. I said, 'Guess they know we're here.'

Ray grunted. 'Mm-hmm. Imagine that.'

Cool T scrambled behind the Monte Carlo and we went to him. Ray said, 'How you doing, Cool?'

'It burns like a sonofabitch.'

Pike examined the wound, then used part of Cool T's shirt to bind it. 'You'll be fine.'

A couple of faces peeked around the jamb, and someone in the house yelled, 'The fuck you doin'? Whatchu want?'

Ray yelled back. 'My name is Ray Depente. We came for Akeem D'Muere and we want to see his chickenshit ass out here.'

A second voice in the house yelled, 'Fuck you.' It was going to be one of those conversations.

Someone pulled the heavy guy out of the door, then a guy in a duster jumped forward, fired two pistol shots, then pulled the door closed.

Ray said, 'You think they'll call the police?'

We left Cool T sitting against the Monte Carlo's wheel and gathered up the pipe and the gas cans and went to the house. We put the pipes across the door and wedged them behind the window bars on either side. As we did it we could hear voices inside. They were trying to figure out what we were up to. Joe Pike came back around the house. 'Back door is sealed.'

'How about the windows?'

'No one's getting out.'

Someone inside yelled, 'The fuck you assholes want? Get away from here.' The closed door muffled the voice.

I stood to the right of the door, reached around, and pounded on it. A shotgun blast ripped through the door about where I should've been standing. I said, 'Hey, Akeem. It's time to pay up for James Edward Washington.'

Another blast came through the door.

'Gunfire is not meaningful discourse, Akeem.'

Another blast came through, this one very low.

I said, 'Here's the way it's going to happen. Everybody's going to put down their guns, and everybody's going to come out one at a time, and then we're going to tell the police what really happened to James Edward Washington. How does that sound?'

Akeem D'Muere shouted, 'Are you on dope? Get the fuck out of my face.'

I said, 'Akeem, I'm going to move in and set up house on your face.'

'You can't get in here. Get the fuck away.'

'It's not a question of us getting in, Akeem. The question is, can you get out?'

Ray Depente popped the top off of one of the gas cans and began splashing gas on the door and the windows and the sides of the house. The smell of it was strong and sharp in the still air.

Akeem said, 'What the fuck you . doin' out there? What's that smell?'

'We're pouring gasoline on your house. You told the Washingtons that you were going to burn them out, didn't you? We thought you'd appreciate the poetic justice of the moment.'

A different voice yelled, 'Bullshit. You wouldn't do that.'

Ray Depente said, 'Watch.'

Ray finished with one can and started with another.

Pike took the third can around to the rear. We could hear banging at the back of the house, but the pipes would hold. Across the street, a door opened and a man in his early seventies came out onto his porch and watched with his hands on his hips. He was smiling.

Inside, you could hear men moving through the house, and voices, and then the tar paper was abruptly torn off the front window and someone fired most of an AK-47's magazine out into the ground at full auto. Ray Depente looked at me and grinned. 'You think they gettin' scared?'

'Uh-hunh.'

He grinned wider. 'These pukes ain't met scared.'

Joe Pike came back. 'Ready.'

Ray Depente took a big steel Zippo lighter from his pocket, flipped open the top, and spun the wheel. He said, 'Welcome to hell, assholes.' Then he touched the flame to the gasoline.

The eastern front corner of Akeem D'Muere's fortified crack house went up with a *whoosh*. Ray and Pike moved around the house, tossing the smoke grenades in through the windows. The grenades had instant fuses, and in two seconds there would be so much smoke that you'd think you were in an inferno. The fire stayed at just one corner of the house, though, and didn't spread. We'd placed the gasoline so that it would smell, but we'd also placed it so that the fire would be small and controlled. The people inside didn't know that, though. There were shouts, and more shots, and someone banged on the front door, trying to get it open. Someone else started screaming for us to let him out, and smoke began to leak from windows and from around the front door. Across the street, more people came out of their houses to watch.

I shouted over the noise. 'The guns come out first.'

'We can't get the goddamn door open.'

'The window.' The smoke was making them choke.

More tar paper was pulled off the windows, and

handguns and shotguns and AK-47s were shoved through the glass. Clouds of thick gray smoke billowed out with the guns.

Ray Depente found a garden hose, turned it on, and sprayed it on the fire. It didn't put out the fire, but it cooled it some.

Someone inside said, 'Let us out. Please.'

I looked at Ray. He nodded. He and Joe took up positions at the corners of the house.

'One at a time. Hands on your heads.'

'Man, I'll put my hands up my ass you let me out of here.'

I unshipped the pipes, pulled open the door, and two men and two women stumbled out, jostling each other to get away from the smoke and the fire. Pike pushed them down and used the plastic restraints. Neither of the two guys was Akeem D'Muere.

Ray Depente yelled, 'You wanna cook, that's up to you.'

No one answered.

Ray looked at me and I held up three fingers and he nodded. Akeem, plus two others. They'd be hard cases, and they would've kept their guns. We could hear coughing.

Pike said, 'Maybe they doubt our sincerity.'

Pike stayed with Cool T to watch the others, and Ray Depente and I went in after Akeem. We went in low and fast, pushing through the oily smoke, and found them in a short hall between the kitchen and a back bedroom. Akeem D'Muere was with a dopey-looking guy with sleepy eyes and another guy who looked like he could have played defensive line for the Raiders. They were coughing and rubbing at their eyes. They heard us, but the smoke was too thick for them to see us. The big guy shouted, 'They're inside,' and started swinging wild. He didn't see anything, he was just swinging, and his first two punches hit the wall. I stepped outside and caught the joint of his left knee with a hard snap kick. The knee went and the big man made a gasping sound and fell. I followed him down and took his gun.

The dopey guy yelled, 'I see the muthuhfuckuhs,' and started firing a Smith .40 somewhere up toward geosynchronous orbit. Akeem D'Muere pushed the dopey guy at us and ran toward the front of the house. Ray Depente slapped the dopey guy's .40 to the outside, then hit him three fast times, twice in the chest and once in the neck, and the dopey guy fell.

Ray said, 'Take his gun.' Ray was already after Akeem.

I grabbed the dopey guy's gun, then used the plastic restraints as quickly as I could. I wanted to get to Akeem D'Muere before Ray got to him, but I didn't make it. Two shots came from the living room, then a third, and I got there just as Ray Depente came up under D'Muere's gun, twisted it free just as he had taught a thousand guys down at Camp Pendleton, then threw Akeem D'Muere through the open front door out into the yard. I went after them.

Akeem D'Muere was standing sort of bent to the side in the front yard, rubbing at his eyes and spitting to try to clear the smoke from his lungs. Ray Depente went down off the little porch, peeled away his shoulder sling, and said, 'Look at me, boy.' Ray didn't wait for him to look. Ray spun once and kicked Akeem D'Muere on the side of the head, knocking him to the ground.

I said, 'Ray.'

Up and down the block, doors opened and people came out onto porches and into yards. Pike and Cool T had the Eight-Deuce Gangster Boys on the ground and out of the play.

Ray Depente went to Akeem and dragged him to his feet. Ray was a couple of inches taller, but thinner, so they probably weighed close to the same. When Ray was lifting him, Akeem tried to grab and bite, but Ray dug his thumbs into Akeem D'Muere's eyes. D'Muere screamed and stumbled back. Ray stood and looked at him and there was something hard and remote in his eyes. Ray opened his hands. 'Hit me. Let's see what you got.'

Akeem D'Muere launched a long right hand that caught Ray high on the cheek and made him step back, but when he tried to follow with a left, Ray blocked it to the inside and drove a round kick into the side of D'Muere's head. D'Muere stumbled sideways, and Ray reversed and kicked him from the opposite side, and this time D'Muere fell. I put a hand on Ray's shoulder. 'That's enough, Ray.'

Ray slapped away my hand. 'Stand away from me now.'

'Ray, you're going to kill him.' Akeem D'Muere struggled up to his knees.

Ray said, 'And wouldn't that be a shame.' He kicked Akeem D'Muere in the chest and knocked him backwards.

I looked at Pike, but Pike was impassive behind the dark glasses.

Ray walked around behind D'Muere, lifted him by the hair, and said, 'You meet James Edward, you tell'm I said hi.' He spun again, and kicked, and Akeem D'Muere snapped over into the ground.

I took out the Dan Wesson. 'Ray.'

'You wanna shoot me for a piece of garbage like this, go ahead.'

He picked D'Muere up again. D'Muere's mouth and nose and ears were bleeding, and most of his teeth were gone. Ray held him up until D'Muere could stand on his own, then Ray punched him four fast times, twice in the solar plexus and twice in the face. Akeem D'Muere fell like a bag of wet laundry. One of the Gangster Girls screamed, 'You're gonna kill'm.'

Ray said, 'You think?'

I aimed the Dan Wesson. 'I don't have to kill you, Ray. I can do your knee. Be hard to teach after that.'

Ray nodded. 'You're right. But think of my memories.'

He lifted D'Muere's head by the hair, aimed, and punched him two hard times behind the ear. Then he let the head drop.

'Damn it, Ray.' I cocked the Dan Wesson.

Pike said, 'He means it, Ray.'

'I know. So do I.'

He reached down and lifted Akeem D'Muere once more.

As he brought D'Muere up, a dark blue Buick stopped in the street by the LeBaron and Ida Leigh Washington got out. She stood in the street, motionless for a time, and then she moved toward us. She was still wearing the clothes that she had worn to her son's funeral. Black.

Ray Depente saw her and let Akeem D'Muere fall to the ground. He said, 'You shouldn't be here, Ida Leigh.'

She stopped about ten feet from him and looked at the smoldering house, and then at the thugs on the ground with their hands bound, and then at me and Joe. She said, 'I wanted to see where he lived. Is that the one killed my son?'

'Yes, ma'am.'

Somewhere far off, a siren sounded. On the way here, no doubt.

Ida Leigh Washington stepped closer and looked down at D'Muere. His face was a mask of blood, but she did not flinch when she saw it. She put a hand on Ray's forearm and said, 'What could turn a boy into an animal like this?'

Ray said, 'I don't know, Ida Leigh.'

She raised her eyes from D'Muere up to Ray. 'This man took my last son. No one could claim my hurt, or my anger. No one could have a greater claim on this one's life.' Her voice was tight and fierce. She patted Ray's arm. 'There's been enough killing down here. We have to find a way to live without the killing.'

Ray Depente didn't move for a minute. Ida Leigh Washington kept her eyes on him. Ray stepped back. He turned away from Akeem D'Muere, and as the police cars began to arrive he helped Mrs Ida Leigh Washington back to her car.

Up and down the street, the people on the porches and in the windows and in the yards began to applaud. It would've been nice to think that they were applauding Ida Leigh Washington, but they weren't. At least I don't think they were. That far away, those people couldn't have heard one woman's softly spoken words, could they?

The cops got out of their cars and looked around and didn't know what to make of it. A Hispanic cop with a butch cut looked at Pike and me and said, 'Weren't you guys at the Seventy-seventh last night?'

'Yeah. We'll probably be there again tonight, too.'

He didn't know what to make of that, either.

CHAPTER 37

When the police went into Akeem D'Muere's house, they found $82,000 in crack cocaine in the attic, along with six cases of stolen rifles. Because the police legally entered the house investigating a crime in progress, the evidence found was admissible and resulted in charges brought against D'Muere. The investigators found no copies of the videotape that Eric Dees destroyed, and Akeem D'Muere, for some reason known only to him, denied all knowledge of such a tape.

The DA went easy on Pike and me. They agreed to trade on all charges except the assault on the police guards when Pike and I escaped from the Seventy-seventh. We were allowed to plead to a misdemeanor, served three days in county jail, and then it was over.

Of the five REACT officers involved in the wrongful death of Charles Lewis Washington, only Warren Pinkworth and Mark Thurman survived. Thurman turned state's evidence and sought neither a plea nor mercy. Warren Pinkworth was indicted on five counts of murder. He attempted a plea, but none was allowed.

Sixteen weeks after the events at the Space Age Drive-In Theater in Lancaster, Mark Thurman was fired from the ranks of the LAPD, losing all benefits that had been accrued. He said he didn't mind. He said it could have been worse. He was right. Four days after that, all administrative and criminal charges were dropped against Mark Thurman due to the intercession of Mrs Ida Leigh Washington. Three members of the city council and one member of the DA's staff objected and wanted, for political reasons, to use Thurman as an example, but cooler heads were only too happy to acquiesce to Mrs Washington's wishes. Negotiations were under way in the matter of her wrongful-death suits against the city. She was suing in the names of both of her sons.

Twenty-four weeks and three days after the events in the Space Age Drive-In, after spring had moved into summer, and then into the early part of fall, I was sitting in my office reading last week's newspaper when the phone rang and I answered, 'Elvis Cole Detective Agency, we're on your case for no money down.'

Jennifer Sheridan laughed. It was a good laugh, nice and clear. She and Mark were living together in Lancaster. She had given up her job with Watkins, Okum, & Beale and had taken a new job with a law firm based in Mojave. She had taken a twenty per cent cut in salary to do it, but she said that it was what she wanted. Mark Thurman had applied for a job with both the Palmdale PD and the Lancaster PD, but had been rejected both times. He had decided to return to school and obtain a degree in physical education. He thought he might like to coach high-school football. Jennifer Sheridan was sure that he would be wonderful at it. She said, 'How do you expect prospective clients to take you seriously if you answer the phone that way?'

I gave her Groucho. 'You kiddin'? I wouldn't work for a client who'd hire me.'

She laughed again. 'You do a terrible Groucho.'

'Want to hear my Bogart? That's even worse.' You get me on a roll, I'm a riot.

She said, 'Mark and I are getting married on the third Sunday of next month. We're getting married in the little Presbyterian church in Lake Arrowhead. Do you know where that is?'

'I do.'

'We've sent you an invitation, but I wanted to call. We'd like you to come.'

'I wouldn't miss it.'

'If you give me Joe's number, I'd like to invite him, too.'

'Sure.' I gave her the number.

Jennifer Sheridan said, 'It won't be a big wedding, or particularly formal. Just a few people.'

'Great.'

'We want a church wedding. We like the tradition behind it.'

She was leading up to something. 'What is it, Jennifer?'

She said, 'I'd really like it if you gave me away.'

Something warm formed in the center of my chest, and then I felt it in my eyes. 'Sure. I'd like that, too.'

'I love him, Elvis. I love him so much.'

I smiled.

She said, 'Thank you.'

'Anytime, kid. Romance is my business.'

She said, 'Oh, you,' and then she hung up.

After a bit I put aside the paper and went out the glass doors and stood on my balcony. It was late afternoon, and the fall air was cool and nice. A beauty-supply company has the office next to mine. It is owned by a very attractive woman named Cindy. She is also very nice. Sometimes she will come out onto her balcony and lean across the little wall that separates her space from mine, and look into my office and wave to get my attention. I did that now, leaning across and looking in her office, but her office was empty. It goes like that, sometimes.

I took a deep breath and looked out over the city to the ocean and to Santa Catalina Island, far to the south, and thought about Jennifer Sheridan and her love for Mark Thurman, and I wondered if anyone would love me the way she loved him. I thought that they might, but you never know.

I stood on the balcony, and breathed the cool air, and after a while I went in and shut the door. Maybe I would come out again in a while, and maybe, this time, Cindy would be in her office.

One can always hope.

Indigo Slam

Dedicated with love and admiration to Wayne Warga and
Collin Wilcox, two worthy men, always overhead.

ACKNOWLEDGEMENTS

The author appreciates the invaluable help of several people:
Howard A. Daniel III of the Southeast Asian Treasury regarding
foreign currencies and printing techniques; Kregg P.J. Jorgenson
for his insights into Seattle, the U.S. Customs Service, and crime
in the Pacific Northwest; and Gerald Petievich for opening many
doors at the United States Secret Service, and to the agents there
who, requesting anonymity, shared their technology and
expertise. Any errors contained herein are the author's
sole responsibility.

A novel is a world built by many hands. Thanks to
Patricia Crais, Lauren Crais, William Gleason and Andrea
Malcolm, Jeffrey Liam Gleason, Carol and Wayne Topping,
Aaron Priest, Norman Kurland, Robert Miller, Brian DeFiore,
Lisa Kitei, Marcy Goot, Chris Murphy, Kim Dower,
Samantha Miller, Jennifer Lang, and, especially, Leslie Wells.

SEATTLE

At two-fourteen in the morning on the night they left one life to begin their next, the rain thundered down in a raging curtain that thrummed against the house and the porch and the plain white Econoline van that the United States Marshals had brought to whisk them away.

Charles said, 'C'mere, Teri, and lookit this.'

Her younger brother, Charles, was framed in the front window of their darkened house. The house was dark because the marshals wanted it that way. No interior lights, they said. Candles and flashlights would be better, they said.

Teresa, whom everyone called Teri, joined her brother at the window, and together they looked at the van parked at the curb. Lightning snapped like a giant flashbulb, illuminating the van and the narrow lane of clapboard houses there in Highland Park on the west side of Seattle, seven and one-half miles south of the Space Needle. The van's side and rear doors were open, and a man was squatting inside, arranging boxes. Two other men finished talking to the van's driver, then came up the walk toward the house. All four men were dressed identically in long black slickers and black hats that they held against the rain. It beat at them as if it wanted to punch right through the coats and the hats and hammer them into the earth. Teri thought that in a few minutes it would be beating at her. Charles said, 'Lookit the size of that truck. That truck's big enough to bring my bike, isn't it? Why can't I bring my bike?'

Teri said, 'That's not a truck, it's a van, and the men said we could only take the boxes.' Charles was nine years old, three years younger than Teri, and didn't want to leave his bike. Teri didn't want to leave her things either, but the men had said they could only take eight boxes. Four people at two boxes a person equals eight boxes. Simple math.

'They got plenty of room.'

'We'll get you another bike. Daddy said.'

Charles scowled. 'I don't want another bike.'

The first man to step in from the rain seemed ten feet tall, and the second seemed even taller. Water dripped from their coats onto the wooden floor, and Teri's first thought was to get a towel before the drips made spots, but, of course, the towels were packed and it wouldn't matter anyway. She would never see this house again. The first man smiled at her and said, 'I'm Peterson. This is Jasper.' They held out little leather wallets with gold and silver badges. The badges sparkled in the candlelight. 'We're just about done. Where's your dad?'

Teri had been helping Winona say good-bye to the room they shared when the men arrived fifteen minutes ago. Winona was six, and the youngest of the three Hewitt children. Teri had had to be with her as Winona went around their room, saying, 'Good-bye, bed. Good-bye, closet. Good-bye, dresser.' Beds and closets and dressers weren't things that you could put in eight boxes. Teri said, 'He's in the bathroom. Would you like me to get him?' Teri's dad, Clark Hewitt, had what he called 'a weak constitution.' That meant he went to the bathroom whenever he was nervous, and tonight he was *very* nervous.

2

The tall man who was Jasper called, 'Hey, Clark, whip it and flip it, bud! We're ready!'

Peterson smiled at Teri. 'You kids ready?'

Teri thought, of course they were ready, couldn't he see that? She'd had Charles and Winona packed and dressed an hour ago. She said, 'Winona!'

Winona came running into the living room with a pink plastic *Beverly Hills 90210* raincoat and a purple toy suitcase. Winona's straw-colored hair was held back with a bright green scrunchie. Teri knew that there were dolls in the suitcase, because Teri had helped Winona pack. Charles had his blue school backpack and his yellow slicker together on the couch.

Jasper called again, 'C'mon, Clark, let's go! We're drowning out there, buddy!'

The toilet off the kitchen flushed and Teri's dad came into the living room. Clark Hewitt was a thin, nervous man whose eyes never seemed to stay in one place. 'I'm ready.'

'We won't be coming back, Clark. You're not forgetting anything, are you?'

Clark shook his head. 'I don't think so.'

'You got the place locked up?'

Clark frowned as if he couldn't quite remember, and looked at Teri, who told him, 'I locked the back door and the windows and the garage. They're going to turn off the gas and the phones and the electricity tomorrow.' Someone with the marshals had given her father a list of things to do, and Teri had gone down the list. The list had a title: *Steps to an Orderly Evacuation.* 'I just have to blow out the candles and we can go.'

Teri knew that Peterson was staring at her, but she wasn't sure why. Peterson shook his head, then made a little gesture at Jasper. 'I'll take care of the candles, little miss. Jasper, get 'em loaded.'

3

Clark started to the front door, but Reed Jasper stopped him. 'Your raincoat.'

'Hunh?'

'Earth to Clark. It's raining like a bitch out there.'

Clark said, 'Raincoat? I just had it.' He looked at Teri again.

Teri said, 'I'll get it.'

Teri hurried down the hall past the room that she used to share with Winona and into her father's bedroom. She blew out the candle there, then stood in the darkness and listened to the rain. Her father's raincoat was on the bed where she'd placed it. He'd been standing at the foot of the bed when she'd put it there, but that's the way he was – forgetful, always thinking about something else. Teri picked up the raincoat and held it close, smelling the cheap fabric and the man-smell she knew to be her father's. Maybe he'd been thinking about Salt Lake City, which is where they were going. Teri knew that her father was in trouble with some very bad men who wanted to hurt them. The federal marshals were here to take them to Salt Lake City, where they would change their names. Once they had a Fresh Start, her father had said, he would start a new business and they would all live happily ever after. She didn't know who the bad men were or why they were so mad at her father, but it had something to do with testifying in front of a jury. Her father had tried explaining it to her, but it had come out jumbled and confused, the way most things her father tried to explain came out. Like when her mother died. Teri had been Winona's age, and her father had told her that her momma had gone home to see Jesus and then he'd started blubbering and nothing he'd said after that made sense. It was another four days before she'd learned that her mother, an assistant night manager for the

4

Great Northwest Food Store chain, had died in an auto accident, hit by a drunk driver.

Teri looked around the room. This had been her mother's room, just as this house had been her mother's house, as it had been Teri's for as long as she could remember. There was one closet and two windows looking toward the alley at the back of the house and a queen-size bed and a dresser and a chest. Her mother had slept in this bed and kept her clothes in this chest and looked at herself in that dresser mirror. Her mother had breathed the air in this room, and her warmth had spread through the sheets and made them toasty and perfect for snuggling when Teri was little. Her mother would read to her. Her mother would sing 'Edelweiss.' Teri closed her eyes and tried to feel the warmth, but couldn't. Teri had a hard time remembering her mother as a living being; she remembered a face in pictures, and now they were leaving. Good-bye, Mama.

Teri hugged her father's raincoat tight; just as she turned to leave the room she heard the thump in the backyard. It was a dull, heavy sound against the back wall of the house, distinct against the rain. She looked through the rear window and saw a black shadow move through the rain, and that's when Mr. Peterson stepped silently into the door. 'Teri, I want you to go to the front door, now, please.' His voice was low and urgent.

Teri said, 'I saw something in the yard.'

Peterson pulled her past a third man in a still-dripping raincoat. The man who'd been loading the boxes. He held his right hand straight down along his leg and Teri saw that he had a gun.

Her father and Charles and Winona were standing with Mr. Jasper. Her father's eyes looked wild, as if at any moment they might pop out right onto the floor. Jasper said, 'C'mon, Dan, it's probably nothing.'

Her father clutched Jasper's arm. 'I thought you said they didn't know. You said we were safe.'

Jasper pried Clark Hewitt's hand away as Mr. Peterson said, 'I'll check it out while you get 'em in the van.' He looked worried. 'Jerry! Let's move!'

The third man, Jerry, reappeared and picked up Winona. 'C'mon, honey. You're with me.'

Jasper said, 'I'll check it with you.' Jasper was breathing fast.

Mr. Peterson pushed Jasper toward the door. 'Get 'em in the van. Now!'

Jasper said, 'It's probably nothing.'

Charles said, 'What's happening?'

A loud cracking came from the kitchen, as if the back door was being pried open, and then Peterson was pushing them hard through the door, yelling, 'Do it, Jasper! Take 'em!' and her father moaned, a kind of faraway wail that made Winona start crying. Jerry bolted toward the street, carrying Winona in one arm and pulling Teri's father with the other, shouting something that Teri could not understand. Jasper said, 'Oh, holy shit!' and tossed Charles across his shoulder like a laundry bag. He grabbed Teri *hard* by the arm, so hard that she had never felt such pain, and she thought her flesh and bone would surely be crushed into a mealy red pulp like you see in those Freddie Krueger movies, and then Jasper was pulling her out into the rain as, somewhere in the back of the house, she heard Mr. Peterson shout, very clearly, 'Federal Marshals!' and then there were three sharp *BOOMS* that didn't sound anything like thunder, not anything at all.

The rain fell like a heavy cloak across Teri's shoulders and splattered up from the sidewalk to wet her legs as they

6

ran for the van. Charles was kicking his legs, screaming, 'I don't have my raincoat! I left it inside!'

The driver had the window down, oblivious to the rain, eyes darting as Jerry pushed first Winona and then Clark through the side door. The van's engine screamed to life.

Jasper ran to the rear of the van and shoved Teri inside. Clark was holding Winona, huddled together between the boxes and the driver's seat. Winona was still crying, her father bug-eyed and panting. Two more *BOOMS* came from the house, loud and distinct even with the rain hammering in through the open doors and windows. The driver twisted toward them, shouting, 'What the fuck's happening?!'

Jerry yanked a short black shotgun from behind the seat. 'I'm with Peterson! Get 'em outta here!'

Jasper clawed out his gun, trying to scramble back out into the rain, saying, 'I'm coming with you!'

Jerry pushed Jasper back into the van. 'You get these people outta here, goddamnit! You get 'em out *now*!' Jerry slammed the door in Jasper's face and the driver was screaming, 'What happened?! Where's Peterson?'

Jasper seemed torn, but then he screamed back, 'Drive! Get the hell outta here!' He crushed past the cardboard boxes to the van's rear window, cursing over and over, 'Always some shit! Always goddamn bullshit!'

The van slid sideways from the curb as it crabbed for traction. The driver shouted into some kind of radio and Jasper cursed and Teri's father started crying like Winona, and Charles was crying, too. Teri thought that maybe even Federal Marshal Jasper was crying, but she couldn't be sure because he was watching out the van's square rear window.

Teri felt her eyes well with tears, but then, very clearly, she told herself: *You will not cry*. And she didn't. The tears went away, and Teri felt calm. She was soaked

7

under her raincoat, and she realized that the floor was wet from rain that had blown in when the doors were open. The eight cardboard boxes that held the sum total of their lives were wet, too.

Her father said, 'What happened back there? You said we were safe! You said they wouldn't know!'

Jasper glanced back at her father. Jasper looked scared, too. 'I don't know. Somehow they found out.'

Teri's father shouted, 'Well, that's just great! That's wonderful!' His voice was very high. 'Now they're gonna kill us!'

Jasper went back to staring out the window. 'They're not going to kill you.'

That's what you people said before! Her father's voice was a shriek.

Jasper turned again and stared at Teri's father for the longest time before he said, 'Peterson is still back there, Mr. Hewitt.'

Teri watched her brother and sister and father, huddled together and crying, and then she knew what she had to do. She crawled across the wet, tumbled boxes and along the van's gritty bed and went to her family. She found a place for herself between Winona and her father, and looked up into her father's frightened eyes. His face was pale and drawn, and the thin wet hair matted across his forehead made him look lost. She said, 'Don't be scared, Daddy.'

Clark Hewitt whimpered, and Teri could feel him shivering. It was July, and the rain was warm, but he wasn't shivering because he was cold. Teri said, 'I won't let anyone hurt us, and I won't let anything happen to you. I promise.'

Clark Hewitt nodded without looking at her. She held him tightly, and felt his shaking ease.

The van careened through the night, hidden by the darkness and rain.

8

Three years later:
Los Angeles

CHAPTER 1

It was plant day in the City of Angels. On plant day I gather the plants that I keep in my office and take them out onto the little balcony I have overlooking West Los Angeles, where I clean and water and feed them, and then spend the remainder of the afternoon wondering why my plants are more yellow than green. A friend who knows plants once told me that I was giving them too much water, so I cut their rations in half. When the plants turned soft as well as yellow, another friend said that I was still drowning them, so I cut their water in half again. The plants died. I bought new plants and stopped asking other people's advice. Yellow plants are my curse.

I was sneering at all the yellow when Lucy Chenier said, 'I don't think I'll be able to get away until much later, Elvis. I'm afraid we've lost the afternoon.'

'Oh?' I was using a new cordless phone to talk to Lucille Chenier from the balcony as I worked on the plants. It was in the low eighties, the air quality was good, and a cool breeze rolled up Santa Monica Boulevard to swirl through the open French doors into my office. Cindy, the woman in the office next to mine, saw me on the balcony and made a little finger wave. Cindy was wearing a bright white dress shirt tied at the belly and a full-length sarong skirt. I was wearing Gap jeans, a silk Tommy Bahama shirt, and a Bianchi shoulder holster replete with Dan Wesson .38-caliber revolver. The shoulder holster was new, so I was wearing it around the office to break in the leather.

Lucy said, 'Tracy wants me to meet the vice president of business affairs, but he's tied up with the sales department until five.' Tracy was Tracy Mannos, the station manager of KROK television. Lucy Chenier was an attorney in Baton Rouge, Louisiana, but she had been offered a job by KROK here in Los Angeles. She had come out for three days to discuss job possibilities and contract particulars, and tonight was her last night. We had planned to spend the afternoon at the Mexican marketplace on Olvera Street in downtown LA. Los Angeles was founded there, and the marketplace is ideal for strolling and holding hands.

'Don't worry about it, Luce. Take all the time you need.' She hadn't yet decided if she would take the job, but I very much wanted it to happen.

'Are you sure?'

'Sure, I'm sure. How about I pick you up at six? We can go for an early dinner at Border Grill, then back to the house to pack.' Border Grill was Lucy's favorite.

'You're a dream, kiddo. Thanks.'

'Or, I could drive over and pull the veep out of his meeting at gunpoint. That might work.'

'True, but he might hold it against me in the negotiation.'

'You lawyers. All you think about is money.'

I was telling Lucy how rotten my plants looked when the outer door opened and three children stepped into my office. I cupped the receiver and called, 'Out here.'

The oldest was a girl with long dark hair and pale skin and little oval glasses. I made her for fifteen, but she might have been older. A younger boy trailed in behind her, pulling a much smaller girl. The boy was wearing oversized baggy shorts and Air Nike sneakers. He looked sullen. The younger girl was wearing an *X-Files* T-shirt. I said, 'I'm being invaded.'

Lucy said, 'Tracy just looked in. I have to go.'

The older girl came to the French doors. 'Are you Mr. Cole?'

I held up a finger, and the girl nodded. 'Luce, don't worry about how long it takes. If you run late, it's okay.'

'You're such a doll.'

'I know.'

'Meetcha outside the building at six.'

Lucy made kissy sounds and I made kissy sounds back. The girl pretended not to hear, but the boy muttered something to the younger girl. She giggled. I have never thought of myself as the kissy-sound type of person, but since I've known Lucy I've been doing and saying all manner of silly things. That's love for you.

When I turned off the phone, the older girl was frowning at my plants. 'When they're yellow it means they get too much sun.'

Everyone's an expert.

'Maybe you should consider cactus. They're hard to kill.'

'Thanks for the advice.'

The girl followed me back into my office. The younger girl was sitting on the couch, but the boy was inspecting the photographs and the little figurines of Jiminy Cricket that I keep on my desk. He squinted at everything with disdain, and he carried himself with a kind of round-shouldered skulk. I wanted to tell him to stand up straight. I said, 'What's up, guys? How can I help you?' Maybe they were selling magazine subscriptions.

The older girl said, 'Are you Elvis Cole, the private investigator?'

'Yes, I am.' The boy snuck a glance at the Dan Wesson, then eyed the Pinocchio clock that hangs on the wall above the file cabinet. The clock has eyes that move from side to side as it tocks and is a helluva thing to watch.

She said, 'Your ad in the Yellow Pages said you find missing people.'

'That's right. I'm having a special this week. I'll find two missing people for the price of one.' Maybe she was writing a class report: *A Day in the Life of the World's Greatest Detective.*

She stared at me. Blank.

'I'm kidding. That's what we in the trade call private-eye humor.'

'Oh.'

The boy coughed once, but he wasn't really coughing. He was saying 'Asshole' and masking it with the cough. The younger girl giggled again.

I looked at him hard. 'How's that?'

The boy went sullen and floated back to my desk. He looked like he wanted to steal something. I said, 'Come away from there.'

'I didn't do anything.'

'I want you on this side of the desk.'

The older girl said, 'Charles.' Warning him. I guess he was like this a lot.

'Jeez.' He skulked back to the file cabinet, and snuck another glance at the Dan Wesson. 'What kind of gun is that?'

'It's a Dan Wesson thirty-eight-caliber revolver.'

'How many guys you kill?'

'I'm thinking about adding another notch right now.'

The older girl said, 'Charles, *please.*' She looked back at me. 'Mr. Cole, my name is Teresa Haines. This is my brother, Charles, and our sister, Winona. Our father has been missing for eleven days, and we'd like you to find him.'

I stared at her. I thought it might be a joke, but she didn't look as if she was joking. I looked at the boy, and then at the younger girl, but they didn't appear to be joking either. The boy was watching me from the corner of his eye, and there was a kind of expectancy under the attitude. Winona was all big saucer eyes and unabashed hope. No, they weren't kidding. I went behind my desk, then thought better of it and came around to sit in one of the leather director's chairs opposite the couch. Mr. Informal. Mr. Unthreatening. 'How old are you, Ms. Haines?'

'I'm fifteen, but I'll be sixteen in two months. Charles is twelve, and Winona is nine. Our father travels often, so we're used to being on our own, but he's never been gone this long before, and we're concerned.'

Charles made the coughing sound again, and this time he said, 'Prick.' Only this time he wasn't talking about me.

I nodded. 'What does your father do?'

'He's in the printing business.'

'Unh-hunh. And where's your mother?'

'She died five and a half years ago in an automobile accident.'

Charles said, 'A friggin' drunk driver.' He was scowling at the picture of Lucy Chenier on my file cabinet, and he didn't bother to look over at me when he said it. He drifted from Lucy back to the desk, and now he was sniffing around the Mickey Mouse phone.

I said, 'So your father's been gone for eleven days, he hasn't called, and you don't know when he's coming back.'

'That's right.'

'Do you know where he went?'

Charles smirked. 'If we knew that, he wouldn't be missing, would he?'

I looked at him, but this time I didn't say anything. 'Tell me, Ms. Haines. How did you happen to choose me?'

'You worked on the Teddy Martin murder.' Theodore Martin was a rich man who had murdered his wife. I was hired by his defense attorneys to work on his behalf, but it hadn't gone quite the way Teddy had hoped. I'd been on local television and in the *Times* because of it. 'I looked up the newspapers in the library and read about you, and then I found your ad in the Yellow Pages.'

'Resourceful.' My friend Patty Bell was a licensed social worker with the county. I was thinking that I could call her.

Teri Haines took a plain legal envelope from her back pocket and showed it to me. 'I wrote down his birth date and a description and some things like that.' She put it on the coffee table between us. 'Will you find him for us?'

I looked at the envelope, but did not touch it. It was two-fifteen on a weekday afternoon, but these kids weren't in school. Maybe I would call a lieutenant I know with the LAPD Juvenile Division. Maybe he would know what to do.

Teresa Haines leaned toward me and suddenly looked thirty years old. 'I know what you're thinking. You're thinking that we're just kids, but we have the money to pay you.' She pulled a cheap red wallet from her front pocket, then fanned a deck of twenties and fifties and hundreds that was thick enough to stop a 9mm Parabellum. There had to be two thousand dollars. Maybe three. 'You see? All you have to do is name your price.'

Charles said, 'Jeezis Christ, Teri, don't tell'm that! He'll clean us out!' Charles had moved from the Mickey phone and now he was fingering the Jiminys again. Maybe I could handcuff him to the couch.

Teri was looking at me. 'Well?'

'Where'd you get the money?'

Her right eye flickered, but she did not look away. 'Daddy leaves it for us. It's what we live on.'

Teresa Haines's hair hung loosely below her shoulders and appeared clean and well kept. Her face was heart-shaped, and a couple of pimples had sprouted on her chin, but she didn't seem self-conscious about them. She appeared well nourished and in good health, as did her brother and sister. Maybe she was making all of this up. Maybe the whole thing was their idea of a joke. I said, 'Have you called the police?'

'Oh no.' She said it quickly.

'If my father was missing, I would.'

She shook her head.

'It's what they do, and they won't charge you. I usually get around two grand.'

Charles yelled, 'Ripoff!' A small framed picture fell when he said it, and knocked over three Jiminy figurines. He scuttled toward the door. 'I didn't do anything. Jeezis.'

Teresa straightened herself. 'We don't want to involve the police, Mr. Cole.' You could tell she was struggling to be calm. You could see that it was an effort.

'If your father has been gone for eleven days and you haven't heard from him, you should call the police. They'll help you. You don't have to be afraid of them.'

She shook her head. 'The police will call Children's Services, and they'll take us away.'

I tried to look reassuring. 'They'll just make sure that you guys are safe, that's all. I may have to call them myself.' I spread my hands and smiled, Mr. Nothing-to-Be-Afraid-of-Here, only Teri Haines didn't buy it. Her eyes cooled, growing flinty and hard and shallow with fear.

Teresa Haines slowly stood. Winona stood with her. 'Your ad said confidential.' Like an accusation.

Charles said, 'He's not gonna do frig.' Like they'd had

17

this discussion before they came, and now Charles had been proven right.

'Look, you guys are children. You shouldn't be by yourselves.' Saying it made me sound like an adult, but sounding that way made me feel small.

Teresa Haines put the money back in the wallet and the wallet back in her pocket. She put the envelope in her pocket, too. 'I'm sorry we bothered you.'

I said, 'C'mon, Teresa. It's the right way to play it.'

Charles coughed, 'Eat me.'

There was a flurry of fast steps, and then Teresa and Charles and Winona were gone. They didn't bother to close the door.

I looked at my desk. One of the little Jiminys was gone, too.

I listened to Cindy's radio, drifting in from the balcony. The Red Hot Chili Peppers were singing 'Music Is My Aeroplane.' I pressed my lips together and let my breath sigh from the corners of my mouth.

'Well, moron, are you just going to let them walk out of here?' Maybe I said it, or maybe it was Pinocchio.

I pulled on a jacket to cover the Dan Wesson, ran down four flights to the lobby, then out to the street in time to see them pull away from the curb in a metallic green Saturn. The legal driving age in the state of California is sixteen, but Teresa was driving. It didn't surprise me.

I ran back through the lobby and down to the parking level and drove hard up out of the building, trying to spot their car. A guy in a six-wheel truck that said LEON'S FISH almost broadsided me as I swung out onto Santa Monica Boulevard, and sat on his horn.

I was so focused on trying to spot the Saturn that I didn't yet see the man who was following me, but I would before long.

CHAPTER 2

Teresa Haines's Saturn turned south past the West Hollywood Sheriff's Station, then east onto Melrose. I didn't careen through oncoming traffic to cut her off, and I didn't shoot out her tires. Teri Haines was driving just fine, and I wasn't sure what to do if I stopped them. Hold them at gunpoint for the police?

Fairfax High School was just letting out, and the sidewalks were dotted with boys toting book bags and skateboards, and girls flashing navel rings. Most of the kids were about Teri's age, some younger, some older, only these kids were in school and she wasn't. Charles leaned out of the passenger-side window and flipped off a knot of kids standing at the bus stop. Three of the kids gave back the finger, and somebody threw what appeared to be a Coke can which hit the Saturn's rear wheel.

Teri cruised along Melrose past hypermodern clothing outlets and comic-book shops and tour groups from Asia until she turned south onto a narrow residential street. Modest stucco houses lined the street, and the curbs were jammed with parked cars. Some of the cars probably went with the houses, but most belonged to people who'd come to shop on Melrose. I stopped at the corner and watched. The Saturn crept halfway down the next block, then turned into the drive of a yellow bungalow with an orange tile roof and a single royal palm in the yard. The three Haines children climbed out of the car and disappeared into the bungalow. Retreating to familiar territory after an unsuccessful meeting with the detective.

I cruised past their house, found a parking space on the next block, and walked back. Screams weren't coming from within, no music was blaring, and no smoke was rising from either windows or roof. Charles had probably passed out.

I stood on the sidewalk in front of the house next door and thought about things. When I was following them I had known exactly what I would do: I would locate their residence, then call one of my friends at Children's Services or the LAPD, and that would be that. Only the house and the yard, like the car and the children, appeared well maintained, and now I wasn't so sure. Maybe these kids were fine, and all calling the cops would get me was a house full of frightened children. Still, all I could see was the outside of the house. Inside, there might be rats. Inside, there might be squalor and vermin. Only one way to find out. When in doubt, snoop.

I slipped past the Saturn and walked up the drive and climbed atop their gas meter to peek into the kitchen. I couldn't see the kids, but the kitchen was neat and orderly and clean. No rats, no flies, no towers of unwashed dishes. I moved to the next set of windows, chinned myself on the sill, and peered through a little dining room to the living room. It occurred to me that Charles might see me peeking in the window and bean me with a brick, but these are the chances you take when you're a world-class private eye. Life is risk. The TV was on, and Charles and Winona were watching *Aeon Flux*. No one was pushing, no one was shoving. Like the kitchen, the living room was neat and orderly and in good repair. Eleven days without an adult, and everything looked fine.

I dropped back to the drive, then went to my car. I

watched the house and tried to look unthreatening so that nervous neighbors wouldn't call the cops. A black guy in a gray LeBaron cruised past. I smiled and nodded, but he looked away. Maybe I wasn't unthreatening enough.

Two hours and ten minutes later I started the car and left to pick up Lucy Chenier. I wasn't sure that I was doing the right thing by leaving them alone, but I wasn't sure it would be best to have them scooped up by a herd of social workers and put into a foster home either. Of course, they might be safer in such a home, but they didn't look particularly endangered where they were. Maybe I should stop advertising in the Yellow Pages.

The KROK studio and corporate offices are on Olympic Boulevard, just west of Doheny Drive along the southern edge of Beverly Hills. It's a large, modern building of steel and glass in an area of chain grocery stores and expensive high-rise apartments and upscale health clubs. Twentieth Century-Fox isn't far away, and neither is Century City.

Olympic was jammed with rush-hour traffic, and the valet parking attendants at the health club across the street from KROK were running double time to keep up with the incoming flux of agents and lawyers and studio execs anxious to pump iron and shoot hoops after a hard day telling the truth. Four guys in Versace suits were standing together outside the health club, staring toward KROK, only they weren't staring at the building; they were staring at Lucy Chenier. Lucille Chenier is five inches over five feet, with light auburn hair and green eyes and the rich, healthy tan of someone who spends a lot of time outdoors. She had attended Louisiana State University on a tennis scholarship, and she still played regularly and was serious about it. You could see it in the way she carried herself, and in the way her muscles

21

worked beneath her skin. I pulled to the curb and felt myself smile as she climbed into my car. 'Did you take the job?'

'Not yet, but they made a very interesting offer.' Her green eyes were amazing. Absolutely without bottom.

'How interesting?'

She smiled wider.

'That's pretty interesting.'

She leaned across the shifter and kissed me, and I kissed her back. 'Did you make a reservation at Border Grill?'

'I did.'

'Fantastic!' She settled back in the seat. 'We can eat, then I'll pack, and then we'll have the rest of the evening to sip champagne and do whatever.'

I smiled at her, and felt an enormous warmth grow between us. 'Whatever.'

Lucy told me the particulars of her interview as we drove toward Santa Monica, and then I told her about Teresa Haines. I told her about Charles and Winona, and how I had followed them back to their home, and as I told it, a vertical line grew between Lucy's eyebrows in a kind of frown. She said, 'They've been alone for eleven days?'

'Yep.'

'With no adult supervision?'

'That's right.' The line grew deeper.

'And you looked through the windows?'

'Everything seemed fine.'

Lucy was squirming so hard that I thought she was going to pop out of the seat. She shook her head and held up her hands and said, 'Seeming fine isn't enough. We'd better turn around.'

I said, 'Hunh?'

'*Turn around*. We're going into that house and make sure.'

I turned. Maternal hormones are awesome to behold.

Twenty minutes later, we left Melrose and once more cruised their house. Everything appeared in order and unchanged, and the Saturn was still in the drive. At least they weren't out joyriding. 'They're fine.' The professional detective makes his pronouncement.

'Stop.'

We parked in the drive behind the Saturn, went to the front door, and rang the bell. Charles threw open the door without checking, and when he saw us his eyes bulged and he tried to slam the door. 'Run! They've come to take us away!'

I pushed open the door and stepped inside, Lucy behind me. He was a game kid, grunting and huffing against the door as he slid across the floor. I said, 'Relax, Charles. No one is going to take you away.'

Teresa Haines said, 'Stop it, Charles.' She said it once, sharply, and he stopped.

Teresa and Winona were in the living room. The TV was off, so they probably hadn't been watching it. Winona was standing behind Teresa, and Teresa looked calm and in absolute control of her environment. She wasn't looking at me; she was looking at Lucy. I said, 'I wanted to make sure you guys were okay.'

Charles said, 'I tol' ya we shouldn't'a said anything! They're gonna put us in a home!'

Teresa crossed the living room, and extended her hand to Lucy. 'My name is Teresa Haines. Who are you?'

Lucy took her hand. 'Lucille Chenier. I'm a friend of Mr. Cole's.'

The house smelled faintly of tomato sauce and garlic. Teri said, 'Are you with Children's Services?'

Lucy smiled, friendly and relaxed. 'Not at all. I don't

live in Los Angeles. I'm just visiting.' Lucy released Teresa's hand, but kept the smile as she walked to the kitchen. 'Mr. Cole tells me that you've been without your father for over a week?'

'I'm sure he'll be back soon.'

'I'm sure he will. Do you mind if I look around?' Her smile was warm and reassuring.

Charles said, 'What about a search warrant? You gotta have a search warrant if ya wanna look around!' He was scowling at us from the door, his hand still on the knob as if he might suddenly throw open the door and run for it if we made the wrong move.

Teri said, 'If it will make you feel better.' Ignoring Charles.

Lucy disappeared into the rear. Teresa looked back at me and cocked her head. I shrugged. 'She's a mother.'

'Did you have second thoughts about helping us?'

'I wanted to make sure that you're okay.'

'So you followed us.'

'Sure.' Grilled by a kid. 'I wanted to see your living conditions. Also, Charles stole a figurine from my office.'

Charles yelled, *I didn't do anything!* He made a big deal out of waving his arms and pulling at his hair. *Why does everyone blame me?* Drama.

Teri said, 'Charles.' Her eyes narrowed and it sounded like a warning.

I held out my hand. 'Give it over, kid.'

Charles dug the Jiminy out of his pocket and threw it on the floor. 'Frig!'

Teri glared lasers at him. 'Charles.'

Charles scooped up the Jiminy, then skulked over with it, ready to run in case I tried to hit him.

He put it in my hand, then scuttled away. I looked at the Jiminy, then tossed it back to him. 'Keep it.'

Charles looked surprised.

Teresa said, 'You don't have to do that.'

'I know.'

She said, 'I'm sorry about this.'

I shook my head. It happens.

Teresa Haines took a breath, then said, 'So you've seen that we're fine.'

'Looks like you've got things under control.'

'So you won't have to call the police.'

I looked into the calm eyes, only they weren't so calm anymore. A tiny flame of fear was burning behind the oval glasses. 'You were aware of that possibility when you came to see me, yet you came anyway. You must be very concerned for your father.'

The flame grew brighter and her face worked, and then the flame was gone and the eyes were calm again. She had fought to control herself, and she had won. Some kid. She said, 'Of course I'm concerned. He's my father.'

Lucy came back and headed into the kitchen. 'Your room is very neat, Teresa. Do you share it with Winona?'

'Yes, ma'am.'

The smile. 'Charles's room is a mess.'

Teresa said, 'I know. You can't get him to make his bed.'

Lucy laughed. 'I know what that's like. I have an eight-year-old son who's the same way.'

Charles made the coughing sound, and this time you could make out the word 'Bitch.'

I said, 'Hey.'

Charles skulked into the dining room as far from me as he could get, put the Jiminy on the table, and pretended to play with it.

I could hear Lucy open the refrigerator and the stove and the pantry. A serious inspection was taking place, and it was coming from somewhere very female. Something was happening between Lucy and Teresa and, in a way I didn't quite understand, I was no longer a part of it. 'What do you and your brother and sister eat, Teresa?'

'I cook for us.'

Winona said, 'I cook, too.'

Lucy came back and smiled at Winona. 'I'll bet you're a good cook, honey.'

'We make spaghetti.'

'My favorite. Did you have spaghetti for breakfast?'

Winona laughed. 'We had Cheerios.'

Lucy smiled at Winona again, then glanced at me and nodded. I said, 'Is there food?'

'Yes.'

Teresa said, 'I shop and cook for us even when Daddy's home. It's no big thing.' She seemed affronted that anyone would think otherwise.

I said, 'We just wondered, that's all. It looks like you're in good shape.'

Teresa looked hopeful. 'Then you aren't going to turn us in to Children's Services?'

I frowned at her. 'You're underage. You can't live here alone.'

Lucy hooked her arm through mine, and squeezed. Tight. She smiled warmly at Teresa. 'He won't call them just yet, dear, but we'll have to consider that as we go.'

Now I frowned at Lucy. 'What's this 'we' business?'

Lucy squeezed tighter. 'But don't you worry about that for now, Teri. Right now, he's going to find your father.'

I said, 'I am?'

Lucy turned the warm smile my way. 'Of course you are. If you know what's good for you.'

I said, 'Mm.'

Lucy turned back to Teresa. 'Have you eaten dinner yet?'

26

'I was about to cook.'

Lucy beamed. 'We were just on our way to a very nice restaurant. Why don't you join us?' She gave my arm a little shake. 'Wouldn't that be fun?'

I said, 'Mm.'

Winona said, 'I want spaghetti.'

I phoned Border Grill and asked if they could make the reservation for a party of five. They could.

The five of us went to dinner – me, Lucy, Teresa, Winona, and Charles. We had to take the Saturn. Winona sat between Lucy and me; Charles threw a sauteed shrimp at the waitress, tried to steal a pepper mill, and ate two desserts. The bill came to a hundred eighty-two fifty.

Mm.

CHAPTER 3

I took Lucy to LAX early the next morning and waited with her at the gate. When it was time to board we held each other, and then she disappeared into the jetway. I went to the observation window, stared at her plane, and tried not to look depressed.

An older gentleman with a walking stick appeared at the glass next to me and shook his head, glum. 'Another visit, another parting.' He shook his head some more. 'Me, I never say good-bye.'

'Good-byes are tough, all right.'

'They're permanent. You say good-bye, you're inviting disaster.'

I looked at him. 'What do you mean, permanent?'

'The big birds come in, the big birds go out, and you never know what's going to happen.' He sighed. 'I hope nobody put a bomb.'

I looked at him harder. 'Do I know you?'

He made a shrug.

'I think I've seen you here before.' He was stooped and balding with baggy, old-man pants.

He shrugged again. 'God knows, it's possible. I spend my whole life in this place, picking people up, sending people off. All without a good-bye.'

'I'm pretty certain.'

He patted my arm and smiled. It was a kindly smile, and wise. 'That's where you're wrong, young man. The only thing certain is death.' He patted my arm again and leaned close. 'I hope you didn't say good-bye. For her sake.'

Great.

I left him at the window, walked out to the car, and took Sepulveda Boulevard north through the city, the footloose and fancy-free detective reentering the workaday world. I was missing Lucy already and feeling grumpy because of it, but I was also excited and hopeful. She felt that the job with KROK was going to work out, and, if it did, she and her son, Ben, would move here and then I could see her all the time. Thinking about that made me smile, and the grumpiness faded. The sun had climbed nicely, the air had warmed, and a slight orange haze was building in the east past Baldwin Hills. Perfect convertible weather even with the coming smog.

I followed Sepulveda north to Washington Boulevard, then turned east past the old MGM Studios to La Cienega when I spotted a gray Chrysler LeBaron edging across the white line three cars behind me. He stayed on the line a few seconds without changing lanes, the way you do when you want to see something ahead of you, and then he disappeared. I thought that maybe it was the same LeBaron I had seen outside Teri Haines's home, but then I said, 'Nah.' I was probably watching too many episodes of *Cops*.

Fifteen minutes later I parked behind Teri Haines's Saturn and went to the door. I kind of expected to find the house in smoking ruins, but I guess Charles had passed out from overeating. *Lighten up, Cole. He's only a kid*. Sure. They probably said that when Attila was a kid, too.

Teresa answered the door in jeans and pink Keds and an oversized white T-shirt. I said, 'Where are Charles and Winona?'

'I took them to school.' I guess she could read my surprise. 'Charles is in sixth grade and Winona is in third. You don't think I'd let them grow up stupid, do you?'

'I guess not.' Put in my place by a fifteen-year-old.

The house was as neat and clean as it had been yesterday, only now it was quiet. A washing machine chunked somewhere beyond the kitchen and street sounds sifted in through the windows. Teresa let me in, and stood well to the side as she showed me into the living room. Watchful. 'Would you like coffee? I always make coffee before I take them to school.' A blue mug sat steaming on the coffee table atop an issue of *Seventeen*.

'What about you?'

'I have a cup.'

'I meant about school.'

She sat at the edge of the couch and laced her fingers over a knee. She was so close to the edge that I thought she might slip off. 'We move around a lot, and I got tired of always being the new kid, so I took the GED exam last year when we moved to Arizona.' GED. General Equivalency diploma. 'I don't go to school.'

'Ah.'

She pursed her lips. 'I'm sorry, but is talking about me going to help you find my father?'

'Maybe. You just told me that you used to live in Arizona, which is something I didn't know. Maybe he went there.'

She flushed a hard red behind the glasses. I guess she didn't like being shown up either.

'If I'm going to find your dad, I'm going to need what we in the trade call a lead. That means I'll ask you a lot of questions, you'll tell me what you know, and maybe we'll get somewhere. You see?'

She nodded, but she wasn't happy about it.

I took out my pen and prepared to make notes. 'Tell me about him.'

Her father's name was Clark Rudy Haines. He was

thirty-nine years old, five feet ten inches tall, one hundred fifty-two pounds. He had light brown hair, though he had lost most of it years ago, and brown eyes. He wore glasses. She told me about the glasses, then she had some of the coffee, and then she stared at me.

I said, 'Okay.'

'Okay, what?'

'I need more than that.'

She looked uncomfortable, as if she couldn't imagine more than that. As if she was suddenly thinking that having me here was a bad idea, and she was wishing that she'd never come to my office.

I tapped my pen on the pad. 'You said he was a printer. Tell me about that.'

'Okay.' She said that her father was a commercial offset operator, and that they had left Tucson for Los Angeles because he had been offered a job with Enright Quality Printing in Culver City. She told me that he had been laid off, and that he had been concerned about finding another job. Then she shut up and watched me some more.

'So you think he left in search of another job?'

'Oh yes.'

'He's done this before?'

'Not for this long.' She explained that printing was a nomadic life because companies got big contract orders and hired printers like her father to fill those orders, but that when the jobs were done, the printers were let go. She said that when her father was let go, he would have to look around for another job and that was why they moved around so much.

'Does he have a girlfriend?'

She looked surprised. 'We move around too much for that.'

'How about friends?'

She frowned, thinking hard. 'I don't think he has any friends here either. He might've in Tucson.'

I thought about her GED. I thought about her not liking being the new kid in school. 'How about you?'

'What?'

'Do you have friends?'

She sipped more coffee and didn't answer. Guess they moved around too much for that, too.

'Does your father have a criminal record?'

'No.'

'Does he gamble? Maybe hit the card clubs down in Belflower or put money on sporting events?'

'No.'

'He drink, or have a history of mental problems?'

'Absolutely not.' The fifteen-year-old face hardened and she gripped the cup with both hands. 'Why are you asking questions like that?'

'Because a man doesn't just walk away from his children.'

'You make it sound like he abandoned us.'

I stared at her, and the washing machine changed cycles.

'He isn't anything like that. He isn't a drunk, or have brain problems. He's a good father. He's kind and sweet, and he's been gone before, but he's always come back.' She shook her head. 'There are too many printers and too few jobs. When you hear of something you have to follow up fast or you'll lose out.' She looked affronted, like how could I suggest anything else? 'I'm worried that he went somewhere and had an accident. What if he has amnesia?' Amnesia.

I circled Enright Printing on the little pad. 'Okay. I'll talk to the folks at Enright and see if they know something. Also, it might help if I had a picture.'

She frowned. 'I don't think we have a picture.'

'Everybody has pictures.'

She bit at her lower lip. 'I don't think so.'

'Well, maybe you have a snapshot.' I knew a friend with a fifteen-year-old daughter. She had about a zillion pictures of her cat and her friends and siblings and vacations and school and things. Boxes of the stuff.

Teresa shook her head. 'I guess we're just not camera people.'

I put away the pad and stood. 'Okay, let's go look in your dad's bedroom.'

She looked horrified. 'I don't think he'd like us snooping in his room.'

I spread my hands. 'When you hire a private eye, you hire a snooper. Snooping is how you find people who walk away without telling you where they've gone. Snooping is what I do.'

She didn't like this either, but we went along a little hall and into a bedroom at the back of the house. It was a small room, sparsely furnished with a double bed and a dresser and a nightstand. There were no photographs on the nightstand or the dresser, but large ink drawings of all three children were thumbtacked to the walls. The drawings were done on coarse construction paper with colored felt-tip pens, and appeared to have been torn from a notebook. They were signed *CH*. 'Wow. Did your father do these?'

'Yes.'

'He's some artist.' The drawings were almost photographic in their realism.

'Unh-hunh.'

When I opened the dresser's top drawer Teresa stiffened, but said nothing. I looked through the dresser and the nightstand. Maybe a half-dozen undershirts and underwear and socks were in the dresser, and not much else. There was a closet, but there wasn't much in it, just a single sport coat and a couple of pairs of thin slacks and a raincoat. 'Does it look like he packed for a long trip?'

She peeked into the closet like something might jump out at her, then shook her head. 'Well, I know he had two coats, and two pairs of pants are missing.'

'Okay. So he packed some things.'

'I guess so.'

I stood in the center of the room and tried to come up with an idea. 'Do you have any pictures of your mother?' If there was a picture of the mother, maybe Clark would be in it, too.

She shook her head. 'I don't think so.' Jesus. I had never seen a house without pictures before.

'Okay. Forget pictures. Where does he keep the credit card receipts and bank statements and things like that?'

'We don't use credit cards.'

I stared at her.

'We pay for everything with cash. When you're on a budget, cash is the best way to manage your money.' She was very certain of herself when she said it.

'Okay. No pictures, no credit cards.' No clues.

'We have a checking account and a savings account, though. Would you like to see them?'

'That, and your phone bills.'

The eyes narrowed again. 'Why would you need to see that?'

'The phone bills will show any toll calls made from or charged to your phone. You see?' My head was starting to throb. I guess she wanted me to find him without clues. Maybe I was supposed to use telepathy.

But she finally said, 'Well, okay.' Grudgingly.

'You know where to find that stuff?'

'Of course I know where to find it.' Offended.

I thought that she might find the stuff in her father's room, or maybe lead me out to the kitchen, but she

34

didn't. She brought me to her room. Two twin beds were set against adjoining walls, a small army of stuffed animals on one, pictures of David Duchovny, Dean Cain, and Gillian Anderson above the other. Again, there were no photographs of Teri or her family. I said, 'Who likes Duchovny?'

Teri turned red and disappeared into her closet. Guess I'd gotten my answer.

She reappeared with a shoe box held together by a large rubber band. She put the box on the empty bed, then sorted out thin packets of paper held together with large paper clips. She knew exactly what was what and where it belonged. 'Are the phone bills in there?'

'Un-huh.' A large wad of cash was mixed in with the packets, even larger than the roll she'd brought to my office. She saw me looking at the cash, frowned, then put it in her pocket. Better safe than sorry.

Far away something chimed, and Teri stood. 'That's the washing machine. I have to put our clothes in the dryer.'

'Okay.'

The checking and savings accounts were from the First Western Bank of Tucson, Arizona. The savings account was a simple passbook account with a balance of $1,104.16, and showed no unusual deposits or withdrawals. The checking account held a balance of $861.47, with the last deposit having been made just before they'd left Tucson for Los Angeles. The entry record was neat and orderly and made in a teenage girl's rounded hand. I put the banking papers aside and paged through the phone bills. Since they had been in Los Angeles for only four and a half months, there were only four bills, and most of the toll calls were in the LA area, with more than half to Culver City. Most of those were in the first month. Probably Clark looking for a job, but maybe not.

Two of the calls were to Tucson, and five to Seattle, three of the Seattle calls made in the last month, and two of them lengthy. When Teri came back, I said, 'Who's in Seattle?'

She stared at me as if she didn't understand what I'd said.

'You've got five calls to Seattle here, three in the last month, two of them for a pretty long time.'

'My mom's up there.'

'That's where she's buried?'

Nod.

'So your dad might have friends there.'

'I doubt it.' She adjusted her glasses. 'We didn't like it there. I'm pretty sure he wouldn't go back.'

'We'll see.'

'I'm positive he wouldn't.'

'Fine.' Like I shouldn't even waste my time.

I tamped the phone bill pages together, folded them, then put them in my pocket. She didn't like it when I did that either. I gave back the rest of her bills. 'Okay, I'm going to try to find your father, but we have to have an understanding.'

She stared at me, watchful and suspicious.

'I will not notify the authorities that three minors are living here alone so long as the three of you appear safe and in good care. Maybe your father will come home today, but maybe not. Maybe I'll find him fast, but maybe not. You're doing okay right now, and that's good, but if at any time I feel it's in your best interest to notify the police, I will do so. Are we clear on that?'

She looked stubborn. 'Will you tell me first?'

'I won't tell you first if I think you'll run.'

She liked that even less.

'I'm willing to let things stay as they are for now, but I won't lie to you. That's the way it has to be.'

She looked at me for a time, and then she looked at her papers. 'Are you finished with these things?'

I nodded. She took the checkbook, secured it to the bank statements and canceled checks with the same paper clips, and returned it to the shoe box. She did the same with the utility bills and the little pack of cash receipts all written in her hand. Fifteen.

'How long have you been paying the bills?'

She knew exactly what I was saying. 'My father is a good man. He loves us very much. He can't help it that she died on him. He can't help it that these things are hard for him.'

'Sure.'

'Someone has to take care of Charles and Winona. Someone has to clean the house.'

I nodded.

'Someone has to hold this family together.'

I thought there might be tears but her eyes were clear and sharp and hard behind the glasses. Determined. She put the remainder of her papers back into the box, put the top on the box, and again sealed it with the big rubber band. The matter-of-fact eyes came back to me and she dug out the wad of bills. 'We never settled the amount of your fee.'

'Forget it.'

The eyes hardened. 'How much?'

We sat like that, and then I sighed. 'A hundred dollars should do it.'

The hard eyes narrowed. 'In your office you said two thousand.'

'It's not as big a job as I thought. A hundred now, a hundred when I find him.'

She peeled off two of the hundreds and gave me both. 'Take it all now. I'd like a receipt.'

I gave her the receipt, and then I left to find her father.

CHAPTER 4

I phoned information for Enright's address, then left Teresa Haines alone with her coffee and laundry, and headed south along La Cienega toward Culver City. I wanted to tell her not to drive, and to be careful if she walked to the mall, but I didn't. She had been living like this for quite a while, and I knew she would ignore me because I would be saying it more for me than for her. That's the way adults often talk to children. You know they're not going to listen, but you want to tell them anyway just so you know that you have.

Enright Quality Printing was located in a two-story industrial building just off Washington Boulevard three blocks from Sony Pictures. On the way down, I was thinking it would be a small copier place like a Kinko's, but it wasn't. Enright was a big commercial outfit with employees and overhead and presses that run twenty-four hours a day, the kind that does large-scale jobs on contract for businesses and government. The building occupied most of the block, and what wasn't building was a neat, manicured parking lot for their corporate customers and a loading dock for the six-wheelers that delivered their product. The loading dock was busy.

I put the car in the parking lot, then went through the front entrance into a little waiting room. An industrial rack was built into one wall, filled with pamphlets and magazines and thick heavy manuals of the kind Enright produced. There were chairs for waiting and a counter with a young woman behind it. I showed her a card and said, 'Is there someone in charge I might see?'

She looked at the card as if it were written in another language. 'Sorry. We don't do cards.'

I took back the card. 'I don't want cards. I'd like to speak with someone in authority.'

She squinted at me. 'You mean Mr. Livermore?'

'Is he in charge?'

'Unh-hunh.'

'Then that's who I'd like to see.'

'Do you have an appointment?'

'Nope.'

'He might be busy.'

'Let's give it a try.'

If we're patient we're often rewarded.

She said something into her phone and a few minutes later a short, thin man who was maybe a hundred years old came out of the offices and scowled at me. 'You want something printed?'

'Nope. I want to ask you about a former employee.'

I gave him the card and he scowled harder. 'This is shit work. Ya oughta get your money back.' He handed the card back and I put it away. Just the way you want to start an interview, getting crapped on by an expert. 'You the cops?'

'Private. Like it says on the card.'

He made a brushing gesture. 'I didn't get that far. I see shit printing, I gotta look away.' This guy wouldn't let up. He said, 'Listen, you wanna talk, I'll talk, but you gotta walk with me. I got some ass to kick.'

'No problem.'

I followed him along the hall and onto the floor of the printing plant, walking fast to keep up with him. I guess he was anxious to start kicking ass.

The plant itself was large and air-conditioned and

39

brightly lit with fluorescent lights. It smelled of warm paper. Machines that looked like cold-war era computers bumped and clunked and whirred as men and women monitored the progress of paper and cardboard and bindings. The machines were loud, and most of the workers wore hearing protection but not all of them, and most of them smoked. A woman with a cigarette dangling from the corner of her mouth was wearing a T-shirt that said EAT SHIT AND HAVE A CRAPPY DAY. 'I'm looking for an employee you let go three weeks ago, Clark Haines.'

Livermore made the brushing gesture again. 'Got rid of'm.'

'I know. I'm wondering if you have any idea where he might be.'

'Try the morgue. All fuckin' junkies end up in the morgue.'

I said, 'Junkie?' I think my mouth was open.

Livermore stopped so suddenly that I almost walked into him. He glared at two guys who were standing together by a large offset press, then made a big deal out of tapping his watch. 'What is this, vacationland? I ain't payin' you guys to flap gums! We got orders to fill!'

The two men turned back to their machines, Livermore set off again, and I chased after. So much ass to kick, so little time to kick it. I said, 'Are you telling me that Clark Haines is a drug addict?'

'Guy was a mess since day one, always runnin' to the john, always shakin' with the sweats an' callin' in sick. I knew somethin' wasn't right, so I started keepin' my eyes open, y'see?' He pulled the skin beneath his right eye and glared at me. Bloodshot. 'Caught'm in one'a the vans, Haines and another guy.' He jabbed the air with a stiff finger. 'Bammo, they're outta here. I got zero tolerance for that crap.'

I didn't know what to say. It didn't seem to fit, but then it often doesn't. 'Have you heard from Clark since that day?'

'Nah. Why would I?'

'Job reference, maybe? He told his kids he was looking for work.'

'Hey, the guy's a top printer, but what am I gonna say, hire a junkie, they give good value?'

Livermore beelined to a short Hispanic man feeding booklet pages into a binder. He grabbed a thick sheaf of the pages, flipped through them, then shook his head in disgust. 'This looks like shit. Redo the whole fuckin' order.'

I looked over his shoulder. The pages and the printing looked perfect. 'Looks okay to me.'

He waved at the pages. 'Jesus Christ, don'tcha see that mottle? The blacks're uneven. Ya see how it's lighter there?'

'No.'

He threw the pages into a large plastic trash drum, then scowled at the Hispanic man. 'Reprint the whole goddamn run. Whadaya think we're makin' here, tortillas?'

I guess printing isn't a politically correct occupation.

The Hispanic man shrugged like it was no skin off his nose, and began shutting down the binder.

Livermore was again stalking the aisles. I said, 'Who was the man with Haines?'

'One of the drivers. Another fuckin' junkie, but him I could figure. Him, he had asshole written all over'm.'

'What was his name?'

'Tre Michaels. I think Michaels was the dealer.'

'Did you call the police?'

'Nah. Hey, I thought about it, okay, but they put up such a fuss, whinin' and cryin' and all. Michaels is on parole, see? I coulda violated him easy, but I figured, what the hell, I just wanted him outta here.'

'Think I could have his address?'

Livermore made a little waving gesture and walked faster. 'Go back up front, and ask Colleen. Tell'r I said it was okay to give you what you want.'

Colleen was only too happy to oblige.

Tre Michaels lived on the second floor of an apartment building just south of the Santa Monica Freeway in the Palms area, less than ten blocks from Culver City. It was just before eleven when I got there, but Michaels wasn't home. I found the manager's apartment on the ground level, told her that I needed to speak with Mr. Michaels about a loan he had applied for, and asked if she had any idea when he might be back. She didn't, but she was only too happy to tell me that Michaels worked at the new Bestco Electronics that had just opened, and that maybe I could find him there. She smiled when she said it and I smiled back. We are nothing if not the finest in West Coast detection.

Five minutes later I turned off Overland into the Bestco's lot, parked, and went inside. Bestco is one of those enormous discount electronics places, and as soon as I stepped through the doors three salesmen in sport coats and smiles surrounded me, anxious to meet or better any advertised price in town. I said, 'I'm looking for Tre Michaels.'

Two of them didn't know the name, but the third told me that Michaels worked in 'big screens.' I walked back to 'big screens.'

Tre Michaels was drinking black coffee from a Styrofoam cup as a gentleman of Middle Eastern descent argued with him about price surrounded by thirty large-format televisions displaying exactly the same image of

Arnold Schwarzenegger throwing a guy through a window. I recognized Michaels because he wore a little plastic name tag that said TRE. The Middle Eastern guy was saying that he could get a better price elsewhere, but if Bestco matched that price, then gave him five percent for cash and threw in free delivery and a free two-year full-service warranty, he might be willing to deal. Michaels said that if the man could produce a published price he might be able to give him an extra two percent, but he didn't seem in a hurry to do it. He seemed more interested in Arnold.

Michaels was an overweight guy in his early thirties with a wide butt and a hairline that hadn't seen his eyebrows in years. He had pale skin and washed-away eyes and dry lips that he continuously licked. The lips made me think he was feeling short and thinking about his next fix, but that's only because Livermore had said he was a junkie. Tre Michaels didn't look like a junkie, but then I've never met a junkie in real life who looked like Johnny Rotten.

Michaels glanced over when he saw me, and I pointed at a fifty-two-inch Mitsubishi. 'When you've got a moment, I'd like to buy this unit from you.'

He nodded.

'Full price.'

Michaels came over without a second glance at the Middle Eastern man and said, 'Will that be cash or charge, sir?'

The Middle Eastern guy started making a big deal out of it, but another salesman drifted over and pretty soon they were gone. I said, 'Do you have an office?'

Michaels smiled like the thought was silly. 'We'll just write you up over here by the register.'

I lowered my voice and went close to him. 'You don't

need to write me up. I want to ask you about Clark Haines.'

Tre Michaels froze as if he was suddenly part of a great still photograph. He glanced at the blond salesclerk. He twisted to look around at the other salespeople and customers, and then he wet his lips some more. He made what he hoped was an innocent smile. 'I'm sorry. I don't know anyone by that name.'

'C'mon, Tre. I'm not here to make trouble for you. I just want some information about Clark Haines.'

More licking. Around us, images of Arnold crashed up through a floor, spraying a hail of lead at faceless bad guys as the world exploded around him. I said, 'That Arnold is something, isn't he? Walks through a world of hurt and all of it slides right off.' I turned the smile back to Tre Michaels. 'Too bad it doesn't slide off the rest of us like that, isn't it?'

Tre nodded, kind of stupid, like he wasn't sure if he should talk to me or not, like he was scared to talk, but scared what I might do if he didn't.

'I'm not the police, Tre. I'm looking for Clark, and I know that you know him. I know that you and Clark know each other from Enright. I know that you're on parole for narcotics, and that you sold Clark drugs at least one time.' I spread my hands. 'Talk to me about Clark and you'll never see me again.'

'Sure.' He kept looking around. He kept licking his lips and looking at Arnold, but Arnold wasn't coming to help.

'Clark's missing and I'm trying to find him.'

'I don't know where he is.'

'Don't lie to me, Tre. I'm betting if I push down your socks or check your arms, I'll find needle tracks. I'll bet if I check your apartment, I'll find dope. If I think you're lying to me, I can call a couple of cops I know. Violation is only a phone call away.'

'I'm not lying. I swear to Christ I don't know where he is.'

'He buy from you often?'

Head shaking. 'A couple of times. Maybe three, four.'

'What did he buy?'

'Dime bags of heroin.' Jesus Christ.

'When's the last time you saw him?'

He shook his head and made a kind of shrug, as if it was tough to remember. 'A couple of weeks ago he calls me. He says he's going away for a few days and he wants to buy enough to get'm through.'

'He say where he was going?'

Michaels shook his head again. An older guy I took to be the floor manager was watching us now. Michaels saw him and didn't like it.

I said, 'Think hard, Tre. Did Clark mention a name or a place? A girlfriend, maybe?'

More shaking. 'Look, that was, what, two weeks ago? I haven't heard from him since, okay? I swear to Christ I haven't.'

The floor manager sidled closer, trying to listen. Michaels leaned toward me. 'These guys beef me out of the job, it's going to go like a bitch with my parole officer. *Please.*'

I left Tre Michaels in the sea of flickering Arnolds and slowly drove north to my office. The day was warm and clear, but the air felt dirty and the weight of the sun seemed heavy as if the light was a burden. I thought about Teresa and Charles and Winona, and how the daddy I was trying to find wasn't the same daddy that Teri was searching for, and I thought how sad it was that we often never really know the people around us, even the people we love.

CHAPTER 5

It was after two that afternoon when I took the winding drive up Laurel Canyon to the A-frame I keep just off Woodrow Wilson Drive in the mountains above Hollywood. It's a long drive up Laurel, but I've found that as you climb through the trees and cut rock to the top of the mountain and leave the city behind, you're often able to leave the clutter and stress of modern life with it. Often, but not always. Less often still when you're thinking about three kids with a missing father who turns out to be a drug addict.

I parked in the carport, turned off the alarm, and let myself in through the kitchen. The home was cool and still and smelled of Lucy's presence, but I probably just imagined it. Wishful thinking. I said, 'Anybody home?'

No answer.

I share the house with a large black cat who has shredded ears and a fine flat head that he carries cocked to the side from when he was shot with a twenty-two. I think it soured him. He is not the world's friendliest cat, and he'd hissed twice when Lucy arrived, then scrambled through his cat door and disappeared. He had watched us drive away that morning, so I thought he'd be inside waiting for me by now, but there you go. He sulks.

I took an Evian from the fridge, had some, then put Clark Haines's phone bills on my kitchen counter and looked at them. Tre Michaels had said that Clark was going on a trip, and the phone bills showed calls both to

46

Tucson and Seattle, but the dope changed things. People died from drug overdoses, and people were often murdered when they were trying to buy drugs, so there was a very real possibility that the only trip Clark Haines had taken was to the morgue. I spent the next thirty-two minutes on the phone with hospital emergency rooms and the Los Angeles County Medical Examiner's Office asking if anyone named Clark Haines or fitting his description had been admitted, living or dead, but no one had. Whew. Dodged that bullet.

I went through the bills, noting the two calls to Tucson and the five to Seattle. Over four months, there were also eighty-six local-area toll calls. The Tucson calls were to two different numbers. The five calls to Seattle were to two numbers, also, one number once, the other four times. I called the Tucson numbers first, getting a woman who answered, 'Desert Moving and Storage,' and asked her if Clark Haines was there, or if she knew how I could reach him. She told me that she knew no one by that name. Clark had probably used them to move to LA from Tucson, and she didn't remember the name. A woman named Rosemary Teal answered the next call. I asked her if Clark was there, and she told me that he'd moved, though she wasn't sure where. I asked her how she knew that he'd moved, and she told me that she was his neighbor. I asked if she'd heard from him since they moved, and she said only once. She said he'd called to ask her to please check and be sure he'd turned off the gas. When she insisted that I identify myself, I hung up. *Turn off the gas.* The junkie as concerned neighbor. I called the Seattle numbers next. When I called the first number, a young woman's voice answered, 'New World Printing.' I again asked for Clark Haines, and she told me that no one by that name worked there. I dialed the second number, and on the third ring a hoarse male voice said, 'Hello?'

'Hi, is Clark there?' Bright, and kind of cheery.

The voice said, 'Who is this?' Suspicious.

'Tre Michaels. Clark said he was coming up and gave me your number.'

'I think you got the wrong number.' Clark Haines had spoken to someone at this number for over an hour on two separate occasions.

'I'm sure I copied the number right. We're talking Clark Haines, okay? Clark said he'd be at this number or that you'd know how to reach him.'

'I don't know anyone by that name.' He hung up, and he didn't sound anywhere close to credible.

I called my friend at the phone company, gave her the area code and number, and asked for an ID. Forty seconds later she said, 'That service is billed to a Mr. Wilson Brownell. You want his address?'

'Sure.'

I copied the address, then hung up and thought about the two hundred dollars I had taken from Teresa Haines. Wilson Brownell clearly knew Clark and, under normal circumstances, would be the next step in the investigation. A ticket to Seattle and a hotel would normally be a billable expense, but having a fifteen-year-old kid for a client wasn't normal. Teresa and Charles and Winona were minor children living alone because their father, unemployed and now established as a drug user with a spotty employment record, had, for all intents and purposes, abandoned them. There was every real possibility that Clark Haines might never return, or even be found alive, and the smart thing to do would be to call the police and let them handle it. If I went to Seattle, I couldn't reasonably expect to recover the cost.

Only I had promised Teresa Haines that I would try to

find her father, and it bothered me to leave the lead to Wilson Brownell untested and unresolved. I thought about the two hundred dollars again, and then I picked up the phone and dialed another number.

First ring, and a man's voice said, 'Pike.' Joe Pike owns the agency with me.

'I'm looking for a guy named Clark Haines, and I believe he's gone to Seattle. He has three kids and I need you to keep an eye on them while I'm up there.'

Pike didn't respond.

'Joe?'

We might as well have been disconnected.

'They're doing okay, but I don't like the idea of them not having an adult around if they need help.'

Pike said, 'Three children.'

'I just want to make sure they don't burn down the house.'

More silence.

I was still waiting for him to say something when the cat came in through his cat door and growled so loud that Joe Pike said, 'Is that your cat?'

The cat trotted into the living room and growled again. Angry. He went from the living room into the kitchen and then back out to the front entry. He would trot hard, then stop and sniff, then growl some more. I said, 'I'll call you back in a few minutes.'

I hung up and watched the cat. 'You okay, buddy?'

His eyes narrowed but he didn't come near.

I sat on the kitchen floor, held out my hand, and after a while he finally came over. His fur was warm and coarse, and he needed a bath. I stroked his back, then felt his ribs and hips and legs. I was thinking that someone had shot him again or that a coyote had gotten him, but nothing seemed broken or tender or cut. I said, 'What's wrong?'

He jumped away from me and disappeared through his door and that's when I saw the blood.

Three drops of red were on the kitchen floor by the door jamb, two overlapping small drops, with a third larger drop nearby. I had stepped over them when I had let myself in. I said, 'Sonofagun.'

I touched the large drop and it was tacky.

I thought that maybe he'd brought in a ground squirrel or a field mouse, but there was no dirt or debris or fur. Sometimes he'll bring a kill up to my loft, so I went upstairs to check. Nothing. I went back down and looked through the living room and the dining room and the pantry, but there were no remains there either, and my scalp began tingling. I checked the doors and the windows, then went upstairs again and once more worked my way through the house. The handguns I keep locked in my nightstand were still there, as was the ammunition. The shotgun and rifle were still secure in the closet. My watches, jewelry, cash, and credit cards were all in their places, and their places looked unchanged, yet maybe not. I was pretty sure that the clothes hanging in my closet had been pushed to the right, but now they were spread evenly across the bar, and someone or something had smudged the dust on the two top shelves of my bookcase. Yet maybe not. Nothing was missing, but I felt an acute sense of difference in the shape and way of things, and a growing suspicion that someone had been in my house, and that they hadn't been here to steal. I went down the slope to check the alarm box on the side of my house. Fresh scratches gleamed in the metal around the screw heads. It looked like someone had beat the alarm, then let himself in through the kitchen. The cat had probably nailed him or her going out because he'd already completed his search. I said, 'Man, this really sucks.'

The cat was stalking around at the top of the slope, still growling, still pissed. He is an obsessive animal and does not let go of anger easily.

I said, 'Come here, you.'

He stalked over, surly and growling and making little noises.

I picked him up and held him close. 'I'm glad you weren't hurt.'

He squirmed until I put him down. Pity any dog that tried to grab him now.

I went back inside, washed my hands twice, then called Joe. 'Someone went through my house.'

'Have anything to do with the father?'

I thought about it. 'I don't know why it would, but I'm not sure.'

'Maybe I should watch you instead of these kids.'

'Maybe.' I told him their address. 'Meet me there and I'll introduce you. I'll take a flight out early in the morning.'

'Whatever.'

Pike hung up, and I stood in the center of the kitchen and listened to the silence. Someone had been in my home, and it made me feel creepy and violated and angry. I pulled out the Dan Wesson, sat it on the kitchen counter, and crossed my arms. 'Let's see'm come back now.'

Acting tough will sometimes help, but not always, and the gun did not lessen the feeling that I was vulnerable and at risk. They seldom do.

I shut off the lights, locked the house, and reset the alarm. It hadn't helped, but you do what you can.

I drove down to see Teri Haines.

CHAPTER 6

It was just after six that evening when I rang their bell and Charles threw open the door. He threw it wide, just as he had before, without regard to who might be on the other side. I said, 'Always ask who it is.'

Charles showed me a twelve-inch serrated carving knife. 'You don't have to ask when you're ready.'

Sometimes you just have to shake your head.

Today Charles was wearing the oversized shoes, the monstrously baggy shorts, and a black Wolverine T-shirt that hung almost to his knees. Teresa appeared over his shoulder, and said, 'Did you find him?' Hopeful.

'Nope. But I've got a couple of ideas. How about I come in and we talk about them?'

Winona was sitting at the dining table, and plates were there for Charles and Teresa. I'd interrupted dinner. Spaghetti, again. Maybe it was all they knew how to make. 'Smells great.' Mr. Cheery.

Teresa said, 'We were just finished, but there's more if you'd like some.'

'That's okay, but thanks.'

'Just let us clear the table.'

'Sure.' I wandered into the living room and sat on the couch. I had to move a library book to sit. Brennert's *Her Pilgrim Soul*.

Winona slid from her seat, placed her silverware onto her plate, then carried the plate and her glass into the kitchen. Teresa gathered her things, too, and so did

Charles. No one had to badger him. Everyone knew what to do and everyone did their job as if it were part of a larger accepted pattern. They gathered their things and brought them into the kitchen, and then Teresa and Charles returned, Teresa picking up the place mats and Charles wiping off the table with a damp cloth. Like they had done it a thousand times and would do it a thousand more, and had accepted it as a natural part of their lives. A ritual. I watched them and wondered at the secrets families keep. Teresa wanted me to find her father, but the man I was finding didn't appear to be the man she knew. And the man that I would eventually find would be different still. It is often that way in my line of work.

When the table was clean, Teresa came over, sat in the big chair, and gave me a smile. 'Would you like a cup of coffee?'

'No, thanks.'

'Well, if you change your mind.' Prim and proper. In absolute control of her environment, and of this meeting with the employee. 'Now, what have you found?'

Water was running in the kitchen. Winona's night to do the dishes. 'Has your father mentioned a man named Tre Michaels to you?'

She shook her head. 'No. No, I don't think so.'

'How about Wilson Brownell?'

She stared thoughtfully as if maybe this rang a bell, but then she shook her head. 'Unh-unh.' Charles skulked in from the dining room and leaned against the wall.

'Tre Michaels worked with your father. He saw your dad a couple of weeks ago, and your father said that he was thinking of taking a trip, but he didn't say where. At about that same time, your dad made five long-distance calls to Seattle and spoke with Wilson Brownell, twice at considerable length.' When I mentioned Seattle Teri and Charles glanced at each other, and Charles crossed his

53

arms. 'I phoned Mr. Brownell, but Brownell denied knowing your father. I think he's lying, and I think maybe your dad went to Seattle to see him. I'm going to fly up tomorrow to ask Mr. Brownell in person.' I didn't mention the drugs, or why Clark had been fired from Enright.

Teresa looked nervous. 'Why do you have to go to Seattle?'

'I told you why.'

She frowned harder. I thought she wanted to object some more, but you could tell that whatever her objections might be, her desire to find her father was stronger. 'Okay. I guess I should pay you some more money.'

I raised a palm. 'Forget the money. I'll take up that part of it up with your father when I find him.'

Charles was frowning, too. He seemed less happy about my going to Seattle than Teresa. She said, 'How long will you be gone?'

'Two days, maybe three. Less if I get what I'm after right away.'

They were watching me now, all big eyes.

'I've asked my partner to come over. His name is Joe Pike, and he'll be around if you need anything.'

Charles looked sulky. 'What are we gonna need? You think we're babies?'

'No, but I'll sleep better if I know there's someone to help you if you need it.'

The doorbell rang. Charles grabbed his knife and raced for the door. I said, 'Ask who it is.'

Charles threw open the door and there was Joe Pike, filling the frame, motionless. Pike is six-one, with long ropy muscles, short dark hair, and a face that gives you nothing unless you know him well. His arms are laced with veins, and bright red arrows had been tattooed onto the outside of his deltoids a long time ago. They point forward. He was wearing a gray sweatshirt with the sleeves cut off and blue Levis and bottomless black pilot's glasses. The glasses tilted toward Charles.

Charles dropped the knife and screamed, *'Run!'* He tried to slam the door, but Pike caught the door without effort, and gently pushed it open.

I said, 'Lighten up, Charles. This is Joe Pike. Joe works with me.'

Charles was leaning into the door with everything he had, making little sounds like 'Grr, grr, grr.'

Teresa snapped, *'Charles!'*

Charles jumped away from the door and ran past Winona into the kitchen, breathing hard. Winona was standing in the kitchen door, hands soapy and dripping, sniffling like she was about to cry.

Teresa said, 'It's okay, honey. He's one of the good guys.' She looked back at me and shook her head. 'We can take care of ourselves. We don't need a baby-sitter.' Charles peeked out from behind the door.

Joe Pike looked at the knife on the floor, then at the children, and then at me. 'Baby-sitter?'

I spread my hands. 'He won't live with you. He'll just be around, and you'll have his phone number. If there's anything you need, you can call him.' I looked at Joe. 'Right?'

Joe's head swiveled so that the flat black lenses angled my way. I thought he might be amused, but you never know.

Teresa's mouth set in a stubborn line. 'It's all right. We're fine.'

I said, 'Look, I'm not leaving you guys here alone. Joe will be outside, and he might drop in a time or two, and that's the way it has to be.'

Teresa wasn't liking it, but I wasn't giving her a lot of

55

choice. 'Well, I guess there isn't much I can do about it, is there?' Stiff.

I shook my head. 'No.'

Charles finished eyeing Joe and skulked out from behind Winona. 'Lemme see your gun.'

Pike picked up the serrated knife, flipped it into the air, then caught it by the blade. He looked at Charles, and Charles ducked behind Winona. Pike walked over and held out the knife. Handle first. 'Put this away before someone gets hurt.'

Charles took the knife and disappeared into the kitchen.

Pike turned to Teresa. 'It's a pleasure to meet you, Ms. Haines. My name is Joe.' He held out his hand and she took it. I think she blushed.

Winona smiled. 'My name's Winona.'

Pike glanced over at me and said, 'Go ahead and leave. We'll be fine.'

That Joe. To know him is to love him.

I left them like that in the deepening purple of twilight, and went home.

I approached my house with a suspicion I do not often feel and let myself in. The three drops of blood were still by the cat's door, and the quiet house still held an air of alienness that I resented. The cat slipped in through his cat door, sniffed the three drops, then snicked across the floor and sat by his bowl. Guess he had moved past it.

I gave him a can of Star Kist tuna, then opened the sliding glass doors that lead to my deck. The twilight air was cool and scented with wild sage. I put Jimmy Buffett on the CD player, then poured a glass of Cuervo Gold, had some, then went out to the side of my house and selected a fat green lime from the tree I planted two years ago. It went well with the Cuervo. My home had been invaded, and I could either let my feelings for the place be changed by that event or not, but either way would be my choice. The event is what you make of it.

I spent the next two hours cleaning both bathrooms and the kitchen and the floors. I threw out my toothbrush and opened a new one, and I washed the sheets and pillowcases and towels. I pulled the plates and the silver from the cupboards and drawers and loaded them into the dishwasher, and vacuumed the couch and the chairs and the carpets. I scrubbed the floors hard, and spent the remains of the day cleaning and drinking until, very early the next morning, I had once more made peace with my home.

I packed, then fell into a fitful sleep as Jimmy Buffett sang about Caribbean sunsets, over-the-hill pirates, and a world where fifteen-year-old girls didn't have to carry the emotional weight of their families.

Later that morning I went to Seattle.

CHAPTER 7

Seattle is one of my favorite cities, and I often think that if I did not live in LA, I might live there. Where the sky over Los Angeles is more often dimensionless and ill-defined, Seattle is capped by a continually redefined skyscape of clouds that makes the sky there a visibly living thing, breathing as it moves, cooling the city and its people with a protective cloak, and washing the air and the land with frequent rains that come and go in a way that freshens the place and its people. You can get the best coffee in America in Seattle, and browse in some of the best bookstores, and fish for silver and blackmouth salmon, and, until recently, the real estate prices were so low compared to those in Southern California that herds of Californians moved there. A friend of mine from Orange County sold her house and used the equity to buy a beautiful home on the water at Bainbridge Island. Cash. She used the balance of her equity to invest in mutual funds, and now she spends the bulk of each day painting in watercolors and digging for butter clams. So many Californians did this that property values in the Seattle area went through the roof and many native Seattleites could no longer afford to live in their own town. Whenever I visit I say I'm from Oregon.

I picked up a Ford Mustang and a street map from the Sea-Tac rental people, then followed Highway 509 north toward Elliot Bay and a seafood house I know that lies in the shadow of the Space Needle. I had a crab cake sandwich and fried new potatoes and mango iced tea for lunch, then asked a parking meter cop for directions to Wilson Brownell's address. With any luck, Brownell and Clark might be sitting around Brownell's place right now. With any luck, I might be on the next flight back to LA and not even have to spend the night. It happens.

Brownell lived across the Duwamish Waterway in an older, working-class part of West Seattle called White Center. It is a community of narrow streets and old apartments and wood-framed homes surrounding a steel mill. Young guys with lean, angry faces hung around near the mill, looking like they wished they could get work there. The ground floor of Brownell's building fronted the street with a secondhand clothing store, a place that refinished maritime metalwork, and a video rental place called Extreme Video. The video place was papered with posters of Jackie Chan and young Asian women tied to chairs with thousands of ropes. Extreme.

I missed Brownell's building twice because I couldn't find the building numbers, then found it but couldn't find a place to park. I finally left the car by a hydrant six blocks away. Flexibility in the art of detection.

Three young guys in T-shirts were hanging outside the video place when I got back, drinking Snapple. One of them was wearing a Seattle Mariners cap, and all of them were sporting black Gorilla boots and rolled-cuff jeans. A stairwell protected by an unlocked wire door had been carved from the corner of the building just past the metalwork place. There was a directory on the wall, and a row of mailboxes with little masking-tape tags for names and apartment numbers, only Brownell wasn't one of the names on the directory and the names on the masking tape had faded to oblivion. I said, 'Any of you guys know Wilson Brownell?'

The one with the cap said, 'Sure. He comes in all the time.'

'You know which apartment he's in?'

'I'm pretty sure it's apartment B. On the second floor.' You see how friendly it is in Seattle?

I took the stairs two at a time, then went along the hall looking for B. I found it, but the apartment across the hall was open and an older woman with frizzy hair was perched inside on an overstuffed chair, squinting out at me. She was clutching a TV remote the size of a cop's baton and watching C-Span. I gave her a smile. 'Hi.'

She squinted harder.

I couldn't hear anything inside Brownell's apartment. No radio, no TV, no voices making furtive plans, just the C-Span and street noises. It was an older building without air-conditioning, so there would be open windows. I knocked, and then I rang his bell.

The woman said, 'He's at work, ya dope.' Just like that, ya dope. 'Middle'a the day, any worthwhile man finds himself at work.' Eyeing me like that's where I should be.

She was maybe seventy, but she might've been eighty, with leathery ochre skin and salt and pepper hair that went straight up and back like the Bride of Frankenstein. She was wearing a thin cotton housecoat and floppy slippers and she was pointing the remote at me. Maybe trying to make me disappear.

'Sorry if I disturbed you.' I gave her my relaxed smile, the one that says I'm just a regular guy going about a regular guy's business, then made a big deal out of checking my watch. 'I could've sworn he said to come by at two.' It was six minutes before two. 'Do you know what time he's due back?' The World's Greatest Detective swings into full detection mode to fake out the Housebound Old Lady.

The squint softened, and she waved the remote. Inside, congressional voices disappeared. 'Not till five-thirty, quarter to six, something like that.'

'Wow, that's a lot later than I planned.' I shook my head and tried for a concerned disappointment. 'An old buddy of ours is in town and we're supposed to get together. I wonder if he's been around.' For all I knew Clark was inside asleep on the couch. You cast a line, you hope for a bite.

She made herself huffy. 'I wouldn't know. I don't spy on people.'

'Of course.'

'People come and people go. You're old and livin' alone, no one gives you the time a day.' She went back to C-Span, and now I could smell cat litter and turnips.

'Well, he's a little shorter than me, thinner, glasses, a hairline back to here.'

She turned up the sound and waved the remote. 'People come, people go.'

I nodded, Mr. Understanding, Mr. Of-Course-I-Wouldn't-Expect-You-to-Remember. Then I slapped my head and made like I'd just realized that I was the world's biggest moron. 'Jeez, he must've wanted me to meet him at work! I'll bet we're supposed to meet there, then go out! Of course!' The World's Greatest Detective employs the Relatable Human Failing technique in an effort to cultivate rapport.

The woman frowned at her television, then muted the sound again. 'What a bullshit story.'

'Excuse me?'

Her face cracked into a thin, angry smile that said she was as sharp as a straight razor, and if a guy like me didn't watch out she would hand back his head. 'If there's something you wanna know, just ask. You don't have to make up a bullshit story about old friends getting together. What a crock!'

I smiled again, but now the smile was saying, okay, you nailed me. 'Sorry about that.' Shown up by the Bride of Frankenstein.

She made a little shrug, like it wasn't a big thing. 'You hadda try, you just went too far with it. A guy making out as nice as you wouldn't be caught dead being friends with an asswipe like Will Brownell.' I guess they didn't get along. 'What's the real story?'

'Brownell's friend owes me six hundred dollars.'

She cackled and shook her head. 'I mighta known. Sooner or later it always gets down to money, doesn't it?'

'Uh-huh.' Everyone relates to greed. 'How about the guy I described? Has he been around?'

She made the shrug again, but it seemed sincere. 'That's not much of a description, young man. Could be anyone.'

'Fair enough. Can you tell me where Brownell works?'

'He works at some printing place.'

'New World Printing?'

'Maybe.' The other Seattle number that Clark had phoned.

I said, 'You won't tell Brownell that I was around, will you?'

She turned back to the television. 'What'd the sonofabitch ever do for me?' Nope, I don't guess they got along.

I went back down the stairs to the street and checked out the building. Two of the kids were gone, but the kid in the Mariners cap was sitting in the doorway to the video store on a wooden stool, inspecting a car magazine. The C-Span Lady's apartment was above the metalwork place at the front of the building, which meant Brownell's apartment was in the rear. I walked down to the end of the block, rounded the corner, then came up the service alley. A rickety fire escape ran up the back of the building to the roof like a metal spiderweb. I counted windows and visualized the location of the C-Span Lady's apartment so that I would know which windows belonged to Brownell. There were a lot of windows. Potted plants nested around some of the windows and drying clothes hung from the rails outside others, and a kid's tricycle rested on the fire escape outside still another. Figure that one. Brownell's windows were closed.

I used a Dumpster to reach the fire escape ladder, chinned myself to the rail, and let myself into Wilson Brownell's dining area. One should always lock one's windows, even in friendly cities like Seattle.

Clark Haines was not asleep on the couch. The apartment was quiet and warm from having been closed, and smelled of coffee and Jiffy Pop. The dining area opened into a living room ahead of me and a kichenette to my right. Beyond the kitchenette was a door that probably led to a bedroom and a bath. A vinyl couch and a mismatched chair filled one corner of the living room opposite a Sony Trinitron and a VCR. A coffee table was angled between the couch and the chair, scattered with magazines and a yellow rotary phone. A small pine table and three chairs sat in the dining area, along with an Ikea shelving unit showing a couple of plants, a bright orange goldfish in an oversized pickle jar, and some photographs of an African-American woman with a pretty smile. The woman looked young, but the photographs looked old, and I thought that the woman might now be, also. Precise, photo-realistic drawings of the woman had been framed and hung on the walls. They were signed *Wilson*, but in style and technique they looked exactly like the drawings that Clark Haines had done of his children.

You hope for the obvious: a sleeping bag and pillows

on the couch, a suitcase, a note stuck to the fridge saying 'meet Clark at 5,' anything that might indicate an out-of-town guest, or the location of same. Nada. A case of beer cooled in the fridge and the cabinets were filled with enough booze for a booksellers' convention, but that didn't mean Brownell had company. Maybe he was just a lush. The magazines turned out to be trade catalogs for commercial printing equipment and industry magazines with dog-eared pages and supply brochures. The marked pages all noted paper and ink suppliers in Europe and Asia. Four of the catalogs still had their mailing labels, and all of the labels were addressed to Wilson Brownell. A hot topic in most of the magazines seemed to be *Digital Micro-scanning Architecture for Zero Generation Loss*. Whatever that meant. I guess if you're a printer, you like to read about printing.

I took a quick peek in the bath, then went to the bedroom. Clark Haines wasn't there either. A neatly made double bed sat against the wall, along with a chest and a dresser and a drafting table. I glanced into the closet. One bed, one toothbrush, one set of toiletries, one used towel, no luggage or alternative bedding. More photographs of the same woman sat upon the chest and the dresser, only some of these showed a smiling African-American man. Wilson Brownell. An in-progress drawing was tacked down onto the drafting table, pen and ink, done with very fine lines, showing an almost photographic reproduction of the Seattle skyline. Wilson Brownell might be a lush, but he was also a gifted artist and I wondered if it was he who had trained Clark. Maybe Clark had come up here for art lessons.

I went through the nightstand and the chest, and was working through the dresser when I noticed a small Kodak snapshot wedged along the bottom edge of the dresser's mirror, half hidden behind yet more photographs of the woman. It was a color shot of two couples standing on a fishing pier, one of the couples Brownell and the woman, the other a much younger Caucasian couple. The Caucasian woman had dark wavy hair, pale skin, and glasses. She looked exactly like an older, adult version of Teresa Haines. She was smiling at the camera, and holding hands with a thin guy whose hairline was already starting to recede. I took down the picture and turned it over. On the back, someone had written: *Me and Edna, Clark and Rachel Hewitt*, **1986**. I looked at the picture again. The Caucasian woman had to be Teri's mother, and the man had to be Clark, only the name wasn't Haines, it was *Hewitt*.

I put the picture in my pocket, made sure everything else was like I had found it, then let myself out the window, walked around to the street, and once more climbed the stairs. The C-Span Lady's door was still open, and she was still shaking her remote at her television. Guess if I watched Congress all day I'd want to shake something, too.

I said, 'One more thing.'

Her eyes narrowed, and she muted the sound.

I held out the picture, and this time I didn't bother to smile. 'Is this one of the people who come and go?'

She looked at the picture, then she looked back at me. 'He owe you money, too?'

'Everybody owes me money. I have a generous nature.'

She held out her hand and brushed her thumb across her fingers. 'How about extendin' some'a that generosity my way?'

I gave her a crisp new twenty.

'He showed up a week ago, Thursday. Stayed a couple of days, then left. You shoulda heard all the carryin' on.'

'What do you mean?'

She made a sour face and waved the remote. 'Moanin' and cryin', moanin' and cryin'. I don't know what all was goin' on in there.' She made a little shudder, like she didn't want to know. 'I ain't seen him since.'

'Appreciate the help.'

She turned back to the C-Span and made the twenty disappear. 'Don't mention it.'

Sooner or later it always gets down to money.

CHAPTER 8

New World Printing was east of the Duwamish Waterway between Georgetown and Boeing Field in a tract of older industrial buildings that were built when red bricks and ironwork were cheap. The front of the building contained a fancy glass entrance and a receptionist who would pick up her phone and tell Mr. Brownell that a Mr. Cole wanted to see him. Considering Mr. Brownell's uncooperative response when I phoned, it was likely that Brownell would (at worst) refuse to see me, or (at best) be warned of my approach and therefore prepared to stonewall. This was not good. I have found that if you can surprise people in their workplace, they are often concerned with avoiding an embarrassing scene, and you can jam them into cooperating. This is advanced detective work at its finest.

I parked at the curb and walked around to the loading dock on the side of the building where two men were wrestling a dolly stacked with about ten thousand pounds of boxed paper into a six-wheel truck. 'You guys know where I can find Wilson Brownell?'

One of the men was younger, with a thick mustache and a hoop earring and a red bandana tied over his head like a skullcap. 'Yeah.' He pointed inside. 'Down the aisle, past the desk, and through the swinging door. You'll see him.'

'Thanks.'

I followed an endless aisle past shipping flats stacked

with boxes of brochures and magazines and pamphlets. I picked up two boxes and carried them with what I hoped was a purposeful expression, just another worker bee lugging paper through the hive.

A balding guy with a potbelly and tiny, mean eyes was sitting at the desk, talking to a younger guy with a prominent Adam's apple. The balding guy was thin in the arms and chest and neck, but his belly poked out beneath his belt-line as if someone had slipped a bowling ball in his pants. He squinted at me the way people do when they're trying to remember who you are, but then I was past him and through the swinging door and into a cavernous room filled with whirring, ka-chunking, humming machines and the men and women who operated them. A woman pushed a dolly past me and I smiled. 'Wilson Brownell?'

She pointed and I saw him across the room, standing at a large machine with two other people, one a kid in a KURT LIVES T-shirt, and the other a middle-aged guy in a suit. A large plate had been removed from the side of the machine so that they could see inside.

Wilson Brownell was in his early sixties, and taller than he looked in the pictures at his home. He was dressed in khaki slacks and a simple plaid shirt, with short hair more gray than not and black horn-rimmed glasses. Professorial. He was using a pen to point at something inside the machine. The guy in the suit was standing with his arms crossed, not liking what he heard. Brownell finally stopped pointing, and the suit walked away, still with crossed arms. Brownell said something to the younger guy, and the younger guy got down on the floor and began working his way into the machine. I walked over and said, 'Mr. Brownell?'

'Yes?' Brownell looked at me with damp, hazel eyes.

You could smell the booze on him, faint and far away. It was probably always with him.

I positioned myself with my back to the kid so that only Wilson Brownell would hear. 'My name is Elvis Cole. I've phoned you twice trying to find a man named Clark Haines.'

Brownell shook his head. 'I don't know anyone by that name.'

'How about Clark Hewitt?'

Brownell glanced at the kid, then wet his lips. 'You're not supposed to be here.' He looked past me. 'Did they let you in?'

'Come on, Mr. Brownell. I know that Clark phoned you six times from Los Angeles because I've seen his phone record. I know that he's been at your apartment.' He wasn't just stonewalling; he was scared. 'I'm not here to make trouble for you or for Clark. He walked out on his kids eleven days ago, and they need him. If he isn't coming home, someone has to deal with that.' Elvis Cole, detective for the nineties, the detective who can feel your pain.

'I don't know anything. I don't know what you're talking about.' He shook his head, and the booze smell came stronger.

'Jesus Christ, those kids are alone. All I want to do is find out if Clark's coming home.' You'd think I wanted to kill the guy.

He held up both hands, palms toward me, shaking his head some more.

'This isn't an earth-shaker, Wilson. Either I'm going to find Clark, or I'm going to turn his kids over to Children's Services, and they're going to take custody away from him. You see what I'm saying here?' I wanted to smack him. I wanted to grab him by the ears and shake him. 'Clark is going to lose his kids unless he talks to me, and you're going to be part of it.' Maybe I could guilt him into cooperating.

Wilson Brownell looked past me, and his eyes widened. The bald guy with the bowling-ball paunch was standing in the swinging doors, frowning at us. Brownell's face hardened and he stepped close to me. 'Do everybody a favor and get your ass out of here. I'd help you if I could, but I can't, and that's that.'

He turned away but I turned with him. 'What do you mean, that's that? Didn't you hear what I said about his kids?'

'I said I can't help you.' Wilson Brownell's voice came out loud enough so that the kid on the floor peeked out at us.

Two men had joined the bald guy in the swinging doors. They were older, with thin gray hair and wind-burned skin and the kind of heavy, going-to-fat builds that said they were probably pretty good hitters twenty years ago. The bald guy pointed our way and one of the new men said something, and then the bald guy started toward us. Brownell grabbed my shoulder like a man grabbing a life preserver. 'Listen to me, goddamnit.' His voice was a harsh whisper, lower now and urgent. 'Don't you mention Clark. Don't even say his goddamn name, you wanna walk outta here alive.' Wilson Brownell suddenly broke into a big laugh and clapped me on the shoulder as if I'd told him the world's funniest joke. He said, 'You tell Lisa I can get my own date, thank you very much! I need any help, I'll give'r a call!' He said it so loud that half of British Columbia could hear.

I stared at him.

The bald guy reached us, the two new guys still in the swinging door, watching through interested eyes. The bald guy said, 'I don't know who this guy is. He just walked in here.'

Brownell kept his hand on my shoulder, letting the laugh fade to a grin. 'Sorry about that, Donnie. I knew this guy was coming by, and I shoulda told you. He's a friend of mine.'

I glanced from Brownell to Donnie, then back to Brownell, wondering just what in hell I had walked into.

Brownell shook his head like, man, this was just the silliest thing. 'This guy's wife has been tryin' to set me up with this friend of hers for three months now. I keep sayin', what on earth am I going to do with a new woman when I'm still in love with my Edna?'

Donnie squinted the ferret eyes at me like he was deciding something. 'What, are you a mute or something? Don't you have anything to say?'

Brownell was looking at me so hard that his eyes felt like lasers. I shook my head. 'Nope.'

Donnie made his decision, then glanced back at the two guys in the swinging door, and shook his head once. The two guys vanished. 'You know better'n this.'

Brownell said, 'I'm sorry, Donnie. Jesus Christ.'

The tiny eyes flicked back to me, and then a smile even smaller than the eyes played at the edges of his mouth. 'C'mon, I'll show you the way out.'

I followed the bald guy out, got into my car, and drove to a Seattle's Best Coffee, where I bought a double-tall mochachino and sat there feeling confused, a more or less natural state. I had flown to Seattle expecting some difficulty in dealing with Wilson Brownell, but nothing like this. Wilson Brownell seemed stark raving terrified to mention Clark's name. In fact, Brownell seemed not only terrified of me but also of his fellow employees. Maybe there was something to it, or maybe Brownell was just a goofball suffering from some sort of paranoid psychosis. Goofballs are common. I could sit here and guess, but all I would have are guesses. I needed to ask

71

Wilson Brownell, and there were only two options: I could shoot my way back into New World and pistol-whip the information out of him, or I could wait and ask him when Wilson left work. The C-Span Lady had said that Brownell got home between five-thirty and a quarter to six, which meant that he probably left work between five and five-fifteen. It was now forty-three minutes after two, giving me two hours and twenty minutes to fill, and I decided to visit Rachel Hewitt's grave. If Clark had visited her grave, he might've left flowers. If he left flowers, there might be a florist's tag, and if there was a florist's tag, I might be able to get a line on Clark. A lot of ifs and maybes, but ifs and maybes define my life.

The Seattle's Best people let me use their Yellow Pages. Twelve cemeteries were listed in the greater Seattle, Mercer Island, and Bellevue area. I copied their numbers on a napkin, traded three dollar bills for quarters, and started dialing. The first four cemeteries I phoned did not have a Rachel Hewitt listed, but a woman who answered the phone at the fifth said, 'Why, yes, we do have a Rachel Hewitt as a client.' Client.

I said, 'Did you know Rachel Hewitt?'

'Oh, goodness, no.'

'You knew she was there without having to look it up.' She had said it that quickly.

'Oh, well, I had to look it up just last week for another gentleman. On a Monday, I believe. Yes, that's right, a Monday.'

'Over the phone, or in person?'

'Oh, he was here.'

I described Clark. 'Did he look like that?'

'Oh, no. Nothing like that. This gentleman was tall and blond, with short hair.'

I got directions, hung up, and eighteen minutes later I

pulled through the gate onto the grounds of the Rest-haven Views Cemetery and parked at the office. The woman I'd spoken with was older and sweet, and named Mrs. Lawrence. She showed me a large plot map of the grounds, and directed me to Rachel Hewitt's grave site. I said, 'The man last Monday, do you know who he was?'

'Oh, a friend or relative, I imagine. Like you.' Like me.

Rachel Hewitt had been laid to rest on the side of a grassy knoll near the western edge of the cemetery with a clear and pleasant view of Lake Washington. I left my car in the shade of a sycamore tree and walked north counting headstones. Rachel Hewitt's was the fifth headstone in, but the headstone was bare. Guess Clark hadn't been out, or if he had, he'd skipped the flowers.

I said, 'Well, damn.'

No flowers meant no lead.

Three cars were parked below me, and I could see people trudging among the graves, some sitting on the grass, some standing, one older gentleman in a lawn chair he'd brought, visiting old friends or loved ones. Above me, twin mausoleums stood on the crest of the hill with what would be sweeping views of the lake. Trees stood sentry around the mausoleums, lending shade, and a couple of cars were parked among the trees, one a faded tan pickup, the other a black Lexus. Someone was sitting in the Lexus, but they were so far away I couldn't see them clearly. Something flashed, and I thought they must be looking through field glasses. Admiring the view, no doubt. Enjoying another fine day with the dead.

I brushed at the headstone and took out the photo-graph that I'd taken from Brownell's apartment and again thought how very much Teri looked like her mother. I put the picture away and stared at Lake Washington and tried not to feel sour. No mean feat when you've spent your own money to fly a thousand miles to stand clueless beside a woman's grave. I was still confident that I could find Clark, but the odds that I could do it within a reasonable amount of time were diminishing, and I would need to do something about the kids. Of course, even if I found Clark, I was thinking that I still might have to call Children's Services. Clark wasn't shaping up as the World's Finest Dad. Rachel might not like it, but there you go. Maybe she should've done a better job of selecting their father.

I left the cemetery and drove south along the lake. It was a lovely afternoon, and the lake was flat. People Rollerbladed along the water and sunbathed on short strips of beach, and none of them were bummed because they had just visited a woman's grave.

I turned west at Seward Park and stopped at a red light next to a woman in a green Toyota. I smiled at her, and she smiled back. Friendly. Then I glanced in the mirror and saw a black Lexus two cars behind. It looked like the Lexus from the mausoleum, but I couldn't get a clear enough look at it to be sure. I said, 'Come on, Cole, you've got to be kidding. First LA and now Seattle?'

The woman in the green Toyota was staring at me. I looked away, embarrassed. 'Get a grip, Cole. Now you're talking to yourself.'

I snuck another glance, and now she locked her door.

The light changed and the Lexus stayed behind me, but two blocks later I slowed, and the Lexus sped by. A guy with a blond buzz cut was driving and a dark man who looked about as big as a Kodiak bear was in the passenger seat. Neither of them looked at me. I said, 'You see? It was nothing.'

The woman in the green Toyota passed me, too. Fast.

I parked a block and a half from the New World main gate at eighteen minutes before five. At five, employees started filtering out both on foot and in cars; at six minutes after, Wilson Brownell nosed out of the lot in a small yellow Plymouth hatchback. I let him get one block ahead, then I pulled out after him. He went west across the Duwamish directly to his apartment and parked at the curb in sight of the C-Span Lady's window. I pulled into the mouth of an alley a block away and waited for him to go into his building, but he didn't. He locked his car, then walked north to the next corner and disappeared. I left the car blocking the alley, trotted after him, and made it to the corner in time to see him go into a place called Lou's Bar. There was a case of beer and damn near a dozen bottles of booze in his apartment, but I guess he wanted to stop off for a couple before he went home for the serious drinking. Or maybe he just didn't want to be alone.

Wilson Brownell watched the bartender pour Popov vodka over ice as I entered. I waited for the bartender to finish and move away, then I took the stool next to Brownell. Two women were hunched together over a little table in the shadows, and three of us were at the bar, but the third guy was facedown on the wood. Brownell saw me and said, 'Jesus Christ.'

I looked serene. 'No, but we're often confused.'

'I got nothing to say to you.' Brownell tried to get up, but I hooked one of his feet behind the stool and pushed down hard on his shoulder, digging my thumb into the pressure point at the front of his neck. I didn't like being tough, but I was willing to if that's what it took to find Clark Hewitt and get his butt home to his kids. No one in the bar seemed to give a damn. He said, 'Ow. My goddamned neck.'

'Relax and I'll let go. If you try to get up, I'll knock you on your ass.'

He stopped trying to get up and I released the pressure.

As soon as I let go, he took a belt of the Popov. 'Goddamn. That hurt.'

I took out my wallet and opened it to the license. 'A fifteen-year-old girl who told me that her name was Teresa Haines gave me two hundred dollars to find her father.'

Brownell took another belt of the vodka.

'I have come up here at my own expense because Teresa, whose name I now discover is really Hewitt, and her two younger siblings have a missing father who has apparently abandoned them.'

Another belt.

'I have discovered that Clark Haines, whose name is also Hewitt, is a drug addict. I have discovered that Mr. Hewitt has come to Seattle, has spent time with his old friend, Mr. Brownell, but that Mr. Brownell doesn't give enough of a damn about these minor children to cooperate in helping me find their father.' I put away the wallet, then took out the picture of Brownell and Clark and their wives and put that on the bar.

The picture was creased from having been in my pocket. Brownell's jaw tightened. 'You went into my home.'

'Yes.'

His jaw flexed some more, then he picked up the picture and put it in his own pocket. He had more of the vodka, and I saw that his hand was shaking. 'You don't know a goddamn thing about anything.' His voice was soft and far away.

'I know Clark was with you.'

He shook his head, and the soft voice came again. 'You're in somethin' now you don't know anything about. If you're smart, you'll just go home.'

'So tell me and I'll go.'

He shook his head and tried to lift the Popov, but his

76

hand was shaking too badly. I didn't think it was shaking from the booze. 'I can't help you and I got nothing to tell you.' He blinked hard, almost as if he were blinking back tears. 'I love Clark, you see? But there ain't nothing I can do. I don't know where he went and you shouldn't be asking about him. I'm sorry about his children, but there ain't nothing I can do about that. Not one goddamned thing.' Brownell's hand shook so badly that the Popov splashed out the glass.

'Jesus Christ, Brownell. What in hell's got you so scared?'

The bar door opened and the blond guy from the Lexus came in. He was maybe six-two, with hard shoulders and sharp features and ice blue eyes that looked at you without blinking. He stepped out of the door to make room for his friend, and the friend needed all the room he could get: He was a huge man, maybe six-five, with great sloping shoulders, an enormous protruding gut, and the kind of waddle serious powerlifters get. His thighs were as thick as a couple of twenty gallon garbage cans. The buzz cut was wearing a blue sport coat over a yellow T-shirt and jeans, but his friend was decked out in a truly bad islander shirt, baggy shorts, and high-top Keds. The big guy had a great dopey grin on his face, and he was slurping on a yellow sucker. The buzz cut said, 'Willie.'

Wilson Brownell said, 'Oh, shit.' He knocked over his stool as he lurched from the bar, then hurried through a door in the rear. Gone. The bartender didn't look. The women didn't look. The guy sleeping on the bar stayed down.

The buzz cut and his friend came over. 'You are coming with us.' The buzz cut spoke the words with a careful, starched pronunciation that made me think of Arnold Schwarzenegger, only the accent was Russian.

'Sez who?' I can slay 'em with these comebacks.

The weightlifter reached under his shirt and came out with a Sig automatic. 'You'll come or we will shoot you.' He said it in a normal speaking voice, as if he didn't give a damn who heard. Another Russian.

I said, 'Have you guys been following me from Los Angeles?'

The weightlifter shoved me, and it felt like getting blindsided by a backhoe. 'Shut up. Walk.'

I shut up. I walked.

Maybe Wilson Brownell was right. Maybe I was in something deeper than I realized, and now it was too late to get out.

Isn't hindsight wonderful?

CHAPTER 9

The buzz cut held the door as the lifter walked me out, then followed behind us. The big guy let the gun dangle along his leg but made no effort to hide it. A woman with two kids came out of a bakery across the street, saw the gun, then grabbed her kids and stumbled back into the bakery. I said, 'Don't you guys know it's illegal to walk around with that thing?'

The big guy said, 'This is America. In America, you can do what you want.'

'I'd put it away if I were you. The cops will be here in seconds.' Maybe I could scare him into letting me go.

He made a little gesture with the gun, as if it were the gun shrugging, not him. 'Let them come.' Guess not.

'Who are you guys?'

The buzz cut shook his head. 'Nobody.'

'Where are we going?'

'To the car.' Everybody's a comedian.

The black Lexus was parked by a fire hydrant at the end of the block. This morning I was boarding a jet to fly to Seattle to find the missing father of three children in what should have been a no-big-deal job, and now I was being taken for a ride by two unknown Russian maniacs. I was willing to walk with these guys, but I did not want to get into the car. There are two crime scenes at every kidnapping. The first crime scene is where they snatch you, the second is where the cops find your body.

The lifter didn't seem to be paying a lot of attention,

but the buzz cut was looking at everything. He scanned the storefronts and alleys and roof lines, his ice blue eyes moving in an unhurried, practiced sweep. I wondered what he was looking for, and I wondered where he had picked up the habit. I said, 'Afghanistan.'

The ice blue eyes never stopped their search.

The big guy said, 'Da. Alexei was Spetnaz. You know Spetnaz?'

The ice blue eyes flicked at the big guy, and Alexei mumbled something soft in Russian. The big guy's eyebrows bunched like dancing caterpillars. Nervous. I guess he was scared of Alexei, too.

I said, 'I know Spetnaz.' Spetnaz was the former Soviet army's version of our Special Forces, but they were really more like Hitler's SS. Motivated zealots with a penchant for murder. 'That's a kind of Austrian noodle, isn't it?'

The ice blue eyes flicked my way, and Alexei smiled. The smile was wide and thin and empty. 'Da, that's right. A little noodle.'

I wondered how many Afghan kids had seen that smile before they died.

The big guy was walking behind me, but Alexei was maybe three paces back and to the side so that he wasn't between me and the gun. If I could put Alexei between me and the lifter, I could use him as a shield from the gun and perhaps effect an escape. Superman could probably do it, and so could the Flash. Why not me?

I slowed my pace, and almost at once Alexei slid sideways, brought up a Glock semiautomatic, and locked-out in a perfect two-hand combat stance. Guess they both had guns. He said, 'The car is safer, my friend.'

I showed him my palms and we went on to the car. So much for effecting an escape.

They put me in the front seat. Alexei got behind the wheel and the big guy got into the back. When he got in, the car tilted. Steroids. We started away and the big guy leaned forward and pushed a CD into the player. James Brown screamed that he felt good, and the big guy bobbed his head in time with the music. He said, 'You like James Brown, the king of soul?'

I looked at him.

Alexei said, 'Turn it down, Dmitri.'

Dmitri turned it down, but not very much. He made little hand moves with the music as if he were dancing, looking first out one side of the Lexus, then out the other, as if he wanted to take everything in and miss nothing. 'I enjoy the king of soul, and the Hootie and the Blowfish, and the Ronald McDonald's. Do you enjoy the Big Mac?'

I looked at Alexei, but Alexei wasn't paying attention. 'I prefer Burger King.'

Dmitri seemed troubled. 'But there is no special sauce.' He spoke Russian to Alexei.

Alexei shook his head, irritated. 'No. No special sauce.'

I said, 'Are you guys for real?'

The lifter said, 'What is that, 'for real'?'

Alexei pointed the Glock at me. 'This is real. Would you like to see?'

'No.'

'Then keep your mouth shut.'

Grump.

A light patter of rain began to fall, and Alexei put on the windshield wipers. We took the Alaskan Way Viaduct up past Elliot Bay into Ballard, then turned toward the water and bumped along an older part of the wharf to a warehouse at the edge of a pier. The warehouse, like the pier, was old and unkempt, with great rusted doors that slid along tracks and peeling paint and an air of poverty. Dmitri climbed out, pushed open the door, and we drove inside to park between a brand-new $100,000 Porsche Carrera and an $80,000 Mercedes SL convertible. Guess the air of poverty only went so far.

The warehouse was a great dim cavern that smelled of fish and rain and marine oil. Dust motes floated in pale light that speared down through skylights and gaps in the corrugated metal walls, and water dripped from the roof. Men who looked like longshoremen were driving forklifts laden with crates in and out of the far end of the warehouse, and did their best to ignore us. Alexei blew the horn twice, then cut the engine and told me to get out. A row of little offices was built along the side of the warehouse, and, with the horn, a pudgy guy with a cigarette dangling from his lips stepped out of the last office and motioned us over. We were expected.

The three of us went through the door into a shabby office in which it was even harder to see. The only light in the place came from a single cheap lamp sitting atop a file cabinet in the corner. Three men were around an oak desk that had probably been secondhand in the thirties, two of the men in their mid-fifties, the third maybe younger. The younger guy was the one who'd waved us in. I had hoped that maybe Clark would be there, but he wasn't. Probably just as well.

An empty folding chair was in the center of the room. The pudgy guy gestured at it and said something in Russian. Alexei said, 'For you.'

'I'll stand, thanks.'

Alexei glanced past me to Dmitri and then an M-80 went off in my ear. I rocked sideways and went down to one knee, then felt myself put into the chair. Alexei leaned toward me. 'No more jokes, now.' His voice was far away. 'That was a slap, do you see? If Dmitri closes his hand, it will kill you.'

'Sure.' His face tilted crazily first to one side, then the other, and I thought I was going to throw up.

A fourth man entered, this guy a little shorter than the others, but wider, and hard to see when your eyes are blurring. He was in his fifties, with crinkly gray hair and a florid face and a dark blue shirt open at the neck to show a lot of grizzled chest hair. He was also holding a McDonald's soft drink cup. Large. I guess that's where Dmitri got it from.

When the new guy entered the other men stood, and murmured greetings of respect. The new man spoke more Russian, and Alexei handed over my wallet. The new man put his cup down and sat on the edge of the desk to look through my wallet. Deciding my fate, no doubt.

I rolled my head one way, then the other. The disorientation was beginning to pass, but the soft tissue around my ear felt tight and hot.

The new guy finished going through my wallet, then tossed it to the floor. His eyes were tired and lifeless and uncaring. Just what you want to see when you're being held in a chair by a four-hundred-pound Russian with steel fingers. The new man said, 'I am Andrei Markov.'

'All right.' He spoke pretty good English.

'Where is Clark Hewitt?' It hung like a chime tone in an empty room. All of this was about Clark.

'I don't know.'

Markov nodded and the steel fingers tightened into my shoulders like pliers. Alexei backhanded me with the Glock and a starburst of pain erupted from my other ear. Some days suck. Some days you shouldn't even get out of bed. I said, 'Who is Clark Hewitt and why is he so important?'

Markov said, 'Tell me where he is, or I will kill you.'

83

'I don't know.' My ears were ringing. I shook my head to stop the ringing but the shaking made it worse.

Another nod, and this time Alexei hammered back the Glock and pressed it hard into my neck. Dmitri stepped back to get clear of the splatter.

I said, 'I've never seen Clark Hewitt, and I don't know where he is. I don't know anything about him.'

Markov said something to Alexei and Alexei answered in Russian. Markov said, 'Do not lie. You were asking about him. You were at his wife's grave.'

'His name came up in something I'm working on so I came up here to find out about him.'

'What thing?'

'I'm trying to find a drug importer from San Francisco. Before he disappeared he said he was going to buy some dope in Seattle off a connection named Clark Hewitt. I came up here to find out.' Good lying is an art.

Markov stared at me some more, thinking about what I had said, trying to decide whether or not he believed me and how far to take this if he didn't. The Glock hovered like a living thing three inches from my left ear. I thought that I might be able to block it away and drive up into Dmitri, and if I was lucky I might be able to live another ten seconds.

Far away a dog barked. Deep and throaty and coming closer.

I said, 'I don't know Hewitt. I don't know you guys. What in hell is going on here?'

The phone rang, and the man to Markov's right answered it and listened without speaking. He put down the phone and said something and Markov's steady eyes wavered.

Something was happening out in the warehouse. The dog sounded closer now, and men were moving and there were voices. Markov murmured more Russian. The

Glock disappeared and Alexei stepped away and the barking came to the door. A guy in a suit stepped inside, holding out a federal badge, and announced, 'Federal Marshal.' He was a tall guy and the suit fit well. He glanced at me, then came over and jabbed a finger into Dmitri's chest. 'Step back, fatso.'

Dmitri squinted at Markov, and Markov nodded. Dmitri stepped back.

The guy in the suit looked at me. 'You okay?'

'Do I look okay?'

'We'll get you some ice.' He turned back to Markov. 'My name is Special Agent Reed Jasper, United States Federal Marshal. The men behind me are with United States Customs. They have some paperwork they'd like to discuss with you.' A powerfully built guy wearing an assault suit and a Browning 9mm was outside the door with the dog, and the dog was straining to get into the room. It was a big, muscular mix, maybe shepherd and Akita, and it looked like it wanted to bite. Behind him, other men were moving through the warehouse.

Andrei Markov spread his hands. 'I am always happy to cooperate with the authorities, Special Agent.'

I said, 'My name is Cole. I'm a private investigator from Los Angeles. These men brought me here against my will and assaulted me. I'd like to press charges.'

Jasper put away his badge, then picked up my wallet and lifted me off the chair as the guy with the dog came in. Jasper never again looked at the Russians, but kept all his attention on me, as if I was the reason he had come and the Russians were now someone else's problem. He said, 'You'll live.'

'I said that I want to press charges.'

'Sure.' He led me out of the room.

Maybe a dozen federal agents were moving through the warehouse. There were a couple more dog handlers in assault suits, but most were wearing blue rain shells that said POLICE – *U.S. Customs*. Jasper led me past them without another word and out into the rain. Maybe Jasper could tell me what was going on. Maybe Jasper could tell me why Clark Hewitt was so important, and why I had been grabbed, and why Andrei Markov had come maybe three seconds from blowing my brains out. I said, 'Man, am I glad to see you guys.'

Jasper said, 'You won't be.'

'What does that mean?'

A guy in a blue shell was waiting beside a nondescript government G-ride. 'Is this the dude?'

Jasper tossed him my wallet. 'Yeah.'

The new guy slipped my wallet into his pocket without looking at it, then went around and climbed in behind the wheel. His blue shell said MARSHAL. I said, 'Would you guys tell me what's going on?' I seemed to be saying it a lot, and no one seemed willing to answer.

Jasper pushed me against his ride, pulled my hands behind my back, and cuffed me. 'You're under arrest, asshole. If you know any good lawyers, you'd better get ready to call 'em.'

Wilson Brownell had been right. I had stepped into something deep, and now I was drowning.

CHAPTER 10

The rain came harder, raging at the G-ride as we made our way southeast across Seattle to the Federal Court Building. Jasper mumbled at the driver a couple of times and the driver mumbled back, but neither of them mumbled to me. The driver's name was Lemming.

First irate Russian thugs, now irate federal cops. Maybe Rod Serling was next.

The rain vanished as we slid beneath the building into the parking garage. We didn't bother with a parking spot; Lemming stopped the car at the elevator where a bald African-American agent was waiting with the elevator locked open. He was wearing a plastic security ID that said SCULLY, WILLIAM P. 'That him?'

'Yeah.'

He stepped into the elevator and unlocked the doors. 'Get his ass upstairs.'

I said, 'If you're Scully, where's Mulder?'

No one answered. Guess they didn't watch the *X-Files*.

They hustled me up to the sixth floor, then along a general issue federal hall as if I were a presidential candidate with an active death threat against him. We went through a door that said UNITED STATES MARSHALS, and into a department room with maybe half a dozen desks and four more agents gathered at one of the desks, talking. Scully took a bag of blue ice from a little fridge by the coffee machine, uncuffed me, then told me to put the blue ice on my eye. 'Put'm in the cold room.'

I said, 'I think I need medical attention. How about calling nine-one-one?'

'Keep the ice on it.'

They brought me to a small room with a table, four chairs, and no windows. Lemming put me in the far chair and said, 'Sit.'

'How about a lawyer?'

'Sit.'

I sat. Jasper sat at the table across from me, but Scully and Lemming stayed on their feet. Scully whispered something to Lemming, and Lemming left. Jasper said, 'First, I want you to know that we're holding you for questioning. We do not plan to file charges against you at this time, but we reserve the option to do so at a later time.'

'Questioning about what?'

'The murder of a federal officer.'

'Come again?'

Scully said, 'Why are you looking for Clark Hewitt?'

I looked at him. First Markov, now these guys. I looked from Scully to Jasper, then back to Scully. They were staring at me the way a circling hawk eyes a field mouse just before she folds her wings and slips down through the air to feed. I said, 'I'm sorry, I didn't catch that name.'

Scully said, 'Knock off the bullshit. We ask, you answer.'

I grinned at him. 'Is that the way it works, Scully?'

'Yeah. That's the way it works.' My eye was burning and flushed with blood. I put the blue ice on it.

Jasper said, 'Who are you working for?'

'I just went through this with Markov. I didn't like it then either.'

'Tough.'

Scully said, 'How do you know Markov?'

'I don't. Two goons scooped me off the street and brought me to see him.'

Scully glanced at Jasper, and Jasper said, 'Alexei Dobcek and Dmitri Sautin.'

Scully looked back at me. 'Why?'

'So they could ask the same questions you people are asking.'

'What'd you tell them?'

'The same thing I'm telling you.'

'It might go easier if you were more cooperative.'

'You might get more cooperation if you told me what was going on.' I'd had enough, and my voice was getting loud. My back was tight and my cheek and ear were throbbing, and the blue ice had lost its cold. I didn't know why any of this was happening, and the not knowing made me feel like a chump. I had flown up on my own nickel to find a runaway dad, only nothing appeared to be quite what I had thought it was, and that made me feel like a chump, too.

I put the ice packet on the table and stood. 'If you're going to charge me, then do it. If you're going to keep me, I want a lawyer.'

'Sit down.'

I looked at Scully. 'No, Scully, I don't think so.'

Jasper stood and leaned across the table at me. 'Get in the goddamned chair.' Yelling.

'You're going to have to put me in the chair, and it's not going to be as easy as you're thinking.' I didn't shout. I was proud of myself for not shouting.

Jasper started to move around the table, but Scully caught him. 'Reed.'

Jasper stood there, breathing hard. I was breathing hard, too, but I was tired of getting shoved around and kept in the dark. Something was going on and everybody seemed in on it but me. I was seeing bits and pieces of it,

89

and I wasn't liking what I was seeing, but I knew there was still more to the picture. Maybe it was time to start sulking. Maybe I could phone Charles for a couple of pointers and sulk these guys into submission. Or maybe Jasper would try to put me in the chair and I could get in two or three good shots before half a dozen federal marshals boiled through the door and rode me down. Might be worth it.

Scully, William P., had stared at me for what seemed like an hour when the door opened and Lemming whispered something in his ear. Scully listened without saying anything, then nodded and the tension seemed somehow lessened. 'Hang on for a minute.'

He patted Jasper's shoulder and the two of them stepped out with Lemming, but now I was feeling better about things. I was probably thirty seconds away from being thrown into jail, but you always feel better when you tough off to a guy.

Three minutes later Scully and Jasper came back without Lemming. Jasper had a nine-by-twelve manila folder and Scully had two Styrofoam cups of coffee and a baggie filled with fresh ice. Scully tossed me the ice, then put one of the cups by me on the table. He sipped from the other. 'We came on too strong and that was a mistake.' He gestured at the envelope. 'The office down in LA faxed up some information on you. You seem like a square guy, Cole, so let's take a step back and start again.'

'I'm listening.' I put the ice where the Glock had bitten me.

Scully said, 'Andrei Markov is looking for Clark Hewitt to kill him. We're looking for Clark to protect him. That's the difference between us and Markov.'

I looked at him without responding. The tough detective refusing to cut them any slack. Or maybe I was just the sulky detective. 'Don't tell me: Clark Hewitt used to be involved with Markov, but he turned state's evidence, and now he's in witness protection.'

Jasper smiled, but there wasn't a lot of humor in it. 'What else do you know?'

'I don't know any of it, Jasper, but I'm a hell of a guesser. Markov wants Hewitt, and so do you. You aren't the cops or the Treasury or the FBI. You guys are U.S. Marshals, and the marshals oversee the federal witness protection program.' I moved the ice to my ear and leaned back. 'And since you guys don't seem to know Clark's location, that means you've lost him.'

Reed Jasper frowned. 'We didn't lose him, goddamnit. He left. You don't have to stay in the program once you're in. You can leave any damn time you want.'

Scully said, 'Did Markov have any idea as to Clark's location or current identity?'

'Nope. That's what he wanted from me.'

'How'd he pick you up?'

'They had someone on Rachel Hewitt's grave.'

Scully whistled. 'Jesus Christ, three years and they're still on that place.' He shook his head. 'When that Russian swears an oath, he means it.'

I said, 'Who's Markov?'

Jasper said, 'Markov is a big macher in the Ukrainian mob. He came over here a few years ago with his brother, Vasily. Vasily was the boss. They set up shop and began expanding the business, and one of these new ventures was printing counterfeit dollars to ship back home and sell on the Ukrainian black market.'

I nodded. Clark the printer. Clark the artist. 'Clark was a counterfeiter.'

Scully said, 'Yeah.'

'So what happened between Clark and Markov?'

'Vasily thought Clark was skimming his print and

laying it off on a couple of locals. Clark got word that Vasily was planning to bump him off, and came to us for help.'

'He turned state's evidence to buy into the program.'

'Didn't have a lot of choice. The Markovs never made a threat they didn't carry out.'

'Was Clark skimming?'

Jasper shrugged. 'Who knows? Because of Clark, Vasily's doing twelve to twenty on Mercer Island, and Andrei swore he'd spend the rest of his life hunting down Clark and his family, and that's what he's doing. It's been three years, and he's still got people on it. Now you show up, and he sees you as a lead back to Clark.' Great.

I said, 'If Clark went into the program, how come you guys lost track of him?'

Jasper stared at me for a time, then wet his lips and looked away.

Scully made a little mouth move as if his lips had gone dry, too. 'The night we brought Clark in things went bad. Middle of the night, raining, we were going to put him and his kids into a safe house, then begin the relocation. We told him not to worry. We told him it was safe.'

I was watching him. 'Only it wasn't safe.'

Jasper's eyes narrowed and he looked back at me. 'Somehow Markov's people found out. We had everything in the truck, we were five minutes from driving away, and they surprised us.' He stopped and stared past me some more and I wondered if he wasn't reliving that night. 'My partner was a guy named Dan Peterson. He was killed.'

Scully said, 'Go get some water, Reed.'

Jasper shook his head.

I said, 'You couldn't get Markov for the shooting.'

Jasper sucked a breath, then focused on me. 'Peterson ordered me to get Clark and those kids out of the kill zone, and that's what I did. He stayed. I didn't see it, and I still don't know for sure what happened. SPD moved on our call. They found Danny inside. He'd been shot in the backyard, then dragged himself in.' He shook his head again. 'We never had a name or a face, but we know it was Markov.' He shook his head some more. 'Everything went wrong that night. It shouldn't have happened.'

Scully said, 'We finished the relocation, but Clark never trusted us after that. He changed his name as soon as they got to the relocation city and the whole family disappeared.' He shrugged yet again. 'That's his choice, of course. You don't have to stay in the program.'

Jasper made a little wave, then suddenly sat straighter, folding his feelings and putting them away. Every cop I've ever known could do that when he or she had to. 'And now you show up, asking about Clark Hewitt.'

Scully nodded. 'A guy from Los Angeles.'

I stared at Reed Jasper, and then at William P. Scully, and then I thought about Teri and Charles and Winona, waiting for Clark to come home. I wondered how much of this they knew, and I thought they must know some of it. Probably why they weren't thrilled about my coming to Seattle. I thought how terribly afraid they must be of losing him to risk bringing me into their affairs. I thought about what it must've been like for them three years ago, and what it must be like to live a life defined by secrets and lies. Secrets never stay secret, do they? Not even when you want them to. Not even when lives are at stake.

I looked Scully squarely in the eyes and spread my hands. 'I don't know where Clark is, or his kids, or anything about him.'

Jasper stared at me, and you could see he didn't believe me. Neither did Scully. 'Look, Cole, it's not our job to protect him anymore, but we feel what you might call a sense of obligation, you see?'

I smiled my best relaxed grin, and said, 'Man, this has to be one of the world's biggest screw-ups.' I told him the exact same story I'd told Andrei Markov. 'I came here looking for a drug connection named Clark Hewitt. I was just following a name, and the name's the same, but my guy doesn't have anything to do with Russians or counterfeiting or any of this other stuff.' I let the grin widen, like I was enjoying the enormous coincidence of it all. 'All of this is news to me.'

Scully nodded, but you could tell he didn't believe me. 'Who are you working for?'

'You know I'm not going to tell you. The card says confidential.'

'This is important, Cole. Clark is in grave danger. So are those kids.'

I shrugged. They had been in grave danger three years ago, too.

Scully said, 'I think you know something. I'm thinking maybe Clark left some footsteps in LA, and if I'm thinking it, Markov will be thinking it, too.'

I shrugged again. 'I'd help you if I could.'

Special Agent Reed Jasper nodded and stood. You could tell he didn't believe me, but there wasn't anything he could do about it. 'Sure.'

'Can I go?'

Scully opened the door. 'Get the hell out of here.'

It was twenty-two minutes after eleven that night when I walked out of the federal courthouse into a hard steady rain. The rain, like the air, was warm, but now felt oppressive rather than cleansing. Maybe that was me.

The world had changed. It often does, I've found, yet

the changes are still surprising and, more often than not, frightening. You have to adjust.

I had come to Seattle to find a man named Clark Haines, and in a way I had, though that no longer seemed to matter. What mattered was those kids, alone in a house with a Russian mobster wanting them dead.

My left cheek was tight and discolored the next morning where Alexei Dobcek hit me. I had been up most of the night, trying to keep ice on my cheek, but the ice had been too little, too late, and I felt grumpy and discouraged, though not very much of it had to do with the ice. I packed my things, brought the rental car back to Sea-Tac, and boarded the plane. Grumpy.

A sandy-haired flight attendant in her early thirties clucked sympathetically and said, 'Rough week?'

I grumped.

She put her fists on her hips. 'Pouting won't help.'

These flight attendants are something.

I settled in beside an overweight man with very short hair and glasses so thick that his eyes looked the size of BBs. He smiled, but I didn't smile back. Tough.

I crossed my arms, frowned real hard, and thought about Teri and Winona and Charles as we lifted up through the northwest cloud layer into a brilliant clear sunshine that stretched from southern Washington to the tip of the Baha Peninsula and the Sea of Cortez. Maybe it would help if I stuck out my lower lip. I had flown to Seattle to find an ordinary missing father, and instead had found that Clark Haines was really Clark Hewitt, and that Clark Hewitt, along with being a drug addict, was a criminal, a former participant in the federal witness protection program, and was actively being sought by both the Russian mob and various federal law enforcement agencies. These are not good things to discover, and were even less good when one considered that, if the mobsters were after Clark, they would also be after his children. For all I knew, Clark Hewitt was dead and would never return, or, if he wasn't dead, perhaps had no interest in returning. I thought that maybe I could get his kids into foster care without revealing their true identities, but this somehow seemed to leave them more vulnerable and exposed. The obvious solution was to take them to the police, identify them by their original names, and allow Jasper and Scully to see to their well-being. Charles and Winona and Teri would still end up in foster care, only an awful lot of people would know who and where they were, and the more people who knew, the greater the possibility that word would get back to the Markovs. This was yet another problem, and all these problems were making me grumpier still. Maybe I should try to get into a problem-free occupation of some kind. Hunting lions, maybe. Or raising the *Titanic*.

The flight attendant stood over me. 'Are we feeling any better yet?'

I stared at her, and then I sighed. 'Is it that obvious?'

'Mm-hm. Could I bring you a nice cup of tea?'

'A cup of tea would be fine.'

She brought the tea, a couple of Tylenol, and a reassuring smile. Two hours and fifty minutes later we let down through a cloudless cathedral of sky and faint orange haze into the wonderland that is Southern California. I still wasn't sure what I wanted to do, but I felt better about not knowing. The attendant smiled a good-bye at the door. 'You look much better.'

'I've achieved a measure of peace with my uncertainty.'

'Sometimes that's the best we can do.' I guess you

develop a certain wisdom when you spend your life at thirty-five thousand feet.

I kissed her hand, then picked up my car from long-term parking, and made the drive up through the city to Teresa Hewitt's house.

It was after three when I arrived, and that meant Charles and Winona would be home. I would've preferred to speak with Teri alone, but there you go. *Tell me, Winona, can you spell 'foster care'?*

I parked at the opposite curb, crossed to their front door, and rang the bell. I couldn't see Joe Pike or his Jeep, but I waved to him anyway. He would be someplace near, and he would be watching. Unobtrusive.

The Saturn was in the drive, and I figured that Charles would throw open the door and we'd go through the same opera again, but this time it wasn't Charles. This time it was a half-bald guy two inches shorter than me with faded hair and skinny arms and glasses. I said, 'You're a hard guy to find, Mr. Hewitt.'

Clark Hewitt made a soft smile that seemed confused. 'I'm sorry, but my name is Haines. I don't use the other name anymore.' He said it as if there were no value to its secrecy, or, if there had been, he'd forgotten. He was heavier now than in the picture with Rachel and the Brownells, and somehow less distinct. He was wearing a loose cotton shirt and ValuMart chinos and brush-burned Hush Puppies that were screaming for a retread. Winona ran up, grabbed him around the legs with an *oomph!*, and looked at me. 'Hi, Elvis. Our daddy's home!'

'Hi, Winona. So I see.' *Can you spell 'reunion'?*

She dangled one of those ugly little trolls that kids have. It had purple hair and a horrible leer. 'You see what my daddy brought me?'

I nodded.

'It's a key chain.'

98

Clark Hewitt beamed at her and patted her head. 'Because she always has the key to my heart.'

Winona giggled, and I wanted to shoot him. Clark looked back at me, and said, 'You must be the detective! Please come in.' The detective.

The house smelled of fresh coffee and baked cookies, and, as we entered, Teresa came out of the kitchen carrying a plate heaped with the cookies. Charles peeked out of the hall that led back to the bedrooms, scowling and hunched, with his hands jammed into his pockets. He didn't look happy, and he didn't come out. Lurking. Teri said, 'I left a message on your machine. Daddy came home this morning.'

'I just got back. I haven't checked my messages.'

Clark Hewitt made himself comfortable in his easy chair. I didn't sit. 'Were you on a trip?'

'Seattle. I guess we just missed each other.'

'Ah. Seattle is a wonderful city, but I haven't been there in years.' He gestured at the cookies. 'Teri baked these cookies, Mr. Cole. Won't you have some?'

Teri said, 'Chocolate chip raisin.'

She held the plate close to Clark, who bent to smell. 'Ah! My favorite!'

Clark beamed at Teri and Teri beamed at Clark. Winona beamed at everyone. Charles stayed back in the hall and glowered, but that was Charles. Maybe this wasn't the Hewitt house. Maybe my plane hadn't really landed in Los Angeles, but had somehow jumped dimensions and brought me to an alternate Los Angeles and these people were the Bradys.

I stayed on my feet, and I didn't take the cookies. 'Clark, you and I need to talk.'

He selected a fat, round cookie and settled back in the chair. 'Mmm.'

'Clark.'

99

Winona perched on the couch and Teresa put the plate on the coffee table near her father. 'Come out here, Charles, and have a cookie with Daddy.'

Charles made a single cough. 'Eff'm.'

Teresa's face flashed into a hard white mask, and her voice came out as rough as a rat-tail file. *'Charles.'*

Charles coughed again, stomped down the hall, and slammed his door. Daddy might be home, but I guess everything wasn't hunky-dory with the Bradys.

Clark chewed and swallowed and smacked his lips as if he hadn't heard. Maybe he lived in one world and they lived in another and the two worlds overlapped only on occasion. 'I'm sorry the kids bothered you with all of this, Mr. Cole, but it's my fault they were worried. A business opportunity came up and I had to leave on such short notice that I couldn't get home to explain.'

'Such short notice that you left three underage children to fend for themselves.' No one had mentioned my face. No one had asked about the swelling or the bruise.

He eyed the plate for another cookie. 'Well, I tried phoning, but I always called at the wrong time.'

Teresa said, 'He phoned during the day when I was out.'

'You told me you don't go out.'

She frowned. 'Well, to the market and to pick up the kids. You know.'

Clark snagged a second cookie. 'I guess I should've tried more often, but there was so much to do.'

Winona said, 'We're going to be rich. We're going to buy a house and a Sega and a really big TV.'

Clark chuckled. 'Well, let's not buy that house just yet, but life is certainly looking up. Yes, it is.' He gave Winona a hug and smiled at Teri, but Teri wasn't looking at him. She was looking at me. He said, 'Our luck is about to change, and, boy, we deserve it. I'll be printing documents for a group of international investors with a long-term contract. A contract spells job security. None of this seasonal employment. No more of this moving every few months.' He tickled Winona and she giggled. 'We'll be able to buy our own home and settle down and not move around so much. Won't that be good, Teri?'

Teri nodded without looking at him. 'Yes sir. Yes, it will be good to stay put.'

Winona twirled the little troll. 'Can I have my own room? I want my own room!'

Clark laughed. 'Well, we'll see.'

I stared at Teri, and Teri stared back. Her lips were a thin tight line and her eyes fluttered and she mouthed the words 'Well, we'll see' as if they'd had this conversation a thousand times, and she knew deep in her soul that it was just talk, that the money would never come, and they would move and move and move. Then she seemed to get the fluttering under control and said, 'Would you like a cup of coffee?'

I said, 'Clark, could I see you outside, please?'

Clark said, 'It's hard being a single parent, but these little guys are just such a help. Their mother would be so proud.' Maybe he hadn't heard me. Maybe he was so filled with wonderful plans and the intricacies of big deals that the words had just flown right past him. Or maybe he was high.

I leaned toward him. 'Markov.'

Clark's eyes focused for the first time, and he stood. 'Well, kids, I'm sure Mr. Cole is very busy, so I'll see him out to his car. Everybody say good-bye.'

Teri and Winona said good-bye, and Clark followed me out to my car. The heat had risen and the sun was bright and hot and the grass on the front lawn looked wilted and spotty. A stocky Hispanic woman walked past on her way up to Melrose. She carried a shopping bag in one hand and used the other to shield her eyes from the sun. She did not look at us. 'Clark, I know who you were and what you did. I was in Seattle. I spoke with Wilson Brownell and a U.S. Federal Marshal named Reed Jasper. I also met Andrei Markov. I did not tell Jasper where you were, or what name you were living under, though I think you should contact him.'

Clark Hewitt was shaking his head before I finished. 'I couldn't do that. I don't want anything to do with those people.'

'The Markovs suspect that there's some kind of connection between us, and they know I'm from Los Angeles. That means they might show up here, nosing around, and even if they don't they're still out there, waiting. Jasper wants to help.'

Clark raised a hand as if I were telling him about a great place to buy discount tires but he was about to tell me of an even better place, his discount-tire secret. 'Thank you, but everything is going to be fine. We're going to leave soon.'

'You should leave *now*, Clark. If you don't have the money, call Jasper. He'll help. So will I.'

Clark shook his head.

'Are you high?'

He blinked at me, then shook his head. 'Oh no. I don't do that.'

I took a breath and let it out. I wanted to shout at him to knock off the bullshit, but Winona and Teri were standing in the front door, watching us. I said, 'I know why you lost the job at Enright Printing. I spoke with Tre Michaels.'

He didn't answer. He was pale, with dark lines under his eyes, and he looked tired. His eyes seemed sad, and I thought he might cry. 'Are you going to tell?'

'Of course not.' Like we were six years old.

Clark Hewitt's eyes filled and he blinked fast. 'Please don't tell.'

My head hurt and my scalp felt tight and the tightness was moving down to my neck. 'Do your children know about any of this?'

He shrugged.

'Do they know what you were, and why you move around so much?'

Another shrug.

'They must know something, Clark. It was only three years ago. You changed their names.'

He looked at the ground. Talk about denial.

Charles appeared in the window, stuck out his tongue, and gave us the finger with both hands. He seemed to be looking more at his father, but maybe it was the angle. 'Clark, I can help you get into a substance abuse program. There are people at the county and at a couple of private places I know who can help. You've got these kids to think about.'

Clark glanced at Teri and Winona. He smiled at them like we were discussing the weather. 'We'll be fine. Everything is going to be okay real soon. I won't leave them again.'

I took out a card and wrote a name and number on it. 'I want you call this number and speak with a woman named Carol Hillegas. If you don't enroll in a program I'm going to call Children's Services. Do you see where I'm going with this?'

Clark took the card, but didn't look at it. 'I understand. I won't leave them again.'

'Clark.'

'Everything's going to be fine. I'll call and I promise I won't leave them again.' He reached into his pocket and came out with an enormous fold of cash. 'I want to apologize for the trouble, and I want to thank you again for taking care of my children. I think you deserve a bonus.'

I stared at him.

He fumbled with the bills, riffling through a roll of hundreds that was even larger than Teri's. 'It's the least I can do.'

Teri noticed Charles in the window and said something. Charles gave us the finger still harder, and started crying. Teri disappeared from the door, reappeared in the window, and grabbed Charles by the arm. He shoved her and ran, and she chased him. She was crying, too. Winona was still in the door, smiling and oblivious and waving. Her face was filled with light.

I said, 'Just call the goddamned number.'

Clark Hewitt was still fumbling with his bonus money when I crossed the street, climbed into my car, and drove away.

CHAPTER 12

Fourteen minutes after leaving the Hewitts, I carved my way through the trees along Woodrow Wilson Drive, then turned onto my little road and saw Joe Pike. Pike's Jeep was parked at the front of my house, and Pike was leaning against the rear hatch, as motionless as a tree or the house or the earth. I put my Corvette in the carport, and met him at the kitchen door. Pike said, 'Nice eye.' No hello, no hey, are you all right? 'Clark do that?' You can always count on your friends for humor.

'How long you been here?'

'I left my position when you and Haines came out of the house.' You see? He'd seen everything.

I let us in, put my overnight bag on the kitchen counter, took two Falstaffs out the fridge, gave one to Pike, then drank a long pull of mine.

I turned on the kitchen tap and cupped the water to my face. I drank most of what was left of the beer, then took a deep breath and let it out. I had pulled the drapes when I left, and the house was dim and still from the close air. Dim and still was good. When it was dark it was easier to pretend that there weren't three kids on the run from the Russian mob with a junkie for a father. Maybe that was why Pike never took off his dark glasses. Maybe it was easier when you couldn't see so much.

Pike said, 'What's wrong?'

'His name isn't Haines. It's Hewitt, and he isn't just your ordinary junkie. He's on the run from the Russian mob, he used to be in the federal witness protection program, and he doesn't have a clue that he or those children are in danger.'

Pike nodded. 'So where's the surprise?' You never know if he means it.

I opened the house, then poked around to see if anyone had been in while I was away. As I poked, I told Pike about Wilson Brownell and Reed Jasper and what Jasper had said about Clark. I described what had happened with the Markov brothers, and how I got the eye. When I told him about the Markovs, Pike's head swiveled about a quarter micron. 'He really Spetnaz?'

'That's what he said.'

'People say anything.' You could tell Pike was interested.

'It's the new world order, Joe. Equal opportunity crime.'

Pike went to the glass doors and looked out. He slid back the glass and the silky mountain air rolled in. 'This isn't good.'

'No,' I said. 'It's not.'

'It won't matter what you told the Russians. They'll figure you've got a line on Clark, and they'll show up.'

'That's what I told Clark. I told him to leave town, or go back to the marshals. They're still willing to help.'

'Will he?'

'I don't know. I told him to call Carol Hillegas. He won't be worth a damn to those kids until he's clean, but who knows what he'll do?' We went out to the deck and stood at the rail and looked down at the canyon. 'Talking to Clark is like talking to your television. He doesn't see that his actions have consequences.'

Pike crossed his arms.

'Also, he told me that our services were no longer needed.'

The corner of Pike's mouth twitched. He'll never smile, but sometimes you'll get the twitch. 'Fired.'

'Well, yeah.'

Another twitch. 'How much money we make?'

'Two hundred, less the cost of airfare and hotel. I'd say we're down about three hundred.'

Pike finished his beer.

'But we picked up some frequent flyer miles.'

Pike said, 'You thinking it was the feds or the Russians who went through your house?'

I thought about it, then shook my head. 'It's possible, but I don't think so. If these Russians had a line on Clark, they wouldn't've bothered with me up in Seattle, and the feds would've just knocked on the door. Besides that, I think I've been followed by a guy in a gray LeBaron, and I'm pretty sure the following started before those kids came to my office.' I told him about the black guy in the LeBaron.

'So maybe there's still someone stalking you.'

'Could be.' Always a pleasant thought. 'You want to stay for dinner?'

'No.'

Pike watched a car move along the canyon floor beneath us for a time, then left without another word. No so long, no see you later. Just left.

I finished the Falstaff, crimped the can, and tossed it in my can bag. Recycling. I unpacked, did laundry, and wandered through the house. I felt empty and unfinished, as if there were more to be done only I didn't yet know what to do. Maybe I was bored.

Clark was home, his kids weren't alone anymore, and he was going to do whatever he was going to do. They would leave or they would stay, he would call Carol Hillegas or he wouldn't, he would ask Jasper for help or not, and there wasn't a whole helluva lot I could do about it short of putting a gun to his head. Life in a free society.

I opened another Falstaff, then called Lucy Chenier at her office. 'It's the world's greatest human being, calling for Ms. Chenier.'

Lucy's assistant, Darlene, laughed. 'I see we've upgraded from the world's greatest detective.'

'They're one and the same, are they not?'

'Only when we're talking about you, Mr. Cole.' To know Darlene is to love her. 'I'm sorry, but Ms. Chenier isn't in.' It was just before six in Baton Rouge. Lucy normally stayed in her office until six, unless her son, Ben, had a soccer game.

'Is she at home?'

'You could call her there and find out, I suppose.'

I kidded with Darlene for a few more minutes, then hung up and phoned Lucy's home. She answered on the first ring with 'Hi, David!'

'David?'

'Oh. It's you.'

'Maybe we should hang up and start this conversation again.'

Lucy laughed and said, 'David is David Shapiro, who just happens to be the most experienced news talent attorney in New Orleans, and who also happens to be representing me.'

'KROK made a firm offer?'

She said, 'Negotiations are officially under way.'

The grin started deep and came out big. 'Lucille, that is totally wonderful.'

'It's only their opening offer, and we have to counter, but we're close, Elvis. We are really, really close, and this is going to happen.' You could hear the energy and excitement in her voice. 'David thinks we'll conclude by the end of next week. After that, it's just a matter of waiting for Ben's school year to end, and then we can move out.' The end of Ben's school year was less than six weeks away.

'KROK doesn't have a problem with waiting?'

'Not at all. They've even offered to put me in touch with a real estate agent to help us find a place to live.'

We talked, and as we did the tension slowly seeped away with our sharing, and my home became my home again, warm and enveloping and no longer a place that had been invaded by another. The cat's door clacked, and the cat walked over, bumped against me, and purred. Maybe he could feel the change, too.

Lucy asked about the Hewitt children, and listened as I told her about my trip to Seattle, and the uncomfortable facts that I had learned about their father. She said, 'You took it upon yourself to fly to Seattle to look for him?'

'There's a sucker born every minute, Lucille.'

She sighed, and I could almost see her smile. I could see her in the big overstuffed chair in her living room. I could see Ben on the floor surrounded by Incredible Hulk comic books while he watched 'Babylon 5'. I could smell the bay leaf and sassafras of the oyster gumbo simmering for their dinner in the warm safe house near LSU. Exactly the kind of house that Teri and Charles and Winona did not have. Or maybe I'd just drunk too much Falstaff and all of it was wishful thinking. She said, 'You're not a sucker, you nut. You're the man I love.'

'Thanks, Luce.'

We talked for another hour, sharing our excitment and the evolution of our love, and then we hung up, Lucy promising to call with periodic updates on her status with KROK, and me promising to send her the real estate section from the Los Angeles Times, and both of us making those sugary kissing sounds. Sometimes I'm so schmaltzy I embarrass myself.

I brought the remains of my beer out onto the deck and listened to the breeze ruffling the leaves and to the shush of the cars down in the canyon and to the silence in my home. The cat came out and sat with me. I said, 'Lucy will be here soon. You'd best get used to it.'

He rubbed his head against my leg and purred.

It hadn't been such a bad day, after all.

CHAPTER 13

I woke the next morning telling myself that I should take a free day and relax. After all, I was officially unemployed, and when you get beat up by Russian weightlifters in Seattle you deserve time off. Teri and Charles and Winona were no longer my responsibility, and Clark had been warned, so there you go. Portrait of the detective with time on his hands. Unemployment had its advantages.

I fed the cat, then worked my way through forty minutes of tae kwon do *katas* in the hot morning sun and considered my options: I could run along the Pacific Coast Highway with Joe Pike or drive up to the Antelope Valley to pick fresh peaches or lay on the deck all day eating venison sandwiches and reading the new Dean Koontz. These all seemed like ideal ways to spend a day, but by nine that morning I had shaved, showered, and made my way down the mountains to the Beverly Hills Public Library to learn what I could about the Markov brothers, and what Clark did to get them so pissed off.

Being unemployed is easier said than done.

The Beverly Hills Library is one of the more wonderful libraries in the city. It is clean and neat and Spanish in its architecture, smack in the heart of BH between the Beverly Hills Police Department and the BH City Hall. A slim woman with very short hair showed me how to use their on-line search service and helped me connect with the *Seattle Times*. I downloaded every article they had about the Markov brothers and Vasily Markov's prosecution and subsequent sentencing, and when I printed the download it came to eighty-six pages. What's a day at the beach when you can spend your time reading about the Russian mob?

It was a crowded morning with no free tables, so I sat at a table opposite a couple of young women who looked about right for UCLA. I smiled at them when I sat, and they smiled back. One of them was tall and blond, with blue glitter nail polish and short, ropy hair. The other was short and dark and might've been Persian. Her nail polish was black. The blonde whispered something to her friend when I sat, and they giggled. I said, 'No giggling.'

The blonde frowned at me. 'No one was talking to you.'

'My mistake.'

The first headline read: MOB BOSS INDICTED ON 39 COUNTS. The basic story was as Reed Jasper described: Vasily Markov headed an organization of Russian émigrés who had long been suspected of involvement in counterfeiting, black marketeering, smuggling, extortion, and murder, but that it wasn't until 'an insider in Markov's counterfeiting ring' turned state's evidence that the grand jury could get an indictment. That insider was Clark Hewitt.

The blonde and her friend giggled again, but when I glanced over they pretended to be studying.

The articles described Hewitt as a professional printer who had been 'coerced' by Markov into printing counterfeit U.S. dollars for export to the former Soviet Union. No mention was made of Clark's family, and no mention was made that Markov suspected that Clark had been skimming and had targeted him for death. Other than minor details, there was nothing new or revealing in the first seventy-four of the eighty-six pages, and I was beginning to feel that I would've been better off reading the Koontz.

More whispering, more giggling.

I glanced over. Fast. 'Caught you.'

The blonde blinked at me with innocent eyes. 'Now that you've caught us, what're you going to do with us?'

I turned red and continued skimming. Flirting can be an ugly business. Especially when your girlfriend is soon to move in.

The blonde leaned toward me and looked at the downloads. 'Why are you reading about criminals?'

'Term paper.'

'You're not writing a term paper.'

'You're right. I'm with the library police, and I'm about to bust you for unlawful flirting.'

Her friend said, 'You started it.'

Three pages later I came to an article that wasn't about Markov, though the headline read MARKOV ONLY THE LATEST. It was a sidebar article about counterfeiting in the Pacific Northwest, and its star subject wasn't Clark Hewitt. I sat up straight and I read the name twice, the second time aloud. 'Wilson Brownell.'

The blond girl said, 'Excuse me?'

I raised a hand and kept reading.

The article labeled Wilson Brownell as 'Seattle's Master Printer' and described Brownell as a key figure in a funny-money ring operating in the late sixties and early seventies. The article said that Brownell had put together a printing operation in his garage and had developed a coffee-based aging process that enabled him to turn out fake currency that, except for the quality of the paper, was almost indistinguishable from the real thing. They estimated that he had placed almost ten million fake dollars into circulation before, in an attempt to acquire actual government currency paper, Brownell met with an undercover Treasury agent whom he believed to be a European paper supplier. The article finished by saying that Brownell had served eight years of a twenty-year federal sentence, was paroled, and was reputed to be living in the Seattle area, though he could not be reached for comment.

I pushed back from the table, crossed my arms, and stared at the articles. The blond girl was concerned. 'Is everything all right?'

I shook my head, went back on-line, and tried to pull up more stories about Brownell, but none were available. Too far back.

I thanked the librarian for her help, said good-bye to the tag team from UCLA, then drove to my office and phoned the North Hollywood Division of LAPD. A woman's voice answered on the third ring. 'North Hollywood detectives.'

'Lou Poitras, please.'

'Who's calling?'

'The world's greatest detective.'

She laughed. 'Sorry, bud. You're talking to the world's greatest.' These cops are something.

'Tell him J. Edgar Hoover.'

She laughed again and told me to hold on.

I hung for maybe forty seconds, then Lou Poitras came on the line. 'It's gotta be you. No one else would have the balls.'

'Hi, Louis. I need to find out about a guy in Seattle named Wilson Brownell. Got time to make the call for me?'

'No.' He hung up. I never met a cop who didn't think he was a riot.

I called back and the same woman answered.

I said, 'This time tell him I've got pictures of the goat.'

She said, 'You sure you wouldn't rather talk to me? I'll bet I could help you.'

'I'd rather talk to you, but Poitras owes me money and this is how he works it off.'

'Hold on.'

Poitras came on maybe ten seconds later and sounded tired. 'Christ, I guess it's go along or have my lines tied up the rest of the day. Beverly's in love with you.'

I could hear Beverly shriek in the background. 'Jesus, Sarge, don't tell him *that*!'

Poitras said, 'What's the guy's name again?'

I spelled it for him. Lou Poitras is a detective sergeant at North Hollywood Division, married, three kids, the youngest of whom is my godchild. He's been pumping iron six mornings every week for as long as I've known him, and he is roughly the size of a Lincoln Continental. I'm pretty sure he could lift one.

Poitras said, 'You know, the taxpayers probably don't like funding your research.'

'At least they're getting something for their money.'

Poitras didn't say anything.

'Sorry, Lou. Just kidding.' Sometimes these cops are sensitive. 'Brownell did time on a federal beef, but now he's out. I need to know if he's keeping clean or if the feds think he's into something.'

'You think he is?'

'If I knew I wouldn't have to put the arm on my friends for free information, would I?'

Poitras said, 'Free?'

A kidder, that Lou.

He said, 'I'll call you later.' Then he hung up.

I pushed back in my chair, put my feet up, and thought about Wilson Brownell and Clark Hewitt, and why Clark would risk returning to Seattle where both the Russian mob and the federal marshals were looking for him. It was obvious that Brownell and Clark were more than just friends. Brownell had probably taught Clark everything he knew about printing money, which is probably how Clark had gotten involved with the Markovs. If Clark was willing to risk going back to Seattle to see Brownell, it had to be because Brownell knew or possessed something that Clark needed, and that suggested Clark's new business plan probably involved counterfeiting. Clark might be goofy, but he probably wouldn't risk getting tagged by the Russians just to pal around with an old bud. Maybe Brownell was even going into business with him.

I pulled out the two one-hundred-dollar bills that Teresa had given me and examined them. They were older bills, well worn and used, and they looked fine to me. I rubbed at the ink and held them to the light and examined the paper. They still looked fine, but I wasn't an expert.

I put them away and leaned back again when two men came through the outer door. The first guy was tall and black, with a shiny bald head and a plain navy suit and a grim demeanor. The second guy might've been a fashion model posing as a cutting-edge corporate executive. He was in his late thirties and in good shape, with immaculate dark hair and a conservative Brooks Brothers suit. I smiled when I saw the black guy because he was the same guy I'd seen in the gray LeBaron outside Teri Hewitt's house. I smiled wider when I saw a thick bandage on the back of his left hand, and I kept smiling as I reached under my jacket, took out the Dan Wesson, and pointed it at them.

The white guy said, 'You won't need that.' He had a light southern accent, and he didn't seem concerned about the gun.

I said, 'That's up to you. We might be here a while waiting for the police.'

The black guy closed the door and leaned against it. I guess he wanted to make sure I couldn't escape.

The white guy inspected my office. He looked at the figurines, and the Pinocchio clock, and then the picture of Lucy Chenier. Especially the picture of Lucy. I said, 'None of it's for sale. You want to tell me why you were in my house, or should I just start shooting?'

The white guy turned away from the picture. Now he was inspecting me.

I said, 'Pal, it's been a rough couple of days and I'm feeling a mite testy.'

He smiled, like me being testy was just what he wanted. He said, 'This is my associate, Mr. Epps. My name is Richard Chenier. I'm Lucy's ex-husband.'

My eyes clicked from Epps to Richard Chenier and I stared. So much for Russian mobsters. So much for federal agents.

Richard Chenier said, 'The gun?'

I remembered the gun and put it away.

'We were going to meet sooner or later, so I decided to introduce myself.' He didn't offer his hand, and neither did I.

'There might've been a friendlier way to say hello.'

Richard nodded. 'Perhaps.' I guess this wasn't going to be a friendly visit.

'Tell me something, Richard. Do you have your man Epps here follow every guy Lucy dates?'

'No. Only the ones who tempt her into moving two thousand miles. And take my son with her.'

I said, 'Richard.'

He smiled, then sat in one of the director's chairs across from my desk. 'My son likes you, so I wanted to find out what kind of guy you are. You can understand that, can't you?'

'I can understand your wanting to know about me. Hiring a guy to B and E my home is stepping over the line.'

'Oh, I didn't hire Mr. Epps for *you*. He works for my company. We're in international oil.'

'Mm.' Maybe I was supposed to be impressed.

'He's very good at what he does, and he tells me that you seem to be a solid man. Stable. Good reputation. All of that.'

'I'm glad you approve.'

'And small. A person we might describe as a minor player in an insignificant game, well beneath what I would want for my wife and my son.'

I stared at him some more, and then I looked at Pinocchio. I sighed, then stood. 'Okay, Richard. We've met. It's been fun. I'm sorry it's going to be like this, but now it's time to leave.'

He didn't move. Neither did Epps. 'Small, but reasonable, so I decided that I should explain things to you so that you understand.'

'I can ask nice, Richard, but, believe me, I don't have to ask, or be nice.' Epps shifted his weight forward slightly, away from the door. 'Epps, you won't believe it even while it's happening.' That probably scared him.

Richard raised both hands and smiled. 'I'm not here to threaten you. Look, I love this woman, and I love my son. What you don't understand is that she still loves me. We just have to work out a few problems, and then she'll come to see that.'

'Good-bye, Richard.' So much for civil discourse. So much for modern men discussing a modern problem in an enlightened manner. I was thinking that it might be fun to beat him to death.

He still didn't move. 'I just want you to consider what's best for Lucy. I know she's been offered this job, but it'll be much better for her to stay in Baton Rouge, and much better for Ben. I'm hoping that you're the kind of guy who wants what's best for them. If you cared, you'd tell her to stay home.'

He really believed it. I glanced at Epps, but Epps didn't seem to care one way or the other. I shook my head. 'You think I should tell Lucy to stay home?'

Richard smiled like a pleased teacher whose slow pupil was finally catching on. 'That's right.'

Maybe that's why their marriage failed. 'Richard, here's something that you don't seem to understand. This decision isn't mine or yours. It's Lucy's.'

Richard frowned, as if I'd failed him in my attempt to understand.

'I love her, and I want her here, but I can't make her come and I can't make her stay, and neither can you. It's her life, and her decision. You see?'

Richard Chenier frowned harder. 'There's always a way to get what you want. That's how I make my living.'

I stared at him. I tried to picture them as a couple, and couldn't.

Richard Chenier glanced at Epps, then stood. Epps opened the door. Richard said, 'You don't think I intend to just let them leave, do you?'

'I don't think you have any choice.'

'You'd be surprised.' He smiled at me, and I didn't like it. I didn't like him.

Richard Chenier walked out of my office without looking back. Epps stared at me, then grinned and turned away, too.

'Hey, Epps.'

He looked back, still grinning.

'That's some cat, huh?'

Epps dropped the smile, walked out, and closed the door. Hard.

I stared at the door for a very long time, and then I shook my head.

'Pleased to meet you, Richard.'

CHAPTER 14

I watched Richard and Epps drive away, then went back to my desk and stared at the Mickey phone and thought about calling Lucy, but what would I say? *Your ex-husband dropped by and told me he loved you?* Nope. *Richard hired some guy to break into my house.* It sounded like tattling.

I looked at the Pinocchio clock, and gave it Stan Laurel. 'Isn't this a fine development?'

Pinocchio's eyes went from side to side, but he didn't say anything. He never does.

I tried to think about Markov. I took out the two one-hundred-dollar bills, looked at them again, but I kept seeing Richard on the bills instead of Ben Franklin. 'For chrissakes, Cole, get over it. You're onto something with Clark. Follow up your lead.'

What kind of guy hires someone to break into his ex-wife's boyfriend's house?

Would you stop?!

I knew from Lucy that Richard Chenier was an attorney with the firm of Benton, Meyers & Dane, and I knew he had graduated from law school at LSU, where Lucy had been an undergraduate, but that was all I knew, and I had never given him much thought. Now he had entered my home and my office in a belligerent and threatening manner, which I could handle, but he had also indicated that he had no intention of allowing Lucy to leave Baton Rouge, which I didn't like at all. Whatever that meant.

I decided that if I couldn't stop thinking about Lucy's ex-husband, the smart thing would be to deal with it. I had met Lucy when I worked a case in Louisiana last year, and while I was there I had made friends with a couple of people on the Louisiana State Police and the Baton Rouge PD. Now I called them, told them what I knew about Richard and Epps, and asked if they could give me a fast background check. They told me that they'd get back to me as soon as possible.

While they were working on that, I called Joe Pike. 'Clark went to Seattle to see a man named Wilson Brownell. Brownell is a master counterfeiter. He taught Clark how to print, and I'm thinking that Clark went back to Brownell because he's getting back in the trade.'

'You think he's printing money?'

'I've got two one-hundred-dollar bills that I'm wondering about, and maybe this explains why Clark won't go to Jasper. If he's setting something up, it might be coming together and he wants to see it through.'

Pike didn't say anything for a moment, like maybe he was thinking. 'There's a woman named Marsha Fields at the Treasury office downtown. I could call her tonight, see if you can drop by with the bills tomorrow.'

'Okay.'

Then he said, 'What?' Like he could hear something in my voice.

'The guy who broke into my house is named Epps. He's the same guy in the LeBaron, and he works for Lucy's ex-husband. They just left my office.'

More silence. 'Want me to do anything?'

'I don't think we need to kill him just yet.'

'Maybe later.' Pike hung up. Sometimes the silence says it all.

I stared at the phone some more, then called the LSU Alumni Office. A little bit after that I phoned Benton, Meyers & Dane, pretending to be a prospective client, and six minutes after that the first of my cop friends called back. One hour and twenty-seven minutes after Richard Chenier walked out of my office, I knew that he had been a second-string cornerback for the LSU frosh team until a blown knee ended his collegiate career. He had dallied in campus politics, graduated summa cum laude, was an unsuccessful Rhodes candidate, and had never been arrested. Impressive. I also knew that he was a full partner at BM&D, a firm specializing in corporate law for international oil concerns, but was currently out of the office (yeah, he was in mine!) and not scheduled to return until next week. Lawrence Epps was a former Louisiana state trooper who had left the job and who now worked as an investigator for BM&D. He had been arrested four times, three of those for assault, and had been convicted one time for misdemeanor battery. One of those arrests was for beating his first wife. Sweet.

All in all, I was feeling better about things when I went home. I still wasn't liking Richard very much, but he seemed like a square guy, and if I tried real hard I thought that I might be going a little crazy, too, thinking that I might lose my child. After all, Lucy had married the guy, and that said something. Of course, she had also divorced him, but that didn't dawn on me until later.

When I got home that evening the cat was sitting by his bowl in the kitchen. I talked it over with him while I was making dinner, and said, 'What would you do?'

The cat blinked, then bent over and licked his anus. Cats lead simple lives.

Joe Pike called me at nine the next morning, telling me that Special Agent Marsha Fields of the U.S. Secret Service was expecting me. I made boiled eggs and English muffins for breakfast, then took my time showering and dressing before winding my way across town to the Treasury Department.

The Treasury has its offices on the seventeenth floor of the Roybal Federal Building in downtown Los Angeles, between the LAPD's Parker Center on one side and the Los Angeles Federal Metropolitan Correctional Center on the other. Cops feel safer when they cluster.

I parked in the basement, then took an elevator to the lobby where I went through a metal detector and gave my name to a guy who looked like he ate a Pontiac for breakfast. Then I took another elevator up to seventeen.

When I stepped off the elevator, a tall, athletic-looking woman with short red hair in a navy pants suit was waiting. She said, 'Mr. Cole? I'm Marsha Fields. Joe Pike asked me to examine some currency for you.' She took my hand with a firm grip and smiled nicely.

'That's right.' I smiled nicely, too, and tried to get my hand back. She didn't let go.

'Mm-hm. And how did you get these bills?' She kept the hand and I was thinking that maybe she wouldn't let go, as if the bills were funny or my answer was wrong she'd slap the cuffs on me and whisk me away to Secret Service Land.

'I cashed a check at a market in Hollywood.'

She kept the hand and the smile a little bit longer and then she dropped both. 'Well, come with me and let's see what we have.'

I followed her along a nondescript hall, past men and women who wouldn't make eye contact. All the better to keep secrets. She said, 'Joe says that you and he work together.'

'That's right. Joe owns the agency with me.'

'Joe's a very interesting man.'

'Mm-hm.'

'We met when Joe was on LAPD. We got to be friends.'
I nodded. She seemed interested.
'We were close.'
I looked at her. 'Joe speaks well of you.'
She brightened and didn't look so suspicious anymore.
'I imagine he's married by now.' I guess love was in the
air. Or at least lust.
'Not yet. But there's always hope.'
She blushed and we went into a small lab that looked
not unlike a doctor's office and smelled of naphtha. A
black Formica counter ran along one wall with a shelf of
little bottles above it and three light trays. A single steel
sink was sunk into the counter, with a binocular
microscope on one side of it and a large magnifying glass
on a gooseneck stand on the other. Modern crime
fighting at its cutting-edge finest.
Someone had taped cutout pictures of the president,
the vice president, and the speaker of the house above
the counter and used a Marks-a-lot to label them Manny,
Moe, and Curley. Someone else had drawn a bozo face on
the president and written *Would YOU take a bullet for
this clown?* These Secret Service agents are a riot, aren't
they?
Marsha Fields said, 'May I see the bills?'
I gave her both hundreds. She put one down and
worked with the other. She examined both sides, then
folded the bill and rubbed it together, then looked at the
face again. She put it on one of the light boxes, then
pulled over the magnifying glass and inspected first the
front face, then the back. She made a clucking sound.
'These babies are righteous fakes.'
'Funny money.' Clark. You doofus.
'You bet. But not schlock. This is good stuff.'
'How can you tell?'
She held the bill under the big magnifier for me to see

and pointed with a Uniball pen. 'Look at the scrollwork around the edge of the bill. You see the vertical lines behind the portrait of Ben Franklin and the spokes in the Treasury seal? All of these lines should be clean and unbroken.'

I looked where she was indicating and I could see that the lines weren't clean and unbroken. The parallel lines were smudged together in some places and in other places were broken or separated. 'Yeah. I see.'

'Real money is made from engraved plates, so all of these lines are clearly resolved and separate. These bills were made from offset plates. The counterfeiter takes a picture of real money, then makes a plate from the picture, only you lose a little resolution with each step so the lines become smudged. Understand?'

She was looking at me expectantly, so I nodded. 'Sure.' If you can at least look smart, people will assume that you are smart.

'The other giveaway is the paper. Real money is printed on a cotton blend made by the Crane Paper Mill in Dalton, Massachusetts. You see these little red and blue lines?'

She showed me the little red and blue filaments we've all seen in money. There were little red and blue lines in this bill, too. 'Sure. I thought counterfeit money didn't have those lines.'

She nodded, pleased not only with me, but with the funny money. 'It doesn't and neither does this.'

'I'm looking at it.'

'Nope, you only think you're seeing it.' She put a drop of something from one of the little bottles on the bill and nothing happened. She frowned, selected another bottle, and put a different drop on another red fiber. This time the fiber dissolved and she smiled. 'The red and blue marks in real money are rayon fibers that are mixed in

the cotton and linen mash when Crane makes the paper.'
She tore the edge of the bill and looked at the fibers.
'This is a pretty good linen fiber, probably from a
European mill, but the red and blue marks were printed
on top of the paper in two separate processes.' She was
smiling broadly now. She was beaming. 'This isn't
schlock work. Someone went to a lot of trouble and they
did a good job.' I guess she could appreciate the
counterfeiter's art.

'Are these new bills?' I was thinking that if Clark was
printing again, this is what he was printing.

'Oh no. I'd say these were eight, ten years old, at least.'
She snapped off the light tray, but didn't offer the money
back to me. 'Looks like you're out two hundred bucks.'

'That's the way it goes.'

She crossed her arms and nodded. 'You want to tell me
where you really picked up this money?'

'I did.'

She smiled again, and stood. 'Sure.'

'You keep the money?'

'That's the way it works. You can file a claim for
reimbursement through this office or any bank.'

'Thanks.'

'Tell Joe to call me sometime.'

I went out through security, down to my car, and
started back toward my office. So Clark and his kids
were living on counterfeit money. That's why they paid
for everything in cash. If they tried to deposit their
money into a savings or checking account, they'd risk
being discovered. The few hundred bucks they had in
checking was probably the only real money they had, but
Teri probably didn't know that, just as she didn't know
that her father was a counterfeiter.

Of course, knowing that they were living on counterfeit money didn't mean Clark was currently printing it

or intending to. This stuff was probably the money he'd skimmed from Markov.

I nosed up onto Temple, then left toward the Hollywood Freeway. The downtown traffic combined with Caltrans construction projects was slowing the streets. I had gone three slow blocks and had just squeaked past a red light when about four thousand horns started blowing behind me. I looked in my rearview and saw the reason for all the noise: A nice new metallic tan Camaro had jumped into the oncoming lane to muscle its way through the intersection against the traffic. A blond guy with a buzz cut was driving, and a man who looked like the Incredible Hulk was filling the passenger seat.

Alexei Dobcek and Dmitri Sautin.

For the first time since Richard Chenier had walked into my office, it was easy to stop thinking about him. The Russians had arrived.

CHAPTER 15

It was just before lunch in downtown Los Angeles, and maybe eighty thousand people were jamming the sidewalks and streets around us, flooding through the crosswalks against the DON'T WALK lights. In New York that would get you killed, but in LA where pedestrians have the right of way, cars collect in turn lanes like debris in a drain cover. Dobcek wasn't used to that; people in Seattle obey the crosswalk signs.

They didn't close the gap between us; they just tried to keep me in sight. Probably picked me up at my office. Probably hoping that I'd lead them to Clark.

I drove with the traffic flow, letting Dobcek stay with me, and turned north under the freeway to Sunset Boulevard, then into a strip mall. Mr. Nonchalant. Mr. Taking-Care-of-a-Little-Errand. Dobcek and Sautin pulled to the curb in front of a menudo shop a block behind and tried to look inconspicuous. Hard to do when you weigh three hundred pounds.

I called Joe Pike from a pay phone outside a florist. 'Dobcek and Sautin are sitting in a tan Camaro fifty yards away, watching me.'

'Shoot them.' Life is simple for Pike. Like with the cat.

'I was thinking more along the lines of delaying them. They probably picked me up at my office, and they're probably hoping I'll lead them to Clark.'

Pike grunted. 'Or they're hoping for another chance to beat it out of you.'

'Well, there's that, too.' I told him where I was, and what I wanted.

Pike said, 'Try to stay alive until I get there.'

Always the encouraging word.

I pretended to talk for another five minutes, went into the florist to kill more time, then climbed back into my car and continued north along Sunset, making sure that Dobcek and Sautin made every light with me.

When I reached Elysian Park Avenue I turned toward Dodger Stadium, and wound my way up past small residential homes through the mountains to Chavez Ravine. Traffic thinned, and I thought that Dobcek might break off the tail, but he didn't.

Chavez Ravine is a broad flat bowl surrounded by low mountains that wall the stadium from the city. Dodger Stadium sits in the center of the bowl, surrounded by black tarmac parking lots like some kind of alien spacecraft resting alone on its launching pad. All you'd need was a big shiny robot, and you'd think Michael Rennie had come back to Earth.

An hour before game time on a cool spring evening and there'd be fifty thousand people driving past. Noontime on a day when the Dodgers were out of town, and the place was deserted. An ideal place for a conversation or a murder.

The roads there loop and roll around the base of the ravine, and little signs direct you toward the stadium or Elysian Park or any number of interesting places. I followed the signs past palm tree sentinels toward the ticket booth, and increased my speed enough to pull away from the Russians. Dobcek would want to stay with me, but not enough to get crazy and blow his tail. After all, he'd figure that he could always go back to my office and wait until I returned, but he would follow because for all he knew I was heading toward a safe house where I'd stashed Clark and his kids. I pressed it going up the hill to the turnoff to the ticket booth, but I didn't turn there. I turned off the road into the grass and backed my car behind a stand of scrub oak and brush. We hadn't had rain in weeks and the soil was hard as the pavement.

Forty seconds later the Camaro cruised past through the gate. I saw his brake lights come on, and I pulled back onto the road, and stopped in the gate, blocking their exit. Pike's Jeep was across the road in front of them. Pike was leaning across the Jeep's hood, pointing a twelve-gauge Beretta autoloader at them. I got out, walked up to their car, and smiled at them. 'Baseball. The great American pastime.'

Dobcek's hands were on his steering wheel. He nodded. 'Nicely done.'

'Welcome to LA, boys. Now get out of the car, keeping your hands where we can see them.'

Dobcek got out first. When Dmitri Sautin climbed out, the little Camaro rocked.

I said, 'Guns.'

Pike came around the Jeep, the shotgun still at his shoulder. Dobcek fingered the Glock from under his left arm and held it out. I tossed it into my Corvette. I looked at Dmitri Sautin. 'Now you.'

Sautin shook his head. 'No.'

Dobcek said, 'Dmitri.'

Sautin said, 'I think they have to take it, if they can.' He lowered his hands and grinned at Pike. Dmitri Sautin was four inches taller than Pike, and outweighed him by a hundred pounds.

Pike said, 'It's going to hurt.'

Sautin said, 'Ha.'

Sautin was still grinning when Pike hit him on the side of the head with a hard fast roundhouse kick. Sautin took one step to the side and looked surprised, but he didn't go down. Pike kicked him again, and this time Sautin staggered. His eyes filled and his lower lip quivered and he began crying. Pike said, 'Gun.'

Dmitri Sautin held out the Sig. I took it and tossed it in with the Glock.

Dobcek smiled, and it was ugly and predatory. His eyes sparkled in the bright sun and stayed with Joe Pike.

I patted them down, took their wallets, and then I told them to step away from the car. They did. I went through their car and found the rental papers. They had arrived at LAX that morning. I took the keys from the ignition and found two overnight bags in the trunk. I looked through them but found nothing but clothes and toiletries. I put their bags in the Corvette, too. Dmitri Sautin wiped at his nose, and said, 'But we will not have underwear.'

'A criminal's life is an ugly one.' I looked through their wallets, didn't learn anything new, and tossed the wallets in with the guns. I said, 'Markov's really going to be impressed when you tell him about this.'

Sautin said, 'You must be stupid to think we would tell him.'

Dobcek said, 'Shut up, fool.' Dobcek's eyes never left Pike.

I said, 'It's like I told you in Seattle, I don't know Clark Hewitt and I don't know where he is. You guys are wasting your time.'

Dobcek said, 'Da.'

'If you're smart, you'll go back to Seattle. If you try to tag me again, I'll kill you.' Mr. Threat.

Dobcek made the little smile again.

Pike said, 'He won't, but I will.'

Dobcek's smile faded.

I said, 'See the little building at the bottom of the hill?'

They could see it.

'Start walking.'

Sautin started toward the ticket building, but Dobcek didn't. Dobcek looked at Pike. 'This one goes to you, but I think we see each other again, yes?'

The corner of Pike's mouth twitched, saying here we are, saying we can take this anyplace you want, but wherever we go I will win and you will lose.

Dobcek made a small nod and followed Sautin.

We watched them for a time, and then Pike said, 'You lie well. Too bad they didn't believe you.'

'Yeah, but it'll buy us enough time to warn Clark. I told Clark they were going to come and now they have, and he'll have to do something. He won't like it, but there you go.'

Pike went to his Jeep and came back with an eight-inch stainless-steel hunting knife. He went around the Camaro and cut all four tires. Buy us even more time.

I said, 'By the way.'

He looked at me.

'The two C-notes were counterfeit.'

Pike nodded.

'Your friend Marsha Fields kept them.'

Another nod.

'Means we're down about five hundred now.'

Pike went back to his Jeep. 'A criminal's life is an ugly one.'

I got into my car and went to warn Clark Hewitt.

CHAPTER 16

Twenty minutes later I turned off Melrose and saw the green Saturn. I parked behind it, then went to the door and rang the bell three times. I was thinking that maybe everyone was pretending they weren't home when Teri opened the door. She wasn't smiling, and she opened the door only wide enough to look out. 'Oh, hello.'

'Great to see you, too.'

Blank.

'I need to see your father.'

'He isn't home.'

I glanced at the Saturn.

'He walked up to Melrose to go shopping.'

I edged closer to the door. 'That's okay. I'll wait.'

She didn't move or open the door. 'He might be a while.'

'No problem. When you make the big bucks like me, time is your servant.'

Something crashed through the house like a runaway buffalo and Charles appeared behind her, his face falling when he saw me. 'Oh, it's him.' Him.

I said, 'Are you going to open the door or make me wait out here?'

Charles jabbed at Teri's back and whispered loud enough for me to hear. 'Tell'm to eff himself.'

I said, 'Charles, for chrissake.'

Teri stepped back to let me in.

Charles screamed, 'Oh, frig!' He thundered back through the house and slammed his door.

I went into the living room, adjusted the blinds, and sat on the couch so that I could see the street. The Russians hadn't arrived, and I didn't expect them to, but you never know. If they found us, maybe I could just give them Charles. 'Where's Winona?'

'In her room.'

The TV wasn't going and Winona hadn't come out to see me. The house did not smell of baking cookies. I watched Teri and Teri watched me, and the close living room somehow felt expectant and tenuous. 'Quiet.'

Teri looked smaller than before, and tired. Her eyes were dark caves. I said, 'What did he go shopping for?'

'Clothes.'

I sat and listened, and her uneasiness was a physical thing that seemed to magnify sounds. I tapped the couch arm, and the tapping echoed like thunder. I sighed, and heard it as a rush of dry wind clawing across the desert. 'He's gone again, isn't he?'

She looked at the floor.

'How long?'

She didn't answer, and I imagined Dobcek and Sautin bombing around town, getting closer and closer, and finally showing up. Maybe it wouldn't be just Dobcek and Sautin. Maybe it would be other guys. Better guys. 'How long has he been gone, Teri?'

'Since yesterday morning.' A voice so small you could barely hear her.

'He didn't take the Saturn.'

'He walked up to Melrose. He said someone was picking him up.'

'He say who?'

She shook her head.

'Did he say when he'd be back, or where he was

135

going?' I wanted to roll my head and hear the bones crack and feel the relief.

She shook her head again. Of course not.

'And he hasn't called?'

'Uh-uh.'

I took a deep breath and let it out. The Russians had landed and Clark had disappeared. Again. Maybe he would be home by supper, but maybe not. Maybe Dobcek and Sautin weren't the only Russians who'd come down, and maybe those guys had Clark right now, but that probably wasn't the case either. Clark might be sitting with the U.S. Marshals right now, asking to get back into the program, but I wasn't willing to bet on it. Either way I wasn't going to leave these kids alone anymore. I said, 'Do you have any Tylenol?'

When I had the Tylenol, I excused myself, went to the kitchen, drank one glass of tap water, then went back to the living room. Teri had not moved, and the house seemed even more still. I wondered how often it had been like this. Maybe more often than I thought. I said, 'You and I need to talk.'

'He'll be back soon.' She tried to sound hopeful. 'He always comes back.'

'I hope you're right.' I sat very close to her and spoke in a quiet voice. I wanted her to know before Charles and Winona. 'We have to talk about some hard things. I don't know how much you know, or what you've guessed, but I don't see any other way.'

'About Seattle.' A statement. Like she knew what was coming and dreaded it.

'That's right. Seattle.'

She remembered the night her family had left, and she remembered the men who had taken them in a dull beige van in the middle of a rainstorm, and the thunder that had not been thunder. She remembered gray federal buildings and airplanes, and she knew that they had moved to Salt Lake City and change their names because bad men were after her father, though she did not know why. I told her. I didn't want to tell her, and I didn't like myself for it, but she needed to know. 'Your father counterfeited money for a man named Vasily Markov. Markov wanted to have your father killed, so your father turned state's evidence in order to buy his way into the witness protection program. Do you know what that is?'

Her lips had formed a hard little knot. 'I'm not an idiot.'

'Your father learned his trade from a man named Wilson Brownell, up in Seattle. Markov's people have been watching Brownell, and they figured that something was going on. They staked Brownell and your mother's grave, and that's where they saw me.'

The hard lips softened. 'You went to my mother's grave?'

'The men who are after your father have come to Los Angeles. They've already found me, because they suspect that I know your whereabouts, and that means they'll stay here until they find your father, too. Do you understand that?'

'Yes.' Without expression.

'These men are dangerous, and I am not going to walk out of here and leave you alone. That is no longer an option.'

She looked from my left eye to my right, not really seeing me, breathing softly. You could tell she was thinking. I heard something creak in the hall. Charles, probably. Eavesdropping. 'What about my father?'

'I think he's going to print money again, but I don't know that. I'm pretty sure that's why he went to see Brownell.' I couldn't bring myself to tell her about the drugs.

137

Her eyes narrowed, and her lips moved, but I couldn't make out what she was saying. She blinked, and I thought she might be trying to keep back the tears.

'I know it's hard.' I said it as softly as I could.

She was hunched over, elbows on knees, arms crossed, lips pursed. A hard, tight knot. She said something, but I couldn't hear her.

'I didn't hear you, Teri.'

She said it again. 'He's such a loser.'

I didn't know what to say.

'He screws up everything. He's screwed up all of our lives.' The blinking grew harder, and her eyes filled. 'I try to make it better, but it just gets worse. I try so hard.' Tears leaked down across her cheeks and into the corners of her mouth, and I put a hand on her shoulder and squeezed, and I started blinking, too.

'Teri.' Something creaked in the hall again and a door closed.

Teri said, 'Please don't let them hurt him.'

For all I knew they had him now. For all I knew he was dead. 'The only way I can help him is to find him before they do, you see?'

She wiped her eyes on her wrist, then took a breath. She hadn't broken all the way, and now she was pulling herself back together. I guess she'd had a lot of practice.

'But not with you here. I am either going to call the feds and have them take you in, or you're coming with me. Either way, you can't stay here.'

She wiped her eyes again, and now the tears were gone. As if they'd never been. 'Where will you take us?'

'We'll go to my house for now, but we'll have to move to a safe house. I'm easy to find, and the Russians might show up there.'

'What about my daddy?'

'I'll look for him when you guys are safe.'

'He's going to come back here.'

'Then I'll wait here for him, but first we have to get you guys to a safe place.'

She was small and folded, sitting on the edge of the couch, and then she adjusted her glasses and stood. 'Okay.' Just like that. 'I'd better get Charles and Winona.' The fifteen-year-old mother again. Taking care of her family.

We went along the hall to their rooms. Both doors were closed. I rapped at each door. 'Charles. Winona. You guys come here.'

Winona's door quietly opened, and she stepped into the hall. Charles's voice came muffled from behind his. 'Eff you!' He'd been listening, all right.

Teri said, 'Charles, we're going away for a few days. We have to pack.'

'Eff!'

I smiled at Winona. 'Hi, honey.' Mr. Friendly. Mr. Don't-Be-Scared-of-the-Man-Who's-Going-to-Take-You-Away.

'Hi.' She smiled back, but it was uncertain. It was the first time I had seen Winona as anything but bubbling. I guess if my dad had blown in and out without warning I would've been uncertain, too. The little troll key chain was clipped to her belt loop. Guess if you couldn't have Daddy, you might as well have the troll. Maybe, sometimes, the two were one and the same.

I said, 'Teri, why don't you help Winona with her things. I'll talk to Charles.'

Charles yelled, 'I ain't goin'!'

Teri said, 'C'mon, Winona. You help me pack and I'll help you.'

They went into their room, and I tapped at Charles's door. 'C'mon, bud.'

'Eff!'

I tapped again, then opened the door, and when I did he ran over and pushed against it as hard as he could, shouting, 'Eff you! Stay out of here! Eff!' He was red-faced and crying, and I felt like a turd.

I forced the door, Charles on the other side, crying louder and pushing hard, sobbing from the mucus in his throat, thin chest heaving, shouting 'You get outta here!' until I had the door open, and then he ran at me, butting head first into me, punching and spitting and screaming for me to get out and I pulled him close and held him, and after a while all the yelling and crying subsided into a sobbing hack. It was a barren room, holding only a single frame bed and a chest, with none of the posters and toys and things you'd expect to see in the room of a twelve-year-old boy. Maybe Charles didn't think he'd live here long enough to bother. I said, 'It's okay, kid.'

'I hope he never comes back!'

I held him.

'I wish he was dead!'

I held him tighter.

Teri said, 'Charles?' She was standing in the door.

I said, 'We're okay, Teri.'

Charles and I stood for a very long time, and when the sobbing subsided I tried to let go, but by then Charles was holding on to me, arms locked tight around my ribs, face buried in my chest. I could feel the wet soaking through my shirt. 'It's okay, kid.' I said it five or six times. Maybe I said it more.

I let Charles hang on to me for another couple of minutes, and then I told him to pack enough for two nights. I told him that we were going to my place, and that when they were safe I would find his father. Charles turned away without looking at me, wiped his nose on the back of his hand, and packed. He said, 'Eff'm.'

Maybe I would kill Clark if the Russians didn't.

CHAPTER 17

I phoned Joe Pike while they packed. 'Clark's gone,' I said. 'Again.'

Pike didn't say anything for a moment. 'You're going to move the kids.'

'That's right. I'm going to take them to my place, but I don't want to keep them there overnight. Sautin and Dobcek could show up anytime.'

'Okay.'

'Think you could come up with a safe house?' Pike knew people, and he'd come up with safe places to stay before. Once an abandoned mansion in Bel Air, once an Airstream trailer in the high desert near Edwards Air Force Base. You never knew. Maybe he owned these places and just didn't bother to tell me.

'Let me make some calls. I'll meet you at your place later.'

By the time I was off the phone, Teri and Winona and Charles were ready to go. Guess they didn't have much to pack, or maybe it was because they'd had so much practice.

We locked their house, put their bags behind the seats, and the four of us made the drive up Laurel Canyon, the three of them bunched together in the passenger seat. Teri had offered to drive their car, but I said no. I wasn't worried that she'd have an accident; I was more concerned that when we got wherever we were going she would simply drive away. Charles said, 'I'm all squished up.'

Teri said, 'Live with it.'

I took it slow because no one was wearing a seat belt. Elvis Cole, the not-quite-responsible parent, looking over his shoulder for a load of Russian hit men.

Teri and Charles were quiet, but after a while Winona began to chatter about how much she liked riding in the convertible. The top was down and the wind blew through our hair, and Winona said that it made her feel like she was in a parade. Charles neither glowered nor flipped off anyone, and Teri seemed lost in herself. I guess everyone had their own way of dealing with what was going on.

Pretty soon we left the city behind and wound through the trees, and a little bit after that we turned into the carport. Winona said, 'Is this your house?'

'Yes.'

'It looks like a tepee.'

'It's called an A-frame. It's tall and steep and shaped like the letter.'

Charles slunk out of the car and peered at the trees and natural hillsides. 'Are there bears?'

'No bears. Just a few coyotes and rattlesnakes.'

He glanced at the ground, then made a sour face. 'What's that smell?'

Winona giggled. 'Charles cut the cheese.'

Teri said, 'Don't be rude.'

'It's the eucalyptus trees.' I pointed them out to him. 'The sun splits their bark, and their sap smells like mouthwash.'

They followed me inside through the kitchen to the living room. I told them to put their bags on the stairs, and I opened the drapes and the big glass doors to let the breeze in from the deck, then checked my answering machine. Lucy had left a message, asking me to call. Teri said, 'Is that Ms. Chenier?'

'Yep.'

'Aren't you going to call her?'

'As soon as we get squared away. You guys can go out on the deck if you want, but nobody climb on the rail. You can play on the slope, just watch out for the snakes.' Summer camp at the Cole residence. They stood in the door and looked at the deck and the slope, but nobody went outside. The snakes.

'There's soft drinks and milk and water in the fridge. You can help yourself. After we get settled, I'll make dinner.'

Teri said, 'You don't have to cook for us.' She hadn't come to the deck. She was standing in the living room by the stairs with her arms crossed.

'Of course I do. But you can help if you like. Is meatloaf okay?'

The three of them shrugged at each other, and Teri said, 'That would be nice. Thank you.'

Charles eyed the loft. 'What's up there?'

'That's my loft. Come on. I'll show you.'

I showed them the downstairs bathroom, then took them up. Charles and Winona wandered through the loft, but Teri went to the rail and looked down into the house. From the rail you can see the living room and the dining area and through the glass out to the canyon. She looked at the big glass triangle of my back wall, then up at the high pointed ceiling. She looked at my bed, and the built-in dresser, and then down at the living room again. 'Do you live here alone?'

'Yes. Except for my cat.'

She let her touch drift along the rail, and then she looked around the room again. 'It's nice.'

'Thank you.' I thought of my house as ordinary, but I

realized then that it was probably a different world to her. Life for them had been a series of temporary furnished rentals, other people's homes and other people's furniture, just a place to stay until their father decided it was time to leave, no more permanent than a daily newspaper.

I showed them the upstairs bath, and then we went downstairs. When we got down again, Joe Pike was standing silently in the entry. Just standing there.

Charles yelped in surprise and shouted, 'Jeezis, you scared me!'

Pike said, 'Yes.'

Charles scrambled outside and peered in from the deck. Guess Joe scared him more than the snakes.

I said, 'I'll make dinner in a minute, but first we have to talk. Charles, come back inside.'

Charles crept back inside and the three of them stared at me, Charles snapping nervous glances toward Joe.

'I'm going to look for your father tomorrow, so I need clues. Did he say anything to anyone while he was home?'

They looked at each other, and shook their heads. Teri said, 'Not like you mean.'

'Nothing that might indicate where he was going?'

Winona said, 'He said we were going to move away soon. He said we could have a really big TV.' Great.

Teri said, 'He made some phone calls.'

'Anyone listen in?'

They shook their heads some more, but Charles wasn't particularly convincing.

'Charles?'

'I didn't do anything.'

'No. But you might've heard something.'

Charles squirmed, then shrugged. 'He said something about going to see someone.'

'You hear a name?'

'Ray.'

'He said the name 'Ray'?'

Shrug.

Pike said, 'How about "Tre"?'

Charles scrunched his face, but this time he didn't shrug. 'Yeah, maybe that was it.'

Pike shook his head and went out onto the deck.

I showed them my videotapes and told them to pick one. Winona picked *Independence Day*. I got them going with that, put two pounds of ground turkey in the microwave to thaw, and was just getting ready to join Pike on the deck when Lucy Chenier called again. I said, 'I was about to call you. Did you close the deal?'

There was a great silence from the other end of the line. 'I'm not sure there's a job offer to be closed.'

I stood in the kitchen with the phone in my hand. Winona and Charles watched great elliptical spaceships enter the atmosphere, but Teri watched me. I said, 'What do you mean, no job offer?' Pike looked in from the deck, curious as to what was keeping me.

'God, I've really needed to talk to you, Elvis.' Her voice sounded hollow and empty.

I held the phone tighter. 'Lucy?'

'When David got back to them, they reduced the term of the contract. They changed every one of the deal points, and said they were reconsidering the amount of my salary.' I could hear the hurt in her voice. 'I just don't understand it.'

'Maybe it's just a negotiating tactic.'

'David doesn't think so. He's done this a hundred times, and he says it's as if they've changed their minds about hiring me.'

I leaned against the counter and frowned. 'Maybe you should call Tracy Mannos.'

'I did. She hasn't returned my call.'

I frowned harder. I thought about Richard in my office, telling me that he wouldn't just let Lucy leave. I thought about it some more and shook my head.

'Richard came to see me.'

Silence.

'He hired a man named Epps to follow us when you were here.' I told her about Epps having searched my house, and about Richard coming to my office. *You don't think I'm going to let her leave, do you?*

She cleared her throat. 'My ex-husband, Richard. Ben's father.' She cleared her throat again. 'He came to see you?'

'Yesterday.'

'And you didn't call me.' It wasn't a question. More a statement, more just wanting to make sure she had the facts of her life straight. 'You didn't think that was worth calling me about.'

I sighed. 'Mistake, huh?'

Silence again. Pike and Teri were watching me until Pike shook his head and turned away. Sometimes you can't win.

'I thought about calling you, but it seemed small. It seemed like something between Richard and me, and I didn't want to bring you into it.'

'A boy thing.' *How do you spell 'moron'?*

'He's upset because you and Ben are moving away, and he stepped over the line with Epps and this other stuff, but it's a stretch to think he could have anything to do with KROK.'

'You don't know, Elvis. This is exactly the kind of thing he would do.' I could hear her breathing. I had never asked about her former marriage, or what led to her divorce, and I didn't want to go there now. She said, 'I think I should come out there.'

146

'Talk to Tracy first. You don't want to come out until you know what you're up against because if you're wrong, it will look bad for you.'

She didn't say anything for several seconds, and then she said, 'Elvis, I'm really sorry about this.'

'You don't have anything to be sorry for.'

'Richard.'

She hung up without another word. I stood in my kitchen, holding the phone and listening to the dial tone, and then I hung up and joined Pike on the deck. The end of the day was approaching, and the sky to the east was hazy with smoke the color of bone. Somewhere, something was burning. Pike said, 'What?'

I told him.

Pike listened without comment, then said, 'Figured we should kill him.' Always with the helpful comment.

'I just don't see it, but you never know. What could some guy from Louisiana have to do with a television station here in Los Angeles?'

Pike crossed his arms and leaned against the deck rail. His head tilted ever so slightly, like maybe it was beyond him. I could see the TV reflected in his glasses. 'First the Russians, now this. You've got a lot to think about.'

'Yes, but I am large.'

He nodded. 'Keep your head in the game. Think about the wrong thing at the wrong time, it'll mean your ass.'

'Thanks.'

'Maybe mine, or those kids'.' You see the way he is? I said, 'You get a safe house?'

'Place in Studio City. Three bedrooms, furnished, phones. We can use it as long as we want.' He told me the address.

'Sounds good. I'm thinking maybe I should stay at Clark's house tonight. If the Russians haven't gotten him, Clark might go back there. He might be there now.'

Pike's mouth twitched. 'Sure.'

'Well, miracles happen.'

Pike told me he needed to buy supplies for the safe house and that he would be back later. I went into the kitchen to start dinner. I had half a head of iceberg lettuce and a fresh bag of spring greens and a couple of tomatoes that would do for a salad, and maybe half a dozen new potatoes that I could roast with the turkey loaf. I was gathering things together when Teri came into the kitchen and said, 'Can I help?'

'Sure.'

I told her what I planned, then showed her the cutting boards and knives, and gave her a small Maui onion and two carrots to dice. She said, 'What are you going to do with the carrots?'

'For the turkey loaf.'

She looked at me.

'We'll toss in raisins, too, along with a little soy sauce and maybe some peas. You'll see.'

'Winona doesn't like peas.'

'Okay, ix-nay the peas.'

She started with the onion. I worked with the potatoes. Teri used the knife carefully and well, and cut the onion into uniform pieces while Charles and Winona watched the destruction of the Earth. Twice I glanced up at her, and twice I caught her looking at me. Both times I smiled, and both times she looked away. After the second time, she said, 'How can Lucy be your girlfriend if she lives in Louisiana?'

'We didn't plan it that way, it just kind of happened.' I guess she'd been listening to my conversation.

'Do you date other girls?'

'No. I did for a while, but I kept thinking about Lucy, so I stopped seeing other people.'

'Does she date other men?'

'No.'

'How do you know?'

I frowned at her. 'She's been offered a job out here and she may move out – if she can work out the terms of the job.' If the job is still hers to be had.

Chopping. 'What if she can't move here?'

I chopped harder. 'We'll deal with it.' This kid was worse than Joe Pike.

When Teri was finished with the carrots I had her add them to the turkey, and then we mixed in the raisins and the soy sauce and a couple of eggs. I let Teri shape the loaf while I dug out a roasting pan. We put the meat in the pan and surrounded it with the potatoes. The fresh potatoes didn't look like enough, so I added a can of whole peeled new potatoes, and sprinkled everything with paprika. We put it in the oven at four hundred and set the timer for an hour. Teri said, 'I'm sorry about what happened at our house.'

'What do you mean?'

She looked embarrassed. 'When I cried.'

I remembered her eyes filling. I remembered a few tears. Then I remembered her packing it away and shutting it down like a SWAT team cop with twenty years on the job. I said, 'You don't have to apologize for that.'

She shook her head. 'I can't afford to lose control.'

'You're fifteen. It's okay to cry.'

She looked at the floor. 'I'm all they have. If I fall apart, who will take care of Winona and Charles?'

I stared at her. 'What about you? Who do you have?'

She pursed her lips. When she spoke, her voice was soft. 'I don't have anyone.'

I shook my head. 'No, that's not true. You have me.'

She frowned at me, then cocked her head. 'Oh, sure.' She stalked out of the kitchen and went up the stairs.

I said, 'Huh?'

I stayed in the kitchen, opened a Falstaff, and stared at the oven. The living room was rocked by alien explosions and Winona laughed. It seemed safer in the kitchen.

Charles edged into the dining room, fidgeting like something was bothering him. I said, 'What?'

'Nothing.'

I had more of the Falstaff. I glanced at my watch and wondered when Pike would get back. This baby-sitting was damned tough work.

Charles sidled into the door. 'I didn't mean it.'

'You didn't mean what?'

His hands were in his pockets and his face was red. 'I don't want him to be dead.'

I looked at him and sighed. 'I know, Charles. It's okay.'

Charles edged back into the living room. I stayed in the kitchen.

Joe Pike got back forty minutes later, and not long after that the timer dinged. Joe and Winona ate. The rest of us weren't hungry.

When the dishes were cleared I drove back to their house to wait for Clark Hewitt.

CHAPTER 18

The Saturn was still in its place. The Hewitts' house was dark, one of only two sleeping houses on their street.

I cruised the house once, parked around the corner, then walked back. The night air was cool, and traffic sounds from Melrose blended with the voices and laughter of children playing and adults taking an evening stroll.

I waited until two young women walking a dog were beyond me, then sauntered up the drive and let myself in using Teri's key. The lights were off, and I did not turn them on. I wanted to search the house again, but not at the risk of alerting either Clark or a passing car filled with Russians. I took off my jacket and holster, put the Dan Wesson near at hand, and settled in on the couch. After a while I slept, but I woke often at sounds made by the strange house, rising when I did to make sure that those sounds weren't Clark or Russian thugs. They never were, and little by little the dark brightened to dawn. Clark Hewitt did not return.

Fourteen minutes after six the next morning, it was light enough to work. I did a more detailed search now than I had with Teri, stripping Clark's bed and checking the mattress seams and the box spring liner, taking out every drawer in the dresser and chest to see if anything was taped behind or beneath them. I didn't know what I was looking for, or even think that I would find something, but you never know. When the phone company offices opened at nine I planned on checking the calls that Clark had made while he was home, but until then it was either search or stay on the couch and watch Regis and Kathie Lee. At least this way I could pretend to be a detective.

I went through Clark's closet, checking the pockets in his shirts and pants and coats, and I looked in his shoes. He didn't have many, so it didn't take long. I went through the bathroom, then once more went through the kitchen, and then the kids' rooms and the living room. At sixteen minutes after eight I was finished, and still hadn't found anything.

I went back into the kitchen, located a jar of Taster's Choice instant, and made a cup with hot water from the tap. At least I found the coffee.

I was sipping the coffee and thinking about phoning Tracy Mannos when I noticed a ceiling hatch in the hall. I hadn't noticed it before because the cord that's supposed to be there so you can pull down the door had been clipped, and also because most houses in Southern California are built without attics because of the heat. If you have anything, you might have a crawl space. I went into the hall and looked up at the door. It had been painted over a few hundred times, but the door seemed free and usable, and, with finger smudges around the edges, looked as if it had been used. Maybe I could detect more than instant coffee after all.

I used one of the dining room chairs, pulled down the door, unfolded the ladder, and climbed far enough to stick my head into the crawl space. Twelve minutes after eight in the morning and it was already a hundred degrees up there.

I went back to the kitchen for a flashlight, took off my shirt, and went up into the crawl space. Maybe ten feet back along one of the rafter wells was a dark, lumpy shape. I boosted myself up, then duckwalked along the prewar two-by-eights to a military surplus duffel bag, as clean and dust-free as if it had just been put there. I opened it enough to look inside and saw banded packs of hundred-dollar bills. I said, 'Aha.'

You hang around an empty house by yourself long enough, you'll say damn near anything.

I dropped the duffel out of the crawl space, opened it on the living room floor, and counted out a little more than twenty-three thousand dollars in worn C-notes that were perfect mates to the bills Special Agent Marsha Fields had confiscated. Markov money. Money that the Hewitts had been living on for the past three years, money good enough to get by with as long as you didn't flash it at a bank or in front of a Secret Service agent. Then I said 'Aha' again.

Mixed with the money were half a dozen printer's catalogs, all of which bore a mailing label addressed to one Wilson Brownell in Seattle, Washington. Clark was definitely printing again, and probably with Brownell's help. Maybe they were partners.

It was two minutes after nine when I put the money back into the duffel, and the duffel back into the attic. I kept the catalogs. I had a pretty good idea who Clark had phoned, and after I stowed the duffel I called my friend at the phone company and had her run a line check on the Hewitts' number covering the past three days just to be sure. It didn't take long. She told me that three calls had been made to two numbers, one of which lasted twenty-six minutes and showed a Seattle area code. Brownell. The other two numbers were both in the Los Angeles calling area, and belonged to Tre Michaels. Charles had called it right on that one.

If I hung around the house long enough, Clark would

return. The money was here, and, as far as Clark knew, so were his kids, but considering Clark's track record I might have to wait for days. Since Clark had phoned Tre Michaels, I was sure he was looking to connect, and that meant either he had been or would be visiting Culver City. Junkies may never go home, but they always go back to their connection. Ergo, Tre Michaels might know something. Maybe they were shooting up together right now.

I washed up, locked the house, and drove south to Culver City and the Bestco. I asked a Pakistani sales-clerk named Rahsheed for Tre, but Rahsheed told me that Tre had the day off. Great. I went along Overland to his apartment, figuring it was a long shot, but as I turned onto his street Michaels passed me going in the opposite direction in a dark blue Acura. Lucky is better than good every time.

I swung around in a fast K-turn, thinking my luck might hold and he might bring me to Clark. He didn't. He turned into the Culver City park and parked next to a rusted-out Dodge van where a couple of younger guys with long, sun-bleached hair were jumping skateboards. The younger guys were well muscled and shirtless, with dark tans and baggy shorts and high-top felony flyers, and they stopped the jumping and opened the van's side door when Tre got out of the Acura. Michaels opened the Acura's trunk, and everybody carried brand-new Sony laser-disc players to the van. Still in their boxes and almost certainly ripped off from Bestco. Tre closed his trunk, and everybody climbed into the van. The van didn't start and didn't move, and its windows were curtained over. Your friendly neighborhood dopemobile.

I parked at the far end of the lot, then crept back to the van and listened. Nothing. Out in the park, two women were jogging with babies in three-wheel strollers and a couple of guys had their shirts off to catch the sun and a half-dozen Latin guys were playing soccer and here in the parking lot Tre Michaels was scoring dope. Life in the big city.

I took out the Dan Wesson, waited for the women with the strollers to pass, then threw open the sliding door, and yelled, 'Police!'

Tre Michaels and the two young guys were sitting cross-legged on the bare metal deck, dividing up money and nickel bags of white powder amid the laser-disc players, all three of them frozen in mid-count, staring at the Dan Wesson with bulging wet eyes. The money was a short stack of worn hundreds, and I wondered if Tre had gotten them from Clark. One of the kids said, 'Oh, shit.'

Tre Michaels said, 'It's you.'

I lowered the gun. 'Good job, Officer Michaels. Couldn't've done it without you.'

The two kids looked at Tre.

Tre Michaels opened his mouth, then closed it and looked at the kids. 'I'm not a cop.'

The bigger kid's eyes narrowed. 'You prick.'

Michaels said, 'Hey. This is bullshit.'

I pulled Michaels out of the van. 'I think we can cut these kids a deal, don't you?' I jerked him harder, then slammed the side door and walked him away. The van's engine roared to life and its tires smoked. Michaels said, 'Are you nuts? Do you know what you did to me?'

'They're kids, Tre. You're not scared of a couple of kids, are you?'

His eyes were wide and bright, and his face was sheened with sweat. 'Jesus, you gotta be nuts.'

I walked him to the car. 'Tell me something. You think Bestco would press charges if they knew you were ripping off goods to turn over for dope?'

Michaels chewed at his lip and didn't say anything, staring after the departing van like it was the last bus to salvation and he had missed it. Across the park, the driver gave us the finger and yelled something I couldn't understand. Charles in five years.

I said, 'Clark Haines.' Tre wouldn't know 'Hewitt.'

Michaels stared at the van.

I jerked his arm. 'Wake up, Tre.'

He looked at me. 'That was my whole score. They got my money. They got the goods. Now what am I going to do?'

I jerked him again. Harder. 'Me or Bestco.'

Tre Michaels wet his lips, still staring after the van. 'Jesus, didn't we go through this before? I dunno where Clark is.'

Another jerk. 'He called you, Tre. Twice.'

He finally looked at me and his eyes were confused. I've never known an addict who wasn't. 'Well, yeah. He came by last night and scored a couple bags.'

Another jerk. 'C'mon, Tre. He's up to something and a crummy two bags wouldn't cut it.'

'He bought eight bags, okay? That was all I had.' He scrunched up his face like he was regretting something. 'I gave him a really good price.'

Eight bags was a lot. Maybe enough to travel on. Maybe he was going back to Seattle. 'Did he say why he needed so much?'

'He said he'd be gone for a few days.'

'He say where he was going?' I was thinking Seattle. I was thinking Wilson Brownell, again.

'Long Beach.'

I looked at him. 'He said he was going to Long Beach?'

Michaels made the scrunched face again. 'Well, he didn't say he was going to Long Beach, but he asked me

156

for a connection down there, so what would you think?'
Long Beach.

'Did you give him a name?'

Michaels frowned. 'Hell, I don't know anyone in Long
Beach.' He started to shake. 'You really screwed me with
those guys.' He waved his hands. 'Now what am I gonna
do, you tell me that? Now what?'

He was crying when I walked away.

I drove to my office. I still wanted to call Tracy
Mannos, but first I needed to call Brownell and ask him
about Long Beach. I would also call Teri and ask her.
Maybe saying the words would ring a bell.

At fourteen minutes after eleven, I left my car in the
parking garage, walked up the four flights to my office,
and found the place filled with cops.

Reed Jasper was sitting at my desk, while three other
guys that I'd never seen before were going through my
files. Papers were scattered around on the floor and the
place had been turned upside down. Jasper smiled when
he saw me, and said, 'Well, well, well. Just the guy we
wanted to see.'

I looked from Jasper to the other guys, then back to
Jasper. They were heavy men in dark rumpled suits with
anonymous faces. Feds. I said, 'What the hell are you
doing, Jasper?'

'Trying to get a line on Clark Hewitt, my man.' He
took a folded sheet of paper from his inside coat pocket
and dropped it on my desk. 'Federal order to search and
seize, duly signed and hereby presented.' He leaned back
in my chair and crossed his arms.

The other three guys were staring at me, and I felt
myself run cold. 'Why?'

'Wilson Brownell was found tortured to death yesterday afternoon. I think Clark Hewitt might've been
involved.'

CHAPTER 19

I said, 'If I wanted to remodel, I wouldn't have called the government.'

Jasper said, 'These are Agents Warren and Pigozzi of your Los Angeles Marshals' Office, and this is Special Agent Stansfield of the FBI.' Warren was black. Pigozzi sported bright red hair, and Stansfield's chin was littered with serious zit-craters. 'We're here because we believe you have knowledge of Clark Hewitt, either under that name or another.'

I dropped onto the couch and frowned at him. 'Didn't we go through this in Seattle?'

Warren said, 'I would encourage you to contact an attorney at this time.'

'Why?'

'Because anything you say will be used against you.'

I spread my hands. 'I've got nothing to hide.' Mr. Confident. 'Other than being pissed off that you guys are ransacking my office.'

Warren went back to the files like it didn't really matter to him either way.

Jasper shook his head. 'I don't get you, Cole. I know you're holding out, but I don't get why.'

I didn't say anything. How do you explain a promise to a fifteen-year-old?

He said, 'Your buddies the Markovs have come to town. If they haven't been around to see you, they will.'

'I hope they're neater than you guys.'

The red-haired agent looked up from the file cabinet, then let six or seven files dribble through his fingers to the floor. The floor was covered with yellow work sheets and billing statements and slim stapled reports. I said, 'That's really bush.'

Jasper looked over and frowned. 'Jesus Christ, Leo.'

Leo said, 'Maybe he shouldn't try to be funny.'

I said, 'That's a good line, Leo. You practice in front of the mirror?'

Leo made a ragged smile. 'Let's see if you're that good when it comes time to renew your license.'

'Pardon me while I catch my breath.'

Leo let more files dribble to the floor.

Jasper came around the desk like we were in his office, not mine. 'Look, Cole, all I want is a little cooperation.'

'You got a great way of showing it.'

'Clark Hewitt is up to his ass here, and so are his kids. You've met the Markovs. You know what I'm talking about.'

I tried to look like it didn't matter.

'My partner got blown away to keep Clark Hewitt whole. You don't think we're going to let anything happen to him now, do you?'

I tried to look like I didn't have a clue as to what he was talking about, but I knew he was right. I also knew that if Clark was printing again these guys would lock him down without a second thought, and that the Markovs would like that just fine. If he was in prison, the Markovs would know exactly where to find him.

Jasper motioned me out onto the balcony. 'Let's talk out here, Cole. It'll be easier while these guys work.'

I went out with him, but I didn't like it much. The sky had filled with a deep white haze that masked the Channel Islands. You could barely see the ocean. I stared at the haze and breathed the sea air. 'Did you guys do my house?'

'Before we came here.'

'You find anything?'

Jasper smiled. 'You know we didn't, and you know we're not going to find anything here either, but we gotta cover the bases.'

'Great, Jasper. That makes me feel better.'

Jasper crossed his arms and leaned with his back to the balcony rail. He was wearing little round government sunglasses and a dull gray suit, fine for Seattle but hot down here. It would be hot, and it just screamed 'fed.' He said, 'I don't like doing this, but I think you're holding out.'

'Moi?'

'I asked people about you, and those people said if you were looking for a guy, then you probably found him. I just can't figure why you won't come clean.'

'Maybe they're wrong.'

He nodded. 'Could be.'

'But maybe I just don't like being muscled, so I'm being petulant.'

He laughed. 'They said that, too.' He let the laugh fade. 'I know that Clark Hewitt was in Seattle. I know from eyewitnesses that a man matching Hewitt's description was seen in contact with Wilson Brownell, a former close associate and master counterfeiter. I'll bet you know that, too.'

'I saw Brownell when I was in Seattle. He didn't know anything.'

'I hope for Clark's sake he didn't.' Jasper watched the men inside work for a while. The black agent discovered the Pinocchio clock and nudged the red-haired agent, then they both stared at it. Jasper said, 'Brownell was tortured to death with a steam iron. I brought down the pictures. You wanna see?'

I shook my head.

'Here's a safe bet, Cole. Whatever Brownell knew, the Markovs now know. If Brownell knew whatever name they're living under, or an address or a phone number, they've got it now. You understand what I'm saying?'

'I get it, Jasper.' I took a breath, and stared south toward Catalina. I tried to see through the haze, but I could only make out the island's outline without seeing what was really there. 'I don't know where Clark is.'

The pocked agent came to the French doors and said, 'Jasper.'

Jasper went in and the four of them gathered by my desk and mumbled in low whispers, the red-haired agent standing with his hand on the pocked agent's back. It wasn't enough that I was ducking Russians and had the weight of the U.S. government on my case, but now I was thinking that maybe Brownell had known exactly where Clark was, and what he was doing, and maybe Dobcek and Sautin were on their way now. Maybe they already had Clark, but if they did there was nothing that I or Jasper could do about it, and I told myself that thinking about it did no good. The kids were the important thing, and the kids were safe. Maybe Clark was still okay, and if I could find him I could save him. If I could find him, maybe I could even bring him to Jasper without having to worry about them nailing him for a counterfeit beef. If he was still alive.

The black agent shook Jasper's hand and walked out of my office. The red-haired agent pointed out the Pinocchio clock to the pocked agent, and the pocked agent shook his head. Jasper came back to the balcony. I said, 'Is the party over?'

Jasper said, 'You're not in the clear. You just get a pass

for today.' He gave me a card. 'I'm staying at the Marriott downtown. I wrote my room number here. You decide to do the right thing, gimme a call.'

'Sure.' The right thing.

He looked at the haze and shook his head. 'How do you people breathe this shit?'

'Makes us tough, Jasper. Angelinos have the toughest lungs in America.'

He nodded, probably more to himself than to me. 'Yeah, sure.' Then he took a deep breath of it and went back to the door. 'I've known Clark Hewitt since he came to us, begging us to save his ass from the Markovs, and I can tell you he isn't what he seems.'

I stared at him.

'He comes across like this doof, but he's more than that.' He smiled at me, but there was no joy in it. 'Whatever you think you know about him, I can promise you this: It ain't what it seems, and neither is he.'

Reed Jasper showed me his palms like he had given me the Rosetta stone and it was up to me what I did with it. Then he walked back through my office and out the door. The red-haired agent and the pocked agent walked with him, and they didn't bother to close the door.

I stayed on the balcony until they left the building and climbed into two dark blue G-rides and melted into the traffic on Santa Monica Boulevard. Then I went in, closed the outer door, and picked up my papers. It took most of an hour, but no more than that because there hadn't been a lot in my files. Nothing seemed to be missing, though a small ceramic statue of Jiminy Cricket had fallen and broken. I threw it away.

When the papers were in their folders and the folders back in their files and the files once more in the cabinet, I opened a longneck Budweiser, sat at my desk, and put my feet up. I said, 'Clark, you'd better be worth it.'

The phone rang then, and I scooped it up. Mr. Happy-go-lucky. Mr. Shirttail-out-and-nothing-on-my-mind, hanging around his office with a liplock on a longneck, the very image of the depressed detective contemplating the loss of his license and livelihood to the weight of the United States government. 'Elvis Cole Detective Agency, professional detection at going-out-of-business rates.'

Tracy Mannos said, 'Are you drunk?'

'Not yet.'

'Well, bag it. Can you come see me?'

I frowned at the Pinocchio. 'Now?' Thinking about Pike and those kids at the safe house. Thinking about following the Long Beach lead. 'You find out something about Lucy's negotiation?'

'I'd rather do this in person, here at KROK.' Ah.

'Why there?'

She sounded irritated. 'Stop being stupid and get over here.' Then she hung up.

I locked the office, then slowly drove to KROK to see Tracy Mannos. No one followed me.

No one that I could see.

CHAPTER 20

KROK Television, Power Channel 8 (*Personal News from Us to You – We take it personally!!*), was housed in a large brick and steel building off Western Avenue in the east side of Hollywood. I parked in the little security lot they have next to the building, and found Tracy waiting for me in the reception area. I hadn't expected her to be waiting, but she was, and she looked anxious. I said, 'Guess you found something.'

'Let's talk in my office.'

Tracy Mannos was a tall, attractive woman in her early fifties. Her hair was streaked with gray and cut close, and she carried herself with an erect, no-nonsense corporate manner, every inch the authoritative station manager. Lucy and I had met her when I was working on the Theodore Martin murder case, and she had been impressed enough with Lucy's bearing and legal analysis to suggest to her bosses that Lucy be offered the job of on-air legal analyst.

She led me through a heavy glass security door and along a sterile hall, near deserted because of the time of day. She said, 'Stu Greenberg's our head of business affairs. I asked him about Lucy's negotiation, and he said that there was nothing unusual about it. In fact, he told me not to worry.'

'Did you ask Mr. Greenberg if perhaps he's had some association with Mr. Chenier?' We went into a sleek white office with comfortable chairs and a cluttered desk. Photographs of a man and three children dotted the walls.

Tracy settled back in the chair and smiled at me. 'A television station is a very political environment, Elvis. People are easily offended, and more than one back around here sports multiple knife wounds.'

I nodded. 'You're saying you couldn't ask him straight out.'

'We have to be very careful that we don't step on something that bites us.'

I nodded again.

'Though I did manage to gain a bit of intelligence when I was in Stu's office.'

'Ah.' I knew that she had. You could see that in her eyes, too. A kind of ferocious twinkle.

'Stuart began his career in Houston, at the home office of Benton, Meyers and Dane.' Richard's firm.

'How about that.' The old-boy network rears its ugly head.

'Yes, but that doesn't prove anything. Greenberg is still the head of business affairs, and how he runs that department is his prerogative.' Then the twinkle became a hard glint. 'Until it becomes an issue that transcends acceptable business practices.'

'Such as an ex-husband pulling strings to limit his former wife's career options.'

'Yes. Then it becomes a larger issue, one to which this corporation would be sensitive.' She spread her hands. 'After all, if such were the case, Lucy might sue.'

'If she had proof.'

'Yes. But proof in such a case is elusive and hard to find. Maybe impossible to find.'

'Um.'

Tracy Mannos leaned toward me. Pointedly. 'Recognizing that, it could be something that simply appears to be proof. After all, if what we're talking about here is an issue of gender politics, the appearance of wrongdoing is something to which this station would be sensitive. When I was in Stu's office, I had the distinct impression that something might be there.'

'Like what?'

She spread her hands. 'You're the detective.'

She stayed with the lean, and I knew it meant something. I thought that she might have a very clear idea of what might constitute that kind of leverage, and where I might find it. I said, 'You got this impression while you were in his office?'

'More like when I was leaving his office and saying good-bye to his secretary.' Ah.

'And has Mr. Greenberg gone home for the day?'

She smiled, like maybe the slow kid in class was coming along after all. 'I'm not sure, Elvis. He usually leaves much earlier than this, but he might still be here.'

'I think I'll go speak with him.'

She settled back in her chair and nodded. 'You do that. I'm sure you'll find it enlightening.'

She told me how to get to Stuart Greenberg's office, and I found my way through the empty halls to the business affairs division. The lower floors of the station were bustling with activity as they mounted the evening broadcasts, but the upper business floors were deserted except for the cleaning crews. No one was around to ask who I was or what I was doing.

Stuart Greenberg had a nice corner office, replete with diplomas and family photographs and plants that were healthier than mine, but I didn't need to go there. I had listened to Tracy closely, and read between the lines, and figured that if anything was to be found it wouldn't be in Greenberg's office, but at his secretary's desk, and if anyone was going to find it, it was going to be me, and not Tracy Mannos. She would go only so far, and no farther. The risk would be mine.

The phone log of Greenberg's outgoing and incoming calls was there, next to the phone. I nodded at the cleaning crew, then sat at the desk and flipped backward through the pages, and found exactly what Tracy Mannos had suggested I would. Three days ago Richard Chenier had phoned Stuart Greenberg twice. There wasn't anything to indicate the content of the conversations, but, as Tracy had also suggested, there didn't have to be. I took the log to a copy machine, copied the page reflecting Richard's calls, then put the log back and drove home.

The cat was sitting in the mouth of my carport when I eased up to the house, one ear up, one down, and his head canted to the side. He looked surly and out-of-sorts, and he did not move even though I nosed the car toward him. I had to park on the street. I said, 'This last week has been hell, hasn't it?'

He ignored me. Snubbed by my cat.

I let myself in through the kitchen and walked through the house to see what the feds had done. Four drawers had been dumped, others left open, and three empty Falstaff cans were sitting on the dining room table. Most of the search seemed to have been in the kitchen and my bedroom, but the mess was not as bad as the office. I guess Jasper had told them to take it easy. Or maybe they were too busy drinking my beer.

I put out a fresh bowl of food for the cat, then called Joe at the safe house. The phone rang twice, and Charles answered. 'We don't want any.' Then he hung up.

I took a deep breath, let it out, and rubbed at my eyes. I dialed again. This time Joe answered on the first ring. I said, 'Can the kids overhear us?'

'No.'

I told him about Reed Jasper and the feds having searched my house and office, and Wilson Brownell turning up dead. Pike said, 'I guess these Russians mean it.'

'They mean it.' I told him about finding the money and catalogs in Clark's attic. 'We have to assume that they know what Brownell knew, where Clark was living and that Clark was using the name Haines. I think we're okay as long as we stay away from there.'

'Where are you now?'

I told him.

'What if Clark goes home?'

I had already thought it through and I didn't like where it led, but there weren't a lot of options. We could sit at the house and wait, but a proactive search seemed better. We could periodically check the house. I told Joe that I had other calls to make, and that I might not come by the safe house until morning 'Besides, my house has been searched by Richard's guy, and now by the feds. Maybe Dobcek and Sautin will come by next, and I can shoot them to death.'

Pike said, 'Take your fun where you find it.'

I hung up, then called Lucy at home. She answered as if she were perched by the phone. I said, 'It's me.'

'Let me change phones.' I waited. Ben was probably there.

When she came back on the line I told her about my conversation with Tracy Mannos, and what I had found in Stuart Greenberg's phone log. When I finished, she said, 'I'm coming out there.'

'Maybe you should talk to Tracy first. Tracy knows what you're up against, and I think she knows how to handle it, but this is pretty flimsy evidence.' In fact, it wasn't evidence at all, but I didn't want to be a defeatist.

She didn't say anything for a while, and then she said, 'I am not going to simply allow this to happen. Richard has no right to use his influence to affect my life. If I do nothing, and Tracy fails, then I'll feel all the worse.'

I didn't answer.

'I'm mad as hell, but I'm also a professional. Now that I know what I'm dealing with, I have no doubt that we can win. These are just two old-boy assholes trying to keep the little woman in her place.'

Pretty much what Tracy had said.

'Well, this is the wrong little woman.' She was quiet for a moment, but I guessed she was thinking. 'I don't care what Richard told you, it's not about Ben. Richard was a lousy father from day one, and he's still a lousy father. This is about me, and about power. That's why I divorced the sonofabitch.' She was mad, all right. 'He's an arrogant, self-involved prick, and if he thinks he can pull a stunt like this on me, I'll cut him a new asshole and stuff his head in it.' Whew.

I said, 'Luce?'

'What?' She almost shouted it.

'Please don't give yourself a stroke.'

She fell absolutely silent, and then she laughed. 'Wow. I'm really mad.'

'Glad I'm not on the receiving end.'

'Not you, Elvis. Not ever.' She laughed some more, and it was good to hear her laugh. Good to hear her sound so strong. 'I have to come out there and do this, even if it makes everything worse. Even if it costs me this job. You see that, don't you?'

'Sure.' I told her about the safe house, gave her the number there, and told her to call Joe with her flight information. After we hung up, I said, 'Richard, prepare to be sawed.'

It took me a little better than an hour to go through the house and put my things in order. I guess if I were a more accommodating person, I could find value in government agents doing such a thorough job.

After all, these were our tax dollars at work.

CHAPTER 21

I drove down the backside of Laurel Canyon into Studio City the next morning, going maybe fifteen miles out of my way to avoid detection. If I couldn't slip the Russians and the feds by slick driving, maybe I could wear them out with LA's morning rush-hour traffic.

The condo Pike had found for a safe house sat in the rear of a quiet, two-level garden building just off Coldwater Canyon near the Studio City Park. It was a classic ranch-style building of the kind constructed in the late fifties, all dark-stained wood and used brick, with mature pine trees lining the sidewalk and a parking lot for residents in the rear. Just the kind of place where unsuspecting inhabitants would never dream that the new people in the corner apartment were being stalked by homicidal maniacs from Seattle.

I parked at the curb, gathered the catalogs I'd taken from Clark's duffel bag, then wandered through the garden courtyard until I found the right door. I rang the bell at ten minutes after nine. Charles's muffled voice came from behind the door as if he'd been waiting there. 'Go away.'

I said, 'Charles.' What a way to start your morning.

The door opened and Pike was there, tall and expressionless. I gave the big grin. 'Well, Joseph, bet you had a fun evening.'

Charles eyed me from the safety of the kitchen. 'It was a joke.'

Pike's head swiveled toward him and Charles ducked out of the kitchen and into the living room. Fun evening, all right.

The entry led past the kitchen to a dining area and the living room beyond, stairs climbing one wall of the living room to open to the second floor. The condo was large and spacious and fully furnished, as if whoever owned the place was away on a short trip. Thriving green plants dotted the room, and the plants were healthy and firm and devoid of yellow. Maybe I should ask whoever owned them for lessons. I nodded at Pike. 'Nice. Better than the Airstream.'

Pike shrugged. Guess it didn't matter to him either way.

Teri and Winona were at the dining room table, and Charles had assumed a position in front of the television. Watching one of those morning exercise shows on ESPN. Kiana Tom doing ab work. Winona said, 'Did you find our daddy yet?' Everyone was dressed and clean and ready to start their day of waiting for the detective to find their father.

'Not yet, hon. But I'm hot on his trail.' Hope is everything.

Teri said, 'Would you like breakfast? Joe and I made cottage cheese pancakes.'

'No, thanks. I ate before I left home.'

She looked disappointed. 'There's fresh coffee.'

I let her pour a cup, sipped some, then nodded. 'Good.'

Teri smiled and seemed pleased.

Joe said, 'We can talk upstairs.'

I followed Pike up with the coffee into one of the three bedrooms. It had been made up as a home office with desk and telephone and fax machine, but there was nothing around to indicate the owner's identity. Maybe

Pike owned the place. For all I knew, Pike owned most of Los Angeles. He said, 'What'd you find?'

'Twenty thousand bucks in counterfeit hundreds and these.' I showed him the catalogs. Several pages were dog-eared, and quite a few items had been marked on the dog-eared pages, including two different grades of offset plate blanks from a firm in Finland, a high-end Hitachi digital scanner from a discount mail-order house in New York, a four-thousand-dollar Power Mac from a mail-order firm in Los Angeles with a commercial graphics software platform that cost almost as much as the computer, something called a dual-side regulator from a commercial printing firm in London, a high-volume paper shear from the same company, and sixty liters each of indigo #7 and canyon orange #9A oil-based ink, as well as lesser amounts of forest green #2, classic red #42, black, kiss blue #12, and yellow AB1, all of which came from three different ink manufacturers, two in Europe and one in Maryland. Pike said, 'He's printing, all right.'

'Yeah, but what?' Hundred-dollar bills are green and black. 'Why would he need indigo and orange?'

Pike took out his wallet and pulled out a hundred-dollar bill. Walking around money. 'Maybe you have to mix them to get the different shades of black. Maybe he uses them to reproduce the security fibers.'

'Maybe if we just took all this stuff to your pal Marsha Fields she could tell us.'

Pike put his hundred away. 'The new hundreds are too hard to copy. If he's making hundreds, he'll make the older series.'

'If?'

Pike flipped back through the catalogs. 'This is almost forty thousand dollars' worth of material. Wonder where he's getting the money to pay for it.'

I was wondering that, too. He almost certainly wasn't sending counterfeit cash through the mail, and he knew better than to try to buy money orders or certified checks at a bank or at American Express. I said, 'If he ordered this stuff, it had to be delivered. Maybe Clark's wherever that is.'

Most of the companies had an 800 number for phone orders, so I took a flyer and called the Los Angeles computer wholesaler first. A young woman with a Hispanic accent answered, 'Good morning from Cyber-World! What would you like to order?' Bright and cheery and wanting to help.

'I placed an order a couple of days ago and the machine hasn't arrived.' Just another customer on just another day.

'Why, let me track down that bad boy!' Wanting to make my phone shopping experience a happy one. 'Your name, please.'

'Clark Haines.' I waited a couple of seconds, then said, 'Oh, you know, my secretary placed the order and she might've used our company name, Clark Hewitt. Heh-heh.' Lame, but what can you do?

The young woman said, 'Gee, we're not showing an order to either of those names. Could she have made the order in another name?'

I thanked her and hung up.

I called three more companies, and none of them had or was processing an order for Haines or Hewitt either. When I put down the phone, I said, 'Hell.'

Pike said, 'Maybe he hasn't ordered yet. Maybe he's going to.'

'Maybe.'

I thought about Clark phoning Wilson Brownell, and how they had spoken often, and how Clark was willing to risk the Russians to go see Brownell. I called the electronics wholesaler in New York and told him exactly what I had told the other four companies, only I told him that my name was Wilson Brownell. He came back on the line almost at once and said, 'Oh yes, Mr. Brownell, here it is.'

I gave Pike a thumbs-up.

The order clerk said, 'Mm, your scanner won't go out until tomorrow. Isn't that what you requested?'

'I wanted it today.'

'I'm sorry, sir. Whoever took the order must've made a mistake.'

'Well, as long as you're on the phone let's double-check the destination. I'd hate to think it was going to the wrong place.'

'Yes sir. We show the airbill addressed to *Pacific Rim Weekly Journal*, hold for airport pickup, on United flight five, direct to LAX.'

I wrote it down. 'And that's tomorrow?'

'Yes sir. It's right here on the form.'

I hung up, then dialed Los Angeles information and asked for the number of the *Pacific Rim Weekly Journal*. The information operator said, 'I'm sorry, sir. We have no listing in that name.'

'Try the valley.'

'Sorry, sir. Still no listing.'

I thought about Tre Michaels. 'Try Long Beach.'

She said, 'Here we go.' She gave me the address and phone, and I said, 'Touchdown.'

'Pardon me?'

'Nothing, Operator. Thanks.'

I dialed the number, and a woman answered with a heavy Asian accent. '*Journal*.'

'May I speak with Clark, please.'

She hung up without another word, and I looked at Pike. 'I think we may be onto something.'

Pike stayed with the Hewitt children, and I took the long drive south to Long Beach, following the Hollywood Freeway to the Harbor Freeway, then dropping straight south for almost an hour before picking up the San Diego Freeway east to the 710 and turning south again to parallel the Los Angeles River all the way to the ocean. Downtown Long Beach is a core of redeveloped modern high rises surrounded by an older landscape of two-story stucco bars and craftsman homes and traffic dividers dotted with palm trees that lend a small-town water-front feel. It would've been a fine place to bring Teri and Charles and Winona for ice-cream cones and a walk in the sun around Belmont Pier to watch the boats coming and going to Catalina Island, only sun walking and boat watching often lose their appeal when you're thinking that your father might've been tortured to death by a steam iron. Maybe another time.

I followed Ocean Boulevard east along the water, then turned north along Redondo Avenue, watching the landscape evolve from small-town waterfront to middle-class residential to lower-class urban, the signs gradually changing from English to Spanish and finally to Asian as the faces changed with them. The *Pacific Rim Weekly Journal* sat two blocks off Redondo in a small three-story commercial building between a tiny Vietnamese restaur-ant and a coin-operated laundry filled with tiny Asian women who were probably Vietnamese or Cambodian.

I cruised the building twice, then parked one block south and walked up past the *Journal* to the restaurant. I glimpsed two people in the *Journal* office, but neither was Clark Hewitt.

It was still before eleven, and the restaurant was empty except for an ancient Vietnamese woman wrap-ping forks and spoons in white cloth napkins. Preparing for the lunch-hour rush. I smiled at her. 'Do you have a take-out menu?'

She gave me a green take-out menu. 'You early.'

'Too early to order?'

She shook her head. 'Oh no. We serve.'

I ordered squid fried rice with honey, and told her that I would wait out front on the sidewalk. She said that would be fine.

I stood around out front with the little menu and tried to look as if I had nothing on my mind except food, and snuck glances in the *Journal* office next door. An Asian woman in her early sixties sat at a wooden desk, talking on the phone. Behind her, the walls were lined with corkboard and about a million little bits of paper and photographs and what looked like posters for community events had been pinned to the board. A couple of ratty chairs were at the front of the office, and another desk sat opposite the woman's, this one occupied by a young Asian guy who looked to be in his twenties. He wore a Cal Tech sweatshirt and tiger stripe field utilities and Top-Siders without socks. He was leaning back, the Top-Siders up on the desk, reading a paperback. A half wall split the space into a front and a back, only you couldn't see the back from here in the front. Maybe Clark was in the back. Maybe I could whip out my gun, charge through the front into the back, and shout, 'Gotcha!' Be impressive as hell if he was really there.

The young guy saw me looking. I smiled and took a copy of the *Journal* from a wire rack bolted to the front of the building, just another bored guy killing time while he waited for his food. It was a tabloid-sized Vietnamese-language newspaper filled with articles I couldn't read and pictures of Vietnamese people that I took to be from the local community. The printing was cheesy and smudged, and I wondered if maybe Clark had been hired to give them a more professional look. 'Do you read Vietnamese?'

The young guy was standing in the door. Inside, the woman was still on the phone, but now watching me.

I shook my head and put down the paper. 'No. I'm just waiting for some food next door. I was curious.'

He grinned. 'They're free. Help yourself, if you want. They make a great birdcage liner.' Mr. Friendly.

I strolled back past the restaurant and up a short alley, looking for the rear entrance. One of the wonderful things about being so close to the water is that the temperatures are so mild that you rarely have to use air-conditioning. It was in the low seventies, so the *Journal*'s rear door was open for the air. I peeked inside. Furtive.

No Clark.

I listened at the door, then stepped in. An Apple laser printer was humming on a little desk beside another door that led to a bathroom. Industrial metal shelves were stacked with reams of paper and office supplies and a well-used Mr. Coffee, but nothing screamed *counterfeiter* and I didn't see any of the things that Clark had marked in his catalogs.

I slipped out, went around to the front again, and this time I walked into the *Journal* office. The young guy was back with his book and the older woman looked up from her word processor. The young guy smiled, but the older woman didn't. I said, 'My name is Elvis Cole, and I'm looking for Clark Hewitt.' I put one of my cards on the young guy's desk. 'His life is in danger and I'm trying to help him. I'm also trying to help his children.' Sometimes honesty is the best policy.

The young guy's smile vanished, and the woman said something in Vietnamese. The young guy answered, also in Vietnamese.

I said, 'Sorry?'

177

The young guy stared at me for a couple of seconds before he shook his head. 'I don't know what you're talking about.' You could tell that he did. You could tell that he knew exactly what I was talking about, and that he did not like it that I had asked, or that I knew.

I glanced at the woman, and she turned away. Fast.

I said, 'I'm driving a 1966 Corvette convertible parked down the block. It's yellow. I'll be sitting in it.'

I went to the restaurant, paid for my food, then walked back to my car, put the top up to cut the sun, and sat. The squid fried rice was excellent, but I didn't have much of an appetite for it.

Twenty minutes later the guy in the Cal Tech sweatshirt came out to the street, looked at me, then went back inside. Sixteen minutes after that, a black 500-series Mercedes sedan circled the block twice, two Asian men in their mid-sixties inside. I copied their license number. Maybe eight minutes after that, a bright red Ferrari Spyder appeared from the opposite direction and eased to a stop a car length away from me. Whoever these guys were, they had money. The Ferrari was driven by a very young Asian guy, but an older man was in the shotgun seat, and, like the people in the Mercedes, both of them were nicely dressed in Italian business suits. I copied the Ferrari's plate number, too. The two men in the Ferrari stared at me for a couple of minutes, talking to each other, and then the young guy rolled down his window and eased next to me to talk. I said, 'Clark Hewitt.'

The young guy shook his head. 'Got no idea who that is.' Flawless English without a trace of an accent. Local.

'I think you do.'

The young guy looked nervous, but the older guy seemed calm. The younger guy said, 'My mother works at the paper, and you're scaring her. I'm going to ask you to leave.' I guess the paper was a family business, but it probably didn't pay for his Ferrari.

'Do you own the paper?'

'I think you should leave.'

I settled back in my seat. 'Can't leave until I see Clark Hewitt.'

The older man said something, and the younger guy shook his head. 'We never heard of the guy.'

'Fine.' I crossed my arms and made like I was going to take a nap.

The older man mumbled something else, and the younger guy said, 'Are you the police?'

'Clark knows who I am. I gave your mother a card.'

The older man leaned past the younger guy. 'If you don't leave, we'll have to call the police.'

'Go ahead. We can talk about Clark and his association with your newspaper.'

The younger guy's jaw flexed, and now he said something to the older guy. 'You're not going away?'

'No.'

The younger guy nodded. 'Big mistake.'

He dropped the Ferrari into first gear and rocketed away, tires screaming and filling the air with smoke and burning rubber. Guess he'd seen someone do that in a movie.

The Mercedes left, too.

I waited. I had found the *Pacific Rim Weekly Journal*, and I had found some people who clearly knew Clark Hewitt. I was making gangbuster progress, and I was feeling proud of myself. Elvis Cole, Smug Detective.

Ninety seconds after the Ferrari roared away three men came out of the alley and approached me. They weren't in Italian business suits, and they didn't look as if they would've been any more impressed by a kid peeling out than I had been. They looked hard and lean and focused with flat, expressionless faces, and all three were wearing long coats. They walked with their hands in their coat pockets, and when they reached the car the one in the middle pulled back his coat enough to reveal a stubby black Benelli combat shotgun. He said, 'Guess what you're going to do?'

'Leave?'

He nodded.

'Tell Clark I'll be back.'

I started the car and drove away.

Honesty might be the best policy, but leaving is the better part of valor.

CHAPTER 22

I drove back to Belmont Pier, parked in front of a shop that sold whale-watching tickets, and used a pay phone there to call Lou Poitras. He said, 'Bubba, you really take advantage.'

'Funny. Your wife said the same thing.'

Poitras sighed. 'Just tell me what you want.' Humor. You break them down with humor, and victory is yours.

I gave him the two license numbers, asked for an ID, and waited while he brought it up on his computer. It took less than twenty seconds. 'The Mercedes is registered to a Nguyen Dak of Seal Beach.' Seal Beach is one of the wealthier communities along the south beach.

'What about the Ferrari?'

'Guy named Walter Tran. He's down in Newport Beach.' Another big-money community.

I said, 'These guys show a history?' Asking him if they'd ever been arrested.

'Couple of speeding tickets on the Ferrari, but that's it. You want to tell me what this is about?'

'Nope.' I hung up, bought an iced tea from a sausage grill, then stared at the bay. The water was clean and blue, and Catalina was in sharp relief twenty-six miles away. A young woman in short-shorts and a metallic blue bikini top Rollerbladed past on the bicycle path. I followed her motion but did not see her. The detective in thoughtful mode. I had never heard of Nguyen Dak or

Walter Tran, but that didn't mean anything. Multicultural crime was flourishing with the Southland's growing diversity, and it was impossible to keep up. I had also never heard of the *Pacific Rim Weekly Journal*, but I was pretty sure I knew someone who had.

I went back to the pay phone, and called this reporter I know named Eddie Ditko. Eddie is old and cranky and sour, but he is nothing if not a joy. 'Christ, I got gas. You get to be my age, even water makes you cut the cheese.' You see?

'You ever heard of the *Pacific Rim Weekly Journal*?'

He went into a coughing fit.

'Eddie?' He was coughing pretty bad.

'Jesus, I'm choking to death.'

'I'll hang up and call nine-one-one.' The coughing was getting worse.

'Screw nine-one-one. They'd probably just put you on hold.' He made a gakking sound, then got the coughing under control. 'Christ, I just popped up something looks like a hairball.'

'That's more than I needed to know.'

'Yeah, well, try living with it. Getting old is hell.'

'*Pacific Rim Weekly Journal*.' Sometimes you have to prompt him.

'Yeah, yeah, yeah. Hold your water and lemme see what we got.' He was probably scanning the *Examiner*'s computer database.

'Check out Nguyen Dak and Walter Tran while you're at it.'

'Christ, you're pushy.' He made a hawking sound, then he spit. Sweet. 'Here we go. It's a political soapbox for nationalist Vietnamese who want their country back. LAPD's Antiterrorist Task Force has them on the monitor list.'

The blader with the metallic top rolled past in the opposite direction. I said, 'Political terrorists?'

'You know how the Cubans in South Florida want to overthrow Castro? It's the same thing. The *Pacific Rim Weekly Journal* raises money and lobbies politicians to discourage normalization with the Commies.' Commies. 'They also advocate the overthrow of the Communist government over there, and under our statutes that qualifies as terrorism, so LAPD has to waste money watching them.'

'What do you mean, 'waste'?'

More coughing. Another hawking sound, and then the spitting. 'Christ, that one had legs.'

'Why a waste, Eddie?'

'We did a feature on these guys in the Orange County edition a couple of years back. Dak and Tran and some of their pals fund the paper, but it's not how they make their living. They're self-made millionaires. Dak washed dishes until he scraped together the money to open a noodle shop. That led to more noodle shops, and pretty soon he was building strip malls. Tran bought a goddamned carpet shampooer to wash rugs after the day shift, and now he's got six hundred employees.'

I thought about Tran in his Ferrari. 'Tran's a young guy.'

'You must be talkin' about his kid, Walter Junior. Walter Senior's gotta be in his sixties. These guys came here with nothing, and now they're living the American dream.'

'Except that they're listed as terrorists.'

'Yeah, well, they didn't come over here for the oranges. They fled Vietnam to escape the Communists, and they damn well want the Commies out so they can go home.'

'Thanks, Eddie.'

I put down the phone and stared at the Rollerbladers and thought about self-made men without criminal records who just want to go home. Good Republicans with a raggy little newspaper and a career counterfeiter on the payroll. Maybe they couldn't quite raise enough money for the cause through strip malls and carpet cleaning and political action committees, so now they were branching out into crime. Crime, after all, is America's largest growth industry.

I made one more call, this time to Joe Pike. 'You hear from Lucy?'

'Yes.' She had given him her flight information, and he passed it to me. She would be arriving on a Delta flight from New Orleans in a little less than two hours, and she would expect me to pick her up. She had made arrangements to stay with Tracy, and, if I couldn't make it, I was to call Tracy.

'Kids okay?'

Pike hung up. I guess too much time with Charles will do that to you.

I worked my way back onto the freeway and made the long drive north to LAX, periodically checking the mirror for Russians, federal agents, and Vietnamese thugs with Benelli autoloading shotguns. If I could bring these guys together, we could have quite a party.

The traffic was dense and sluggish, but I found myself smiling more often than not, and feeling pretty good about things. I was getting closer to Clark, and I was only minutes away from seeing Lucy. I had been neither shot nor beaten in almost three days. Happy is as happy does.

I was still happy when Lucy Chenier came out of the jetway, saw me, and opened her arms. She was wearing a charcoal suit and carrying an overnight bag. She wasn't smiling, but that was okay. I was smiling enough for both of us.

We hugged, and I could feel the tension in her back and shoulders, and the strength there. I whispered into her hair, 'It is so good to see you. Even for a rotten reason like this.' Her hair smelled of peaches.

She hugged harder, and an overweight man with no hair scowled because we were blocking his way.

'You want me to take you to Tracy's?'

'I want to spend some time with you first. There's something that we need to talk about.' Her face was composed and empty of emotion, and I thought it must be her game face. The same face she would use in court; the face she had used when she was working her way through college on a tennis scholarship.

'Okay. Do you have bags?'

'Only this.' She let me carry her bag, and as we walked to the car she said little. Focused, I guess. Sleek and stripped down and ready for war. Or maybe she was just scared.

Once we were on the freeway, she brought my hand into her lap, holding it tight with both of hers. I thought she might fear letting go. I said, 'Does Ben know what's going on?'

Her eyes were not quite on the creeping red lights ahead of us. 'No. I've always kept the bad things between me and Richard from him. I've thought that was best.'

I nodded.

'I didn't want him in the middle.'

'Of course.'

She glanced at me. 'I don't want you in the middle either.'

I looked at her. A woman in a black Jaguar cut in front of us and I had to brake. 'Luce, there is no middle here for me. I love you, and I'm with you. I'll help any way I can.'

A tiny smile worked at her lips. The smile was so

small that it was almost impossible to see. I almost didn't. She said, 'I know that you do, but I have to do this without you.'

I didn't say anything.

'It's important to me that you understand that I'm not being selfish. This isn't about Ben.'

'All right.'

'When we got divorced, I offered Richard open visitation rights. He never took advantage of it. When Ben would stay with Richard on weekends, or during the summer or on holidays, Richard was never there. He would hire a sitter, or drop Ben at his grandmother's. What's happening now isn't about Ben, it's about me, and Richard's need to control me, so please don't think that I'm this horrible woman who's stealing a man's child.' She looked at me then, and something in great pain was peeking through the composure. 'I am not the villain here.'

'Luce, you never could be.' She said it all as if she'd spent most of the flight thinking it through. I guess that she had. 'And you don't have to explain yourself or your former marriage to me.'

She looked at our hands, twined there in her lap. 'I know you want to help me through this. You already have, and I'm grateful, but you can't help me anymore.' She tugged at my hand, and when I looked over I think she was trying not to cry. 'I will not have my life defined by triangles. It's not fair to you, and it's not fair to me. Richard is my mistake, and I have to live with it.'

I didn't know what to say.

'What's going on now is between me and Richard, and only us. I need it to be that way. Do you understand?'

'No.'

She frowned. 'This is all about control, and he has to know that he can't control me, or intimidate me.' She frowned harder. 'I have to know that, too.'

I stared at her. Lucy Chenier seemed like the most uncontrollable woman I'd ever met, but maybe she hadn't always been so, and maybe she needed to remind herself.

'I could just shoot him. That would solve the problem.'

She smiled, and it was warm. 'I know, but then you would have saved me, and I wouldn't have saved myself. This is for me.'

'Okay.'

'I am the saver, and not just the savee.'

'You don't want me to be with you at KROK.'

She squeezed my hand again. 'No, you can't be there.'

I didn't like it, but I tried not to look sulky.

'Richard and I will be the only two players on the court, and when I kick his ass, and get his good-old-boy buddy up the proverbial creek, Richard will think twice about ever trying anything like this again.'

I looked at her, and thought that she was the most beautiful woman I had ever seen. 'Can I shoot him later?'

She smiled again, and this time patted my hand. 'We'll see.'

Something to live for.

'When are you going to see the KROK people?'

'Tracy arranged a meeting for tomorrow afternoon.'

Tomorrow was when the scanner arrived at LAX. Pike and I would be there waiting. We would be following the scanner, and hoping it brought us to Clark. 'I'll be working.'

She squeezed my hand again. 'Of course you will, my dove. That's as it should be.' She squeezed my hand another time. 'And I will be loving you.'

'Good.'

We continued up through the Sepulveda Pass into the Valley, and then on toward the safe house, riding in silence.

CHAPTER 23

The condo in Studio City smelled of rosemary and baked chicken. Joe and Teri were in the kitchen, and Winona and Charles were in the living room, but the TV wasn't on. Guess Pike had drawn the line. I said, 'That smells terrific.'

Winona bounced in from the living room. 'Teri and Joe made chicken. Hi, Lucy.'

'Hi, sweetie.'

Charles peered at Lucy from the dining room and grunted hello. Teri didn't say anything. She was behind a little forest of pots at the stove, frowning.

Lucy went into the kitchen and gave Teri a hug. 'How are you doing, dear?'

'Fine.' Tight and terse and futzing with the pots.

Lucy said, 'That smells wonderful. What is it, rosemary chicken?'

'Um.'

Lucy came back to me and took my hand. Teri frowned harder, then suddenly smiled brightly at me as if Lucy wasn't there. 'I saved some for you, Elvis.' The bright smile turned sad and she looked at Lucy. 'But I don't think there's enough for two.'

I stared at her.

Lucy said, 'Oh, that's all right. I should call Tracy and tell her how to get here.'

'I'll take you there.'

Lucy grinned, and you could tell she was trying to

keep the grin from growing wider still. 'No. We made plans to discuss strategy over dinner. She wants to take me out.'

I stared at Teri some more, then showed Lucy to the living room phone. She sat on the edge of the couch to make the call.

Teri beamed at me from the kitchen. 'Heating the chicken shouldn't take long. When would you like to eat?'

'Later.' What was with this kid?

Teri bustled away in the kitchen, the pots and pans rattling. 'I'll get started now. Then you can eat whenever you want.' Happy is the little homemaker, happy as a bee. 'Can I bring you a beer?'

'No.'

Winona said, 'Did you find our daddy yet?'

'Not yet.'

Charles eyed Lucy on the couch, then edged closer and craned his head. I watched all the craning, then figured it out. He was trying to see up Lucy's skirt. I said, 'Charles.'

He scuttled away. 'I didn't do anything.' Just another fun evening hiding out with the Cole posse.

Lucy spoke with Tracy, then asked me to give Tracy directions. I did, then they spoke a few more minutes, and Lucy hung up. 'Tracy says it should take her about a half hour to get here.'

Pike glanced up the stairs. 'We should talk.'

Charles said, 'Why ya gotta go upstairs? Why don't ya just say it here in front of us?'

Teri said, 'Elvis knows what he's doing. Leave him alone.' Teri turned back to the stove, and put cool eyes on Lucy. 'I'll call you the second your friend arrives.'

I looked from Lucy to Teri, then back to Lucy. Lucy's eyes glittered and she pulled me toward the stairs.

When we got upstairs and closed the door, I said, 'Do you have frostbite?'

Lucy smiled wider. 'You don't know?'

'Know what?' Mr. Idiot.

Lucy glanced at Pike, and Pike's mouth twitched. I said, 'What?'

'She's got a crush on you, dopey.'

I looked back at Pike. 'You think this is funny?'

Another twitch. Everyone was having a good time with this but me.

Lucy said, 'Think about it. She's always been the caregiver. She's never had a male authority figure take care of her before, and now you're doing that.'

'Great.'

'Also, you're cute.' Lucy bumped me, and her eyes said she was enjoying this, even if I wasn't. 'I can hardly blame her, can I?'

Pike said, 'Tell me about the newspaper.'

I told them, the three of us sitting there on the office floor, me holding Lucy's hand. I told them about the paper, and about the Ferrari and the men with the shotguns, and what I had learned from Eddie Ditko about Dak and Tran. Just having Lucy here made me feel better about things, and I wondered if this is what it would be like when she lived here full time. When I finished, Lucy said, 'They don't sound like terrorists to me.'

I shrugged. 'No, and they don't sound like criminals either, but they've hired a counterfeiter, and three of their people flashed me with shotguns.'

Pike nodded. You could tell he liked the part about shotguns.

Lucy said, 'What are you going to do?'

'The scanner arrives at LAX tomorrow. I'm thinking that Joe and I meet it, then follow whoever picks it up and see if they take it to Clark.'

Lucy's mouth tightened and she shook her head. 'This has grown far and above finding a missing father. I think you should turn this over to the police.'

'If I turn it over to the police, they'll arrest Clark.'

'Perhaps Clark deserves to be arrested.'

'I'm not doing it for Clark. I'm doing it for these kids. Clark isn't the world's greatest father, but if he's arrested, the Markovs will be able to get to him. If I can find him before he does anything stupid, I might be able to scare him into doing the right thing.'

She didn't seem convinced.

'Also, I promised Teri.'

Lucy sighed. 'Everyone else falls for a doctor or an engineer. I fall in love with Batman.'

Pike said, 'It's the cape. Women love the cape thing.'

Someone banged hard on the door, and Charles yelled, 'Some woman is here!' He said it so loud that half the apartment complex probably heard him.

Lucy said, 'That's Tracy.'

We looked at each other and I held her hand tight, feeling that if I let go she would go her way and I mine, and, having lost her, I might not find her again. 'I wish you could stay.'

'I know. Me, too.'

The three of us went down.

Tracy Mannos was standing in the entry, looking tired but determined. I hugged Lucy again, and so did Pike, and then they left. I said, 'Hell.'

Teri said, 'Your dinner's ready.' She said it with a broad bright smile.

I looked at her, then at Charles and Winona on the couch, watching television. 'I might have a line on your father, but to follow it I'm going to need Joe's help. Can you guys stay by yourselves tomorrow?'

Teri filled a plate with rice and chicken and something

that looked like stewed tomatoes. She brought it to the table and put it down at a place that had been carefully set. 'Of course, silly.' Silly? 'When we met we'd been alone for eleven days, hadn't we?'

I nodded. I sat.

Teri said, 'Can I bring you a beer now?'

'I'll get it.'

I started to rise but she pushed me down. Hard. 'I'm already on my feet.'

She got the beer, opened it, and set it on the table by my plate. I said, 'Thank you.'

She smiled and sat with me.

'You don't have to sit with me.'

'I want to.'

Pike went upstairs. Guess he couldn't stand it.

I looked at Teri. She looked back. 'Is it good?'

I nodded. 'Very.'

She fluttered her eyes and sighed.

Man.

CHAPTER 24

Pike and I left for LAX early the next morning, leaving the apartment as the sun was torching the eastern sky. That part of the morning, the air was still and cool, and we made good time; the southbound traffic moved easily, even though dense with commuters from the Simi and Antelope Valleys grinding toward the Los Angeles basin. I said, 'We're just another couple of guys on their way to work.'

Pike said, 'Uh-huh.'

The Beretta autoloader was on the floorboard behind our seats. I had the Dan Wesson, and Pike had his Python and maybe even an MX missile. Just another couple of guys.

We left the San Diego Freeway at Howard Hughes Parkway and dropped south through Westchester to LAX. The scanner was due in at nine that morning, and, according to the dispatcher in New York, was to be held at the airport for pickup at the Small Package Delivery office in the baggage claim area. Being a small package, it would come down the carousel with the luggage, where a United employee would pick it up, then take it to be held in the SPD office until it was claimed by someone from the *Journal*. That person might be Clark, but more probably it would be someone that we couldn't recognize, so we had to be in position to identify the package and follow its movements.

We left Pike's Jeep on the arriving flights level as close

to baggage claim as we could, then went into the SPD office. An attractive African-American woman was behind the counter there, stacking small packages for a guy in a gray express delivery uniform. I said, 'Excuse me. Could you tell me which carousel the luggage from United flight five will come down?'

'That would be carousel four. But that flight isn't due in until nine. You're awful early.'

I smiled at her. 'The wife's coming in and I miss her.' The wife.

'Oh, isn't that nice.'

The people in the terminal ebbed and flowed with the early morning flight schedule of the big cross-country flights to New York or Miami or Chicago, then grew steadily as the number of flights increased. At eight-thirty we separated and positioned ourselves with a view to all points of egress in case Clark showed. He didn't. A family of Hare Krishnas came through snapping finger chimes and offering pamphlets for money, moving from person to person until they reached Pike, and then they hurried past. Strong survival instinct.

At exactly nine a.m. the arrival monitor indicated that flight five had landed, and a few minutes later the carousel kicked on and luggage began sliding down its ramp. The fourth piece down was a white cardboard box taped with a bright yellow airbill. Pike drifted to the carousel, watched the package pass, then came back. '*Pacific Rim Weekly Journal.*'

Twenty minutes later, almost all of the crowd and luggage was gone. The attractive African-American woman appeared, and took the package into the SPD office. I said, 'Watch for the package, not the people.'

People carrying packages came and went through the SPD office, but none of them had the white box.

We waited some more.

Pike said, 'Maybe you scared them off.'

Nothing like support from the home team.

We were still waiting at sixteen minutes after ten when an Asian guy went into the office and claimed the white box with the yellow airbill. I looked at Pike. 'Ha.'

We followed him out to a plain white van, then out of the airport to the San Diego Freeway, then south. It took almost an hour and forty-five minutes to reach Long Beach, but the white van didn't seem to be in a hurry, and neither were we. Pike said, 'Paid by the hour.' Cynic.

The white van left the freeway at the Long Beach Municipal Airport, then cruised north along the west side of the airport into an area of warehouses where he turned into the parking lot between two enormous modern storage buildings. The buildings were painted a plain beige and bore no identifying signs. We cruised past to the next building, then turned back, slowing long enough to see our guy carrying the white box into the north building. I said, 'Want to bet Clark is in there?'

Pike shook his head. 'We could shoot our way in and grab him.'

You never know when he's kidding.

The street was lined with similar buildings, most of which were occupied by carpet wholesalers or appliance outlets or metalworking shops. We parked across the street and trotted back, Pike going around the north side of the building, me strolling across the parking lot. The building was divided into sections, with offices in the front and three big truck doors evenly spaced along the parking lot, and no windows. All the better in which to do crime. The people door at the front was heavy and industrial, and it was also closed. The guy from the van had entered a door on the side of the building, but that door was closed, too. In fact, all the doors were closed. Maybe the Roswell aliens were in there.

I had just reached a row of Dumpsters at the rear of the building when the people door kicked open and the guy from the white van came out with three other men, the four of them laughing and yucking it up. One of the men I had never seen before, but the other two had leaned on me outside the *Journal*. Pike drifted up beside me, and we watched as the four men climbed into the van and drove away. 'The middle two guys fronted me yesterday at the newspaper.'

Pike didn't respond. Like it didn't matter to him one way or another.

I said, 'Anything on the other side?'

'Two doors, both locked. No windows.'

'I'm thinking Clark's inside. There might be other people inside, too, but with four bodies out, now might be our best shot.'

Pike said, 'We could always just call the police.'

I frowned at him.

'Just kidding.' Then he looked at me. 'What if Clark won't come?'

I looked back at the door. 'Clark will come if I have to put a gun to his head. He will come and we'll sit down with those kids and we'll figure out what to do next.' I think I said it more for me than for Pike. 'But he will come.'

'Optimist.'

We drew our guns, and went through the side door into a long colorless hall that smelled of Clorox. The hall branched left and straight. Pike looked at me and I gestured straight.

We moved past a series of small empty offices to the door at the end of the hall, then stopped to listen. Still no sounds, but the Clorox smell was stronger. Pike whispered, 'Stinks.'

'Maybe they're dissolving bodies.'

Pike looked at me. 'Acid to cut litho plates.' I guess he just knows these things.

We eased open the door and stepped into a room that was wide and deep and two stories high, lit by fluorescent tubes that filled the space with silver light. A lithograph machine sat in the center of the floor, surrounded by long cafeteria tables that had been lined with boxes of indigo ink and acid wells and printers' supplies. A high-end Power Mac was up and running, anonymous screen-saver kittens slowly chasing each other. The scanner was still in its box, the box on the floor by the Macintosh. A color copier was set up on one side of the litho machine, and three front-loading dryers stood in a row against the far wall. The smell of oil-based ink was so strong it was like walking into a fog. I said, 'Clark's going to print, all right.'

'Yeah, but what?'

Pike nodded toward a row of wooden crates stacked on pallets near the door. The crates were labeled, but the printing wasn't Arabic. Pike said, 'Russian.'

The top crate had been opened and you could see blocks of paper wrapped in white plastic. One of the blocks had been slit open to reveal the paper inside. The sheets were something like eighteen inches by twenty-four, and appeared to be a high-grade linen embedded with bright orange security fibers. The sheets also looked watermarked, though I couldn't make out the images. I said, 'Our money doesn't have orange security fibers.'

Pike drifted to one of the long tables.

'You think they're going to counterfeit Russian money?'

Pike reached the table. 'Not Russian, and not ours.'

Pike held up what looked like a photo negative of a series of dollar bills, only when I got closer I could see that they weren't dollars. The denomination was 50,000, and the portrait wasn't of Washington or Franklin or even Lenin. It was Ho Chi Minh. Pike's mouth twitched. 'They're going to print Vietnamese money.'

I put down the negative. 'We still have to find Clark.'

We went back along the hall toward the front of the warehouse, passing more empty offices. The hall reached a kind of lobby, then turned right to more offices, and as I passed the first office I saw a small camp cot against one wall, covered by a rumpled sleeping bag. 'In here.'

We went in. 'Guess he's supposed to stay here until the job's done.'

Clark had been here, but he wasn't here now. An overnight bag sat on the floor beside the cot, and a cheap card table with a single folding chair stood against the opposite wall. A little radio sat on the table, along with a few toiletry items and a couple of printers' magazines. Diet Coke cans were on the floor, along with crumpled bags from Burger King and In-n-out Burger and a large bottle of Maalox and a mostly used tube of cherry-flavored Tums. The room smelled of sweat and body odor and maybe something worse. A candle and a box of matches and a simple rubber tube waited on the table. Drug paraphernalia. I said, 'Goddamn. The sonofabitch is probably out scoring more dope.'

Pike said, 'Elvis.'

Pike was standing by the overnight bag, holding a rumpled envelope. I was hoping that it might be something that would lead us to Clark, but it wasn't. The envelope was addressed to Clark Haines in Tucson, and its return address was from the Tucson Physicians Exchange. It was dated almost three months ago, just before the Hewitts had left Tucson for Los Angeles.

I felt cold when I opened it, and colder still when I read it.

The letter was from one Dr. Barbara Stevenson,

oncologist, to one Mr. Clark Haines, patient, confirming test results that showed Mr. Haines to be suffering from cancerous tumors spread throughout his large and small intestines. The letter outlined a course of treatment, and noted that Mr. Haines had not returned any of the doctor's phone calls about this matter. The doctor went on to state that she understood that people sometimes had trouble in dealing with news of this nature, but that it had been her experience that a properly supervised treatment program could enhance and maintain an acceptable quality of life, even in terminal cases such as Clark's.

The medical group had even been thoughtful enough to enclose a little pamphlet titled *Living with Your Cancer*.

I guess Jasper was right; Clark Hewitt was more than he seemed. I looked at Pike. 'Clark's dying.'

Pike said, 'Yes.'

That's when a hard-looking man with an AK-47 stepped through the door and said, 'He's not the only one.'

CHAPTER 25

He was an older guy with a hard face that looked as if it had been chipped from amber. He waved the AK. 'Hands on heads, fingers laced.' The accent was thick, but we could understand him.

I said, 'The building is surrounded by the United States Secret Service. Put down the gun and we won't have to kill you.'

'Lace your fingers.' I guess he didn't think it was funny.

He took a half-step backward into the hall, and when he did Pike shuffled one step to the right. When Pike moved, the older guy dropped into a half-crouch, bringing the AK smoothly to his shoulder, right elbow up above ninety degrees, left elbow crooked straight down beneath the AK's magazine, the rifle's comb snug against his cheek in a perfect offhand shooting stance. Perfect and practiced, as if he had grown up with a gun like this and knew exactly what to do with it. I said, 'Joe.'

Pike stopped.

The older guy yelled down the hall without taking his eyes from us. A door crashed and Walter Tran, Junior, came running up, excited and sweating, expensive shoes slipping on the vinyl tiles. When he saw me, his eyes got big and he barked, 'Holy shit!' He clawed at his clothes until he came up with a little silver .380 that he promptly dropped.

I said, 'Relax, Walter. We're not going anywhere.'

He scooped up the .380, fumbling to get the safety off and pointing it at the older guy who snapped at him in Vietnamese and slapped it out of his hands. The old man shifted to English. 'You're going to shoot yourself.'

I said, 'Walter, take a breath.'

Walter Junior pointed at me. 'This one was the guy at the paper. I've never seen the other one.' Pike, reduced to 'other' status.

The older guy narrowed his eyes again. 'He said they were with the Secret Service.'

Walter Junior said, 'Holy shit,' again, and ran back down the hall.

'I was kidding. We're private investigators.'

The older guy shrugged. 'Gives the boy something to do.'

The door crashed once more and Walter Junior was back, skidding to a stop just ahead of Nguyen Dak and two of the shotgunners who had fronted me at the *Journal*. I said, 'We could sell tickets.'

Nobody laughed at that one either.

Nguyen Dak was wearing a fine wool suit that had probably cost three grand. He looked at me. 'We told you to stay away.'

'Clark Hewitt has three children, and I have them. A bunch of Russians from Seattle are looking for Clark because they want to kill him. That means they're looking for his kids, too.'

'You should have listened.' Guess none of it mattered to him.

'We're here because we're working for Hewitt's children. We don't care about the printing.'

I guess that didn't matter to him either.

They made us lie face down with our fingers laced behind our heads, then searched us as if they were looking for a microphone or a transmitter. I guess maybe they were. Dak positioned the two shotgunners in the front corners of the room so they could cover us without shooting each other. The guy with the AK took our guns and our wallets, tossed them to Dak, then tied our hands behind our backs with electrical utility wire. Dak called him Mon. When our hands were tied, they lifted us into the two folding chairs. I said, 'It started out like a pretty good day.'

Dak made a gesture and one of the shotguns punched me on the side of the head. Seattle all over again.

Dak looked through my wallet first, then Pike's, then handed them to the guy with the AK. 'Private investigators.'

'I told you that.'

'You told this gentleman you are with the Secret Service.'

'Bad joke.'

Dak stared at me some more.

I said, 'We came here to find Clark Hewitt. We know he's working with you, and we know he's been here.'

Dak lit a Marlboro and looked at me through the smoke. The guy with the AK said something in Vietnamese, but Dak didn't respond. He said, 'We now have a problem.'

'I kinda guessed.'

'Who do you really work for?'

'Clark Hewitt's children.'

More cigarette, more smoke. 'I think maybe the FBI.'

I shrugged at him. 'If that's true, your problem's bigger than you think.' You could tell he knew that, and didn't like it. 'If we're feds, then other feds know where we are. If they know where we are, and we turn up dead, you're history.'

Dak clenched his jaw and waved the cigarette. 'I told you to stay away, and you did not. You came onto our property, and you have seen things that you should not have seen.'

I said, 'I don't give a damn what you're going to print, or why, or what you're going to do with it. I came here because Clark and his children are in danger.'

The AK spoke Vietnamese again, louder this time, and Dak shouted back at him, the other Viets looking from one to the other like some kind of tennis match was taking place, maybe yelling about killing us, maybe saying murder us clean right here in the room, then sweat it out with the cops and pretend they didn't know what happened or how or why. They were still going through it when Clark Hewitt came in with Walter Senior and another younger guy. Clark was wearing a cheap cotton shirt and baggy trousers over busted-out K-mart canvas shoes, and he had the vague, out-of-focus look of someone who'd just shot up.

Clark saw us and said, 'Oh, dear.'

Dak's eyes flashed angrily, and he jerked the cigarette. 'Get him out of here.'

The younger guy was pulling Clark back into the hall when I said, 'The Russians are in LA, Clark. I've got your kids stashed, but they're in danger.'

Clark jerked his arm away and came back into the room. 'Where are they?'

'At a friend's.'

Dak told the younger guy to get Clark out of there again, and when the younger guy grabbed his arm, Clark swatted at him. 'Get away from me!'

I looked back at Dak. 'I've got his children, goddamnit. Shooters from Seattle are down here looking for him, and he knows it's a fact.' I looked back at Clark. 'The Russians killed Wilson Brownell, and that means they know everything that he knows.'

Clark's face worked. 'They killed Wil?'

The AK screamed again, and this time he shoved past the others and leveled the gun at us. When he did, Clark shrieked, 'No!' and lurched forward, shoving him away. Both Walters and the other Viets swarmed around him, and Dak slapped him hard, twice. Clark didn't quit. He punched at Dak, throwing awkward punches with nothing on them, but he kept throwing them until a Walter hung onto each arm and a third man had him around the neck. Clark was just full of surprises.

Pike said, 'Payback's going to hurt.'

The three men pulled Clark out of the way, and Dak waved at us, saying, 'Kill them.'

Clark said, 'If you kill them I won't print your goddamned dong.' Vietnamese money is called dong.

Dak's face went dark, and he shook Clark's arm. 'You agreed to print for us and you will make the money!'

Clark said, 'Like hell I will.' When he said it a little bit of spit hit Dak on the shirt.

The AK had had enough with all the talk. He pushed past Dak and ran at us again, barking in Vietnamese. When he did, Dak yelled 'No!' and grabbed him from behind.

Dak and the AK and the other two older guys shoved and screamed at each other, and I knew what it was about. They were revolutionaries, but they were also businessmen with families and property and things they would lose if they were discovered. They were shouting about killing us, and it was clear that they wanted to. Pike tensed beside me, probably thinking that if the younger shotgunners looked at the older guys he would come out of the chair and risk the charge, maybe hit the near guy hard enough to knock free the gun, maybe get the gun and do some damage even with his hands tied behind his back.

Helluva morning. Drive down to Orange County to die.

I said, 'Clark, whatever Brownell knew, the Russians know. They'll have your address and phone number, and that gives them a place to start looking. If I can find you, they can find you, too.'

Clark was nodding, trying to hear me past all the yelling. A faint sheen of sweat covered his face, and he looked pale and more than a little nauseated. I thought that even with the dope whatever was eating him up must hurt like hell.

I said, 'I've got the kids stashed in a safe place, but you're going to have to do something. Either go back into the program or get out of town.'

Clark was looking from me to the Viets, me to the Viets, over and over again. 'I need this money.' Whatever they were paying him to do the job.

'Clark, what good's the money if they murder your children?'

All the screaming had peaked, and Dak jerked the AK away from the other guy and used it to shove Clark toward the door, screaming, 'We have the paper now, we have the machines! Go into the other room and print the dong!'

But Clark didn't go into the other room. He grabbed hold of the AK, and shouted, 'I'm not going anywhere! If you kill them I won't print your money.'

Dak was breathing so hard he sounded like a bellows. One of the other guys ran up beside him and tried to wrestle the AK away but Dak shouted a single Vietnamese word and the man stopped. Now they were both breathing loud, and Clark was breathing loud, too. Clark grabbed Dak by the front of his jacket and shook him. Clark's face was so pale I thought he might keel over. He shouted, 'My children are in danger and these men are taking care of them.' He looked back at me. 'If they let you go, you won't tell, will you?'

'No.'

'You won't stop me from printing the dong?'

'Clark, if they let us go, we'll do everything we can to help.' I wanted Clark Hewitt to get his money.

The other man shouted and Dak raised the gun. Dak was shouting, too, and with all the shouting I thought that no one could understand anything and that the moment had taken on an inevitable life of its own. I thought that Dak would shoot right through Clark, the 7.62mm bullets ripping through Clark into me and Pike and ending us all, but then the shouting stopped and Dak muttered a single coarse Vietnamese curse, and he looked at me with an expression of infinite weariness. He said, 'All right.'

He told Dak to cut us loose.

My heart began to beat again.

CHAPTER 26

The one named Mon didn't like it. He stomped around, waving the AK and making a big scene until Nguyen Dak slapped him and took the gun away. The others started shouting and arguing, but when Dak finally had them quiet, he said, 'Make the dong and let's be done with this.'

I said, 'How long will it take to print the dong?'

Clark frowned. 'Well, after I make the plates, a couple of days.'

'How long start to finish?'

'Three days.'

'Okay. Your children can stay with you here while you print the dong, and you can decide what you want to do.' I wanted to get the kids out of LA, and I was hoping that I could work on getting Clark and his children back into the witness protection program while he was down here guarded by Dak's people. 'When you have the money you can leave from here without going back to Los Angeles. That way it's a clean miss for the Russians.'

Clark was liking it. 'That sounds good.' He turned to Dak. 'We'll have to go to Los Angeles to get my family.'

Dak shook his head. 'Absolutely not. Print the money first, then do what you want.'

I said, 'Forget it, Dak. His kids are in danger as long as they're in Los Angeles. So is he.'

Dak glared at Clark. 'You agreed to make the dong.

We've bought the press and the materials. We have an enormous investment.'

Clark frowned. 'I'm still going to do it. I'll make the dong when I get back.'

Dak shook his head again. Adamant. 'No dong, no money.'

'I'll make the dong. I just want to get my children.'

Dak waved at me and Pike. 'You stay and make the dong. They can go get the children.'

Clark pursed his lips and scowled, and suddenly I could see Charles in him. 'No, I'm their father and I'm going to get them.'

I said, 'They're just up in Studio City, for chrissake. It's not like they're on Mars.'

Dak put his hands on his hips.

'We're talking about three hours round-trip.'

'No.'

I spread my hands. 'Look, if you're that scared Clark won't come back, why don't you come with us.'

Pike stared at me.

Dak huddled with the other Viets. There was more handwaving, but this time no one was shouting or pointing a gun at us. I guess they were getting used to the idea. Finally Dak came back to us and said, 'All right. Let's go get them.'

Pike sighed. 'Now it's 'us.' '

Dak looked at Pike. 'We have a large investment here that's worthless if he doesn't come back. We're going to protect it.'

Pike shook his head and stared at the floor.

I said, 'Clark, are you up to this?' He looked pale and clammy, and I was wondering just how much longer he could stay on his feet. He looked like he should be in a hospital.

208

Clark Hewitt pulled away from me. 'I'm fine. Just let me get my bag.' His drugs were in the bag.

They made me draw a map detailing how we would get to the safe house, and then we left, Dak and the two Walters following in Dak's Mercedes, Mon riding with us. The other guys stayed to guard the warehouse. I wasn't sure from whom, but you never know. Mon seemed sullen and resentful, and made sure we all knew he had a pistol tucked in his pants. He must've been something when he was younger.

We drove in silence for the first twenty minutes or so. I glanced in the rearview mirror at Clark every few minutes, but all he did was stare at the passing scenery without really seeing it. 'Clark, why didn't you tell someone about the cancer?'

He still didn't look at me. 'How do you know about that?'

'We found the letter from your doctor.'

He nodded.

'Does Teri know?'

'How could I tell them something like that?'

Pike said, 'You shoot dope for the pain.'

Clark glanced at Pike. It was the first time he had turned from the window. 'I don't have health insurance, and I can't afford prescription painkillers. Dealers buy and sell their drugs with cash, and they rarely put anything in the bank, so I just use the funny money.'

I looked at him some more. Even in the mirror I could see the faint sheen of sweat that covered his face. He was pale and he looked nauseated. 'Does it help?'

'Not as much as it used to.'

Pike said, 'How long?'

Clark turned back to the window, almost as if he was embarrassed. 'A few months.' He shrugged. Like that was the way he'd found to deal with it. Shrug and keep going.

'That's why you're printing for these guys.'

'I don't have any savings. I don't have insurance. I had to do something to take care of my children, and this is it. Printing is all I know how to do.'

'Sure.'

'I print the dong, and Dak will pay me real money that I can put into a bank. Enough to get them grown and through school. Maybe even enough for college.' He nodded to himself as he said it, almost as if he was saying it because he needed to hear it to keep himself going, telling himself that it would all work out, that his kids would be fine. It made me want to cry.

'You don't have family who can take them?'

'My wife and I were both only children. Our parents are dead.' Another shrug. 'They don't have anyone but me.' He finally looked at me through the mirror. 'I want you to know how much I appreciate everything that you've done. You're a very nice man.'

I stared at the road.

'When I get paid I'll pay you for all this.'

I stared harder and nodded.

We made good time in the late afternoon traffic, and would've made even better time except that the Mercedes kept falling behind. After about the eighth time, I said, 'What's wrong with that guy?'

Mon said, 'Dak won't go over the speed limit.'

'He's willing to kill us to protect his revolution, but he won't break the speed limit.'

'Dak wants to be a good American.'

I could see Pike out the corner of my eye. Shaking his head.

Clark said, 'These people aren't criminals. They're revolutionaries.'

'Sure. Counterfeiting dong.'

'They have this idea that if they put a lot of counterfeit money into the Vietnamese economy, it will destabilize the Communist government and force Vietnam toward a democracy.'

Pike said, 'Patriots.'

Clark shrugged. 'It was their country. They want it back.' Same thing Eddie Ditko had said.

I asked Clark if he wanted to stop at their house first, but he said no. I asked if there was anything we could get for him at the drugstore, but he said no again. He just wanted to pick up his children and go back to Orange County and print the dong. He sounded tired when he said it.

'I've got a doctor friend, Clark.'

'It wouldn't do any good.' Like he wanted to lie down and go to sleep for a long time.

I drove harder, and kept waving Dak faster. Dak didn't like it much, but as long as I didn't go too fast he kept up.

The late afternoon rush caught us in Hollywood and traffic began to back up, but twenty minutes later we were through the Cahuenga Pass and dropping off the freeway into Studio City. When I exited the freeway at Coldwater Canyon in Studio City, Clark sat up and seemed more alert. I wondered at the dull ache he must live with, and what it must be like for him to keep it muted by shooting drugs. Jasper was right. There was a lot more to Clark than it seemed.

Clark said, 'Are we close?'

'Yes.'

Two minutes later I parked at the curb in a spot that left room for Dak's Mercedes, and then the four of us climbed out of Pike's Jeep. Dak jerked his thumb at the building, and Mon said, 'Let's go.'

Clark was walking fine, though every once in a while he made a little wince. The cancer.

We reached the condo, knocked twice, and waited for Teri to unlatch her door. It should have been a surprise homecoming, and it should've been nice, but it wasn't.

Teri opened the door the third time I knocked, and I knew something was wrong. 'Teri.'

Her eyes made little round O's when she saw Clark. 'Daddy!'

Clark said, 'Hi, sweetie.'

'Teri, what's wrong?'

Teri's eyes filled and she threw her arms around Clark and wailed. 'Charles ran away.'

CHAPTER 27

Mon ran back to the Mercedes, and the rest of us went inside, Clark with an arm around Teri. Winona jumped off the couch when she saw Clark and ran to him, shrieking and grabbing him around the waist. Guess she wasn't all that worried about Charles, or maybe she was just that much happier to see her father. I said, 'How long has Charles been gone?'

Teri wiped her nose. 'Since before lunch.' It was after three now.

'Do you know where he went?'

'Uh-uh.' She wiped her eyes again. 'He said he wanted to look around the building. He said he'd be back soon, but he never came back.'

I gave her a hug and tried to look confident. 'It's okay, kiddo. We'll find him.' Charles might be anywhere.

Mon came back with Dak and the two Walters, and nobody looked happy. They stood in a little clump in the front door, Dak angry and firm. 'Now what?'

'Clark's son is missing.'

Dak glared at me as if I had to be kidding.

'We can't just drive away. We have to find him.'

Dak looked angrier still. 'You said this wouldn't take long. You said we would pick them up and leave.'

Teri had stopped sniffling and was looking at Dak and his pals. She said, 'Who are these people?'

Clark said, 'These are the men I'm working for,

honey.' Like they were Sears, and had a great retirement plan.

I said, 'What can we do, just leave him?'

Dak stalked past me, slumped onto the living room couch, and shook his head. Walter Senior and Walter Junior sat next to him. Mon stood by the coffee table and gave Dak a smug smile, the look saying 'I told you so.' They talked among themselves, then Dak sighed and looked defeated. 'Describe the boy and we will help you look for him.'

Teri told us that Charles was wearing big shorts and the black Wolverine T-shirt, and after a bit the four Viets left, Dak telling them to meet back at the condo in thirty minutes. Revolutionary operation.

I said, 'Did Charles take anything with him?'

Teri said, 'No.'

'Winona?'

Winona shook her head without looking at me.

'Did he say anything about the park or a 7-Eleven or anything like that?' The Russians didn't know where we were and had no reason to be in Studio City, so I wasn't worried about them. The Studio City Park was a block away, and two convenience stores were within a couple of blocks. The convenience stores would have video games and magazines and comic books, any of which would be an ideal way to kill a few hours if Charles was bored.

Teri said no and Winona shook her head again.

Pike and I split up. I cruised the park, getting out of the car and walking around the community center they have there. Half a dozen moms with babies were in the sand pit, but none of them had seen a boy matching Charles's description. Eight guys were playing basketball, but they hadn't seen Charles either. I cruised the surrounding streets, then stopped at the little market and the two convenience stores, again describing Charles and again being told that no one matching that description had been around.

Thirty-eight minutes after I left the safe house, I was back, and so were the Viets and Joe Pike, and none of us had found Charles or anyone who had seen him. When I came in empty-handed, Nguyen Dak put his face in his hands. More delay. Teri said, 'Didn't you find him?'

'Not yet. But we will.' I was thinking that if Charles had met another kid here in the complex, he had probably gone home with that kid to hang out. Probably playing Sega right now. I told Clark what I was thinking. 'You and the girls could go down to Long Beach with Dak, and I can wait here. When Charles shows up, I'll join you.'

Dak stood. 'That's an excellent idea.' I think he smiled for the first time in hours.

Clark considered it, but didn't seem convinced. 'Well, maybe.'

Teri said, 'What's in Long Beach?' You could hear an edge in her voice. Tired of always moving. Tired of all the new places.

Clark said, 'That's where I work, honey.'

Winona looked uneasy. 'I want to go home.'

I shook my head. 'If you need anything there, Joe and I will pick it up for you. Best if you guys go straight to Long Beach.'

Winona looked even more uneasy, and picked at her shoe. 'I think we should go home first.'

I stared at her. Teri looked at her, too. 'Winona, you know something?'

'No.' Stubborn.

The muscles in my shoulders and neck tightened, and now I didn't like what I was thinking. Now what I was thinking scared me. 'Winona, did Charles say anything to you?'

She shook her head.

'Did Charles tell you that he was going home?'

She picked harder at the shoe and a little piece of rubber came away. 'Charles said he'd beat me up if I said.' Charles.

Joe said, 'Little girl.'

Winona snuck a glance at him. Joe was standing against the wall with his arms crossed, eyes dark and hidden behind the glasses. If you were Winona's size he probably looked twelve feet tall. He said, 'I'll protect you.'

Winona still wasn't happy about telling. 'He said he thought waiting around here was dumb because we all knew that Daddy would come home. He said he was going to go wait for him.'

Clark said, 'Oh, dear.'

Winona said, 'He made me give him my key.' The little troll key ring.

Walter Tran Senior looked at his son and nodded. 'Children are a source of great misery.'

I glanced at Pike, and neither of us were liking it. The Russians knew about their house. 'Home is pretty far away. Would Charles know how to get there?'

'Charles is good with directions.'

If Charles headed home, he'd probably use Laurel Canyon to get over the mountains to the basin side. If he was walking it would take a long time and he might still be on the road, but Charles didn't seem like the type who'd hesitate to put out his thumb. If he caught a ride, he might be there now. Of course, the Russians might be there also.

I dialed their number and let it ring fifteen times. No one answered.

Teri said, 'Maybe he's scared to answer.'

'Sure.' I didn't believe it, and that gave me hope. If Charles was there he'd have to answer just to say something smart. 'Okay. I'll drive over and see if he's there.'

Clark and Teri both said, 'I'm going, too.'

'No. Stay here and pack your things. If Charles is there, we'll leave as soon as we get back.'

Dak put his hands together like he was praying. Mon smirked, and rolled his eyes.

I left Pike with them, and drove along the route that I thought Charles would take, cruising slow enough to check out storefronts and lawns and the knots of people standing at pay phones and bus stops. I cruised the parking lot of every minimall I passed, looking in the 7-Eleven and the Subway and the game arcades, and Charles wasn't in any of them, and little by little, I worked my way over the mountain and down into the basin and along Melrose to the house that the Hewitt family called home.

It took me almost an hour and fifty minutes to reach their house, and when I got there I checked the street for Dobcek's tan Camaro. The Camaro wasn't around, and that made me feel better about things.

I parked behind the Saturn, went to the front door, and was just fitting the key into the lock when someone opened the door from the inside. I thought it was Charles, but it wasn't.

Alexei Dobcek stared at me with his bottomless Spetnaz eyes, then pointed a pistol at me. 'We knew one of you assholes would show up sooner or later.'

I guess they had parked the Camaro a couple of streets over.

CHAPTER 28

Dobcek stepped away from the door, and waved me inside. The house was warm and dark and close, and quiet the way empty houses are quiet. I called, 'Charles?'

Dobcek smiled. 'What? You think we'd tie him in the bathroom?' He dangled Winona's key ring, the one Clark had brought her from Seattle, and the one she had given to Charles. The little troll was matted and ugly, and looked pleased with events.

'The boy better be all right, Dobcek.'

Dobcek smiled, telling me that I could be as tough as I liked, but he still had the boy. Sautin was in the living room, sitting in Clark's chair, watching the Food Channel without sound. The Too Hot Tamales were goofing with each other, smiling and kidding around in total silence, and Sautin was smiling with them. His eye and the side of his face was swollen and purple where Joe had kicked him. Dobcek said, 'Don't you hate being found out a liar, you telling us you know nothing about these people?'

'Sure. I wake up sweating about it every night.'

The house had been turned inside out. Drawers had been emptied onto the floor and plates smashed and living room furniture upended and slit open. Even the dining room table was upside down, its legs pointing to heaven like some dead beast. I guess they'd been searching when Charles showed up. I wondered if he had tried to fight them. I wondered if they had hurt him, and, if they had, I thought that I might kill them. I said, 'Where's the boy?'

'Somewhere safe.'

'Where?'

Dobcek put his hand under my jacket to get the Dan Wesson, and when he did I caught his gun with my left hand and twisted it up and out at the same time that I drew the Wesson and pointed it at his nose. 'The boy.'

Dobcek made the shark smile. 'Dmitri, you should have seen what he did. That was pretty good.'

'Da.' Dmitri Sautin was still watching Susan and Mary Sue.

I thumbed back the hammer.

Dobcek made the shark smile harder. 'And then what happens to the boy?'

I stared at him past the gun. Sautin said, 'Da, the boy,' but still didn't move.

Dobcek said, 'What we have here is what you call a Mexican standoff.'

'I've got Clark, and you've got Clark's boy.'

'Da. Put away the gun and let's deal with this.'

I breathed deeply, and then I stepped back and lowered the gun. He held out his hand, and I gave back his gun. A nice new Sig P226. Nine millimeter. Easy to shoot. Since Pike and I had taken his other gun, I wondered where he'd gotten this one. 'I reach into my pocket, okay?'

'Sure.'

He took out a hotel card from the Sheraton-Universal. 'We're staying here. The boy isn't, but we are.' The boy was probably with Markov. 'You ask Clark if he wants to see his boy again, then you give me a call and we talk about it.'

'The boy for Clark.'

'That's right.' He said something in Russian to Sautin,

and Sautin came around the chair. The swelling was nasty, and I hoped it hurt.

Dobcek winked at me, and then they left.

I stood in the house without moving for maybe five minutes, watching the Too Hot Tamales, and thinking. The Hot Tamales were making something with ancho chiles and tequila, and laughing a lot. They looked like they were having fun, and I wished I was with them and laughing, too, but I wasn't. I was in a devastated house that had just been vacated by a couple of Russian hit men who were holding a little boy, and I was trying not to let panic overwhelm me. Panic kills. I felt like a juggler with too many balls in the air and more being added. Okay, Cole, take a breath. I said, 'Good-bye, ladies,' and turned off the Tamales.

The house had been turned upside down because Dobcek and Sautin were looking for a clue to find Clark. Then Charles had walked in, and Charles was better than a clue. He was a don't-pass-go E-ticket straight to the big money payoff.

I went into the hall and looked at the attic door and saw that it was undisturbed. I pulled down the door, and went up for the duffel. It was where I had left it, and I thought that maybe I could use it. I wasn't sure how yet, but maybe. I dropped it out of the attic, closed the hatch, then locked the house and drove back to Studio City. I drove slowly, and thought about Markov, and what he wanted, and Clark, and what he wanted, and little by little the bits and pieces of a plan emerged.

When I let myself into the safe house, Joe and Clark and Teri were at the dining room table, and the Viets were still clumped together in the living room. Winona and Walter Junior were watching *Animaniacs* on television. Everyone in the room looked at me, and Teri and Clark spoke at the same time. 'Did you find him?'

'Dobcek and Sautin were at the house. They have Charles.'

Clark drifted one step to the side, then caught himself on the back of a chair. Teri squinted. 'Who are Dobcek and Sautin?'

Pike said, 'They work for the man who wants your father.'

'What's that?' She was staring at the duffel.

I didn't answer. I looked at Clark instead. 'Charles is okay, but we need to talk about this.' Clark was staring at the duffel, too.

Teri said, 'That's what this is all about, isn't it? That's his counterfeit money.' Her voice getting strained.

Clark said, 'Teri, please take Winona upstairs.'

Teri didn't move.

'Teri, please.'

'Don't treat me like a child!' It was a sudden, abrupt shriek that caught Clark by surprise. 'I'm the one who takes care of him. I'm more his mother than you're his father! Why don't *you* take Winona upstairs?' She was shouting, and Winona was crying, and Clark was looking like he must've looked the day he found out he had cancer, as if a truth that he'd believed in with all his heart had now been proved a lie.

Dak turned away. Embarrassed.

I said, 'Teri.' Soft. 'Teri, it's not your fault.'

Teri came around the table and hugged me, mumbling something that I could not understand. I think she was saying, 'I will not cry. I will not cry.'

I stroked her hair, and held her, and after a time she took Winona and went upstairs.

Clark stared at the floor.

'Clark.'

He looked up at me. 'Yes?'

I told them what Dobcek had said. The father for the

boy. While I was saying it, Clark ran one hand over the other in a kind of endless wringing motion, and when I was done, he said, 'Well, I guess we have to call them.'

Pike said, 'They want you dead.'

'They have Charles.' Clark's face was tinged a kind of ochre green. 'I can't let them hurt Charles.'

Mon said something to Dak in Vietnamese. Probably seeing their revolutionary dream crumble.

I said, 'We don't want them to hurt Charles, but trading you isn't the answer. They won't let Charles go if they have you. They'll kill you both because that's the only way they can protect themselves.'

Clark shook his head. 'What do you mean, protect themselves?'

'Think about it, Clark. They want to kill you. If they do that, and anyone is left alive, what's to keep Charles or me or someone from going to the police?'

Clark pinched his lips together. 'But what do we do?'

Mon mumbled something again, and Nguyen Dak said, 'We make them want to keep you alive.'

I looked at Dak, and Dak seemed dark and enclosed and dangerous. I thought he must have looked this way many years ago. War is war.

Pike said, 'Yes.'

Dak said, 'The Russian wants vengeance, but he will trade his vengeance for greed. All criminals are this way.'

I watched him. 'Are you willing to help?'

'I want the dong. If I have to help you in order to get the dong, then I will help.' There was something hard in his eyes, and maybe a bit of a smile at the edges of his mouth.

Mon said, 'Russians.'

Pike's mouth twitched, and I knew Pike was seeing it, too. Old wars merging with new wars. The Russians had supported the North against Nguyen Dak, and the

Russians still supported the North's Communist regime today. It would all be the same to these guys. A war they needed to win to go home.

I touched the duffel with my toe. 'Is this Markov's money?'

Clark nodded. 'Uh-huh.'

'Will Markov know it, and will he know it's counterfeit?'

Clark dug a packet of the bills from the duffel and flipped through them. 'He won't know they're his, but he can tell they're counterfeit. He has people who know how to tell.'

Pike said, 'What are you thinking?'

'Markov knows what Brownell knew. That means he knows that Clark is printing again, but he may not know what. He knows Clark is good, but what if he thinks Clark is even better now?'

Clark shook his head. 'I don't understand.'

'What if we buy Charles back?'

'With what?'

'Funny money.'

Clark said, 'But he'll know it's counterfeit. He can get counterfeit money anywhere.'

'Not just any counterfeit. What if it's counterfeit that's so good that it looks exactly like the real thing, so good that Markov couldn't tell it was funny money, and neither could a bank inspector.'

Pike nodded. 'Like the super notes from Iran.' Iran was rumored to be counterfeiting U.S. hundred-dollar bills that were so good they were undetectable.

'Exactly.' I looked at Clark. 'Markov knows you're good. What if we tell him that you're as good as the Iranians?'

Clark was shaking his head. 'But I can't print anything

like that. The Iranians use intaglio presses from Switzerland just like our Treasury. They use a paper just like ours.' He kept shaking his head. 'I couldn't duplicate that paper. I can't get an intaglio press. They cost millions.'

Pike said, 'Real money.'

Clark opened his mouth, then closed it.

I said, 'We flash a few thousand bucks in real hundreds, only we tell them it's counterfeit. We let Markov examine them, whatever he wants, and we offer to buy back the boy. All the funny money he wants for Charles.'

Clark said, 'But when we give him the counterfeit dollars, he'll know. He'll be able to tell that they aren't the same.'

'I know, Clark. That's why we'll need the police.'

Clark simply said, 'Okay.'

Walter Tran, Jr., gasped, and Mon turned a dark, murky color. Dak said, 'Why the police?'

'We need the police to get Markov off the board. Markov takes possession of the funny money, we get Charles, and the feds make the bust, taking down Markov both for the funny money and the kidnapping.' I turned back to Clark. 'If we give Markov to the feds, they might be willing to let you print the dong.'

He stared at me.

'That way you still get your money from Dak.'

He nodded.

'For your kids.'

Clark looked past me at something far away. You could almost see an exit light come on a door at the far end of a hall in his mind.

Nguyen Dak crossed his arms, still looking dangerous, but now looking thoughtful, too. Maybe thinking about his own children. Or maybe just wondering how he could get out of this without losing everything he'd worked for.

I said, 'I can call Dobcek and set a meet, but we still need the flash money. A few thousand in hundreds that we may not get back. Markov might want it. We might even have to destroy it to convince him that it's fake.'

Clark rolled his eyes and made a deep sigh. 'Oh, that's great. Where can we get that?'

Nguyen Dak said, 'Me.'

I was staring at him when he said it, and he was staring back. 'All right,' I said. 'All right.'

Mon looked happy, liking the idea of getting back at the Ruskies.

CHAPTER 29

Dak made two phone calls to arrange for the money. After that, I called Dobcek and told him I thought we could work out a trade, but that we would have to talk about it. I didn't mention the money, but I made it sound like Clark was willing to exchange himself for the boy. It was a classic bait and switch, promise them one thing, give them something else. Whether they like it or not. Dobcek said, 'You will bring the father.'

'Right. And you'll bring the kid.' Classic.

Somebody said something behind Dobcek. Background noise. Then he said, 'We will not discuss the details now. Give me your phone number.'

'Why?'

'I will have to discuss this with our friend. I will call you tomorrow with the details.' Our friend. He meant Markov.

'Forget it, Dobcek. I'll call you.'

Dobcek snickered. 'You don't trust us. You think we find you with the phone number?'

'I'll call you.'

Someone spoke behind him again, then Dobcek's voice hardened. 'Call us exactly at nine tomorrow morning. Be ready to act immediately. Do you understand?'

'Dobcek, I am the master of understanding. Remember that.'

'Da.'

'I am also the master of vengeance. That boy better not be harmed.'

Dobcek gave a single raspy laugh, then hung up.

Clark, Joe, and the Viets were looking at me. 'We'll set the time and place tomorrow at nine. Will the money be here?'

Dak said, 'Twenty thousand dollars in one-hundred-dollar bills will be here in a few hours.'

Pike nodded. 'You're okay, Dak.'

I was climbing the stairs to see Teri when the phone rang. Pike answered, then held it out. 'Lucy.'

'What happened?' My heart began hammering. Worse than with the Russians. Worse than when Mon was holding the AK on me.

Pike held the phone.

I ran down, took it, and said, 'Luce?'

'We won.' Two words that cut through the adrenaline like a sharp edge. 'Elvis, it's over. We won.'

'You got the job.'

'Yes.'

Pike was staring at me. I nodded at him, and he gripped my shoulder and squeezed. 'We've got time. Go see her.'

I looked at Clark. I frowned toward the stairs.

Pike said, 'Jesus Christ. Go.'

Tracy Mannos lived in a small contemporary home on a lovely street off Roscomare Drive at the top of Bel Air. It was almost ten when I got there, but Lucy and Tracy were bright and excited and celebrating their victory with a bottle of Mumm's Cordon Rouge Brut. Tracy opened the door, but Lucy almost knocked her down getting to me. We hugged hard, the two of us beaming, and Tracy laughed. 'If you two start taking off your clothes, I'm calling the police.'

Lucy and I started laughing, too, as if someone or

something had pulled a plug and an ocean of tension was draining away. Lucy said, 'How long can you stay?'

I stepped back, and the laughter faded a bit. 'Not long.' I told her about the money. I told her what we were going to try to do. 'I don't know how long this is going to take. I might be busy the next couple of days.'

She had one of my hands in both of hers again, squeezing hard. 'I know. I'll have to get back to Ben tomorrow.' Two ships passing. The price of adulthood.

'Yes, but you'll be back.'

Her smile widened again. 'You bet your buns I will, Studly.'

'Tell me about it, Luce. Tell me everything that happened today.'

They did, some of which they now knew as fact, and some of which was supposition. It was neither complicated nor elaborate, because such things never are. It was merely ugly. Stuart Greenberg wasn't the evil, old-boy-crony that we'd suspected. When Richard had learned it was KROK that offered Lucy the job, he used his position at BM&D as an entrée to KROK's parent firm, then suggested to them that Lucy was erratic in the workplace. When the parent firm, concerned that KROK was in the process of hiring an uncertain (not to mention, untested) on-air personality, passed along their concerns to Stuart Greenberg, Greenberg questioned this information, and was told to contact the source, namely one Richard Chenier, a highly respected partner at the Baton Rouge office of Benton, Meyers & Dane. Greenberg had only been reacting to what Richard reported. Tracy said, 'When Stuart realized what had happened, he spent the rest of the meeting apologizing.'

Sometimes you just have to shake your head. 'And that was it? You've got the job?'

Lucy smiled. 'We agreed to agree. Stuart promised to

phone David Shapiro and wrap up the negotiation as quickly as possible.'

Tracy leaned toward me. 'She has the goddamned job.'

I said, 'What about Richard?'

Lucy's game face reappeared. 'I've phoned his office. I've also phoned his boss.'

Tracy said, 'I think she should sue the sonofabitch.'

Lucy's mouth formed a hard knot. Thinking of Ben, maybe. Thinking how far do you take a war like this when some of the fallout might rain on your child. She said, 'Yes. Well. We'll see.' Then she seemed to force the thoughts away, and took my hand again. 'I want to thank you.'

'I didn't do anything.'

'Of course you did. You supported my need to fight this without you.' She smiled and jiggled my hand. 'I know you. I know it couldn't have been easy.'

I shrugged. 'No big deal. You said I could shoot him later.'

'Well, yes. I guess I did.'

Lucy glanced at Tracy, and Tracy smiled. Voiceless female communication. Tracy kissed my cheek, and handed me the bottle of Brut. There wasn't much left. 'You take care of yourself, doll.' And then she walked away.

I said, 'Did you just send her away?'

'I did.'

'Good.'

Lucy and I sat in Tracy's living room, holding hands. It was late, and getting later, but I did not want to leave. Lucy said, 'I do wish I could stay, Elvis.'

'I know.'

She looked at me carefully, and then she touched my face. The bruise from Seattle had faded. 'I'll be out soon to find a place to live. As soon as Ben finishes school, we'll move.'

I nodded.

'You damn well better still be here.'

I nodded again.

'Please be careful tomorrow.'

'Careful is my middle name.'

'No, it isn't. But it should be.'

'I'll be here when you move out, Lucille. You have my word.'

She kissed my hand, and we sat like that, and not very long after, I drove back to Studio City.

CHAPTER 30

I let myself back into the safe house a few minutes after one that morning to find Mon hiding behind the door with his pistol. Mon shrugged when I looked at him, and said, 'Can't be too careful.'

Walter Junior was stretched out on the floor, sleeping. Dak and Walter Senior were at the dining room table, playing cards. Clark was sitting with them. 'Money come yet?'

Dak was concentrating on his cards. 'Soon.'

'Where's Pike?'

Mon said, 'He left, but he did not say anything.' His eyes narrowed. 'I no like that.'

'He never says anything. Forget it.'

Clark's skin seemed greasy, and if you looked close enough, you could see that his hands were trembling. 'Clark?'

Clark shook his head.

'How're the kids?'

'Sleeping.'

I joined them at the table and waited. No one spoke. The waiting is often the worst.

At twenty minutes after two that morning, someone knocked softly at the door and handed Dak an overnight bag containing twenty thousand dollars in nice neat hundreds. Real hundreds, printed by the U.S. Treasury on paper milled at the Crane Paper Mill in Dalton,

Massachusetts. Dak probably kept them under his mattress.

Clark pronounced them too clean, put the bills in a large Ziploc plastic bag with a half pound of ground coffee and one pound of dried kidney beans, and put the bag into the dryer. It wouldn't hurt the money, Clark said, but it would uniformly color the money as if it had been falsely aged.

Joe Pike returned at just after four. He gave Clark a small brown vial of prescription pills, and murmured something to Clark before moving to a dark corner of the living room. Clark looked at the vial, then stared at Pike for a long time before he went into the bathroom. A little while later he appeared to be feeling much better.

None of us formally went to bed; instead, we perched on the couch or in the big chair or on the floor, and drifted in and out of nervous uncertain catnaps, waiting for the dawn.

Sometime very early that morning, Teri came downstairs and moved between the napping men and cuddled against her father.

I phoned Dobcek at nine the next morning, exactly as I said I would. He said, 'We meet you on the Venice boardwalk in exactly one hour.'

'Let me speak with the boy.'

He put Charles on the line, and I told him that everything would be fine. I told him to stay calm, and to trust that Joe and I would bring him home. Dobcek came back on the line before I was finished. 'You know the bookstore they have there?'

'Yeah.' Small World Books.

'Wait on the grass across from that. We come to you.' Then he hung up.

I looked at Clark. 'You up to this?'

'Of course. Charles is my son.'

'Then let's go.'

Dak agreed to stay with Teri and Winona while Joe and Clark and I went to the meet. We used Joe's Jeep, with Joe driving. Two long cases were on the rear floor that hadn't been there yesterday. Guess he'd gotten them last night.

We used the freeways to get to Santa Monica, then turned south along Ocean Boulevard, riding in silence until we came to Venice. Pike turned onto a side street and stopped. He said, 'What's the deal?'

'They want Clark and me across from the bookstore on the grass. They'll come to us. They're supposed to have the boy, but I wouldn't bet on it.'

Clark leaned forward. He was holding the overnight bag on his lap like a school lunch. 'Why won't they have Charles?'

'They'll say that the boy is in a car nearby, and maybe he will be, but probably he won't. They're not coming here to trade, Clark. They're coming here to kill us. Keep that in mind.'

'Oh.'

'They'll say the boy is somewhere else to get us to go with them to a place they've picked out. It will be a private place, and that's where they'll do the murder. We in the trade call that the kill zone.'

Clark said, 'You say that so easily.'

Pike shrugged. 'It is what it is.'

'But how will we get Charles?'

'We'll show them the money. Your job is to stay calm and convince them that you printed this money and that you can print more. That's very important, Clark. Can you do that?'

Clark nodded. 'Oh, sure.' Oh, sure.

'Markov wants you dead, but if he thinks he can get

something from you before he kills you, he might go for it.'

'What if he doesn't?'

Pike said, 'Then we'll kill him.'

When we were two blocks north of the bookstore, Pike turned into an alley, got out, and slipped away without saying a word. He took one of the cases. Clark said, 'Where's he going?'

'He's going to make sure they don't kill us while we're waiting for them.'

'You think they'd do that?'

'Yes, Clark. They would do that.'

I climbed behind the wheel, and at nine forty-two, I left Pike's Jeep illegally parked in a red zone behind the Venice boardwalk. 'Let's go.'

I led Clark along the alley to the boardwalk, and then to the bookstore. It was a bright, hazy day, just on the right side of cool. Street people were already up and walking their endless laps of the boardwalk, and shop merchants were hawking tattoos and sunglasses to tourists come to see what all the excitement was about. Tall palms swayed in the breeze. Joggers and Rollerbladers and male and female bodybuilders with great tans moved through the streams of people with practiced indifference. Clark said, 'Where's Joe?'

'You won't see him, so don't look for him. The Russians will wonder what you're looking for.'

He locked his eyes forward, afraid now to look anyplace other than directly ahead. 'Do you see them?'

'No, but they're probably watching us.'

'Oh.'

The bookstore had just unlocked its doors, and a dark-haired woman with glasses was pulling a wire magazine rack onto the walk. I walked Clark into the store and told him to wait inside with the bag and watch me through the window. I told him not to come out until I waved for him. The dark-haired woman eyed us suspiciously. Probably thought we were shoplifters.

I walked back across to the grass and waited. Three homeless men were lying on the grass there, one of them holding a fat dog. The man with the dog looked at me, and said, 'Spare any change?'

'Sorry.'

'Don't be cheap. It's for the dog.'

I shook my head. 'No change.'

The man smirked at his friend. 'Cheap.'

I looked along the boardwalk first one way, then the other, then along the beach behind me, and into the parking lots and alleys, just another guy hanging around on the boardwalk wondering if he could get his gun out in time to save Clark Hewitt's life, not to mention his own. I eyed the fat dog. 'Looks like he could use a little exercise.'

The homeless man was affronted. 'Mind your own goddamned business.' So much for small talk.

Six minutes after ten o'clock, Alexei Dobcek walked out of the bookstore's parking lot and came directly toward me as if we were the only two guys on the beach. I said, 'Where's the boy?'

'Near. Let's get Clark and go see him.'

I lifted the bag. 'We had a different idea.'

Dobcek glanced at the bag, then past me and to both sides, like maybe someone might be coming up on him fast. He smiled like I should know better than to try anything like this. 'We know Clark is in the bookstore. Why you want to get stupid like this?'

I dropped the bag at his feet. 'Look in the bag.'

He glanced at the bag, but didn't pick it up. The homeless man was eyeing the bag, too. Dobcek said,

'Markov is near with the boy. We had an agreement, did we not?'

'Look in the bag. It won't bite you.'

The homeless man said, 'Can I look?'

Dobcek pasted the homeless man with dead eyes. 'Leave here before I crush your dog.'

The homeless man gathered up the dog and scurried away.

Dobcek said, 'Fucking trash.' All heart, these guys.

'Look in the bag, Dobcek.'

He glanced at me again, then squatted and opened the bag. He reached in, felt the paper, then closed the bag and stood. 'So?'

'It's Clark's new project. Bring it to Markov, have him look at it, and tell him we'd like to work out a different arrangement.'

Dobcek stared at me, then shook his head. 'What do you mean?'

'Bring it to Markov and have him look at it. I'll wait here.'

Dobcek leaned close to me. 'We'll kill the boy.'

'Have him look at the money, Dobcek. I'll wait and so will Clark. We're not going anywhere, and Markov will want to talk about it. Tell him this is a sample.'

Alexei Dobcek looked one hard long time at the bookstore, then walked away with the bag.

I watched couples share coffee and breakfast at the little restaurant next to the bookstore, and I thought I might bring Lucy down here. She'd like the bookstore, and we could sit at one of the little outdoor tables and watch the street performers and enjoy ourselves. Read a little, eat a little. Be nice to do if I survived the next ten minutes or so.

Dobcek reappeared between the street vendor tents, and this time Sautin and Andrei Markov and a fourth man were with him. The fourth man was wearing jeans and a green polo shirt, and he was carrying the bag. Markov was wearing a sharkskin jacket and gold chains, and looked like a second-rate Vegas lounge act. A young woman in a green bikini looked at him as she Bladed past and laughed. Probably wasn't the fashion reaction he was hoping for.

When they reached me, Markov made a little wave at the bag. 'I always worry when someone change the plan on me.'

'So why didn't you just kill the boy and drive away?'

'Maybe I still gonna do that. Maybe the boy and you and Clark, too.' Markov smiled toward the bookstore, then waved toward the bag again. 'Why you wanna show me this?'

'Clark printed it. He's going to print more, and we were thinking you might like some of it instead of killing Clark and his boy. We were thinking that you might like so much of it that you'll forgive Clark for the little problem in Seattle and let bygones be bygones.' They would either go for it or they wouldn't. We could either convince them it was counterfeit, or we couldn't.

The fourth guy put the bag on the ground, and took out one of the hundreds. He snapped the bill and sneered at me. 'You sayin' this is funny?' He snapped the bill again. 'My goddamned ass it is.'

The fourth guy wasn't Russian. He sounded like he was from Georgia or Florida, and I didn't like it that he was here. He sounded like he knew about printing, and he might be able to call Clark a liar and get away with it. Maybe he was Markov's current funny money specialist. I said, 'Who the hell are you?'

'The guy sayin' you're bullshit.'

I smiled at Markov. 'You're not interested, that's fine.' The homeless guy with the dog had set up shop ten yards down the boardwalk in front of a stand selling African robes. I called, 'Hey, dog man.' When he looked over, I closed the bag and tossed it to him. 'Have a party.' I turned back at Markov and spread my hands. 'Your loss, Andrei. We're sitting on a couple million more of this stuff.'

Ten yards away, the homeless guy looked in the bag and shouted, 'Yeow! Jesus has returned!'

Markov sighed and tilted his head. 'Dobcek.'

Dobcek trotted over and pulled the bag away from the old man. The old man didn't want to let go, so Dobcek punched him once in the forehead. Hard. I kept the smile on my face like it didn't matter to me. I kept the smile like I didn't want to take out my gun and shoot Dobcek to death. Like I didn't feel like a dog because I had brought it on the old man.

The fourth guy said, 'Hey, Mr. Markov, if those bills are righteous I'd like to know how.' Wounded and whiny, as if his feelings were hurt that Markov doubted him.

I said, 'Clark's in the bookstore. You give him a pass to come out here and talk about it?'

'Da.'

I waved Clark out. When Clark reached us he stood a little behind me, and kept his hands in his pockets. The sun made him squint so much that his eyes were little slits. Markov said, 'You look like shit.'

Clark said, 'Hi, Mr. Markov.'

The fourth guy toed the bag. 'This is intaglio, not offset. This is Crane paper.' He shook his head. 'My ass you printed this.'

Clark blinked at me, and I gave him an encouraging smile. 'Guy thinks you're bullshit. Guy wants to know how you did it.' I crossed my arms so that my hand was near the Dan Wesson and hoped that Pike was zeroed on

238

Dobcek because I was planning on shooting Sautin. I would shoot Sautin first, then Markov, and then the fourth man, and hope that I could do all that before someone shot me. We were maybe twenty seconds from all the shooting, and if we survived the boy would still be lost, all because some cracker who knew a little printing just happened to be with Markov.

Clark blinked at me again, and I said, 'Tell the man, Clark.'

Clark blinked once more, then took a bill from the bag, snapped it just as the cracker had, and smiled at Andrei Markov. 'Of course it's Crane paper. You can't fake that wonderful sound.' He snapped it again, then held up the bill. 'They used to be one-dollar bills.'

The cracker frowned.

Clark said, 'Real U.S. money printed on real Crane paper.' He held the bill to Markov. Markov took it. 'But they were ones. I washed them, Andrei. Bleached the original ink, then washed them and pressed them and reprinted them as hundreds.' Clark's smile widened. 'You wouldn't believe the wonderful technology we have now, Andrei.'

The cracker took a bill from the bag and frowned harder at it.

Clark said, 'I bleached eight hundred pounds of paper, and I've got an intaglio press. It's older, but it's one of the Swiss originals that a printing firm in France had until they went out of business last year.' Clark let the smile turn shy. 'Well, it's not mine, really, but these people I know have it. I'm printing for them just the way I was printing for you.' I was staring at Clark. Staring, and impressed as hell.

Markov said, 'You gonna steal from them, too?'

'If I have to.' He said it directly to Markov and he said it well.

The cracker said, 'Where'd you get the plates?'

'Scanned them off a series of mint collector notes, all perfect hundreds printed between 1980 and 1985. I used a high-density digitizer to get a pretty clean line, then created a photoneg off the digital image and used the photoneg to acid-etch the plates.' Clark pointed at the hundred the cracker was holding. 'You can see the inks are a little off, but I think I got pretty close.'

The cracker squinted at the bill and nodded. 'Yeah, a little too dark.' Afraid that Clark was showing him up in front of Markov.

Markov watched them talk with no more understanding of what they were saying than any of the rest of us, but he seemed to be buying it and that was all I cared about. I said, 'It doesn't matter that the inks are a little off. What we're talking here is bank-quality notes, counterfeit bills that will fool a bank or a cop or a Secret Service agent. Clark can print some extra for you. You get the money, and he gets his boy and you let them walk.'

Markov stared at me. Probably thinking about his older brother sitting in prison.

I rested a hand on Clark's shoulder. 'And when he finishes this job, maybe you guys can go into business again.'

Markov's eyes shifted to Clark, then back to me. They went to Clark again. 'How much of this paper you have?'

'Eight hundred pounds, like I said.'

'When it's gone, can you make more, da?'

Clark shrugged. 'Maybe, maybe not. The chemicals were very hard to get. I won't lie to you about that.'

Markov nodded, thinking, then looked at the cracker. The cracker shrugged. 'It's good, Andrei. It's the best I've ever seen.'

I picked up the bag and held it out to Markov. 'Here.

You keep it. You got any doubts, go see how it spends and think about getting more of it.'

Andrei Markov took the bag but didn't look into it or think anymore. He said, 'Five million.'

I looked at Clark. 'Can you print five million extra?'

Clark said, 'Oh, sure. No problem.'

I smiled at Markov. 'How about letting the boy go as a sign of good faith?'

'Don't be stupid. You'll get the boy when I get the money.'

I nodded. 'And after that Clark and his family are done with it. You give them a pass?'

'Sure.'

'I'll call Dobcek at the same number when we've got the money.'

Andrei Markov nodded again, and then the four of them walked away. I took Clark by the arm and we walked away in the other direction. I said, 'You did fine, Clark. We're going to get your son.'

Clark didn't say anything. Just past the bookstore he collapsed to one knee and threw up. I waited until he was done, then helped him to his feet.

Now all we needed were the cops.

CHAPTER 31

Joe Pike reappeared at his Jeep five minutes after us, the long gun in its case. I said, 'Anyone follow us?'

Pike shook his head. 'How'd it go?'

I helped Clark into the backseat and patted his leg. 'Fine. Clark, you did fine.'

Clark smiled, but it was tired and weak, and two blocks later he hung his head out the window and threw up again.

We drove directly to my office to make the calls. I wasn't worried that the feds had tapped the phone because that's who I was calling. We left Pike's Jeep in my parking spot, then took the elevator up to the fourth floor. Normally, I would walk, but not with Clark.

I let us in, then opened the French doors for the air. 'You want anything to drink?'

'Uhn-uhn.'

'You need the bathroom, it's down the hall.'

'Thank you.' He sat on the couch and stared at the Pinocchio clock. I took a breath, organized what I wanted to say, then called Marsha Fields. When she came on the line, I said, 'Are you familiar with a Seattle mobster named Andrei Markov?'

'No. Should I be?'

'Markov and his organization are in your system. A U.S. Marshal named Jasper is down here now because of him. I'd like to call you back in five after you've checked this out.'

She seemed impatient. 'Does this have anything to do with your counterfeit money?'

'Yes.'

I hung up and leaned back. Pike was standing in the French doors, watching the city. Clark was on the couch, hands in his lap, breathing gently. He was smiling at the Pinocchio clock and the little figurines. He said, 'Your office isn't what I would've expected.'

'Neither are you.'

He looked at me and nodded, and I nodded back. 'Thanks again for doing all this.' He wet his lips like he was going to say more, but then he said nothing.

I gave Marsha Fields ten minutes, then called. She said, 'Okay, your boy Markov is a real sweet piece.'

'That's one way of saying it.'

'I understand Jasper's down here looking for a printer who turned state's against Markov's brother.' Marsha Fields had done a lot in ten minutes.

'I can give you Markov for possession of counterfeit currency and for kidnapping.'

'Kidnapping who?'

'Markov is holding Hewitt's twelve-year-old son.'

'Well, good Lord.' She didn't say anything for maybe ten seconds. 'Is Clark Hewitt printing?' She had done more than a lot.

'Markov's people murdered a guy named Wilson Brownell four days ago in Seattle. They're using the boy to try to get to Hewitt, and then they'll kill the whole goddamned family. Do you want Markov or not?'

'You want something for Hewitt, don't you?'

'Hewitt will testify for you, just as he did in Seattle, and he will participate to such a degree as will allow you to bust Markov, but his other activities are not to be investigated and must not be questioned.'

Marsha Fields said, 'No one can agree to that.'

'That's the deal.'

I could hear her breathing on the other end.

'I will tell you this much: Clark Hewitt is not printing U.S. currency, and his activities involve no other crime, either civil or criminal. It's a one-shot deal, and you'll never have to worry about Clark Hewitt again.'

'How do I know that?'

'He's dying of stomach cancer.' When I said that, Clark Hewitt did not react in any way. I guess he was used to it.

She took a single breath, then let it out. 'How do I know that's true?'

'Your own doctor can examine him if you want.'

She hesitated.

'Come on, Marsha. You'll get Markov and half a dozen of his people, and maybe his whole operation. It's either worth it to you, or it isn't, and all I want you to do is let Clark Hewitt walk away when it's over.'

'Where are you?'

I gave her the number, and she told me that she would call back within the hour. It only took forty minutes. She said, 'No one is agreeing to anything at this time, but we're willing to talk about it. Will Hewitt come in?'

'No.'

'You're really being a prick.'

'He'll come in after you agree to the deal, but not before.'

'My office at noon.'

We phoned Dak and told him we were on our way in. Pike dropped me at my car, then he and Clark went back to the safe house while I made my way downtown to the Roybal Building. I got there at three minutes after noon. Reed Jasper was there with his red-haired pal from the LA office of the U.S. Marshals, along with a muscular balding guy with little square glasses named Lance

244

Minelli. Minelli was Marsha Fields's boss at Treasury. The last person there was a chunky African-American woman with gray-flecked hair from the U.S. Attorney's Office. She was wearing a dark green linen business suit, introduced herself as Emily Thornton, and from the way everyone kept glancing at her you could tell she was the one with the juice. I said, 'Man, Jasper, you get around.'

Jasper didn't offer to shake my hand, and neither did the other marshal. 'I knew you had something going with Hewitt. I could smell it on you like stink.'

Emily Thornton cleared her throat. As soon as she sat, the others sat, too. She said, 'Special Agent Fields indicates that you have information regarding a man named Andrei Markov.'

'Did the special agent describe that information?'

Jasper said, 'Describe. Can you believe this guy?'

Thornton's eyes flicked to him and her eyebrows went up maybe an eighth of an inch. 'You're here by invitation, I believe, aren't you, Mr. Jasper?'

Jasper frowned but said nothing. I was liking Emily Thornton just fine. She came back to me. 'Ms. Fields did tell me the situation, but I'd like to hear it from you.'

I went through it again, telling her that I could offer them Andrei Markov on a count of possessing counterfeit U.S. currency with intent to distribute and defraud, and for the more serious charge of kidnapping a minor. I told them that I could offer Clark Hewitt as a witness to both counts. Thornton listened without speaking until I was done, and then she said, 'Who is this minor?'

'Hewitt's twelve-year-old son.'

She wrote something on a pad. 'Is Hewitt now printing this money?'

'Hewitt is in the Los Angeles area.'

Jasper's pal said, 'Oh, to hell with this guy!' He put his

forearms on the table and made a face at Minelli. 'Christ, Lance. Fuck this guy.'

Thornton's eyes went to him. 'Would you get us coffee, please?'

He blinked at her.

Emily Thornton repeated herself. 'Coffee for everyone, with sweeteners and a creamer of some kind.'

Jasper's pal's face went dark red, and he forced out an angry smile, like she was confused about something and he was going to set her straight. 'You want coffee, lady, I think you oughta ask someone in the hall.'

Emily Thornton didn't move, but Lance Minelli said, 'Step out of the room, please.' His voice was quiet and his face said absolutely nothing.

The red-haired man opened his mouth, closed it, then abruptly walked out and closed the door. He closed the door so softly that you could barely hear it. I guess he was the one confused.

When he was gone Thornton pursed her lips, and tapped one immaculately enameled nail on the table. 'I would think your Mr. Hewitt would come to us anyway, with his son in danger.'

'We're going to get his son back with or without your help, Ms. Thornton. Your help will make it easier.'

A microscopic smile touched the corners of her mouth. She said, 'You were involved with Ida Leigh Washington, weren't you?'

'Yes, ma'am.' Ida Leigh Washington was a woman I'd helped a few years ago. I'd proven that a small group of corrupt police officers had murdered her son, and then I'd helped her recover damages from the city.

The smile broadened for just a moment, then vanished. 'Yes, well, I imagine you could get the boy back.' She tapped the nail again. 'What is it you want?'

'Clark Hewitt is dying of stomach cancer. He is

currently engaged in an activity to earn money to care for his children after he dies. I want him to be able to complete that activity free of investigation or prosecution.'

Emily Thornton shook her head. 'I couldn't possibly agree to that.'

'Then we have no deal.'

Jasper said, 'How about we just throw your ass in the tank?'

I spread my hands. 'On what charges?'

Jasper frowned and Minelli shrugged. 'We could probably think of something.'

'So play it that way if you want.'

Marsha Fields said, 'What is Hewitt doing?'

I looked at Emily Thornton when I answered. 'He is not printing U.S. currency, or any other paper negotiable in the United States. He is not committing fraud, nor is he engaged in any other crime for which he could be charged.' I spread my hands. 'Should you agree to this arrangement, you don't want to ask any more or know any more.'

Emily Thornton was nodding. 'If we knew more, and approved it, we'd be stepping over the line into entrapment.'

'Yes. We want Markov off the board, and you can do that for us. That's why I'm here. I can get the boy back, but there's less risk if you're involved. That's also why I'm here. But everything that I want to happen is going to happen whether you're a party to it or not. If you're a party to it, you get Markov and you'll bring down his entire operation.' I leaned back and waited.

Lance Minelli said, 'How do you see the scam?'

'Markov is going to receive a large amount of counterfeit U.S. currency as ransom for the boy. When I learn the time and place of that transfer, I'll let you know so your people can be there. You get to arrest Markov in possession of the counterfeit money, and Hewitt will testify against him in the kidnapping.'

Marsha Fields was gently rocking in her chair. She was staring at me, and I could see that she was liking it. She said, 'You know, the more funny money Markov has on him, the more we could charge him with.' Everyone looked at her. 'He had about a million bucks, say, we could hit him with a manufacturing count, as well as possession with intent to sell. A million dollars would do just fine.'

Emily Thornton said, 'That's dangerously close to plotting an entrapment, Special Agent.'

Marsha Fields blinked at her. 'Oh, I wasn't suggesting anything. I was just thinking out loud.'

'Mm-hm.'

Lance Minelli smiled.

Reed Jasper said, 'Markov is responsible for the death of a U.S. Marshal. His organization is suspected in at least fourteen unsolved homicides in the Seattle area.' He shook his head. 'I don't give a damn what we have to do to get Markov as long as we get him.' Way to go, Jasper. But then Jasper leaned forward, and jerked a thumb at me. 'But my interest is in keeping Hewitt safe, and I wouldn't trust this sonofabitch any farther than I can spit. If we go along with this, we should have someone on the site to make sure things don't get out of hand, and I'm here to volunteer.'

I frowned at him. 'What do you mean, on site?'

Lance Minelli looked at Thornton. 'I go along with having someone there, Emily. I'd want to make sure Hewitt doesn't cut and run as soon as he gets his kid.' He shook his head and looked back at me. 'I don't believe this cancer thing for a minute.'

Marsha Fields nodded. 'Agreed. I could see my way

clear to buy into this, but I'd like to know what's going on even if we're not going to follow up.'

Emily Thornton said, 'That's it, then.'

I said, 'Wait a minute. I've got other people involved, and they may not go along.'

Emily Thornton stood. 'They don't have any choice. I think we can do business here, but only if we have one of our people on the inside to maintain a level of control.' She offered her hand. 'That's our final offer, and now you can take it or leave it.'

I stared at her for maybe a thousand years, and then I took her hand and we shook. 'I guess we'll take it, Ms. Thornton.'

She smiled nicely. 'I knew you would.'

Juice.

CHAPTER 32

Thornton and Minelli left first. I thanked Marsha Fields, and told Jasper that I would call him as soon as I had talked with Clark and the other principals. Jasper said, 'I'll wait here until I hear from you.'

'It might be late.'

He shrugged. 'I don't have anything else to do.'

I drove back to Studio City, and reached the safe house at six minutes before three o'clock. Joe Pike was standing beneath a pine tree on the front sidewalk. He said, 'We on?'

'We're on. They went for it, but a fed has to come along. Jasper.'

'Dak won't like it.'

'We didn't have a choice, and neither does he. They agreed not to investigate.'

Pike's jaw moved imperceptibly. 'But they'll still know.'

'Yes. They'll know. You ready to go?'

'Always.'

We went inside and explained the setup to Clark and the others. When I got to the part about Jasper coming along, Dak made a hissing sound, and both Mon and Walter Senior said, 'No, no, no, no. They will know everything about us.' Like they'd rehearsed it. Walter Junior was asleep on the floor.

'Stop saying no and listen. The feds have given you guys a pass. Jasper is just going to be there to make sure we're not scamming them. They've agreed not to investigate you, or interfere with Clark in any way.'

Mon said, 'I can't believe this is happening.' He was running his fingers through his hair, and fistfuls of gray hair was coming out. 'We'll be ruined.' So much for revolutionary fervor.

I said, 'Look, their only interest here is Clark and Markov. If you're worried about it, go down to the warehouse and remove anything that could connect you or your people to that location. Just leave whatever Clark will need to print the money.'

Mon was still pulling his hair, but Dak nodded. 'What about the dong?'

'When the business with Markov is finished, we'll come back with Clark and print the dong.'

Dak said, 'We could all end up in jail.'

'You knew that when you conspired to break the law, but you're safer now than you were before. Before, they might've gotten wind and investigated and thrown your asses in jail. Now, they're going to look the other way and not even ask your name.'

Walter Senior said, 'Can we trust these people?'

'Yes.'

Mon started to say something else, but Dak shook his head and spoke in Vietnamese. Twenty seconds later they were gone. I looked at Clark. 'Can you set up to print U.S. currency?'

'Oh, sure.' Like it was nothing.

'How long will it take you to run off a million dollars?'

He frowned. 'Markov said five million.'

'That's what he wants, but it's not what he's going to get. All we need to do is make sure he's busted with a million in his possession. One million is the magic number.'

Clark nodded. 'Three or four days.'

'You're printing for Charles, damnit. You have to do it faster than that.'

Clark frowned again. 'Well, I don't have the right kind of paper. I don't have the right inks.'

'It doesn't have to be good, Clark. All it has to be is phony and add up to a million.'

'But Markov will take one look at it and know right away that it isn't like the money you showed him.'

'He won't have a chance to look at it. He'll be listening to Marsha Fields reading his rights.'

Clark thought some more, then looked at his watch. 'Well, I know where we can get some paper that might be good enough. And we'll need something to carry the money after it's printed.'

Pike said, 'How big is a million bucks?'

'About five suitcases worth. We'll need five regular Samsonite suitcases. That should do it.' The voice of experience.

'Okay. I can get the suitcases.'

'How long, Clark?'

More thinking. 'Tomorrow by noon.'

I looked at him. 'You can print a million dollars by tomorrow at noon.'

He frowned. 'Well, it won't be my best work.'

I used the kitchen phone to call Dobcek at the Sheraton. 'Da?'

'We can have the money for you by mid-afternoon tomorrow.'

'Five million dollars.'

'Sure. Five million. How about we meet at Griffith Park?'

Dobcek laughed. 'Call us again when you have the money. I will tell you when and where.'

'Whatever you want.'

252

I hung up. 'We're on. Everything will happen tomorrow afternoon. We should leave as soon as possible.'

Clark took his vial of pills into the bathroom, but this time he brought his bag, too. The pain was getting worse. I went upstairs to the second-floor office to Teri and Winona. Winona was coloring and Teri was helping her, but she looked up when I stepped in. I said, 'How're you guys doing?'

Teri's face was flat. 'Fine.'

'We need to leave you and Winona here again. Will you be okay?'

'Of course.' Angry about being excluded. And maybe about something else.

'There's plenty of food in the fridge, and there's a market on the corner.' I took forty dollars from my wallet and put it on the desk. 'Here's some money.'

Teri didn't look at the money. 'How'd it go for your friend?' Lucy.

I sat on the floor beside her. Winona was drawing a picture of the troll. It looked sad. 'It went okay. She got things worked out.'

'How nice for you both.' She said it so cold that we might as well have been sitting in a Subzero, but then she realized that and turned red. She adjusted her glasses and looked away. 'I'm sorry. That was so bush.'

I put my arm around her and squeezed. Fifteen going on thirty, and feeling all the pain at once. 'Been tough on you.'

'You like her a lot.'

'Yes, I do.'

'You'd rather be with her, right now, wouldn't you?'

'That's right. But my obligation is to see this through for you and your father and Charles.'

Pike rapped softly at the doorjamb. 'Clark's ready.'

Teri's eyes were wet and she reached under the glasses to wipe them. She said, 'I really like you, too.'

Winona said, 'Oh, yuck.'

I smiled at Teresa Hewitt. 'I like you, too. But Lucy's my girlfriend.'

'Can I hug you, please?'

She hugged me hard, and then she said, 'Please take care of my daddy. Please save my little brother.'

'That's what this is all about, Teresa.'

I went downstairs to Clark and Joe. We decided that Clark and I would get the paper, and Pike would pick up Jasper and the suitcases. I called Reed Jasper in Marsha Fields's office. Marsha Fields answered. 'We're on. Is Jasper there?'

She gave him the phone without a word, and he said, 'We ready to rock?'

'Joe will pick you up in forty minutes.'

'I've got a car. Just tell me where to meet you.'

'Joe will pick you up. If you're happier driving, follow him.'

I hung up before he could say anything else, and we went to print the money.

CHAPTER 33

Clark phoned paper suppliers until he found one that had the kind of paper he wanted. 'It's a nice cotton blend, but it should look okay.' Like he was talking about sheets.

'Remember, Clark, it doesn't have to be perfect. It doesn't even have to be pretty good.'

'Well, you want it to look like a legitimate attempt to counterfeit money, don't you?'

'Yes.'

He looked sulky. 'Believe me, no one will confuse this stuff with Crane paper, but at least it won't look like Monopoly money.' I guess he had an artist's temperament about these things.

The paper supply house was in a little red-brick building on Yucca Street in Hollywood, a block north of Hollywood Boulevard. The clerk had two boxes of the paper waiting for us, each box about the size of a standard moving box. It didn't seem like much, but the boxes were heavy. I went inside with Clark because I had to pay for the paper. On my Visa.

When we had stowed the boxes in the little bay behind my car's seats, I said, 'Doesn't seem like very much paper.' Clark had said that the million dollars would fill five Samsonite suitcases, but this paper only filled two boxes.

'Air. Factory bundles are packed tight. When the

255

sheets have been printed and cut and stacked, they'll take up more room.'

'Ah.'

The drive to the warehouse in Long Beach was in the worst of the evening rush-hour crush, and took almost three hours. For most of that time, Clark seemed in a kind of peaceful half-sleep. The eastern sky purpled, slowly fading to black as the sun settled on our right and, around us in the heavy traffic, people ended their day in a slow, frustrating march toward home.

We turned into the parking lot next to the warehouse just before eight that night as a huge Air Korea 747 thundered into the sky. The lot was empty except for a single white Pontiac that probably belonged to someone who worked at the adjoining building or across the street. Dak and his people were gone, but the parking lot was lit and a single light burned at the warehouse front door. 'Clark.'

Clark opened his eyes.

'We're here.'

He nodded. 'We have a lot to do.'

I used Dak's key to open the side door. They had left some of the inside lights on, but not all, and the still space of the empty building made me feel creepy and afraid. I took out the Dan Wesson, but no one was waiting behind the door or in the long hall or in the big room with the printing equipment. I hadn't expected anyone, but I felt better with the gun all the same. Thirty-eight-caliber pacifier.

Clark turned on the banks of fluorescent lights and filled the printing room with a cold blue light. He looked over what Dak's people had left on the tables, then powered up the litho printer and the plate maker and the Macintosh. I said, 'Is there anything I can do?'

'Turn on the radio.'

I turned on the radio and tried to stay out of his way. Help at its finest.

The crates of Russian paper were gone, as were the dong plates and most of the boxes of inks. I said, 'They took damn near all the ink.'

Clark didn't bother to look. 'All we need is black and green. I told Dak what to leave.' He checked something on the litho machine. 'You could bring in the paper.'

I went out and got the two boxes of paper. Didn't trip even once.

Pike and Jasper arrived forty-five minutes after us, first knocking at the door, then coming through with the suitcases. A black guy with short hair was with them. Clark stopped connecting the scanner to the Macintosh when Jasper walked in. 'Hello, Mr. Jasper.'

Reed Jasper smiled. 'Damn, Clark, you're a hard man to find.'

I was looking at the black guy. He was wearing a navy suit, and he was trying to see everything at once. 'Who are you?'

'Claude Billings, Secret Service.' He was chewing gum. 'I thought it was just Jasper.'

Billings blew a bubble the size of a grapefruit and walked over to the litho press. 'Guess they wanted the first team in the game.' Secret Service, all right. Cocky.

Jasper and Pike put down the suitcases by the long tables, then Jasper came over and shook Clark's hand. Clark seemed embarrassed.

Jasper put his hands on his hips and looked at the lithograph press and the plate maker and the computer. 'Well, I don't blame you for being scared after what happened that night, but you should've stayed in the program. After that night, you would've been fine.'

Clark said, 'I'm sorry about your friend.' Peterson.

'Yeah, well.' Jasper walked over to the big press and

ran his fingers along it. Billings took off his jacket, folded it, then put it on one of the long tables. Jasper said, 'I understand there's a problem with your boy. I'm sorry about that.'

Clark stopped futzing.

'We'll try to do a little bit better by you this time.' Jasper offered a friendly smile when he said it.

Clark turned back to the Macintosh and scanned a one-hundred-dollar bill. I watched him, and Billings came over and watched with me. Clark scanned the Franklin side, then turned the bill and scanned Independence Hall. When the images were scanned, he brought them up on the Macintosh, enlarged them, and began isolating sections of the bills. I said, 'What are you doing?'

'I have to make plates, and to make the plates I need a clean image. We're making Federal Reserve notes, and that means we need three plates. A back plate because the back of the bill is printed in a uniform green, and two front plates because the face of the bill is printed in black, but the serial numbers and Treasury seal are printed in green, so those images have to be separated.'

'Oh.'

Clark stopped what he was doing and looked at me and Billings. 'Do you have to watch me?'

'Sorry.'

Billings and I went to the table. There were five people and only two chairs, so I sat cross-legged on the table. Billings took one of the chairs.

The time oozed past like cold molasses. Clark worked steadily and hard, but the rest of us could only watch. Pike went into the far corner and stood on his head. I did a little yoga and felt myself getting sleepy. Jasper paced. Billings blew bubbles. Crime fighting at its most exciting.

Jasper said, 'I'm starving. Is anyone else hungry?'

Pike and Billings and I said, 'Yes.'

'Saw an In-n-out Burger on the way.'

I said, 'Joe doesn't eat meat.'

Jasper frowned, like that was the world's biggest problem.

Clark said, 'There's a Chinese place close by.'

Billings said, 'I could go for that.'

Pike and Jasper went for Chinese, got back just before ten, and we ate. Clark never stopped working, and didn't eat. Maybe the dope killed his appetite, or maybe he was thinking about Charles.

When Clark had perfect separate images, he had the computer reverse them and build perfect photonegatives, then copied the negatives in a pattern that would let him print twenty bills at a time. One million dollars was ten thousand hundreds, but if you could print twenty bills per every sheet, that meant only five hundred sheets. Of course, you had to run each sheet through the press three times, but it still meant that the press only had to run for three or four hours. All the time was in getting ready.

When Clark had the three master negatives, he mounted them in a plate maker and burned a positive image on a thin aluminum sheet, then, one by one, washed the sheets in a chemical bath to ready the plates for the ink. It took Clark about six hours to make the plates, and it was time that passed ever more slowly, with nothing for me or Pike or Jasper or Billings to do except offer the occasional word of encouragement. The In-n-out Burger was open twenty-four hours, and once Jasper went for drinks, and once I went, but most of our time was spent doing nothing. Clark grew pale again, and his skin seemed clammy, and twice he sat down, but neither time for very long. I said, 'Clark, why don't you take a break. Let's get some air.'

'It won't be very much longer.' He said it even when I didn't ask. He said it maybe a hundred times.

Jasper would watch Clark, then walk away, then watch some more, then walk away, like he was nervous about all of this and losing his patience. Finally, he said, 'It doesn't have to be perfect, for chrissake.'

Clark stopped working and stared at him. Jasper walked away.

At ten minutes after six that morning I went out into the parking lot and breathed the cool night air and watched the first traces of pink freshen the eastern sky. Moths swarmed around the parking lot lamps, banging into the glass with a steady tap-tap-tap, and I wondered if they welcomed the dawn. At dawn, they could stop slamming their heads into the thing that forever kept them from the light. People don't have a dawn. We just keep slamming away until it kills us.

Clark had worked steadily through the night, and I thought that his pain must be terrible, but, unlike the moths, he was doing it because he loved his son. I guess I would do it, too, and I hoped that the love helped with his pain.

When I went back inside, Clark Hewitt was still working. Billings had fallen asleep.

At eight minutes after seven that morning, Clark brought the plates to the lithograph machine, fitted the portrait plate to the printing cylinder, then filled the inkwell with black ink. He looked at me and said, 'I think we're ready.'

Jasper said, 'About goddamned time.'

Pike was still in his corner. I don't think he had moved for hours. Billings sat up, blew another bubble, then stared at Pike. I think he found Pike odd.

Clark said, 'We'll run some test sheets through, first. Just to see.'

I brought over a bundle of the paper. It made me feel useful.

Clark fitted a stack of the paper into the paper feeder, then ran through two sheets. The big machine made a whirring, snapping sound as the paper went through, and the paper went through faster than I'd expected. It came out smudged and dark. Clark said, 'Sucks.'

He made some adjustments with a little screwdriver, then ran through two more sheets. These looked fine to me, but Clark frowned again. Jasper rolled his eyes. Clark made another adjustment, printed two more sheets that I thought were identical to the last two, but this time he seemed pleased. 'This should do. I think we're ready to print.'

That's when Joe Pike said, 'Listen.'

Billings said, 'What?' He blew an enormous pink bubble.

Jasper said, 'For chrissakes, let's just print the money and get going.'

Pike moved to the lithograph and slapped the shut-off switch. The drum whined down and the humming stopped. Clark said, 'It's going to take a while to reheat.'

Jasper said, 'What are you people talking about?'

Pike held up a finger, his head cocked to the side, and then he took out his gun. 'Listen.'

There might have been the faint squeal of a door hinge, and there might've been the faraway thump of something hard bumping into a doorjamb or a wall. My first thought was that it was Dak and his people, coming to check on us, but it wasn't, and I didn't have time for another thought.

Claude Billings trotted to the door, stepped into the hall, and that's when Alexei Dobcek shot him once through the great pink bubble and blew out the back of his head.

CHAPTER 34

Pike pushed Clark down behind the litho press. I ran for the door, shooting three times into the darkness and once into the wall. Dobcek yelled something in Russian, and he and another guy fell back along the hall into the parking lot. I fired twice more, then pulled Billings back into the big room, but he was already dead. I said, 'The Russians. We're outta here now.'

I saw a flash of men moving in the parking lot, and I heard crashing at the front of the building.

Jasper checked Billings. 'Jesus Christ, how in hell did they find us? How many you see?'

'Five. Maybe more. They were running toward the front, so they'll probably enter that way.'

Clark said, 'But what about the money?'

Pike pulled him to his feet. 'That's over now.'

'What about Charles?'

'If they get you they won't need Charles.'

Jasper snuck a fast look out the door and down the hall that led to the parking lot. That door was closed, and there was probably a man with a gun waiting for whoever opened the door. All the noise was coming from the other hall, which led to the front. Jasper said, 'Shit, man, they've got us boxed.'

Pike said, 'Up.'

I pushed Clark toward the metal stairs and told him to climb. 'There's a stair at the front door and offices on the second floor. If we move through the offices and they stay on the ground, we can come down behind them and get out of here.'

Clark and Jasper and I clattered up the stairs to the catwalk and into the offices as Pike went back to the hall, fired four fast shots in the blind, then followed.

The upstairs offices were dark and hot, and we could hear the Russians moving beneath us, faint and faraway. I thought we were going to make it just fine until a squat guy with a thick mustache turned a corner, saw us, then ducked back behind the corner, shouting. I pushed backward into Jasper and Clark, yelling for them to get back, when the mustache popped out again, snapping off two shots that hit the ceiling above us. I shot back, then Alexei Dobcek darted across my field of fire into an adjoining doorway, firing as he ran. Jasper said, 'This really bites.'

We fell back along the hall, retracing our route onto the catwalk and down the stairs into the warehouse, reaching the bottom just as Dmitri Sautin and the guy with the mustache blew through the catwalk door, firing as they came. Dmitri Sautin was wearing a HAPPIEST PLACE ON EARTH T-shirt from Disneyland.

I yelled, 'Joe,' and pushed Clark down behind the plate maker as Joe Pike spun around and shot Sautin once with his .357.

The guy with the mustache dove back into the upstairs hall, but Sautin didn't. Sautin weighed three hundred pounds, but the .357 pushed him into the wall and knocked the gun from his hand. He looked down at his chest as red soaked through the HAPPIEST PLACE shirt. He said, 'Alexei?' Then he fell head first over the rail and hit the cement floor like a bag of damp flour.

A blond guy appeared in the hall door, fired twice, then disappeared.

The shooting stopped and no one was shouting and the

only sounds in the place were my own heart and a bubbly wheeze from Dmitri Sautin. He coughed twice, and then he started to cry. Jasper was under the stairs.

Dobcek said, 'I think we got you trapped. What do you think?' He said it from behind the catwalk door.

'I thought we had a deal, Dobcek.'

'Da. An' I think you were going to set us up.'

I was looking at the truck door. It was big and electric with a red open-close switch next to it on the wall about twenty feet away from me. All I had to do was run over there, hit the switch, then run back and hope that no one shot me.

Dmitri Sautin managed to roll onto his side, but that was as far as it went. He was crying the way a small child cries, with little gasping whimpers. He said, 'Oo, it hurts, Alexei. I need help.'

Dobcek called back, 'Shut up, fool.'

The sobbing became a wet, phlegmy cough.

Dobcek said, 'You give us Hewitt, maybe we let you live, yah?'

Pike snapped his fingers and pointed at the truck door.

I nodded. Somebody was probably waiting out there to shoot us, but if the door was up at least we could see. If we could see, maybe we could lay down a suppressing fire so that we could get out.

Pike reloaded the Python, and I reloaded the Dan Wesson. I said, 'Jasper, are you in?'

'Sure.'

'Joe.'

Joe Pike swung out from behind the plate maker, popping off two shots at the hall door, then three shots at the catwalk. I moved when he moved, sprinting hard to the door and slapping the big red button. The door started up with a lurch, and Dobcek yelled something and suddenly the Russians upstairs and the Russians in the hall were shooting as hot and as heavy as they could and I knew that they were coming.

Bullets slammed into the big door like hammers. The noise from the firing hurt my ears and made me squint, and I tried to stay low and close to the floor as I fired back. The closed space filled with smoke and the stink of gunfire and the shouts of men in a foreign tongue. I heard Jasper shout, 'I'm out,' and then his magazine hit the floor. Pike was reloading the Python and I was futzing with the Dan Wesson and the Russians in the hall door opened up again, pouring out rounds. One of them came through low and fast and made it to the base of the stairs to set up a cover position so that another could follow and then there came the surprising *boom-boom-boom* of a combat shotgun. Men in the parking lot screamed, and the big door was finally up enough for us to see Mon and two other guys running hard from the warehouses across the street as a black BMW with more Vietnamese guys screeched into the parking lot.

The three men running across the street had the shotguns, and all three of them stopped at the front of the warehouse and cut loose at two Russians in the parking lot, kicking one of them up and onto the Pontiac. The other Russian scrambled for cover behind it.

The Russians in the hall were shouting and running and shooting. One of them must've run to the parking lot door and seen the Viets. Dobcek was shouting more Russian, and shooting down through the doorway at us, but then the shooting stopped and there was a crashing noise from the second floor and Pike said, 'They're pulling back.'

'Stay down. Clark, you okay?'

'Uh-huh.'

'Jasper?'

'What the fuck just happened here?!'

Mon and another guy ran in through the big door with their shotguns, and I pointed upstairs. Mon and the other guy went up the stairs with practiced moves.

'Dak must've wanted his people to keep an eye on us. His people were across the street, and when they heard the shooting, they came.'

There was more shooting at the front of the building, and then from the street, and then a couple of cars roared to life and screeched away and the shooting was done.

Pike said, 'Charles.'

I ran to Sautin, kicked the gun away from his hand, and grabbed him by the shirt. 'Where's the little boy, Dmitri?'

Dmitri Sautin was making gasping noises. Mon and another guy ran back into the room, looked around, then high-fived each other like they'd just won the big game.

I shook Dmitri by his shirt. 'Damnit, where's the little boy?'

'With Markov.' You could barely hear him.

I shook him again. 'Where's Markov?!'

Dmitri Sautin made a soft gurgling sound, his eyes rolled back in his head, and all three hundred pounds of him died.

I pounded on his chest, and started CPR, yelling at him about Charles, demanding that he tell me where Markov had the boy, but Dmitri was beyond that now, and finally Jasper said, 'Jesus Christ, Cole, he's over. Lay off.'

I kneeled there, the points of my knees hurting from the cement floor. I said, 'Mon!'

Mon stopped all the high-fiving and looked at me with a big smile just as Dak walked in through the big door. He looked scared.

'They leave any cars?'

Mon shook his head. 'Two cars come, two go. We got three of the bastards!'

Pike said, 'I'm on it,' and trotted out through the big door.

I shoved between Mon and his pal. 'Get on the phone and describe their cars to the police.'

Mon's eyes went wide and he pointed the shotgun at me and when he did I rolled it away from him and hit him in the face with the barrel. 'You're safe from the cops, goddamnit. Now get on the phone and maybe we can find those people before they kill the kid.'

Mon looked like he wanted to kill me, but Dak said something in Vietnamese and Mon hurried away.

Sautin's shirt was wet with blood and the wet was spreading to his pants and along the cement floor. I didn't think about it. I rolled his body over and tore out his shirt pocket, and then his front pants pockets, hoping to find something that would point toward Markov. There was nothing. I felt something gritty in my eyes and I wanted to kick his dead body. Instead, I pushed up out of the warehouse and ran out into the parking lot to help Pike, but Pike had already found it.

Pike stepped away from the guy on the Pontiac with a hotel key card and said, 'I know where they are.'

It was a key card from the Disneyland Hotel.

CHAPTER 35

Disneyland was fifteen minutes away.

I used Dak's cell phone to call Marsha Fields, who said that she would contact the Orange County Sheriff's Department, as well as dispatch both Secret Service and FBI agents from the Orange County field office to the Disneyland hotel. She told me not to leave the crime scene. I said, 'Sure, Marsha.'

When I broke the connection, Pike said, 'If Dobcek tells Markov that it's over, Markov will kill the boy just so he can't testify in a kidnapping beef.'

'I know. You drive.'

Jasper didn't like it, but he came, too, the four of us piling into Pike's Jeep. We cranked hard onto the Garden Grove Freeway, then east to Anaheim. The Garden Grove was a nice straight shoot, but it was heavy with morning traffic, and Pike spent more time on the shoulder than on the freeway, blowing his horn and pegging his brakes, then jumping hard on the accelerator to shoot through gaps in the flow. Reed Jasper said, 'Do you have a death wish?'

Pike said, 'Pretend it's fun.'

We careened off the freeway at the Harbor Boulevard exit, then turned north toward the park and pretty soon we could see the peak of Matterhorn Mountain and then we were at the hotel. An Orange County sheriff's highway car was waiting beneath the monorail station, both deps sitting in the front seat with the doors open.

One of the deps was a tall ropy guy with a mustache, the other a slender African-American woman. Jasper flashed his marshal's badge, and the mustache said, 'They told us to wait here for the FBI.'

'You do that.'

We went inside. Jasper badged the desk clerk, then gave her the key card and asked for a room identification. Markov had four rooms blocked together on the ninth floor, one of them a suite. Jasper said, 'Okay. We'll wait for the others.'

I said, 'Come on, Jasper. If he's already taken off with the boy we're wasting time.'

Jasper looked worried. 'But if he's up there, we should go in with as many people as possible.'

Pike pushed past him. 'Forget it, Jasper.'

Jasper said, 'Ah, hell,' and followed.

The four of us walked fast across the back grounds past the swimming pool and into the rear building, and took the elevator to the ninth floor. Housekeeping carts were parked along the hall, and Andrei Markov's suite was open, the sound of a vacuum cleaner coming from inside. Markov was gone. We went through all four of Markov's rooms, trying to figure out what to do next when one of the housekeepers smiled at us. 'You looking for the man and the boy?'

All four of us stared at her. She was short and squat, and had probably come up from Ecuador. I said, 'That's right.'

She pursed her lips. 'They only go a few minutes ago. They said they were going into the park. The big man, he say he want to ride the mountain.' The big man. Markov.

Clark frowned. 'Matterhorn Mountain?'

She described how they were dressed as well as she could remember, then we thanked her and went back to the lobby. Clark was making little huffing sounds as we walked back past the pool, and I said, 'You okay?'

He didn't look at me. 'Fine.'

Two more Orange County deps had arrived, along with an FBI agent named Hendricks. They were standing with the manager and a tall blond guy named Bates who introduced himself as an executive with park security. When I introduced Clark, I said, 'This is the boy's father.'

Both Hendricks and Bates nodded, and Hendricks said, 'Maybe you should wait outside, sir.'

'But he's my son.'

Hendricks said, 'Please.' Polite.

Clark went outside. Jasper and I told them what we knew, and what the housekeeper had told us. More feds and Orange County cops were on the way, along with representatives from the Secret Service. Bates was calm and competent, and after we told him what the housekeeper said, he nodded. 'If they've gone into the park, we own them. We can put people at every egress, then just wait until they walk out.' He nodded, but maybe the nod was meant to bolster himself as much as us. 'We've worked with the authorities before. We know how it's done.'

It sounded workable. Markov wasn't likely to harm the boy inside the park, even if Dobcek found them. There was too great a possibility of being seen, and if he hurt the boy inside the park, what would he do with the body? So all we had to do was wait, and then we could recover Charles with a minimum of risk.

Pike and I left them to work out the details, and went back to the car to tell Clark, only Clark wasn't in the car. He wasn't standing around outside the hotel or in the lobby rest room, either. Pike said, 'He's on the monorail. He's going to get his son.' The monorail was pulling away from its station.

I yelled inside for Hendricks, and Pike and I were climbing the stairs to the monorail station when they ran out of the lobby. Jasper said, 'Hey, where are you guys going? Where's Clark?'

I told them, and I told them we were going in after him.

Hendricks said, 'Goddamnit, we said we'd wait. We got more people coming in.'

'He's going after them, Hendricks. If he gets to Markov or Dobcek, those guys are going to kill him. Then they might kill the boy, too, and the whole damn thing will blow up.'

Hendricks ran up the stairs after us, Jasper and Bates and three of the Orange County deps behind him. Bates talked us past the gate guard, and then we stood on the platform, waiting for the next monorail. We waited for two minutes that seemed like forever, and then the monorail came and Bates asked the people in the front car to please get off. He was polite and professional, but you could tell he was nervous about doing it. I guess things like this just don't happen at the happiest place on earth. When the car was clear we hustled aboard like an airborne assault team piling into an attack chopper, Bates talking into a Handie-Talkie. He said, 'I'm really not sure about this.'

Hendricks said, 'It'll be fine.'

'The shift supervisor's going to meet us at the station with some of our people.'

'It's going to be fine, goddamnit.' Hendricks's jaw was working and he looked like he wanted to hit someone. Probably me.

We glided silently over the parking lot, me describing Markov and Dobcek and Clark and Charles to the cops. Hendricks told them that our first goal was to find Clark, and remove him from the park before he stumbled into the Russians. After that, we would locate Markov and the boy, but he didn't want any move to be made against them until they had exited the park. When he said that part Bates looked relieved. Hendricks said, 'We'll hang back and watch them until they're in a safe place, then we can neutralize them with no danger to the boy.' Neutralize. There's a good word.

A small army of park security officers with hand radios met us at the Tomorrowland monorail station, and nobody looked like Mouseketeers. They looked like hard-core professional men and woman who would be more than happy to quell a small rebellion. Hendricks went through it again for them, and I once more described Markov and Charles and Clark. The park security people didn't want me or Pike involved, but we were the only ones besides Jasper who had actually seen the people we were looking for. Hendricks said, 'Just give 'em the radios, for chrissakes. They're for real.'

So they gave us little Handie-Talkies even though they weren't happy about it, and told us to take no action if we spotted Markov. They said hang back and call. I said, 'Fine.'

When Bates found out we had guns, he got red in the face and demanded we hand them over.

Pike said, 'Screw that.'

Jasper said, 'Look, it's private property and they're being damned cooperative. We don't want another goddamned war.'

Hendricks rolled his eyes, sighed, and looked at me. 'Please give 'em your guns and let's get this show on the road.'

Pike looked at me and I shrugged. I gave them the Dan Wesson and Pike gave them the Python. The security guy looked mollified, but not a whole lot. I guess he was thinking about lawsuits.

They gave us the radios, told us to check in, and then Pike and I went down the escalator and into the park. The security people broke into teams, and they moved out also, everyone going in a different direction.

We were walking past a cotton candy cart when Pike said, 'Over here,' and moved behind the cart like he was going to tie his shoe. He took a little Sig .380 from his left ankle and palmed it to me.

I smiled. 'What about you?'

'I've got something for me.' Always prepared.

We worked our way up past the Submarine grotto toward Matterhorn Mountain, doing our best to search the twenty or thirty thousand people we passed, with the grim and depressing awareness that we couldn't see everything and everyone, and that we might've passed Markov and Charles and Clark a dozen times without seeing them. Maybe they were in a rest room. Maybe they were standing in line for a hot dog or riding one of the submarines.

We split up at the Matterhorn, Pike circling to the left and me to the right, but we met again on the other side without having seen them. Pike said, 'The housekeeper said the mountain.'

'Yeah, but maybe they already took the ride, or they're on it. Maybe they're going to do something else and ride the mountain later.' Maybe a million things.

Pike's dark glasses were empty.

I said, 'You stay with the mountain, I'll follow the flow to Fantasy Castle. I'll go as far as the bridge, then circle back.'

Pike disappeared into the crowd as I continued along the walk. I moved past a pretty young woman selling frozen bananas, then between a small group of British sailors when Markov, Charles, and a hard-looking guy with leathery skin stepped out from behind a Kodak film

273

kiosk and turned away from me. The hard-looking guy had a hand on Charles's shoulder. Charles was wearing a Mickey Mouse hat, but he didn't look happy about it. Markov was eating an ice-cream cone and wearing a set of Mickey Mouse ears, also. His name had been embroidered on the back of the cap in red. *Andrei*. I guess it's a magic kingdom even for mobsters from Seattle.

I stepped behind an overweight couple and keyed the Handie-Talkie. 'It's Cole. I've got 'em.'

Hendricks's voice came back. 'Where?'

I was telling him when Dobcek pushed through a tour group of elderly people from Florida, shouted something in Russian, then shot at me three times fast.

Around me, forty thousand people jerked as if hit by an electric current.

The shots went high and wide into a monorail support, and then Dobcek was running toward Markov. Markov dropped to the ground at the shots, but now he was up, grabbing for the boy as he listened to Dobcek. Markov pulled the boy close, using him for a shield as he scuttled backward through the panicked crowd and I gave Hendricks our location. Hendricks said, 'Stay the hell away from them.'

'Just get your people over here, Hendricks, but tell them to come in soft. Markov's using the boy as a shield.'

They ran toward Fantasyland, and I followed them, giving Hendricks a play-by-play, and trying to keep Markov in sight without getting too close. When they crossed the bridge into Fantasy Castle, I lost them. I told Hendricks, and ran faster, pumping across the bridge into the castle, and there was Markov and Charles, Markov's arm locked around Charles's neck, a small black pistol in his free hand, standing by Mr. Toad's Wild Ride like they were waiting for me. Dobcek was maybe ten yards

274

behind him, but I couldn't see the leathery guy. Markov said, 'You lying prick. You tried to set me up.'

I wanted to stall him. I wanted the security people and cops to get here and cut him off and clear the crowds. 'Let him go, Andrei. The park's tied up. You can't get out.'

Markov said, 'You be surprised.' That's when the leathery guy stepped out from behind a juice bar cart, put his gun into my back, and said, 'Kiss your ass good-bye.'

When he said it, Clark Hewitt lurched past the line waiting to board Mr. Toad's Wild Ride, and shouted, 'You let him go!'

No one was expecting Clark.

Markov jerked sideways and so did Dobcek, and when they moved I spun into the leathery guy's gun side, forcing his gun away and bringing the little Sig up into his ribs. I pulled the trigger one time and its *pop* sounded hollow and faraway. A deep, larger *bam* sounded in almost the same instant, and Andrei Markov was slammed down onto the ground, the crowd of people in the small place suddenly surging in a panic, unsure where to go, moving in every direction like flake in a human blizzard.

Joe Pike was standing above us on the castle's parapet with a foot-long stockless shotgun. Dobcek fired five fast shots – *powpowpowpowpow* – to drive Pike down, then ran to Markov. I rode Charles and Clark to the ground, yelling for them to stay down. I thought Pike would shoot again, but he didn't.

I listened to my heart beat, and I took careful breaths, and felt the sobbing father and son beneath me as the herd of people ran around and over us with all the thought and caring of Cape buffalo. All the while I was on them, Clark said, 'We got you, Charlie. We got you.'

Over and over. I had never thought of Charles as a Charlie before.

I looked around until I spotted Pike, still high overhead on the parapet like some kind of avenging angel. I mouthed, 'Markov?'

Pike shook his head.

Markov and Dobcek were gone.

CHAPTER 36

Hendricks and Jasper came running up, and the Orange County cops set about securing the area. Hendricks said, 'Is everyone okay?'

Clark nodded. Charles made little breathy sounds, and squirmed around in his father's lap to see the leathery man. 'Is that guy dead?'

'They're okay, Hendricks. Markov's hit.'

Hendricks pumped his fist once and made a wide grin. 'Then we got the bastard.'

Jasper took out a cell phone. 'How bad?'

Pike said, 'Took a load of number four high in the right shoulder. Here.' Pike touched his shoulder to show them.

Jasper punched a number into his cell phone. 'Okay. Which way they go?'

Pike told him, and Jasper waved over Bates. While Bates was on his way, Jasper said, 'I gotta to be in on this, Cole, but I wanted to thank you.' He put out his hand, and helped me up. 'You did okay.'

'Thanks.'

'Where you gonna be? I wanna give you a call later, talk a little more.'

I gave him the number at the safe house, then he and Bates trotted away, Jasper talking into the phone as Bates deployed his security people. The clock was ticking, and it wouldn't be long before Markov was had.

Hendricks was frowning at me and Pike. 'I thought we took your guns.'

Neither of us answered.

Hendricks shrugged. 'Yeah, well, I guess it worked out.'

I took Hendricks aside. 'You understand the situation from Marsha Fields?'

Hendricks nodded. 'We're going to need to talk to the father to make the kidnap case. We'll need the boy, too.'

'I know that.'

He looked past me at Clark and Charles. They were still on the ground, Charles sitting in Clark's lap, Clark holding on tight. Clark looked shaken and scared, but Charles didn't. He was flipping off the dead man, and making faces at the body. 'Hang around a little while longer till we get this wrapped up. It shouldn't take long.'

'Sure.'

'You can wait at the hotel, you want. Get the kid something to eat.'

'Sure.'

'I'll get back there soon as we find this clown.'

Two more FBI agents, another half dozen Orange County deputies, and the representative from the Secret Service arrived. Everyone was smiling and patting each other on the back because they figured Markov was in the bag. Only so many ways out, they kept saying, and all points of egress were covered.

One of the cops took us back to the hotel, but Charles didn't like it much. He said, 'I wanna go on Space Mountain. I wanna ride the submarines. I wanna climb the Matterhorn.'

Some things don't change.

I called Teri from the hotel lobby and told her that we had Charles and that everything was fine. Teri passed word to Winona, and they both shrieked and clapped their hands. It made me smile.

We had hamburgers at the hotel cafe, then hung around the lobby and the monorail station for another two hours, but when Hendricks finally showed up they still hadn't found Markov or Dobcek. Pike said, 'You want me to come back in and find them?'

Hendricks scowled. 'I think we can manage, but thanks.'

Pike shrugged.

I said, 'I want to get these people home, Hendricks. You can talk to them later and arrange the statements.'

Hendricks said, 'Okay,' but you could tell he didn't like it.

Charles coughed. 'A-hole.'

Hendricks glared at him, then stalked away shaking his head.

Pike took us back to the warehouse for my car. The FBI and Long Beach cops were still standing around the place, but Dak and his people were gone, and so were the bodies. The big truck door was open, revealing the litho press and the computer and plate maker, but no one seemed to be paying attention. Marsha Fields was there, as was a representative of the U.S. Attorney's Office, both of them talking to a couple of Long Beach PD detective-supervisors. When Marsha Fields saw me, she came over, introduced herself to Clark and Charles, then smiled at Joe. 'Hi, Joe.'

Pike's mouth twitched. I guess they knew each other, all right.

She smiled at him a little longer, then put the smile on Charles. 'You're a good-looking little devil.'

Charles turned a nice plum red.

She said, 'Mr. Hewitt, we're very anxious to speak with you.'

Clark was still in the Jeep. Too tired to get out. 'Of course. Anytime you want.'

I took Marsha Fields aside and said, 'So where do we stand with this?'

She watched three Long Beach cops laugh about something at the far end of the parking lot. Nothing had gone as we had planned. Markov hadn't been arrested as a counterfeiter, and instead we'd managed to shoot up both Long Beach and Disneyland. A small army of cops had seen the printing equipment, and each and every one of them knew what it was. The bodies had to be explained, and I still wanted Clark to get his money, and that meant he still had to print for Dak. I told her what I was thinking.

Marsha watched the cops laughing, and nodded. 'We made the deal in good faith, and so did you. We'll still want Clark's testimony on the kidnapping count.' She looked back at me. 'A deal's a deal. Just have Clark get this finished, and tell whoever is behind this operation that if they break the law again, I'll make them my hobby. Are we clear on that?'

'Clear.' I offered my hand, and she took it. I gave her the safe house number, and she said that she would call as soon as she heard anything. I thanked her.

Marsha Fields took three steps away, then stopped, looked back, and raised an eyebrow. 'Dong?'

I spread my hands. I wondered how she knew.

When I rejoined Pike and Clark, and told them that we were free to go, Charles said he wanted to ride home with me. He liked riding in the Corvette with the top down, he said. He thought it was cool. It took an hour and thirty-five minutes to drive up to Studio City, and Charles talked constantly about Marsha Fields, and never once mentioned Markov. I didn't mind. He seemed fine, and I guess he had fallen in love.

We arrived at the safe house maybe a dozen minutes after Joe and Clark. Charles was disappointed. He said, 'What a gyp! They beat us.'

This kid is something, isn't he?

When we went in, Teri and Winona scooped up Charles in a big hug, everyone crying, but this time they were happy tears. I got hugs, too, and then I asked Pike if Hendricks had called. He hadn't, and that worried me. If Markov and Dobcek slipped through their net, we were back where we started. I didn't think they had, but you never know. I went up to the office and phoned Dak. He wasn't happy to hear from me, but at least he was cordial. He said, 'The boy is all right?'

'Yes. And so is Clark. I spoke with Marsha Fields about this, and the deal still stands.'

'The police have been asking questions.'

'Those questions will go away. The paper will not be investigated about the printing equipment found on its premises, nor will you.'

Dak said, 'How will we explain the bodies?'

'It's already been explained. Employees of the *Journal* discovered a robbery in progress and the bad guys drew guns. Your employees acted in self-defense.'

Dak didn't say anything for a moment. 'She can do this?'

'It's the government, Dak. She can do anything.'

Nguyen Dak said, 'You're a man of your word, Mr. Cole. I have much respect for that.'

'Not me, Dak. Her.'

I told him that Clark would call tomorrow and arrange for the printing, then I hung up, and stared at the phone in the quiet of the room. I could hear the others down below, but up here was peaceful and the peace was soothing. I didn't feel particularly noble, and I didn't feel like I'd won anything. I felt lucky. I had come very close to being shot. Charles and Clark could have died, and I had killed men whose faces I could not recall. I looked at my hands. Dmitri Sautin's blood was still crusted around my fingernails. I felt myself start to shake, and I closed my eyes and waited for the shaking to pass, and when it did I went into the bathroom and washed my hands and arms. I had to wash twice, and then I showered.

When I went downstairs, Teri said, 'We've decided to have a party. We're going to get pizza.'

'Great.'

The phone rang then, and I thought it might be Marsha Fields, but it wasn't. Reed Jasper said, 'Have you heard yet?'

'Heard what?'

'We got 'em. Snagged Dobcek and Markov trying to sneak out of a maintenance exit on the north side of the park.'

I cupped the phone, told everyone that Markov had been captured, and Jasper laughed at the shouts and applause. He said, 'You guys going to be around?'

'Sure. We're going to have a little party, then I guess I'll take them home.'

'I want to swing by and talk to Clark. I'll probably head back to Seattle in the morning.'

'Sure, Jasper. That'd be fine.' I gave him directions.

We ordered the pizza, and Joe and Winona walked to the little minimart for soft drinks and beer. I volunteered to make a salad. The Hewitts wanted to go home after the pizza, and I thought that would be a good idea. Let them be a family again. Let them fall asleep under the same roof without wondering if someone would come through the door and shoot them. Teri and Charles went upstairs to pack. Clark hovered at the pass-through, watching me mince garlic. I said, 'You're going to have to tell them.'

'I don't know how.' He fidgeted like he was nervous. 'I've thought about it a lot, but nothing I come up with sounds good.'

'You just tell them, Clark. You sit them down and tell

them you're sick and that you're going to die. Let them cry, and you cry with them.'

'They're so young.'

'They're older than you think.' I took tomatoes and a cucumber from the fridge. 'You feel bad, why don't you rest over there on the couch?'

He frowned at the couch.

'Would you rather help?'

'Huh?' He looked surprised.

'Would you like to help make the salad?'

Clark Hewitt stared at me. 'Sure.' He came around into the kitchen. I told him to wash the tomatoes and cucumbers, then slice them. As he did it, he nodded. 'I get it.'

'What?'

'I could sit on the couch over there and feel bad, or I can help make the salad.'

I put the garlic in a little jar and added some olive oil. 'Yep.'

'Either way I'm going to die.'

I nodded. It wasn't anything he didn't already know. The deal with Dak proved that.

'Maybe I should tell them tonight.'

'That would be good. If you want, I could sit with you.'

He thought about it, then shook his head. 'Thanks, but that's okay. I can do it.'

Good for you, Clark.

We were tossing the salad when someone knocked at the door, and Clark said, 'That's the pizza.'

I opened the door, but it wasn't the pizza. Reed Jasper came in, and Dobcek and Markov pushed in behind him. Dobcek pointed his gun at me, then backhanded me with it two hard times, knocking me into the wall. Clark said, 'Ohmigod,' and then Dobcek pointed the gun at him and touched his lips, going, 'Sh,' as he pushed us back into the living room.

Markov came in behind him. Markov was pale and shaky and standing hunched to the side with a windbreaker draped over his shoulders to hide the blood. He looked at me with the kind of look that said he wanted to eat me while I was still alive, while the blood still pumped and he could feel it warm and hot in his mouth. I looked from the hungry eyes to Jasper, and I said, 'You sonofabitch.'

Jasper shrugged. He was holding his service gun loose along his leg. 'Hey, it's a living.'

Markov smiled when he saw Clark. His tongue raked dry lips. I guess you dry out when you're bleeding to death. 'I'm going to do you myself, you termite.'

Clark turned white and trembled. 'Please don't hurt my children.'

I said, 'Pike's upstairs. He's got a machine gun.'

Jasper pointed with his gun. 'Shut up and sit down.'

Markov slumped heavily on the couch, and Dobcek moved to the stairs.

I stared at Jasper. 'How'd you get them out of the park?'

Jasper looked in the salad bowl, nibbled at a piece of cucumber. 'It was touch-and-go there for a bit, but I managed. Dressed 'em up in a couple of maintenance uniforms.'

Markov shifted on the couch; you could tell he was hurting. 'Don't say a goddamned word.'

Jasper shrugged. 'What's it matter? He ain't going anywhere.'

'How long has Markov owned you, Jasper?'

Jasper ate more cucumber.

'That's why your buddy was killed the night Clark went under. You sold out three years ago, and it got a marshal killed.'

Jasper made a big-deal shrug. 'If he hadn't tried to play hero it wouldn't've been a problem.'

I stared at him, and then I looked at Markov. I was thinking that Pike and Winona should have been back. It was only two blocks to the market, and two blocks back. I was trying to remember if Pike still had his gun. I had left mine in my trunk. 'You've lost a lot of blood, Markov. You might not make it.'

'I'll make it. I'm gonna kill this bastard first, and then I'll get fixed up just fine.'

I looked at Markov, and then Jasper. 'You going to let him kill these children, too?'

Jasper nodded. 'Sure. Why not?' Like it was nothing.

Something thumped upstairs, and Charles said, 'Quit shovin', ya frig!' Charles and Teri came down the stairs with Dobcek behind them. Dobcek was holding Charles by the back of the neck, and Teri looked angry.

Dobcek said, 'Where's the other one?' I didn't know if he meant Pike or Winona.

Jasper looked irritated. 'Who gives a shit? Let's just do it and get out of here.'

Markov said, 'Da.'

When he said it, someone knocked on the door and Dobcek clamped a hand over Charles's mouth and aimed his gun at Clark. 'Sh.'

Jasper went to the door, raising his gun, and Markov pushed to his feet, holding his own gun loosely at his side. Pike and Winona had a key, but maybe Pike had seen Markov and Dobcek coming in. Maybe he'd seen Markov's blood trail leading to the door. Or maybe it was just the pizza man.

Jasper peered through the peephole, then frowned and stepped away from the door. 'I can't see shit.'

If it was Pike, he would make a move.

If it was Pike, the knocking would have been to focus our attention there while he came in from another place.

I looked at Teri and Charles and Dobcek. Dobcek was breathing hard and staring at the door with the kids in front of him and the muzzle of his gun maybe three centimeters from Charles's head. I stood. 'I'd give up, if I were you. It's the cops.' I said it in a normal speaking voice.

Dobcek pointed his gun at me. 'Shut up.'

Markov waved his gun at Dobcek and hissed, 'Make him shut up.'

Something creaked above us, and Dobcek glanced up the stairs, like maybe he'd heard it but wasn't sure. A drop of sweat worked down from his hairline and along his temple.

I spoke even louder. 'What's that smell, Dobcek? You so scared you messed your pants?'

Dobcek took a single step toward me, but he was still between the kids. I wanted him away from them, and thought maybe I could bait him to me. Of course, he might decide to shoot me instead.

I spoke louder still. 'Why don't you chickenshits just open the door and see who it is?' I took a step toward Markov. 'Christ, you want me to do it?'

Markov hissed angrily at Dobcek, 'Make him be silent, goddamn you.'

Dobcek surged past Charles and Teri, and put his gun to my head. He clamped his hand over my mouth and kept the gun there and smiled horribly. His face was red, and his snow-blond buzz cut stood sharp and spike-like up from his head. 'When this is done I will kill you slow.'

I caught Teri's eye and snapped a glance at the floor. She grabbed Charles and pushed him down.

Everything in the room was focused on the door when Markov wet his lips and told Jasper, 'Open it.'

Jasper threw open the door, but no one was there

except Winona's little troll, hanging over the peephole. It looked angry.

Jasper blinked. 'What the hell?'

A shadow flicked at the top of the stairs and Alexei Dobcek must've caught the move because I felt him tense a tenth of a second before Joe Pike shot him once through the temple and Dobcek collapsed away from me as the pressure wave and burnt powder residue blew past me like a hot rain.

Jasper jerked at the blast, but I was already moving. I put my shoulder into Markov, twisted the gun out of his hand, then shot Jasper three times, knocking him through the open door and out into the breezeway, shooting until he was over and out and gone.

When I turned back to Markov, Joe Pike was on him. Markov was still on the floor, confused and blinking up at us, profoundly surprised at how fast his life had taken a downward turn. I said, 'Close.'

Pike shrugged with an absolute lack of expression. 'Not even.'

That Pike is something.

The Hewitts were fine. I said, 'Clark, why don't you make a citizen's arrest, and we'll call the police.'

Pike said, 'Already called them. They're on the way.'

Charles ran over to Markov and kicked him. 'A-hole!' Pike had to lift Charles away to get him to stop.

The police didn't get there in time.

Little by little the angry wolf hunger drained from Andrei Markov's eyes and he was gone. Bled to death before the police arrived.

Pike went out and brought in Winona. He'd put her in his Jeep after he called the cops.

I put my arms around the Hewitt family, and I told them that it was over, and this time it was.

CHAPTER 37

The courtyard and the sidewalk by the street filled with police and gawkers, and pretty soon a news crew from the local ABC affiliate showed up.

The cops on the scene got pretty tense about finding three bodies, especially when one of the bodies was identified as a U.S. Marshal. I called Marsha Fields, but she was still in Long Beach. I finally reached Emily Thornton, and after she spoke to the lead cop, he was only too happy to accept my version of events. It pays to have friends in high places. When the pizza arrived, Charles ate some and the cops ate the rest. No one else wanted it.

When the lead detective told Clark that he could go, Clark came over and asked if he could speak with me. He looked embarrassed.

I took him aside, and he said, 'What about Dak?'

'Call him tonight and set it up for tomorrow. He'll probably send a limo, he wants the dong so badly.'

He looked at his children. The three of them were standing in a little group under a pine tree by the street. He said, 'Well, I might be down there a couple of days. I don't want to just leave them alone.'

I had to smile when he said it. 'Call me, Clark. They can stay with me.'

Clark looked uncertain, and then he went back to his family and the four of them walked away. Joe drove them home.

I left not long after, stopping at Gelson's for a nice salmon steak and a couple of fresh baking potatoes and a six-pack of Budweiser. I would've preferred Falstaff, but they didn't have it. As in all things, you do what you can.

When I got home I set the coals in my Weber, popped the potatoes in the oven, then took a shower while they cooked. After the shower I called Lucy. It was after eight in Baton Rouge by the time I called, and she answered on the second ring. I said, 'It's done.'

She asked me about it, of course, and I told her, speaking for most of a half hour as I watched the coals redden, their heat visibly rising in the cooling evening air. Stuart Greenberg had been good at his word, and now, one day after her meeting with him, he had finalized her deal with David Shapiro, the deal that would bring her to Los Angeles and, I hoped, make her a part of my daily life.

When the coals were ripe for the salmon, I told her so, and promised to send her Sunday's real estate section. She said, 'I love you, Elvis.'

'I love you, too, Lucy.'

Just talking to her made me smile.

I doused the salmon with soy sauce, placed it on the grill, and then the phone rang. I thought it might be Lucy calling back, or Joe, or Clark to tell me when he needed me for the kids, but it wasn't. A man's voice said, 'You didn't win anything.'

It was Richard Chenier.

He said, 'You think it's over, but it's not.'

Then he hung up.

I took a deep breath, then went back to the grill and turned the salmon. It dries quickly if you don't watch out.

I could have called Lucy, I suppose, but, as before, I did not. Before, it would have felt like tattling; now, to call her would have given him more weight in our lives than either of us wanted him to have.

I drank the Budweiser and ate the salmon, sitting on my deck in the liquid night, listening to the coyotes singing against the stars and the black cutout shapes of the mountain. Late that night I fell asleep there, thinking how very lucky I was that she loved me and no one else.

As Pike said, we could always kill him later.